CENTURION

CENTURION

L.D. Alford

WATERFORD, VIRGINIA

Centurion

Published in the U.S. by:
Capstone Publishing Group LLC
P.O. Box 8
Waterford, VA 20197

Visit Capstone Fiction at
www.capstonefiction.com

Cover design by David LaPlaca/debest design co.
Cover image © iStockphoto.com/Luke Daniek

Copyright © 2008 by L.D. Alford. All rights reserved.

With grateful thanks to the following sources:
The *Holy Bible,* New English Version, © 1976 by Oxford University Press, Inc. Used by permission. All rights reserved.
The Jewish New Testament, copyright © 1979 by David H. Stern. Published by Jewish New Testament Publications, Inc. www.messianicjewish.net/jntp. Distributed by Messianic Jewish Resources. www.messianicjewish.net. All rights reserved. Used by permission.

ISBN: 978-1-60290-012-7

Centurion is a work of fiction. Names, characters, places, and incidents either are the product of the author's imagination or are used fictitiously. Any resemblance to actual events (other than historical connections), locales, organizations, or persons, living or dead, is entirely coincidental and beyond the intent of either the author or the publisher.

*To one
who already knows
and believes:
The Story of Our Joy
and Her Adam.*

Preface

To convey the feel of the language differences of the time, I employ many words and names used during the actual historical period. In the narrative and for Aramaic conversations, I use transliterated Aramaic names instead of the more common anglicized equivalents. In general, I use anglicized names when the characters speak Greek or Latin, and except in some rare cases, I apply this pattern throughout the book.

I introduce most of the original language items in the text but have provided a lexicon at the end of the novel for easy reference.

*Against thee, thee only, I have sinned
and done what displeases thee,
so that thou mayest be proved right in thy charge
and just in passing sentence.
In iniquity I was brought to birth
and my mother conceived me in sin;
Yet, though thou hast hidden the truth in darkness,
through this mystery thou dost teach me wisdom.*

Psalm 51:4-6

One

Naomi walked swiftly across the screed hillsides toward the village. The sun was as merciless as her tormenters. She shaded her eyes. She shouldn't be going for water during the hottest part of the day, but it was the only time she could approach the well and find no other women there.

The women—pah. She had no time for them, and they had too many opportunities to harass her. Their cold, hard stares were painful enough, and though Naomi had brave intentions, she could not make herself face them. Hot tears pressed between her eyelids. She shook her head and dashed them like twin raindrops into the dust. Alone in her small house she had time enough for sorrow; she didn't need to display her grief to the world. She didn't need to tell her tormenters they succeeded.

Perhaps with the newest scandal in the village, they would forget her. Naomi had heard the rumors before and had not believed them; the youngest daughter of Eli had conceived a child. Eli's daughter was the last girl anyone would have imagined caught in that sin. She was always so disconcertingly truthful—and naive. Who would have thought her capable of it? Especially when her prospects were so good. The betrothal was fresh on her and her bridegroom had not taken her to the marriage bed. He had not even had time to prepare the bed, and no one knew whose child she carried.

Naomi supported her own swelling belly. No one knew whose child Eli's daughter carried, but unfortunately, everyone knew the father of Naomi's child. Naomi was the most beautiful girl in Natzeret—perhaps in all of the Galil. Had she not been chosen out of all of them to be the wife and consort of Abenadar Iustus, the Roman emissary to the court of Herod the Great?

Naomi had lived the past ten years like a great gentlewoman. All that time, she served as a lady in Herod's court, and she lived with Abenadar Iustus in a large house in Yerushalayim. She learned to speak Latin and Greek, and unlike most women, she could read and write a little. She had servants and slaves to wait on her. And for the whole time, her family and countrymen despised her as a whore and a traitor.

Naomi knew Abenadar Iustus had a family and a wife back in Rome, though that knowledge came to her gradually. She was once as naive as Eli's daughter. The existence of the Roman's family was well-known. She was foolish to believe it could have been otherwise. All of the highborn Romans who served the Emperor in Palestine took local "wives." Naomi refused to use the word *concubine*.

When the officials' appointments came to an end, they were recalled to Rome and new responsibilities. They left their heathen countrywomen and gladly returned to their rich and cultured Roman brides.

Naomi knew all this, and as the time approached for Abenadar Iustus to leave her, she tried every wile, at first, to convince him to stay. Then she begged him to take her with him, if only as a slave. Of course, he could not—would not—take her, an uncultured countrywoman who would be entirely out of place even as a slave in his house in Rome. Naomi could hear the contempt in his voice as he held her in his arms and conceived his child upon her. In ten years, she could not produce a child for him, and now, the Lord, Adonai, blessed be He, punished her with the blessing of a child.

Tears again threatened to fall, but she valiantly cut them off. Though he had left her, Naomi still loved Abenadar Iustus. She was still a young woman. She still held to notions of love. Yet he condemned her to the life that she, without realizing, had chosen ten years before— the life of an outcast among her own people.

Ahead of her, the village of Natzeret swam in the midday heat. Palms and brush surrounded the well at the edge of the small town. As Naomi stepped into the path and neared the place, she caught sight of another woman already there. Naomi stopped short and started to turn. Better to wait until there was no one at the well. Better to go hungry and thirsty than to face the taunts of the wives and unmarried women.

But then Naomi recognized the slight figure bending over the well; it was Eli's daughter.

The woman was very young and small. She had long dark hair that flowed in a heavy braid out from under her veil, a petite face, and large brown eyes. Naomi thought her pretty, but not nearly as beautiful as she. The girl barely showed her pregnancy, but her small belly pressed out through her robes, displaying for all the world her abomination.

Naomi nearly turned around in the path again. She did not want to gloat, and she understood the solitude the girl desired…knew what she must be feeling. But Naomi was also hot and the clay pot on her head was heavy. She didn't want to make this trip again today. Neither did she want to face this young woman. Who knew what the daughter of Eli thought of Naomi?

While Naomi stood in the path, still undecided, the young girl at the fountain glanced up and noticed her. The girl cocked her head.

Naomi instantly made up her mind. She could take any taunt from this one and turn it back twice.

The girl smiled as Naomi walked cautiously to the well. "Good day, Naomi."

"Good day, daughter of Eli." Naomi set her pot beside the open well.

"I am called Miryam. Surely you remember me, Naomi? I am the betrothed of Yosef."

Miryam, thought Naomi, *the cuckold of Yosef. That was surely not Yosef's child.* But she only acknowledged Miryam with a nod.

"Let me help you with the water bag," said Miryam. She pushed the leather bag back into the well and brought it up heavy with water.

Naomi held her pot under the bag, and together, she and Miryam poured the water into the pot.

"Thank you," said Naomi pertly.

"Here, cool yourself from the bag," and Miryam held it for Naomi.

Naomi drank deeply until her thirst was slaked; then she splashed the dust from her face and hands.

"Why are you here now, Miryam?" Naomi wished she could take back her words the moment they were said.

"For the same reason you come at noon, Naomi." The girl hung her head. "I can't stand the cruel ridicule of the women."

"Yes. I'm sorry. Thank you for helping me with the water." Naomi touched her pot. "I haven't seen you for a while."

"I was visiting my cousin Elisheva."

"She is expecting a child, isn't she?"

"Yes," Miryam laughed, "a child in her old age, and Z'kharyah cannot speak. He cannot praise the Lord, Adonai, blessed be He, with his own lips."

Naomi had heard the story. It was reported throughout the country. How Z'kharyah was the priest offering the daily incense in the Holy Place, who could not bless the people because he was struck dumb. "When is she due?"

"In a few months. Z'kharyah still cannot speak, but we are blessed with an abundance." She stroked her swelling belly with her palm.

Naomi glanced at Miryam to see if she spoke with sarcasm, but the girl just stared back at her with large, trusting eyes.

"When are you due?" asked Miryam.

"Soon. One or two months." Naomi glanced again at the girl to see if she spoke with mockery.

"Who will be with you?"

"No one. I will give birth by myself."

Miryam touched Naomi's arm. "You will not be alone. I will be there, and I will ask Puah to midwife you."

"Puah will not come."

"I will ask her. May I visit you, Naomi? I am alone, too. Although Yosef is kind, and he helps me, he is a man and doesn't wish to speak about women's things."

Naomi almost sat in the dust. "You would visit me?"

"Yes, anytime." Miryam paused. "You may visit me too."

"No, daughter of Eli, I cannot visit you. You, like me, are disgraced already. You don't need the taint of Rome in your house."

Miryam glanced up in gratitude. "I will meet you at the well tomorrow at this time and then we will go to your home."

Naomi's eyes filled with tears. "Yes, Miryam, daughter of Eli, come visit me anytime you wish."

Miryam looked down at the ground, then took up the heavy pot and turned toward the village. "I would stay longer, but Yosef expects me. Shalom, Naomi."

"Oh, thank you, Miryam, thank you," Naomi whispered as Miryam walked away. Then she said loudly, "Shalom."

Miryam paused a step and slowly nodded, then continued into the village.

Naomi picked up her water pot, set it on her head, and wept all the way back to her small house.

But thou art he who drew me from the womb,
who laid me at my mother's breast.
Upon thee was I cast at birth;
from my mother's womb thou hast been my God.

PSALM 22: 9-10

Two

The next day, Miryam followed Naomi to her house. Naomi lived in a small clay-brick hut set precariously on the side of the hill near the approach to Natzeret. Though only a stone's throw from the road, the house was well hidden from the highway that ran from Natzeret to Kanah. The roof of the building was made of sticks with palms for thatch. That didn't look, to Miryam, like it would keep out the rain or much of the summer heat.

The hut reminded Miryam of one of the booths for Sukkot, the Feast of Tabernacles. She remembered, as a child that she wanted the Festival of Booths to never end. It was her favorite celebration. As an adult, she couldn't imagine living in Naomi's boothlike house every day without end.

Naomi pulled back the reed mat covering the doorway and waited until Miryam entered. The inside of the hut was very different from its rude exterior. It was small but swept clean, and tiny refinements accented its bleakness. The dirt floor was covered with fine mats and a small colorful rug. On the cooking hearth sat one copper and two bronze pots. In the corner was a low cot covered with rushes and a wool covering.

Miryam said a blessing as she entered the house that Naomi acknowledged with a nod. Miryam sat on the floor and Naomi eased herself heavily onto the cot.

As Naomi sat down she said, "The child is heavy within me. I hope it is a boy. I need a strong arm here to keep me safe."

"It is not safe for you here?" returned Miryam.

"Nowhere is safe for me, daughter of Eli. I have no man to keep me and no family to look after me."

"How do you live?"

"Abenadar Iustus left me with enough money to keep me fed. I have some comforts. I make things from reeds and clay to sell in Kanah and when I visit Tzippori. It is not much, but it is enough."

"What of your child. When it is born, what will you do?"

"I will live here. Abenadar Iustus promised me the child would be a citizen of Rome." She spat. "It is enough. That is all he left me."

"I have dreamed a dream about your child, Naomi. Would you like to hear it?"

"Oh yes, Miryam." Naomi bent over as much as she was able and moved closer to the girl. She had often heard about Miryam's dreams. Many said they foretold the future, but others now thought they represented only the ramblings of misspent youth.

Miryam stared at her feet. "I don't know whether you will think much of my dreams. Once the village awaited them as though they were important. They don't listen to me anymore."

"What was your dream? Please tell me. I will listen to your dreams though no one else will."

"Very well." Miryam's bright eyes turned to her. "I will tell this one to you. I saw your child and mine. We will both have boys. They will know each other, and they will be fast friends. They will be as different as the day and the night. Yours will be fair and handsome and mine ruddy and dark. They will be bound in life in some way I cannot understand. There is some greatness for them both. Your boy will be great. I saw him wearing a helmet." She paused. "What do you think that means?"

Naomi sat back again and held her belly. "The child leapt," she said with amazement. "I do not know, daughter of Eli. Do your dreams sometimes come true?"

Miryam looked down at the mats on the floor. "They have always come true before. Shall I tell you the dream that no one believes?" She stopped. "That is, everyone but Yosef and Elisheva."

Naomi smiled at her. "Tell me your dream."

"It wasn't really a dream. I saw an angel who said I was to bear the Son of the Highest."

"Of the Lord, Adonai, blessed..." Naomi stared at Miryam suspiciously. "Of Adonai?"

"So the angel said." Miryam looked up at her. "I have never known a man."

"Never?"

"Never." Her voice became very quiet. "I don't even understand what it is to know a man. Yosef will not tell me."

Naomi's mouth was dry. "I will not tell you either."

Miryam smiled. "I was not seeking to know. I just wanted to tell you the dream."

"You should not be here, Miryam, daughter of Eli. I am a defiled woman. You are something else."

"You don't have to believe me."

"I am not sure that I do, but my child moved at your words."

"That is what Elisheva said. She has a child in her old age. I have a child and I am not sure where he came from. Except what the angel told me. That is enough for me. Now you are the only woman who will speak to me in Natzeret."

"What? Won't your mother speak to you?"

"No." Miryam's voice was forlorn. "You are not evil, Naomi."

"I was foolish...I was a foolish girl. I will pay for my foolishness. I am paying for it."

"Would you repeat it?"

Naomi's eyes glazed for a moment as she contemplated the city of Yerushalayim far away; the events of ten years seemed to pass across her sight. "I'm not sure," she answered truthfully. "But if I could live it all over...if I could live it over, I might do it all again." She glanced down, shamefaced.

"We are all foolish in some way. Adonai blesses us nonetheless, and we live on. Ah, show me how you weave your mats. I would learn, and I could tell you of the events in Natzeret."

The silence stretched out between them. Naomi absently took down her latest work and bent over it.

Miryam got to her knees and watched Naomi's nimble fingers as they quickly built up the fine mat. "This is much better than anything made in Natzeret," Miryam said.

"It is the style of the court."

"I will bring my own rushes tomorrow. Will you help me learn?"

"Yes, and if you bring cloth and thread, I will show you how to sew a fine garment and decorate it in the court style. I have no money for cloth myself."

"I have cloth and thread. I will bring some to you if you will teach me. I could sell it in the marketplace. That is, if I could learn to sew as well as you." Miryam examined again the fine hangings in the small house.

"I will teach you, Miryam."

The women both hunched over the mat, and Naomi showed Miryam how she made the reeds take on a design. They spoke of the village and many other things until the late afternoon.

As Naomi saw Miryam out of her house, the younger woman said, "I will come again tomorrow. And I will talk to Puah." She put her hand on Naomi's arm. "You are like the Naomi of the past, and I will be like your Ruth."

Naomi bowed slightly and smiled for the first time in a long time.

As she watched Miryam make her way down the side of the hill, she thought to herself, *Miryam is as innocent as a child. She could have known no man. A rape? No, she knows nothing of consort between men and women. An angel told her?*

But Naomi could not laugh. Perhaps it was as the girl said.

Miryam, her eyes large and bright in the darkness, held on to Naomi's shoulders. The firelight and lamplight were barely enough to illuminate Naomi's small house. Old Puah coaxed her. She touched Naomi's spread thighs and spoke gentle words that Naomi only caught with half her mind. The pain, real and imagined, was all she could contemplate.

Miryam whispered to her, but Naomi couldn't understand those words either....

Finally, in a moment, it was done. The pain and pressure gave way to an abrupt release and the old woman smiled. There was a hearty cry. "It is a boy," she cackled, and Naomi understood that.

"A boy!" shouted Miryam.

Puah tied off the umbilical cord and placed the child on Naomi's stomach. Crying for joy and pain, Naomi took the child to her swollen breast. "A boy," she mumbled. She arched slightly as her womb expelled the afterbirth, but her thoughts were only for the child. He nuzzled her breast and suckled her.

"He is a strong one," said Puah.

"A boy, Miryam. A boy, just as you dreamed. And he is fair and beautiful."

"They are all beautiful," said Puah. Her old voice seemed to crack. Puah took her flint knife and cut the umbilical cord. "There is much blood in this one." She put the cord and afterbirth in a small burial urn.

"Is that good?" Naomi asked. She could barely get out the words for her fatigue.

Puah put Naomi's knees together and gently lowered her legs. "Yes it is very good. He is a strong boy." She glanced around the room. "I have done all I can. Send for me if you bleed. I cannot help you with the child much."

"I understand, Puah. Thank you," Naomi said wearily.

Miryam let down Naomi's shoulders and made her comfortable; then she held open the reed door covering for Puah. "If I ask, you will help, won't you?"

"Yes, yes, if you ask, Miryam. Anything for you. Everything I can do is done for now. Naomi—" Puah spat the name, then spoke more kindly—"Naomi won't need much. She is strong. The child is strong. There is not much more we can do. It is Adonai, blessed be He, who heals and saves."

"Yes," said Miryam.

The mat door covering dropped as Puah took her lamp and walked down the hill.

The inside of the house was much darker now. Miryam put another piece of dung on the fire.

Naomi gazed at the nursing child; he was almost asleep.

"Is he cold?" said Miryam.

"No, but help me swaddle him."

Naomi held the child up a little from her body as Miryam wrapped the wide strip of cloth around him.

Naomi changed her position on the cot and moaned a little. "It still hurts, but it is much better than a little while ago." She pointed toward the far wall. "Miryam, I made that mat for Puah. Take it to her tomorrow. She will know who sent it, but don't remind her; I want her to accept it."

"It is beautiful." Miryam stroked the reed mat. "She will accept it. If only to sell."

"That is good too. Thank you for bringing her."

"I told you she would come."

"I didn't believe you." Naomi turned her head toward the fire.

"Did you believe my dream?"

"I hoped it was true."

"What do you think now?"

"It is true. Do you have more dreams?"

Miryam was evasive. "It is late, and you must sleep. I will come in the morning with food and to help you with the child."

"Just one more word before you go. What else have you dreamed?"

"It is late, but I will tell you one other thing that Adonai, blessed be He, has shown me. I needed to help you. I would have anyway, but I needed to see your child's birth. I know I will give birth without any woman to help me. I am afraid, but now I know how it will be."

Naomi grasped Miryam's arm. "I will be with you, and Puah will be there."

Miryam shook her head. "I have dreamed it. There will be Yosef and no one else. In the village, girls are not allowed in the birth chamber. You know we are taught nothing of this, and we see nothing. This is a mystery of womanhood held from us until we are ready—until we are wives. Your child's birth has let me know what I must do. I am ready now."

Miryam put her veil around her thin face. "I don't want to leave you, but I must see to my household. I have no one to take care of things while I am gone. I will be back in the morning. Shalom."

"Thank you, Miryam. Shalom," said Naomi as she nodded off to sleep.

The wind blew cool through the doorway for a moment, and then it was cut off as the reed covering fell back into place.

*Thou art my hope, O Adonai,
my trust, O Adonai, since boyhood.
From birth I have leaned upon thee,
my protector since I left my mother's womb.*

PSALM 71: 5-6

Three

Naomi finally screwed up enough courage to visit Puah. Miryam had not come to see her for many days, and the time for Miryam to give birth was very close. Naomi still would only approach Natzeret in the middle of the day, the time when she was sure most of the women would be inside, and the streets less populated.

She carried her babe, Abenadar, at her breast. He was already a large boy. She could not have wished for a better child. He was fair, but his personality seemed almost brooding. His light gray eyes would follow her quietly as though they already comprehended something of her disgrace. He seldom cried.

At Naomi's first call, Puah came to the door.

"What do you want?" said Puah. When she noticed the child, she smiled and her voice gentled. "Well, he looks healthy. What do you need, Naomi?"

"I came to ask after Miryam."

"Ah. She is gone."

"Gone. She didn't say anything to me."

"She is gone. Haven't you heard about the census? No, I suppose you don't hear much about such things. There has been a decree from that Roman."

Naomi knew she meant the Emperor Augustus.

"He has called for all men to register in their own cities and be taxed," Puah continued. "Yosef was born in the village of Beit-Lechem. He has taken Miryam with him, and, you know, the trip to Beit-Lechem and back takes almost a week."

"But she is so close to her time."

"That doesn't mean anything to the Romans," Puah hissed. "They would as soon we all die, much less a woman with child. She is riding on Yosef's donkey. The old fool coddles her as though she were a virgin bride."

"They will be back soon?"

"As soon as they register and pay, I suppose." Puah wiped her hands on her robe. "That is all I know, Naomi of the hill. Here." She peered up and down the street and shrugged. "Since you are here…let me see him." Puah gently took the child from her arms. "Ah, he is a big one." She stiffened. "He is not circumcised! What will you do to this child?" All the while, Puah held the boy, crooning to him.

"No one…"

"Yes, I know no rabbi will circumcise a Roman child. Well, perhaps that is best. Perhaps he will be a friend to us, no."

Puah smiled at Naomi and handed the child back to her. "Miryam has gone with Yosef. They will be back in two Shabbats. Don't have such a long face; your friend has not gone forever. Now I did have one question for you. About the mat?"

"What was wrong with it?"

Puah put out her hands. "Nothing was wrong with it. I would like more." She opened the door a little wider, and Naomi saw the mat she made on the floor beside the hearth. "Every woman in this village told me how beautiful they think it is, and I cannot figure how you put those designs in it. Since I can't make it, I must buy from you."

"You would buy from me?"

"Don't look at me that way. Are we not of the same clay? Are you not a woman of the Galil? Make me another one like it, and I will try to save you a trip to Kanah. Well, what do you say?"

"Yes, oh yes." Naomi took her hand. "Thank you, Puah."

"I will soon be the one thanking you, Naomi."

Naomi bowed her head slightly and began to turn.

"Shalom, Naomi," called Puah from her doorway.

Surprised, Naomi turned with a thankful look. "Shalom, Puah."

Naomi bundled her child close to her breast and walked back to her house, shaking her head. What a story she would have to tell Miryam when she returned.

Miryam did not return.

Yosef and Miryam settled with Yosef's family in Beit-Lechem. Later Puah told Naomi that they escaped to Egypt just before Herod killed all the children of Beit-Lechem looking for a child prophesied to be the King of Y'hudah. "Better Hordos should kill Romans instead of his own subjects," Puah told her, making a sign to ward off the evil eye.

In time, the women of Natzeret came to tolerate Naomi. Her sewing and reed work were considered the best in the countryside and won some fame for her in the town.

Naomi's son, Abenadar, grew quickly and straight. Abenadar was known as Able to the people of Natzeret. Most had forgotten his origins, or they didn't care anymore. He had the cast of a boy of the Galil with the face of a Roman. His eyes were gray and constantly sober. Even as a child, he was given to a fixed and disconcerting gaze that many times took his opponents by surprise.

Abenadar's mind and limbs were fit and strong. At 17 he did a man's work—when he could find it. Alone, no one bothered him, and he had long ago shown the boys of Natzeret that even a group was not a good match against the child of Naomi of the hill. When they tried to beat him, he outran them and picked them off one by one. They gave up their persecution of him early and let him join, an unwelcome and always isolated playmate—never a friend.

Except to Yeshua.

Five years after they had left for the census, Miryam and Yosef returned to Natzeret. Their son, Yeshua, was an amazing child. He was fine-boned like his mother and dark-haired. His eyes were a very deep brown, almost black…large and solemn. But his face was never solemn; it always sported a smile that stretched from every point of his features. His smile wasn't insipid, nor was it out of place. It was contagious. He was a child who never seemed to know sadness, but in some way he was as out of place as the Roman bastard, Abenadar.

Yeshua was a good boy. He worked with his father most days and went to Torah school every day he could. Abenadar envied Yeshua's easy grace, his quick wit, and his compassion. They knew each other well. Their mothers often visited, for Naomi could come into Natzeret now without censure.

Abenadar and Yeshua played together as children. They grew up in the same world but different realms. Yeshua lived in the village, attended the Torah school, and had a father as his example. Abenadar had no father, lived outside the limits of the village, and only gained formal learning from what his mother taught him. Naomi taught him Latin, the language of Rome, some Greek, and the little knowledge of Latin and Greek reading and writing she knew. Abenadar attacked his lessons with zest and was never content, though his mother taught him everything she could.

Yeshua was Abenadar's connection to the village of Natzeret. When he was free, Abenadar would wait every day outside Yosef's shop until Yeshua was finished with his work.

"Shalom, Yeshua," said Abenadar as Yeshua left the workshop.

"Abenadar. Where have you been today?"

"I gleaned Shim'on's fields and he gave me a kodrant for the work." Abenadar held up the copper coin.

"A whole kodrant?"

"Yes, I guess I gleaned too much."

"Are you going to give the kodrant to your mother?"

"What do you think?"

"I think she could have used the wheat more than you could use the kodrant."

"Zeus," cursed Abenadar.

"What makes you angry, friend?"

"You're right. You're always right. I'll probably do as you say."

"What have I said for you to do?"

"Nothing." And Abenadar flashed a smile.

Yeshua smiled back. "Shall we climb the hill on the road and see if a caravan will pass today?"

Abenadar stopped abruptly. "A caravan, eh. What makes you think one will pass within the whole next week?"

"Why don't we see? The climb will be goal enough."

The two boys ran until they reached the base of the plateau, then started to climb the large hill on its north edge. They pulled and pushed each other up the steep slope until they sat at the very crest.

Yeshua pointed down into the valley. Below them, a caravan of laden camels and horses wended toward Natzeret. "It will pass by without getting near Natzeret," said Yeshua. "I suspect it is going to Yerushalayim."

"You are probably right, although I can't figure out how you know when these things will happen."

"I make a good guess?" Yeshua shrugged.

Abenadar shrugged also. "I will be leaving soon."

"Yes," Yeshua said as though he wasn't surprised. "Where are you going?"

"I am 17 now, only a little older than you. Tomorrow my mother will take me to the palace in Tzippori. At the Roman consul she will have me registered as a Roman citizen."

"A citizen of Rome. Do you think the Primus Pilus will acknowledge you as a child of Rome?"

"Primus Pilus? My mother will seek an interview with the Roman ambassador, not the legion's chief centurion. She has a letter from my father that will prove my claim."

"And then what will you do as a citizen of Rome?"

"Why, I will join the legion."

"The legion." Yeshua didn't seem all that surprised. "Does your mother know?"

"Of course not." Abenadar glared at Yeshua. "Do you disapprove of my plans?"

"I rarely advise at all. On the contrary, I applaud your choice and ambition."

"You do?"

"Of course I do. Why would I steer you otherwise?"

"I'm not sure." Abenadar rubbed his bristled chin.

"Have I given you the impression that I don't approve of the profession of arms?"

"No. But we have seldom spoken about the subject."

"David was a king of Y'hudah. David was a 'man after Adonai's own heart.' How could I not approve such a man myself? Adonai will have much for you to do in the army of Rome."

"I did not intend to serve Adonai," said Abenadar almost painfully.

"I knew that." Yeshua drew with his finger in the dust. "I warn you, my friend Abenadar, although I doubt you will heed my words for a long while. Do not forget Adonai, and do not forget me. This moment is like so many moments in our childhood, but more than any other time of your life, your choices will determine your fate."

Yeshua's face tilted upward, blazing with the brightness of sunshine. "I guarantee, you will find glory in the service of Rome. You will find a necessary place in the legion." He stared back at Abenadar. "You will forget Adonai, the Lord of your mother…of your people. Though I give you this warning, you will forget. You will forget, and you will be brought back to righteousness only if you do not bow to foreign gods. In other ways you will fail Adonai, but in this one thing, promise me."

"Yes. I think I can promise you this thing."

Yeshua said, "Abenadar, my friend, a time will come when you will wish you could wipe away all of your glorious past. Though you will be clothed in glory, you will be ashamed."

Abenadar smiled crookedly at him. "What? Are you now a prophet?"

"Perhaps that is my calling. Yours is a legionnaire," said Yeshua, brushing the dust from his hands as he stood up. "Don't forget what I said."

"I will try not to," said Abenadar, himself standing. He wasn't offended by Yeshua's words, but surprised at the intensity of them. Their past conversations were often serious, but rarely was Yeshua so direct.

They began climbing back down the hill. "You act as if I will be accepted into the legion very soon. That is not such an easy thing."

"I didn't say it will be easy. I said you might find you are a legionnaire sooner than you expect. I also warned you not to forget my words."

They reached the bottom of the hill. Yeshua grabbed Abenadar around the shoulders and then released him. "Farewell, my friend. I shall look after your mother while you are gone. Shalom."

"I had not thought about my mother," said Abenadar. "Thank you."

"I know."

Abenadar turned toward his mother's house as Yeshua started down the trail. Then almost as an afterthought, Abenadar turned around and shouted at Yeshua, "You have been my only friend. If I am to go so soon, thank you, friend. I will remember your words. Shalom." Yeshua turned and waved. Then Abenadar watched as Yeshua walked toward the village and was eventually lost from sight around the hill.

The next day, Naomi and Abenadar traveled the caravan road to Tzippori. Since Herod Antipas reinforced the city and moved his capital there, Naomi had taken many of her mats and needlework to Tzippori to sell instead of to Kanah. To remind themselves of the language, Abenadar and Naomi spoke nothing but Latin on the way.

The road was empty; they didn't meet any caravans or any other travelers. The major festivals of the year were over, and little was left from the late fields to sell. The area around the city of Tzippori was still thinly settled, and the city itself was a fortress. It had been built in the valley between Rumah and Besara, one of the few easy approaches into the Galil between the coast and Lake Kenneret. The city was erected over the ancient tombs there, so not many of the faithful in the Galil would enter the city and that pleased both the Romans and Herod.

Naomi took Abenadar straight to Herod's palace in the fortress city. The Latin parchment with Abenadar Iustus' seal and her command of the language conducted them through the gate and into the Roman court. She requested an interview with the Roman emissary, but instead of meeting the Roman ambassador immediately, she waited with Abenadar for hours. Finally, a legionnaire showed them into the quarters of Iulius Valens, the Primus Pilus of the III Gallica Legion.

Abenadar followed his mother into the court.

The chamber of the Primus Pilus was large and garishly decorated. The floor was adorned with colorful tiles and bright Oriental rugs. The Primus Pilus sat in an ornamented chair with a lion-skin cover on the seat. He was dressed in a white toga with a purple stripe, and in one hand he held a richly decorated baton. Iulius Valens was still a young man; he was only 35 and already a noted centurion in the legions of Rome. He was a member of the class of equestrian knights. Through this heritage and his father's name in Rome, the Emperor granted him a commission as a centurion. Iulius Valens had served with distinction in more than one legion, and a year before, by order of the Emperor Augustus, he was posted as Primus Pilus of the III Gallica Legion.

Iulius Valens had a large open face. His features were well defined but not garish. Although he rarely let any idea of the contents of his thoughts bleed into his countenance, he was considered a just man whose intentions were always open to scrutiny. His friends said he was a careful man, while his rivals, probably more rightly, considered him impenetrable.

"Come forward," ordered Iulius Valens.

Naomi and Abenadar walked toward the man. On either side of the Primus, two armed legionnaires watched them carefully. They each held a heavy spear and carried a short iron sword. They wore an armored cuirass and bronze helms.

Naomi bowed to the Primus and waved Abenadar to do the same. Abenadar and his mother fell to their knees before him.

Her head bowed, Naomi said, "I am Naomi, the consort of Abenadar Iustus who was once the Roman emissary to Herod. I bring his son for you to approve as a citizen of Rome."

The Primus leaned forward. "You have proof of this?"

Naomi pulled the letter from her bosom and handed it to the Primus.

Iulius Valens cut the heavy seal and read the letter under his breath. When he reached the end, he chuckled. "Do you read Latin, woman?"

"Only a little."

He shook his head. "Abenadar Iustus always had fine taste in women, but infinitely poor timing. You may leave. I wish to speak to your son."

Naomi stood up and gazed anxiously at Abenadar; then she backed out of the chamber.

"Stand up, young Roman, and let me look at you," said Iulius Valens. "Yes, you are truly your father's child."

"Did you know my father, sir?" asked Abenadar.

"Yes, I know him. I know him well. We are friends, and you do look like him. Now what do you wish of me?"

"Sir?"

"Your came here with your mother. You are a strong-looking young man with a young man's ambitions. You are a Roman citizen, or so I pronounce you. What do you wish from me?"

The words came out in a rush from Abenadar. "I wish to be a legionnaire."

"You and every other young Roman in the Galil. Why should I choose you? Are you trained in the use of any weapons: the pila or the gladius?"

"No, sir."

"What skills do you have which would make you useful to me?"

"What skills do you need?"

"A fair question. Burthus, what kinds of men do we still need in the III Gallica?"

The legionnaire to the left of the Primus answered him, "I am not sure, Primus. Should I get the Cornicularius?"

"Yes, call in Fonteius."

The legionnaire saluted and left. In a few moments, a burly man in a short tunic and leggings followed him into the chamber.

"Yes, Primus," said the Cornicularius while saluting.

"What skills do you still need, Fonteius?"

"Chiefly in the librarii, I need men who can translate and speak to the people of the Galil."

"You—" the Primus pointed at Abenadar—"Abenadar, the Roman, can you speak the language of the Galil?"

"Yes, Primus. I can speak it as well as anyone born here."

"I know you can speak Latin; what other skills do you have?"

"I can write some Latin, and I know the language of the Greeks."

"Better than your mother can read Latin, I hope. Will this one do, Fonteius?"

"Yes, Primus, this is just the kind of man I am looking for."

"Very well, Abenadar, consider your probatio to be at an end. I shall accept you as a librarius, but I have few immunii in this legion. You will answer to Fonteius as a librarius, but you shall fight for Centurion Capolinius in the Hastatus Posterior Century. Centurion Capolinius commands the sixth century of the tenth cohort. They are the last of the centuries in the accounting of this legion, but they call themselves the Lions. You will find with them an appropriate beginning. The Cornicularius Fonteius will instruct you and place you with your century. Follow his teaching and prove yourself a worthy Roman and you shall not be sent back to your mother's house."

"Thank you, Primus."

"Now, Abenadar, are you ready to take the sacramentum and accept the Emperor's viaticum?"

"What are these, sir?"

The Primus smiled. "The oath and your first payment."

Abenadar did not hesitate. "Yes. I am ready."

"Cornicularius, administer the oath!"

Fonteius took a standard from an honored position behind an altar in the corner of the chamber. The standard sported a golden Roman eagle perched on the top of a pole. "Abenadar, place your hand on the aquila of the III Gallica and repeat the sacramentum after me."

Abenadar touched the golden bird and repeated after Fonteius, "I Abenadar from Natzeret, son of Abenadar Iustus, a citizen of Rome, swear to follow the consuls to the wars to which the Republic is called. I swear never to desert the aquila nor do anything against any law prescribed by the consuls and the Republic. I will follow all orders of the consuls and of any official placed over me by them. I promise to always act on the behalf of the Republic, and I will not leave my post or responsibilities until I have served my full term. I swear never to shrink from death on behalf of the Roman state. These things I do swear by all that I hold sacred and honorable and present my own life as my bond."

Fonteius slapped Abenadar on the back. "Welcome to the III

Gallica, boy. Ha, but we will make a man of you."

The Primus took three gold aurei out of his pouch and motioned for Abenadar to come to him. The Primus handed Abenadar the coins. "I also welcome you, young Abenadar. If you have the strength and wisdom of your father, you will bring great honor to us. Go with the Cornicularius Fonteius and he will settle you in your new responsibilities."

"Thank you, Primus." Abenadar tried to salute like he had seen the others do.

Fonteius led Abenadar out of the chamber by the side door that he entered.

"Cornicularius Fonteius—" Abenadar caught the man's sleeve— "may I say good-bye to my mother?"

"Yes, certainly, boy. Send her off with a big kiss, and then I'll set you up with your things."

Abenadar held the three aurei on his palm. "How much money is this, Cornicularius?"

Fonteius laughed. "Each is worth 25 denarii."

"How much will I need for myself?"

"That depends on how much drinking and whoring you want to do."

"No, I mean to acquire clothing and weapons."

"You will need at least 50 denarii. Give one aurei to your mother and that will leave you with enough to buy your kit. If that isn't enough, I will loan you the difference."

"Thank you, Cornicularius."

Naomi was waiting outside the Primus' chambers. She took hold of Abenadar when he came up to her. "What did the Primus say, my son?"

"He pronounced me a child of Rome."

"All is well, Abenadar. Come now; we can make it back to Natzeret before the sun sets." Naomi turned to leave the officium.

When Abenadar didn't follow, she stopped in the doorway. "Why do you tarry, Abenadar?"

"I will not be returning with you, Mother."

Naomi could not contain her shock. "Why, why not, Abenadar? Where will you go?"

"The Primus offered me a place in his legion."

She spat in Aramaic, "You would serve Rome?"

"I would take my place like a man. I can send money home with you." He handed an aurei to her.

Naomi stared at the gold in her hand. She raised her arm as though she were about to throw it at him. Then she slowly lowered her arm, and her shoulders sagged. "And what about me? I now have neither a husband nor a son."

"This is true, but Yeshua promised me he would look after you if you needed it."

"While you are off with the legions of Rome? You will certainly be killed. You will bow to their idols and their gods."

Abenadar colored. In taking the oath on the image of an eagle, he had done just that. He took small comfort in the fact that he had not worshiped their aquila. Angrily he said, "That is the risk I run. I cannot turn back now. I have taken the sacramentum, their oath, and accepted this money, the viaticum." Then, more gently, he said, "Mother, will you be able to make your way safely home today?"

"Yes, I have made this journey many times without you. Why not once again?" Naomi's shoulders sagged even further. "Kiss me, my son. I know this is the last I will see of you."

Abenadar smiled and shook his head. "It is not the last you will see of me. I will visit you when I can. You have your friends in Natzeret. I will make something of myself, and you will be proud of me."

"Shalom, my son, shalom is all I can offer you." Naomi pushed away from him and shuffled out of the building.

Abenadar sadly watched her go. He was at once exhilarated, apprehensive, and unhappy. He knew his mother would never forgive him for joining the legion—at the same time, he could not believe his good fortune.

Grasp shield and buckler, and rise up to help me.
Uncover the spear and bar the way against my pursuers.
Let me hear thee declare, "I am your salvation."

PSALM 35:2-3

Four

After Naomi left, Cornicularius Fonteius was waiting for Abenadar. Fonteius said, "Well, son, are you ready to become a legionnaire?"

"Aren't I a legionnaire now?"

"You will not truly be a legionnaire until the Primus Pilus pronounces you fit to carry the gladius and the pila. I'll take you to your quarters."

The Cornicularius led Abenadar through the officium where the Primus had his quarters. Behind the officium lay the camp proper. The legion camp was a large, flat compound surrounded by a six-foot wall. A series of large buildings covered almost half the area. The officium that Abenadar and Fonteius had just left was a long, two-story building aligned parallel to the main gate. On the other side, and perpendicular to the officium, stood six long, low barracks and several smaller buildings. Fonteius led Abenadar to the last of the barracks.

The structure was rudely built but seemed substantial enough. It was not made from brick and daub like the common buildings of the Galil, but was almost entirely stone and wood. To Abenadar the barrack had a strong foreign look. Over the front, the words *Decimus Cohort* and an *X* were inscribed on a board. The door was a simple flap of leather tied back to let the light autumn breezes blow through. The odor of unwashed bodies and stale hay wafted from the opening. Abenadar followed the Cornicularius through the doorway.

Inside, wattle, reed mats, wood, and stone subdivided the barrack into compartments. On each side of the central corridor, Abenadar counted 20 wide doorways—a total of 40 rooms.

Fonteius led Abenadar down the row of openings until they arrived at the last set of portals. In the bowels of the building the smells were stronger. He turned into the left doorway and Abenadar followed closely behind him. In this room were 20 cots arranged in orderly rows. Three legionnaires sat on two of the rear cots and rolled knucklebones.

"Lupus, Portius, Euodus," called out Fonteius. When they recognized the Cornicularius, all three stood up. "This is Abenadar, your new librarius. Treat him well. He'll be keeping the duty rosters and records for your century, and—" Fonteius paused for effect—"he can speak to the people of the Galil."

The legionnaires picked their money up off the cot and came over to examine Abenadar. Lupus was a thin man with a flat, broken nose and a heavy scar across his face. His voice was thick and distorted by his deformed nose. Because he could only breathe through his mouth, it was always open, but he seemed intelligent in spite of his dull look and contorted speech.

Lupus said, "Can you really speak to the people of the Galil? Can you speak to the women around here? They will have nothing to do with us."

"I can speak to them," said Abenadar, "but I don't think it will do you any good. They will have nothing to do with me either." He guessed that if they were anything like the women of Natzeret, no legionnaire would ever get close to one.

The men laughed.

"Portius," said the Cornicularius, "take Abenadar over to the quartermaster and get him a kit and armor. Show him what he needs and don't cheat him, or I will have all three of you flogged. Where is Tero, your optio?"

"If he is not in the next chamber," said Portius, "he is with our centurion working out the duties for tomorrow." Portius was a large man. His face was mobile and expressive. It had a tendency to draw into a half smile only partly echoed by his eyes—half a smile, but there was no menace in him. He seemed more like a storekeeper than a legionnaire, but Abenadar would discover, when pressed in battle, that Portius' placid strength and calm fortitude became a supreme asset.

"You take Abenadar. I will find the optio." The Cornicularius left them and, after sticking his head into the compartment Portius had gestured to, he headed out of the building.

"Where are you from, youngster?" Portius asked Abenadar.

"I came from Natzeret in the Galil."

"From Natzeret?" said Euodus. "Is the Primus now accepting trash from the provinces?" Euodus was as fancy a man as Abenadar had ever seen. His short hair was carefully shaped to form oiled ringlets in the style of a Persian warrior. His face was angular but well made. He wore a colorful tunic with pins and decorations all over it.

"No, I'm a Roman citizen," answered Abenadar.

Euodus smiled. "Another bastard child of Rome. You are well placed in this century. We are all bastards of one type or another."

Portius laughed out loud, but Lupus protested, "I, for one, have a family in Italia."

"Yes, but does your family claim you?" riposted Euodus.

"They will welcome me back when I am released from service."

"If your throat is not cut first by these rebels, you may see Italia again."

Lupus rubbed his throat and made a face. "I wish you wouldn't put it like that, Euobus."

"Don't get carried away, Lupus," said Portius. "The people fear us."

"Yes, they fear our blood will splatter their clothing when they slit our throats."

"Shut up, Euobus," said Portius. "Come, Abenadar. Don't listen to his rambling. It is meaningless. As long as we stay together, we are in little danger, and we're always safe while in camp."

Without waiting for Abenadar, Portius walked out the door. Abenadar quickly followed behind him.

As Portius exited the barracks, Abenadar hurried to catch up. "The camp is huge. How many legions does it hold?"

Portius chuckled. "It doesn't hold even one."

Abenadar was shocked.

Portius noted Abenadar's look and laughed again. "That's right. This camp holds only two cohorts: the I Cohort, Primus and the X Cohort, Decimus—the first and the last in the III Gallica. Admittedly, the Primus Cohort is the largest and best, but the Decimus isn't a training cohort. It isn't made up of inexperienced recruits." Portius glanced at Abenadar. "You excepted. You will get along well if you can translate in the marketplace, especially if you can speak with the barmaids and whores. I predict you will be a very popular man in the Decimus Cohort."

"How many men are in our cohort?" asked Abenadar.

"During your training, you will learn how the legion is organized, but I guess I can start your education early. The Decimus Cohort is formed of six centuries. They are called the Pilus Prior, the Pilus Posterior, the Princeps Prior, the Princeps Posterior, the Hastatus Prior, and the Hastatus Posterior. We are part of the Hastatus Posterior, the Lion Century. Each century contains about 80 men. The men are organized into 10 columns of eight each. All the other cohorts from the second to the tenth are put together the same way, but the Primus Cohort is different."

"How is it different?"

"I'll tell you if you stop interrupting me," growled Portius. "The Primus Cohort has only five centuries: the Primus Pilus, the Princeps, the Hastatus, the Princeps Posterior, and the Hastatus Posterior. But they are double centuries of 20 columns each. The centurions of the Primus Cohort make up the Primes Ordines that help the Primus Pilus command the entire legion."

"A centurion commands each century?"

"Yes, and below each centurion are four principales: the optio, the signifer, the tesserarius, and the librarius."

"Then I am a principalis?" Abenadar said, amazed.

Portius stopped in midstride. "Don't try to push your rank around. A librarius is technically a principalis, but in your position, you have no authority and a lot of responsibility."

"What does a librarius do?"

Portius gave Abenadar a strange look and started walking again. "A librarius keeps the duty roster and helps the optio and the centurion with any writing and all that business." He spread his arms in a gesture of depreciation. "I'm not exactly sure of everything you will be required to do because I cannot read or write. If I could, I would be a librarius myself. Now, are you going to keep asking questions or are you going to listen?"

"I'm listening."

"The tesserarius is in charge of the guards and ensures the men properly accomplish their assigned duties. He collects and marks the tessera of the guards on duty. If he finds you sleeping, he will not take the tessera plaque from around your neck and you will be flogged—or worse. The signifer carries the century's signum and keeps track of the men's money. The optio is in charge of training and helps the centurion lead the century. There, does that answer your questions?"

"Many of them, but where are the rest of the cohorts and how does the Cornicularius fit in?"

"Like our cohort, the other eight in our legion are billeted in their winter camps. Usually two cohorts share a camp, but I have been in a camp that held two whole legions. It makes no sense to do that here; there is too much territory to patrol and no organized resistance to Roman authority. The other cohorts of our legion, the III Gallica, are stationed in the cities of Capernaum, Caesarea-Philippi, Tiberius, and Julias.

"Finally—" Portius mimed that he was exhausted—"you will find a whole host of other principales like the Cornicularius and Aquilifer, who are assigned to the officium. The most important to you is the Cornicularius; he is in charge of all of the librarii."

As Portius lectured Abenadar, they walked past two other buildings as large as the barracks of the Decimus Cohort. The first smelled of men and the second of horses. In the center of the camp stood a smaller two-story building. Half of the lower level was open and enclosed a large smithy. Portius took Abenadar to the enclosed half of the building.

"This is the quaestorium and that is the forum." Portius pointed to a twin building about 50 feet to the north.

A split door marked the center of one wall of the quaestorium. Portius knocked on it, and after a moment the top of the door opened to reveal an armory and storeroom. Abenadar was more intrigued by the man who opened the door. He was ancient and grizzled. As hoary a veteran as any Abenadar was likely to see still in service. The man was very tall, but bent with age. His skin was deeply scored with scars and wrinkles. They faded into each other and accentuated the sharpness of his nose and cheeks by creating parallel tracks down his face. His mouth almost disappeared in the profusion of canyons of skin.

As the veteran spread his large hands over the bottom half of the split door, Abenadar saw his hands were as scared and misshapen as his face. In spite of his frail appearance, he moved with combat quickness, and his voice was sure. "Portius, who is this? And what do you want? Have you already broken the pila I issued you yesterday?"

"No, Piso," Portius addressed the ancient legionnaire. "This is the new librarius of the Decimus Hastatus Posterior Century, Abenadar of Natzeret. He needs a kit and armor."

Piso stretched over the edge of the door toward Abenadar and squinted. "He is tall. He will have to be fit, but I have armor for him." Piso didn't open the door. He handed a mail hauberk over the top. "Here is his lorica hamata and his belt."

Abenadar examined the armor Piso called a lorica hamata. It was formed of fine iron rings woven into one another and sewn to a leather jerkin.

Portius said, "Put it on, Abenadar. Let's see how it looks on you."

Abenadar glanced at Portius and then with perplexity at the armor.

Portius laughed. "Here, let me help you." He lifted the bottom end over Abenadar's head and pulled it down. The lorica hamata clung to him, but it wasn't too tight or too loose. Portius pulled the shoulder flaps from the back to the front and attached them with their hooks and an iron ornament. An extension of the mail around the loose square collar covered Abenadar's shoulders. The leather jerkin that undergirded the rings extended beyond the mail in wide overlapping strips. All of the edges of the armor were finished with leather. The whole garment reached down to Abenadar's lower thigh.

"Now you're starting to look like a legionnaire." Portius clapped him on the back.

Piso nodded in wry approval then disappeared for a moment. He returned with a helmet.

Abenadar gingerly took the helmet from Piso. It was polished bronze and shaped like a half sphere. An inch above the lip at the front of the helmet, a thin bill projected three-quarters of an inch. Below the front bill and even with the lip, another bill, this one three inches long, projected from the back of the helmet. An empty clip projected from the very top of the helmet. On all the helmets the legionnaires wore, Abenadar noticed this projection held a plume. On either side of the helmet, large side plates protected the face, and thin bronze stays ran from these to the long bill at the rear. The inside of the helmet was covered with a thick leather pad.

Abenadar tipped the helmet onto his head. "Where's the plume?"

Portius stepped up to Abenadar and fitted the sides and braces to adjust the balance of the heavy helmet on Abenadar's head. As he tugged on the leather straps, he said, "When you have finished your training—after the legion's training officer, the Praefectus Legionis, awards you the plume of a fallen legionnaire—then you can wear a legionnaire's plume, but not before." Portius half turned to the old man in the quaestorium. "Piso, you always seem to fit a man with just a glance. How do you do it?"

Piso cackled. "If you're still alive when I get ready to leave the Emperor's service, then and only then will I teach you my secrets. For almost 15 years, those secrets have kept me the quartermaster in the officium."

"Phew, Piso, at that rate, you will still be quartermaster when I muster out."

Piso cackled again. Over the top of the door, he handed a sword, the gladius and scabbard. These were quickly followed by two pila—one light, the other very sturdy. Piso tossed a pair of heavy sandals to Portius, who passed them on to Abenadar.

"Here," said Portius, "is a real pair of sandals, your caligae."

"And, the rest of the issue," said Piso. "Here is his basket, bucket, axe, leather strap, sickle, and chain. All one size," he quipped. "The last is also." Piso handed a large rectangular shield through the top of the door. "Your scutum will keep you in the land of the living—if you learn to use it well."

Abenadar took the shield from the old man. It was made of curved laminated wood backed with metal reinforcements. Attached to the back were a leather loop and a strap. A long hanging strap was connected to the top and bottom of the shield.

"You may have to adjust the straps of the shield to yourself," said Portius. "How do the caligae fit?"

Abenadar knelt over, still tightening them. "I think they will be fine. They are comfortable enough."

"They better be. You will be marching most of your life in them. Come, thank Piso." Portius whispered to Abenadar, "You always want to stay on his best side." Then he continued more loudly, "We have one other place to go before you will be fully outfitted."

Abenadar nodded to Piso and thanked the old man. Then he and Portius picked up the rest of Abenadar's gear and walked across the yard to the forum.

"This is the camp market," said Portius. "You can buy almost anything you need here, and you will not be cheated by much. You have your issue." Portius fingered the sleeve of Abenadar's brown homespun robe. "But now we need to make you look like a legionnaire when you are not on duty."

Like the quaestorium, half of the lower part of the building housing the forum was open. Clothing, cloth, jewelry, trinkets, pots, food, and wine were displayed on tables under the overhanging roof. A large man with heavy Roman features watched them carefully from the back of the forum. When they stepped up to the displays of goods, he rushed leisurely forward.

"Gentlemen," he said, "I heard there was a new recruit in the legion, and a fine Roman at that." The man's accent was unlike any Abenadar had heard before.

The accent wasn't the only thing that made Abenadar stare at the man. The merchant was large and rotund and looked nothing like a legionnaire. Still, his face was scarred by a long slash that ran from his left eye across his cheek and neck and disappeared under the toga at his shoulder.

"Varro means you." Portius poked Abenadar with a finger.

"Oh," said Abenadar. He couldn't keep his eyes off the large man's mobile but disfigured features. Each word Varro spoke remolded his face.

Varro called to a young boy sitting in the shade of the forum, "Here, boy. Bring us chay."

While they waited on the child, Portius helped Abenadar out of his armor. They stacked the issued equipment out of the hot sun under the edge of the building.

After a few moments, the boy came back with three steaming clay cups of chay on a bronze platter. At Varro's prompting, Abenadar took one of the cups and found it was full of a hot, thin, brownish-green liquid. Varro and Portius both took loud sips. After watching them, Abenadar tentatively tasted the drink. The chay was slightly bitter but refreshing.

When Varro finished his chay, he put the cup down on the platter with a flourish and, turning to Abenadar, he asked, "Now, young master, what do you wish?"

Except for the master of thieves or the master of bastards, no one in the Galil had ever called Abenadar the master of anything. "Portius," whispered Abenadar, "what do I need?"

In answer, Portius pointed at Abenadar. "This is Abenadar, Varro."

"Pleased to meet you, Legionnaire Abenadar," said Varro, bowing. "You will be assured of a centurionate if you buy from me."

"There is no one else to buy from," said Portius.

"Couldn't I go to the market?" asked Abenadar.

"Wouldn't sell to a Roman." Varro didn't seem offended.

"Is that true?"

"In the main, yes. They would cheat you too. Or they would try," said Portius.

"I will not cheat you," said Varro, opening his hands. "The prices here are set by the Legatus Legionis."

"But Varro will make you a bargain, nonetheless," said Portius.

"I will not cheat you," reiterated Varro, "not on the price of the goods in the forum."

"In the price of whores," said Portius, "he will take your last denarii for a disease-ridden, toothless bitch."

Varro smiled broadly. "This is also true. But in the forum I market articles for the good of Rome. In the brothel, I sell the flesh of women. In the forum I can imagine the best of the legion. In the brothel, the least of its characteristics."

"Except for my issue, I have nothing a legionnaire needs," said Abenadar. "What can you sell me?"

Varro stepped behind the tables of goods. He brought out an iron spit, a bronze cooking pot, a woolen blanket, and a bronze cup. "These are the things you will need the most in camp and on campaign. I also suggest you purchase something to carry them in." He lifted a leather pack from the table beside him. "I will sell you these things at the fair legion price. But—" he squinted at Abenadar, measuring him up—"you will also need two tunics and perhaps a belt. A fancy chain might also agree with your youth and vanity. These things I will sell you altogether for 15 denarii."

"For 15 denarii," said Abenadar warming to the bargaining, "I would have to see the chain and the tunics. They would have to be of a very fine quality to merit such a figure."

"Certainly they are fine. This would fit you, I am sure." Varro lifted two tunics with a blue trim at their edges and fingered the trim. "This is the color of the Decimus Cohort."

"Is this the color I should wear on my tunic?" said Abenadar to Portius.

"Yes, though you might wish a tunic that is all blue."

"I would like the tunics to be entirely in the cohort's color. Do you have any of this type?"

"Yes," answered Varro as he took two all-blue tunics from the tables and placed them before Abenadar, "but the cost is greater."

"Before you state a number, what if I wished to buy the white-and-blue tunics you first showed me, and these? I would then give you 15 denarii for the lot."

"Fifteen for the lot? I should be soon too poor to keep the girls in the back. But for 17 denarii I might think of giving you the whole."

"I cannot say yes to that figure until I see the chain and belt you promised."

Varro took a leather belt and a bronze chain from behind the tables.

"Surely not a bronze chain," said Abenadar. "That is not much better than the iron one Piso gave me in the issue."

"Very well," said Varro, "here is a silver chain."

"It is not very high quality; certainly all this is worth no more than 15 denarii."

"Sixteen with the tunics and the kit."

"Fifteen and 8 copper asses is what I will give you."

"Fifteen and 12 copper asses, and I will have the tunics fitted to you."

"I thought it was included," said Abenadar.

"I did not say it was."

"Twelve copper asses at 16 to the denarius is a lot. Is this a fair price, Portius? What do you think?"

"I think it is a fair price. Take it and the fitting and you will be ready for anything—in the field, the city, or the camp."

"Very well, Varro, I will accept your offer for 15 denarii and 12 copper asses."

"Good, young master." Varro snapped his fingers and the chay boy came running. "Call Kepra to me." Varro chuckled. "Abenadar, you have spirit and a way with words."

A woman, stooped but not old, shuffled from behind the forum. Her face was almost as disfigured as Varro's but from disease and not any wound.

"Kepra, fit these tunics to this young legionnaire," ordered Varro.

Abenadar was obliged to change into each of the tunics, and Kepra marked the fit with a crease. Then he and Portius sat and drank chay with Varro until Kepra returned with the clothing. Abenadar and Portius gathered Abenadar's issue and new acquisitions. They waved to Varro as they made their way back across the camp to the Decimus Cohort's barracks.

*Blessed is Adonai, my rock,
who trains my hands for war,
my fingers for battle;
my help that never fails, my fortress,
my strong tower and my refuge,
my shield in which I trust,
he who puts nations under my feet.*

PSALM 144:1-2

Five

Portius poked Abenadar awake. The barracks room was dark and warm. The smell of unwashed men and rancid hay greeted Abenadar out of his slumber.

"Get up, Abenadar," hissed Portius. "Put on a tunic and your armor."

"I can't see to put on anything."

"Put on your tunic then and bring the rest outside. I'll help you with it there. It's already dawn," said Portius.

Abenadar felt around under his cot and gathered his things. After a moment, he followed Portius out of the barracks building. The sounds of waking men engulfed the chambers. Abenadar could hear clanking weapons and armor as the men dressed in the darkness.

Outside, with Portius' coaching, Abenadar shrugged on his lorica hamata and clasped it at the shoulders and breast. He put on the belt and hung his gladius from it. Portius strapped Abenadar's kit bag to his side and his scutum on his back. When Portius was finished, he studied Abenadar as he stood, uncomfortably weighted down by his armor and awkwardly holding a pila in his hand.

"Good," said Portius as he adjusted Abenadar's grasp on the pila. "At least you look like a legionnaire."

Tero, the optio of the Hastatus Posterior Century, strode out of the barracks. Portius pointed him out for Abenadar. This was the first time Abenadar had seen the optio. Tero was a brick of a man. Large and squat, his muscles were enormous. They bulged around his armor. He moved with a fluid gait that didn't match his appearance at all. As soon as the men caught sight of the optio, they quietly lined up on the signifer and formed into columns of about eight men each with 10 columns across the front of the century. The signifer stood by himself at the right of the century. Only a couple of the columns were totally manned with the full complement of eight legionnaires; the rest contained only seven men.

Abenadar didn't know where to go. He stood to the side of the formation until Portius waved him into the last position in the third column to the right of the signifer. This was the same column as Portius, Lupus, and Euodus. He stood directly behind the dour Euodus.

To the left of their century, the fifth century, the Hastatus Prior was forming up, and to the left of the fifth was the fourth, and so on to the first century in the cohort.

Tero, their optio, walked to stand in the center at the front of the century between the fifth and sixth columns. He barked a command Abenadar couldn't understand. Immediately, the legionnaires came to attention. Abenadar quickly imitated their stance. He was glad no one stood behind him to observe his untrained response.

Across the camp, the centurions appeared from their quarters in the officium. They carried arms and armor similar to the rest of the troops, but they sported cloaks in the blue of the cohort, and gold and silver decorations covered their armor. Instead of a pila, each carried a baton similar to the one Abenadar had seen in the Primus' hands. Abenadar learned later that the baton was called a vitis. It was the badge of a centurion's rank. The centurions marched with practiced precision toward their centuries.

As soon as Capilolinus, the Centurion of the Hastatus Posterior came to the front of the century, Tero called out another command. At that order, the signifer dipped the signum to salute the centurion and then came back to attention.

The signum was a long pole with metal decorations on it. On the top was a bronze wreath that encircled a silver *X*—the number of their cohort. Below the wreath, two short arms stretched at a 90-degree angle from the pole. From these arms, chains held three unit decorations. Abenadar noted that the signum of the Hastatus Posterior Century had six silver phalerae down the center of it. Phalerae were thick, four-inch-wide disks made of precious metals. These six phalerae were arranged below the wreath, one after the other on the pole. Following the last phalerae near the center of the pole was a gilded lion's head. Abenadar discovered later the center phalerae denoted the position of the century in the cohort while the gold and silver phalerae mounted with chains on the arms of the signum were awarded for valor in battle. That the Hastatus Posterior's signum displayed two silver and one gold decoration on the crossbar was significant.

Later, from Portius, Abenadar also found out that individual legionnaires could be awarded phalerae. These were usually given for outstanding initiative and actions that led directly to a unit's victory in battle. In addition, a legionnaire could earn a torque, a gold or silver necklace for killing an enemy in single combat or by show of conspicuous courage and prowess during battle. A metal armband called an armillae might also be bestowed for conduct of an even more remarkable character.

Centurion Capilolinus marched up to Tero, and the optio saluted him. Without another word Tero faced right and marched across the front of the century. At the signifer, he smartly turned right again and marched to stand at the last row facing forward and directly behind the signifer. Capilolinus took the optio's place at the front of the century. These were the positions normally kept during a march, Abenadar found out. The only variation to this was during battle when the centurion usually moved to stand beside the signifer.

To the left of the Hastatus Posterior Century, the five other centuries executed exactly the same drill. When all of the centuries had formed up with their centurion in front, the Pilus Prior Centurion, the centurion of the first century of the cohort, marched to stand in front of the entire group. He was the commander of the cohort, responsible for the first century as well as the overall control of the cohort.

The Pilus Prior called out his orders to the centuries. They were Latin words Abenadar couldn't fully understand. After a moment, their Centurion, Capilolinus, called out an order and the men quietly fell out. Capolinius handed a piece of papyrus to the optio, who saluted him, and then, the morning muster complete, Centurion Capilolinus returned to his quarters in the officium. The men gathered expectantly around the signum. With impatience, the optio called out, "Where is the Lion's new librarius?"

Portius, Lupus, and Euodus pointed at Abenadar, who still stood in his last position. The optio walked up to Abenadar. "I am Tero, the optio of the Lion Century. You are Abenadar, the new librarius. Is this not so?"

"Yes, sir," said Abenadar.

"You will read the duty roster every day." Tero squinted at him. "You can read?"

"Yes, sir."

Tero handed the sheet of papyrus to him, eyed him a moment from head to foot as if to take his measure, and walked away.

Abenadar examined the heavy sheet of papyrus in his hand. He had never handled papyrus. It was beautiful and felt strangely soft and supple against his skin. The sheet was marked with a matrix of lines. To the left, a column listed the names of the legionnaires, and across the top were written the numbers of the days and the name of the month. Each of the blocks contained words and abbreviations.

"Come on, Abenadar," insisted Portius, "what are the duties?"

Abenadar stared at the sheet. He read the first name. "Andreus."

The man stood right in front of him. He was tall and broad. "Yes, what is my duty today?"

"What day of the month is this?" asked Abenadar.

"The fourth."

"It says your duty is ad stercus."

Andreus groaned, then cursed. "The latrines."

"Callistus," read Abenadar.

"Yes, yes." Callistus raised his hand.

"Strigis."

"Patrol. I'll be lucky to come back alive." He winked.

Abenadar worked his way through the long list. The abbreviations stumped him a couple of times, but when he read out the letters, the men seemed to know what they meant and what they were supposed to do. The work was difficult for him. As he neared the end, Abenadar found his own name; for this day, the entry said "stakes."

The optio and signifer still stood near Abenadar speaking to each other. After a while, they noticed Abenadar alone beside them.

"Well," said Tero to Abenadar, "where are you supposed to be?"

"The roster says 'stakes,'" said Abenadar, "but I don't know what 'stakes' means."

"It means you are to be trained as a legionnaire."

"Where should I go?"

"Come with me." Tero took the papyrus from Abenadar's hands.

Abenadar followed the optio toward the back of the camp. When they passed the end of the barracks, the buildings gave way to a large enclosed field. Across the field, Abenadar saw the six-foot wall of earth topped with stakes that marked the boundary of the camp. The space between the earthen wall and the end of the barracks was at least 300 yards wide; from side to side it was more than twice that. At the right of this area lay a large square of raw earth with about 20 six-foot poles that stood straight up in it. Near these were reed targets and long wooden beams covered with hide. In front of the poles stood a giant of a man surrounded by about 20 men without plumes on their helmets.

Tero led Abenadar toward this group. "Hey, Nico, here is a new man for you to train."

Nico was the giant. He was as broad and tall as one of the huge doors leading into the camp. His name in Latin meant "battering ram," and Abenadar never learned if Nico was a nickname or really his own. Like all of the veterans, Nico's face and arms were covered with scars, and though his armor was complete, it showed signs of frequent repair. He carried a baton similar to the vitis of the centurions, but without decorations. This, Abenadar learned, was a training baton.

"So, who is this?" boomed Nico in a voice as large as he was.

"I am Abenadar of Natzeret."

"Are we now taking men from the Galil?" said Nico.

"I am a citizen of Rome."

"All men are the same here," said Nico. "What matters is not where you come from but how well you learn to be a legionnaire."

"That is why I'm here," said Abenadar.

Tero slapped Abenadar on the back. "I like this man already, Nico. Train him well." He turned and walked back toward the front of the camp.

Nico said, "Good, Abenadar. Join the group. I was just explaining the march. Today, like every day, we march. Put on your shields."

All the men except Abenadar had taken off their shields. They now used the long strap to loop them over their backs.

"We march, but first we need some fuel to march on. Follow me, and we'll see if any breakfast is left for starving Romans—even one from Natzeret." Nico led them to the front of the camp.

The men followed closely behind Nico. As they walked, they pulled their bowls and drinking cups from their packs. Abenadar copied them. He wound up at the end of a long line that curved around the barracks toward the officium. Because they were trainees and not full legionnaires, they had to wait for all the other men before they could eat.

The line moved quickly. When Abenadar finally stepped around to the front of the barracks, the single line became four separate queues that passed before large iron cooking pots. The first pot in each queue steamed from a fire below it. As Abenadar stepped to the front of the line, a cook dished cibaria, thick wheat gruel, into his bowl. The cook filled his bowl almost to the top, and added a large splash of olive oil to it from an amphora. From the second large pot, a kitchen slave ladled a thin mixture of water and beer that was almost entirely water into Abenadar's cup.

As soon as he had his food, Abenadar paused and scanned around. Nico and the trainees sat on the ground near the quaestorium. Abenadar joined them there.

The cibaria was palatable and filling. It was the most food Abenadar had ever eaten at one time. He downed it and scraped the bottom of the bowl with his fingers to get the last scraps.

Nico finished quickly too. When he was done, he scrubbed out his bowl with sand and ordered the men into formation.

"Fall in," roared Nico. "Now we march."

Abenadar imitated Nico; he cleaned his bowl with sand and stashed his bowl and cup away in his leather kit bag.

At Nico's instructions, the men formed three columns of seven. Abenadar found himself again at the end of a column. Nico took his place at the right where the optio normally stood and called out, "Forward, h'arch."

"Keep in step," ordered Nico. For a while, he counted the pace out loud and watched each man's feet. When someone fell out of step, Nico tapped him with his baton. When Nico had to correct the same man more than once, he struck his legs. A third mistake brought the baton down with a whistle on the man's back.

Abenadar was hit twice, but he soon fell into the rhythm of the march and wasn't struck again. Many weren't so lucky. The columns marched in step to the end of the camp, turned around, and marched to the other end. Without a rest, they repeated this same pattern over and over for hours.

While they marched, Nico came up beside Abenadar. Abenadar flinched. He expected to feel the sting of the baton. Instead, Nico began to instruct him in the basic courtesies of the camp. He told Abenadar how to salute and to whom and how to address the different officials. Nico explained the marching steps and gave Abenadar hints on how to march correctly. This advice allowed Abenadar to take much of the strain off his back and legs.

After a while, Nico went back to calling the pace. While the morning waned, from time to time Nico increased their pace to a quick-march. At least once each hour, he pushed them to a run. By the time the sun rested straight overhead, Abenadar was exhausted. He could tell the other men had also just about reached their limit. His armor was heavy and uncomfortable, and his new sandals where stretching out and did not fit as well as when he had begun.

At last Nico called, "Halt."

Abenadar almost ran into the man in front of him.

"Very good," said Nico, when all the men stood at attention. "Now, not a sound, not a movement. You must discipline yourself." He walked all the way around the formation. "Don't move a muscle until I tell you to—fall out."

The men let themselves drop to the ground. They lay quiet and exhausted. Nico allowed them to stay there for about half an hour. That was not long enough for Abenadar or for any of the other men.

"Okay, trainees, get up. Now it's time for weapons training."

The men groaned, but not too loudly.

"You'd better get used to it," Nico warned. "Every day for the rest of your training, the morning is for marching and formations, and the afternoon is for weapons training. The quicker you learn, the quicker we can get this over. Let's move!"

Nico led them in an unorganized quickstep to the dirt area that bristled with six-foot stakes. When they got to the practice field, the other men immediately headed for a small shelter and picked up heavy wooden training swords.

Nico pointed at Abenadar. "Get a practice gladius for yourself and come back over here."

Abenadar picked up one of the swords. It was the same shape and size as the gladius Piso issued to him, but instead of iron, the blade was made of hardwood weighted with lead. Through constant use, the grip of the practice sword was well polished, and its dull blade was nicked in a thousand places. Although Abenadar was unfamiliar with any sword, he could immediately tell this was much heavier than the regular gladius that hung at his belt.

Abenadar quickly rejoined the men gathered around Nico at the stakes. These poles were a little taller than a man and were placed in staggered rows at about 10-foot intervals. Each stake was covered with about as many nicks and marks as the wooden sword Abenadar held.

Nico was explaining: "You attack your man by going for the body and head. A strike against the legs or arms may injure, but it puts you in danger of his attack. This is how I want you to fight the stakes today: remain behind your shield and strike only at the top and middle of the stake. Stay at your practice until I order you to halt. Now take your places."

The men unlimbered their shields from their backs and picked out a stake. Abenadar mimicked their actions and stance.

"Practice gladius ready; attack!" bellowed Nico.

The men began striking at the stakes. As Nico had instructed, they hid behind their shields and made cautious blows at the pole. Abenadar attempted to copy them, but before he made more than one attack, Nico was immediately at his side.

"Okay, Abenadar," said Nico, "you missed a few days of training. Let me show you the proper way to use the gladius and scutum."

Nico instructed Abenadar on how to properly hold the sword and the correct way to attack—not with the edge but with the point of the gladius. After Abenadar demonstrated a basic understanding, Nico left him and moved so he could oversee the rest of the practice.

Abenadar was soon covered with sweat, and not much later, his shield and sword arm started to ache. After a couple of hours, he couldn't remember how long ago they started, and with each attack, he wondered aloud when they would rest.

If the men slacked off during the exercise, Nico reminded them of their assignment with a baton prod. Finally after what seemed like hours, Nico called a halt. The men let their practice swords fall to the ground and sat exhausted with their backs against the stakes. They didn't take the time to remove their shields. No one had any breath left for talking. They all sat with their head back, gasping.

After a few minutes, Nico said, "Okay, all you trainees, are you ready for chow or are you going to sleep the afternoon away?"

The men grumbled. Some seemed to be giving consideration to Nico's alternative.

Nico growled at them, "You'll need all your strength to practice after dinner, so you have to eat. I don't want any excuses. Up you go."

The men climbed stiffly to their feet.

Abenadar lay on his back beside his stake. He stayed there until Nico prodded him with his baton. "Abenadar, aren't you ready for chow?"

Abenadar tried to stand up. "How about a hand?"

Nico smirked a grin from ear to ear and with one hand pulled Abenadar—armor, shield, practice gladius, and body—to his feet. Nico smiled broadly at Abenadar's astonishment. "Come on, youngster. Let's go eat."

It was a repeat of the long lines of the morning. This time the cooks again filled their bowls with cibaria and olive oil, but they poured new wine mixed with water into their cups. Again, the drink contained more water than wine.

Like the morning, the trainees and Nico sat on the ground in the shade of the quaestorium and ate the hot cereal with their fingers. The water-laced new wine was good. Abenadar had never tasted wine before. He was very pleased with the rations and surprised to hear complaints from some of the men.

"This could get old," said the trainee at his left.

"You'd better get used to it, Thermus," said Nico. "That is why you are paid so well."

Thermus scoffed. "The pay won't last long enough to feed you meat at the temple. Not for more than a few days."

"Is it meat you want?" asked Nico. "You could go hunting."

"And become meat for the altars of the rebels in the Galil."

"When I'm finished training you," said Nico, "you will fear no man."

"I personally fear only devils and no man," said Thermus.

"Then I will have to be a devil," said Nico, still smiling. "Aren't you finished yet? It's already time for the stakes again."

The men groaned but rushed to clean their bowls and cups and followed the huge man back to the practice field.

Abenadar felt refreshed. He'd rarely had so much to eat at once. It was a pleasure to work hard and then be well fed. Unfortunately, he felt more like sleeping than practicing.

At the field, Nico immediately ordered them back to the stakes. So they could pace their energy through the rest of the afternoon, the men fought their imaginary foes more carefully than before.

It didn't work. By the time the cornicen's horn sounded the next watch, they were again completely exhausted. Nico allowed them a short rest, then gathered them around to critique their practice. The large legionnaire seemed to remember every stroke each of them made during the long afternoon.

"Okay," said Nico when he was done, "one more practice and you are released from the day's training." He waited for the groans to subside. "All you have to do is show me a correct salute. I will stand here with the baton. Imagine I am your centurion, and you are reporting to me. When you report correctly, I will return your salute, and you are cleared off. If you report incorrectly, you get to feel the baton."

The men formed a line and started through, each saluting Nico. Whenever he sent a man to the back of the line, Nico explained exactly what the trainee had done wrong.

Abenadar listened carefully. When it was his turn, Nico returned his salute, and he dragged himself off to the barracks.

The camp served no evening meal. Two meals a day was more than Abenadar was used to, and he was too tired to eat anyway. He didn't say a word to anyone. He just crawled out of his armor.

Before the sun set, he fell into a dead slumber.

*Test me, O Adonai, and try me;
put my heart and mind to the proof.
For thy constant love is before my eyes,
and I live in thy truth.*

Psalm 26:2-3

Six

Abenadar awoke the next morning with a jab from Portius' foot in his back. He wouldn't thank Portius for the generosity, though sleeping through the morning muster meant additional duties and possibly lashes. During yesterday's training, Nico had explained all the infractions and their punishments to Abenadar and the other trainees.

In the unlit barracks, Abenadar tried to put on his armor, but he was still too unfamiliar with the fittings to accomplish that feat in the dark. Like the day before, he gathered everything up and took it outside. He didn't ask for aid, but two legionnaires from his century helped him put everything on. Before the optio called them to attention, Abenadar already was in his place. He stood through the formation with confidence borne of yesterday's brief instruction. He almost felt like a legionnaire.

As soon as the Decimus Cohort's Pilus Prior Centurion dismissed them, Capilolinus again handed the duty roster to optio Tero and left. Tero immediately released the men and passed the thick papyrus to Abenadar.

Abenadar was more comfortable with the roster today. He rattled through the abbreviations. When he forgot one, though none of the other men could read, they reminded him of the meaning.

Abenadar could spare more time to look over the document today. The top of the sheet listed the names of the century's officers. They were listed by rank. First was Centurion Capilolinus. Below his name in a single row came Optio Tero, Signifer Stechus, Tesserarius Rufus, and in a new hand, Librarius Abenadar. Like the men, Abenadar had a row that indicated his duties, but the centurion and other principales did not. Their work was to supervise the activities of the legionnaires in the century. Again today, Abenadar's duty was at the stakes.

After Abenadar read the legionnaires their duties, he handed the duty roster back to Tero and reported to Nico on the practice field. As soon as all the men reported for training, Nico led them over to another breakfast of hot cibaria and weak beer; then he marched them back to the practice field.

"Today," said Nico, "we really begin your training."

The men groaned, Abenadar along with them. He already anticipated the day's fatigue.

"Come on," Nico protested. "Do you want to be legionnaires or would you rather work for Varro? Maybe as one of his pleasure items." Nico snorted at them. "Come on; get your practice weapons and shields. We are going to march."

"But the practice weapons are twice as heavy as the regular weapons," complained Thermus.

"Thermus, you are getting smarter with each passing day," said Nico. "Today, because I feel nice—" he frowned—"you won't have to carry your own weapons too. And you may carry your field pack instead of the practice pack."

Some of the men, including Abenadar, limped slightly. Nico pulled them aside and helped them properly adjust the leather straps of their caligae.

After all the men gathered their heavy wooden weapons and wicker shields, Nico formed them into the three columns of seven. He stood in the optio's place. "Forward, h'arch!"

For a while, until Nico was satisfied with their progress, he marched the columns at the normal pace back and forth across the field. Today Nico didn't have to warn the men as much. Only one or two reached the third infraction and felt the heavy baton full on their backs. Abenadar was certain he was out of step a couple of times, but either he was lucky or Nico was more lenient today.

The columns just turned at the end of the field for the fifth time when Nico called, "Quickstep, h'arch." The columns accelerated to double the march pace.

There were moans from all around, but Nico countered them with a laugh. "Be happy. In the quickstep, sometimes you get to rest every hour." Nico began to call the steps and drove them to a steady march. They marched at this pace for an hour before Nico called a halt. He gave them 15 very short minutes, then formed them up to march again. Abenadar legs ached already.

"Forward, h'arch," said Nico, then right away, "Quickstep, h'arch."

This time they didn't just march. Nico directed them to the edge of the field. Where the rain ran from the flat field under the walls, ditches cut deeply into the sandy soil. They jumped the ditches at the quickstep pace. Any man who didn't jump high enough or far enough felt Nico's baton on his buttocks or back. Any man who wasn't back in step within two paces also felt the warning nudge of the baton. After a while, Nico allowed them another insufficient rest. When they started again, they jumped the ditches while running and Nico varied the pace from the quickstep to a run and back to the regular gait. The pace was grueling.

Abenadar was surprised no one fell out from exhaustion. After a while, Abenadar realized Nico was too shrewd an instructor to allow that. In some way yet unknown to Abenadar, Nico expertly sized up each of the men and knew almost intrinsically their limitations. From this untutored observation, Abenadar concluded, Nico must be a master at training soldiers.

After that, Abenadar watched Nico's actions and decisions more carefully. He noted how the man operated, how he worked with and appraised the men. After one particularly strenuous march left them all breathless, Nico gave them a long half hour of rest, and after the last hour of march, which seemed particularly easy, he let them off early for chow. These seemingly unplanned generosities bound the men to Nico and made the hard and sometimes cruel training acceptable. Abenadar realized Nico's generous acts were intentional.

At dinner, Abenadar found the food even more palatable than the day before. He offered to take any leftovers off the hands of the men in his training group. Though they grumbled about the food, he got only a little extra cibaria for his efforts.

"Abenadar, the insatiable," Thermus kidded him.

After dinner, they returned to the field—now, like the day before, they practiced against the stakes. They toiled until their arms felt like lead weights. With goads from the baton, Nico kept them at it. When the day was over, they crawled like whipped dogs to their cots. Abenadar slept like a log until, like the previous day, Portius roused him with a hearty kick.

Each day, as soon as the morning muster was over, Nico had them fed and marching. Each day, Nico increased their load and the vigor of the march. The training was intense, but Abenadar enjoyed it. The exercise gave free play to his young strength, and he was not disappointed at his progress or his innate abilities.

Every afternoon they practiced at the stakes. From individual practice, they began controlled exercises. They practiced specific parries and thrusts at Nico's command. By the ease with which Abenadar could now wield the practice weapons, he knew his muscles were growing larger and stronger. In the camp, he had no time for anything except the training.

After about a month, Nico introduced them to a new game. "Okay," said the scarred veteran, "today we will make an ambulatura, and you learn how to make a camp."

"A camp?" said Thermus. "You want us to build a whole camp?"

Nico grinned. "A small camp. One fit for a century. Grab your kits. Full field pack. Real weapons. Stakes and digging equipment."

This time, Nico himself took a pack and gear. He put on his helmet with the full plumes of an optio. The rest of them wore their plain helmets without plumes.

"Are we going outside the camp?" protested Thermus. When Nico nodded, Thermus continued, "We don't have the plumes of a legionnaire. What if the Zealots of the Galil notice that and attack us?"

For almost a full minute Nico stared at Thermus, his grin widening. "Then you will get better training than I can give you. And you won't have to do the stakes this evening. I promise. Or perhaps Abenadar can explain to the Zealots that you are not quite up to the fight, and if they let you pass by," he paused, "then you will still have to practice at the stakes."

No one except Nico laughed.

Like every day before, Nico formed them into three columns and they started out across the camp. "Forward, h'arch."

A couple of men started with balked steps. "Keep your march

perfect, or all the Galil will know you are a bunch of untrained dolts," Nico growled in warning.

They marched in perfect step to the gates, and at Nico's command, they came to a halt.

"Open the gates," commanded Nico.

With a loud creak, the guards opened both heavy wooden portals.

"Forward, h'arch," bawled Nico.

Within a few paces they entered the streets of Tzippori, or Sepphoris, as the Romans called it. Through the city, Nico marched in the centurion's place at the front of the columns. He didn't correct them or appear to look at them, but from experience, Abenadar knew Nico could tell from the sounds of the march when they were out of step…and who was out of step. Nico marched with his head held high, an explicit Roman threat in his every move. Each of his trainees tried to follow his example, and their lines were good, though not perfect.

As soon as they passed through the gates of the city, Nico ordered, "Quickstep, h'arch."

They sped at the ground-covering pace and the miles began to flow beneath their feet. As soon as the city fell out of sight, Nico berated the men who had not kept perfect step through the city. His baton reminded them with a couple of heavy clouts that they must show themselves at their best or they risked no less than the jeers of Herod's troops and the ridicule of the people of the Galil.

Nico didn't censure Abenadar, so Abenadar guessed he'd kept the step along with the proper decorum. For their corporate failings, Nico didn't let them rest until they marched over an hour and a half, and then he put them at normal pace instead of letting them stop. They marched west through the valley of Sepphoris and then turned to the south into another shallow valley. Soon a village—Abenadar guessed it was Simonias—came into sight. The grassy valley turned into a dusty path that widened into a rutted roadway.

The people of Simonias stood warily outside their houses and watched the approaching columns of legionnaires. There were no cheers—never any for the Roman oppressor, especially since the reign of Herod Antipas. The people had once welcomed them, and some of the older legionnaires had told Abenadar of the adulation they'd received when they'd helped free the land from the heavy hand of the Greeks. But in Herod, the people had their own devil now, and together with the cruel king, the Romans experienced the people's censure. The villagers stood silent, their eyes slightly downcast.

The soldiers' steps reverberated between the buildings and back into the street. The three columns sounded overloud in the small village. The children didn't chase after them, not like they had when their columns marched through Sepphoris; the adults held on to them as though they feared the Romans would suck them away. Outside of the village, the road turned back into low grass and then into dusty scree. For a while, they saw no signs of any human habitation; then they entered a backcountry of grasslands, fields, and small farms.

"Quickstep, h'arch," called Nico.

In an hour, the columns came across the wide shallow bed of the Kishon River. At this time of year, the Kishon was only a trickle as it wound its way toward the Great Sea. They crossed the river and Nico stopped them on the other side. One column stood watch while the other two drank from the dirty stream of the Kishon and ate a handful of parched uncooked wheat, their cibaria ration. After half an hour, Nico rotated another column to the watch and let the first column eat and drink.

The Kishon River indicated they had truly come into a fruitful place—the plain called Esdraelon. Here, the ripe land full of villages and cultivated fields mocked the hilly desolation typical of much of southern Judea. The mountains towered in the purple horizon, looming on three sides over the grand flat expanse. The green and fertile earth hid completely the bones of thousands of warriors.

The Esdraelon was a killing field—in appearance only an easy approach to the interior. The valley of Sepphoris was the one straightforward avenue of invasion from the coast into the Northern Kingdom. Generations of the men of Judea and the Galil had ambushed their attackers as they tried to cross the steep valleys at the east end of the Esdraelon.

After all the men ate and drank, Nico reformed their columns, and they marched straight out into the fields. He led them out toward the center of the plain paralleling the stream of the Kishon and not into the mountains, where they would have been certain to meet rebellious members of the Essenes, Zealots, and any of the other groups who patently resisted the rule of Rome.

After a couple hours, Nico finally let them stop. He chose a flat area near the open streambed of the Kishon. They still couldn't all rest; he posted four men at corners of the open area and gathered the others around him. "First, we eat," he said. "Then we build a camp."

Nico marked out the boundaries of the camp they would build and checked the guards while the rest of them opened up their packs and ate again from their cibaria rations. They had only the dirty water of the Kishon to drink and the dry-roasted wheat to eat. It was a dusty meal, but it satisfied Abenadar.

After Nico changed out the guards, he gathered them together again and explained the rudiments of the legion field fortifications. Then he set them to work. Abenadar and the others began digging a ditch where Nico scored it in the earth. Nico had marked a square 50 feet on a side. They dug the ditch with their simple spades and piled the dirt on the inside to form a wall. The ditch was to be four feet deep and the wall four feet high. They only rested when Nico rotated them onto guard duty.

The ground here, like most of the Galil, was solid and brittle. They used the points of their digging tools to break apart the rock-hard soil and the flat parts to shovel it out. The work was slow and backbreaking.

"You would have thought Nico chose this place because it has the hardest dirt in the Galil," said Thermus to Abenadar.

"Don't worry," returned Abenadar, "all of the Galil is like this. I've dug enough fields here to know."

By evening, they finished the ditch and its low wall. Then, under Nico's guidance, they embedded the stakes they carried in their field packs into the top of the wall facing outward. As the sun fell beneath the plain, Nico set four men to guard and let the others sleep.

In the middle of the night, Nico woke Abenadar, "Get up, Abenadar; it's your turn to guard." Nico directed him to a corner of the camp, and Abenadar stumbled sleepily to his post. There, the guard handed him the wooden tessera of the watch. While the man shuffled gratefully off to sleep, Abenadar put the tessera around his neck and stared, straining, out into the darkness. To keep awake, he walked slowly back and forth.

Just as the sun started to rise between the mountains, Nico came to him and retrieved the tessera. "Good. I'm glad you stayed awake. Otherwise…"

Yes. Abenadar knew what Nico meant—a flogging or death. Abenadar realized the gravity of his charge, and he was glad to take it. He had never before held any real responsibility. Here, he shared responsibility for the safety of all twenty-two of them. As the sun edged above the mountains and began to throw long shadows over the ground, he stood a bit straighter. Thermus replaced him.

While the trainees refilled in the ditch and stamped the dirt into place, Nico allowed Abenadar and the other three late guards to sleep. A little before they formed up to make the march back to Sepphoris, Thermus shook Abenadar awake. Nico let them eat—another meal of dry wheat and water. Already Abenadar longed for the hot cibaria of the camp.

"On your feet," Nico ordered. "Form up." He stood in front of the columns. "Never," he said while striding back and forth along their three ranks, "never fail to build a fortification when you stop for the night, and never leave any fortification for your enemies to use. That little rule may save your rotten hides one day. Now let's get back to your soft beds in Sepphoris."

Nico stepped to the optio's march position and called, "Forward h'arch." He let them warm their blood for a couple of hours at the regular march pace, then called out, "Quickstep, h'arch."

When they entered and marched through the city of Sepphoris, the men held their heads a little higher, their steps were precise, and Nico was obviously pleased with their entry into the legion fort. He was so pleased with the performance of his trainees during their first ambulatura, or march in the field, he let them off early that day.

After the afternoon meal, Abenadar sat with the men from the training columns. With a free period until sunset for the first time in their training, they spoke about the Galil and the different places they had been.

"I entered the service in Rome," said Thermus. "They sent me to this godforsaken place right off."

"I met my probatio in Egypt," said Pallas, a recruit from the fifth, the Hastatus Prior Century, the same century as Thermus.

"Which city?" asked Thermus.

"Alexandria."

"Why didn't they keep you in the Egyptian Legion?"

"My family came from Napoli," Pallas explained. "They don't like full Romans in the Egyptian Legion."

"Why didn't they leave you in Rome, Thermus?" asked another.

"Ah," growled Thermus, "my father wasn't wealthy enough and my family couldn't get me a letter of introduction to the Praetorian Guard. This is a good billet until I can make my way back to Rome."

"You were lucky they didn't send you to the Isle of Britain."

"I'm not so sure," said Thermus. "I hear the women there are at least more accommodating."

"More accommodating, but ugly."

"What do you know about it?"

"Piso was stationed there, and he said it was always bleak and dreary. The women, he says, are all ugly and dirty. They would as soon cut your throat as accommodate you."

"Here they won't even speak to you," said Thermus.

"You have to know their language, and then the women here will be as willing as the women of Britain. What do you say, Abenadar? You speak their tongue."

Abenadar wasn't sure what to say. "I don't know," he finally stuttered. "I haven't spoken to any women in Sepphoris. The first time I ever stayed in the city overnight was after I made my probatio. The girls of the villages are careful of their virtue, and it is considered a great sin to speak to a foreigner."

"We have no hope, then?"

"I don't know what the women of the city are like," said Abenadar.

"They are all the same no matter where you are," said Pallas. "A little money goes a long way to convince them. Abenadar, you will speak for us when Nico lets us go into the city?"

"Why not?" said Abenadar, shrugging.

Thermus clapped him on the shoulder. "Good man. They will

certainly take our obols for their comfort then."

"You'll need to trade your copper obols and asses for kodrantes and leptons; that is if you don't want to waste your money. The people of Sepphoris do not traffic in the money of Rome. They are too poor."

"What do you say? We need to change our currency?"

"Yes, the copper Judean coins are the city's currency," said Abenadar.

"Already you are worth your weight, Abenadar. When we go into the city, you must show us the way."

"I cannot show you the way," snorted Abenadar, "but I can get you the proper rate and with coppers in our purses, we can find a tavern and women who will give you more than a cold shoulder."

The cornicen sounded the beginning of the night watch.

"It's time to sleep," said Thermus. "When we are finally legionnaires, then we will see what prospects there are in the city of Sepphoris."

The next morning Nico began their training in the battle formations.

"You didn't expect to enter combat in column formation," he bawled at them. "You'd be cut to ribbons. So we never enter a fight in columns. The first formation I will teach you is the single line."

He walked them through the steps to turn a column of rows into the single line. Although this was just a single line of men, it was not so easy to get into from the columns, at least, not easy without practice. And practice they did.

Nico sent them around and around the practice field. While they marched at a full tilt, he expected them to immediately and correctly reassemble into the line formation. At first he had them make the line following a halt, then they formed a line without a pause. Finally, he ordered them into the line while running. If anyone moved out of place, Nico struck him with his baton. As the morning ended, like always, they were exhausted. When Nico finally released them for the afternoon meal, every one of them fell into a heap in place.

After dinner, they began something new. "Training in the pila," announced Nico. "Get two training pilum, the pilum praepilata, and form a single line on me."

Abenadar picked up two of the practice spears. They were at least twice as heavy as a regular throwing pila—all the practice equipment weighed more than twice as much as the normal equipment. Abenadar quickly found his place in line.

Nico struck the last man in place. "You were late. Move faster next time. Everyone, put down your pilum in place and get a wicker shield. Hang the shield on the knob on your stake and reform your line."

All the men ran to carry out Nico's instructions. No one got a reminder this time.

Nico lined them up about ten yards from the stakes. Their wicker shields hung on the stakes at about the normal height for a shield carried by a soldier.

"You know by now," said Nico, "there are two types of pilum, the light pila and the heavy pila. Both can be thrown, but the light pila can be thrown farther. You use this weapon when the enemy has not engaged your line. The light pila, properly thrown, will cause a man to discard his shield. And without a shield he is much easier to kill. When the light pila strikes a shield, it punctures it and the barbs on the point make it almost impossible to pull out. Also, because the metal shaft is weak, it will bend, both so it is harder to remove and so it can't be thrown back at you. A shield with a pila stuck in it is practically useless. Remember this; it may save your life: a pila that has struck almost anything is useless. That is why you take care of them in the field. You can also use a light pila against a man. The weapon will cause a painful wound, but don't use it for anything except throwing. Only in the direst emergencies, when you have nothing else should you think of using it against a charge. A gladius is better—even the scutum is a better weapon against a charge.

"The heavy pila can also be thrown, but it will not have the same effect. If you throw the heavy pila at a man, you don't want his shield; you want to strike him. But remember this; if you don't strike him, he will throw your pila right back at you. The heavy pila is a defensive weapon. It can stop any charge. And in the double and triple line formations, you can use it to reach forward to strike beyond the froward ranks.

"Do you all understand?" He paused to look up and down the line. "Good. Let's hit the shields. Light pila first. Ready. Throw."

Their line stood close enough to the stakes that almost every wooden pila hit the shield and stuck. A few that weren't thrown hard enough fell to the ground in front of the stake. Nico growled at those men, but he didn't do anything but warn them—this time.

"Ready with the second pila. Light pilum. Ready. Throw."

As they struck and stuck in the shields, the rattling of 20 wooden pilum reverberated across the field. This time all the pilum remained fixed in the targets.

Nico smiled. "Good. Go get your pilum, then back to the line."

For the rest of the afternoon, they threw pilum at the wicker shields on the stakes. By evening, like each evening, every one of the trainees was worn out. Nico's solution to a tired arm was to have them use their other arm to throw, and this time, when their pila didn't stick in the target, he chastised them with his baton.

The rest of the month they learned how to make not only the single-line formation but also the double line, triple line, square, wedge, and circle. They learned and practiced how to assemble into and from every formation, and they practiced every single combination until they could perform them without a pause. If they responded sluggishly or with confusion, Nico beat them until they got it right.

Now they alternated practicing against the stakes with both the pila and the gladius. With the pilum, they backed away from the stakes until they could hit the shields consistently at 75 feet with either arm.

Once a week Nico took them away from the camp to practice the muli marinani. Eventually on these long ambulatura, they carried a full field pack with 17 days of rations and constructed the two types of camps. The simple camp they made on their first muli marinani, and the fortified camp with 12-foot ditches nine feet deep with four-foot walls. When they built the fortified camp, they stayed out for a week.

Abenadar didn't know which was worse, building the camp or taking it down, and Nico never let them build a camp in the same location twice. To enhance their practice, Nico made sure the ground was always hard and untouched.

After two months, when the men reported to the stakes, a centurion stood beside Nico. The centurion was dressed in full field gear. His lorica hamata was a finer quality than the halburk the men wore, and it was decorated with awards of valor, the gold and silver phalerae of an experienced and successful combat veteran. The centurion's arms and legs were scarred, the ever-present marks of a survivor of close fighting. He was a tall man and the plumes of a centurion made him look taller. The cheek guards of his helmet also sported gold phalerae.

Today, Nico didn't hold his ever-present baton.

Without his usual banter, Nico immediately ordered the men into their full field gear with weapons and formed them into columns. The trainees found their places with quiet precision. They realized they were about to embark on a new portion of their training.

"This is Praefectus Legionis Aemilius Regulus," said Nico. "He is the centurion of the third century, the Hastatus of the Primus Cohort. He will judge your training today. If your capability pleases him, you will progress to the armatura training. If you fail, you will receive barley rations instead of wheat until the Praefectus Legionis judges you fit. If many of you fail, I will get barley rations and none of you will know peace in this world.

"The Praefectus Legionis selects the training for today. He has instructed me that he wants to observe you in the ambulatura and at the stakes." Nico turned smartly toward the centurion and saluted him. "Praefectus Legionis, the men are ready for your examination."

Centurion Aemilius spoke with a taut baritone, but his voice carried as well as Nico's deeper bass commands. He raised his vitis to return Nico's salute. Nico turned and took the optio's normal march position at the back of the formation.

The centurion called smartly, "To the gates."

Nico ordered, "Forward, h'arch." And like a single man they stepped off together. The hours of practice were evident. Though Nico didn't mark any cadence, they marched in perfect step. Their turns and movements were precise. Without a falter or a change step, the men marched like veteran legionnaires through the camp and gates and into the streets of Sepphoris. They were dauntless and silent; only the pound of their heavy caligae gave evidence of their passing.

As soon as they passed through the gates of Sepphoris, the Praefectus Legionis ordered, "Quickstep."

"Quickstep, h'arch," called Nico in time, and the column leapt forward. Like a lion on the trail of its prey, Centurion Aemilius lengthened his stride. His plumes waved with his steps and the men followed with a heavy unconscious grace. They were like an oiled war machine, a mechanical phalanx, and they thought they could face anything.

Aemilius let the men warm to the march. He could feel the strength in these recruits. With the miles, their stride lengthened, and he became confident they would keep the pace and the step. "Nico, change out the ranks."

"First rank, to the back, h'arch." The men in the first rank moved to the end of their columns.

Aemilius let them march in this new position to see if the men were all able to keep their precise steps through the change. After a while, he shifted the ranks again and then again and again, until the first rank was back in the front. All the time, the mechanical phalanx kept pace. "Nico, at a run."

"Ready, ready, charge."

The pace increased and the men began to breathe hard. Their exhalations came in hard puffs, quick and deep. The columns remained even and unbroken.

Aemilius smiled. They rushed like an unstoppable chariot. He glanced back at Nico. "Slow to a normal march."

"March step, h'arch." The columns slowed in two steps and

without a break marched on apace. Sweat dripped from under their helmets and showered their lorica hamata. Where their tunics could be seen under their armor, they were dark and saturated. But the men were barely winded. Nico had tried them harder than this. Their reserve of strength was perceivable; Aemilius could feel it in them. Instead of letting them rest, he said to Nico, "Formations."

Nico took the columns through the formations. They formed the single line, double line, triple line, square, wedge, and circle. Aemilius tried to confuse them. He changed the ranks more than once and kept them at the march pace throughout.

Finally, Aemilius told Nico, "Call a halt."

"Columns, halt." The men stopped as one. Except for their breathing, almost in time with the pace of their last march, they were silent.

Aemilius stepped out of his position and turned to face them. "I am very pleased with what I see so far, Nico. Give the men a rest and let them refresh themselves."

Nico took the centurion's position. "Half a ration. First column, on guard. Fall out."

The men found places to sit on the ground while the first column formed the guard. After 15 minutes, Nico changed the guard to the second column. The men stayed unusually quiet during the break. They knew the gravity of this exercise, and they wanted to make a perfect impression, not for Nico, but because they all wanted to be legionnaires. They knew this was a test of their training.

After half an hour, Aemilius strode back through the men. He didn't say a word. He raised his baton in a salute to Nico.

Nico stood up and called the men back into formation. They began the march again, and almost immediately, he increased the pace to the quickstep. Aemilius turned them up into the rough terrain. They headed into the hills on the south side of the valley of Sepphoris. Nico had put them through many grueling marches, Aemilius knew, but he had most likely not dared to take them into the mountains. The danger of attack from the Zealots was great. But Aemilius wanted to see if they were capable of facing the Judean warriors.

Almost immediately, the terrain began to rise. They didn't have any problem until they reached rough ground clogged with large rocks and brush. At this, Nico called the formation to open and let the men vary their steps. Aemilius nodded his approval.

They marched for hours through the mountain tracks, up and down slope, but didn't see a sign of anyone. Aemilius was disappointed; he'd wanted to try the men in real combat. Instead he ran them through the formations on the scree-covered hillsides, then led them into the valley, and they made an easy march back to the camp.

Aemilius planned their expedition precisely; they returned in time to eat the afternoon meal. But they didn't get much of a break. Nico called them back into formation at the stakes before Centurion Aemilius returned.

The work at the stakes wasn't much different than any other day, except it was easier. Aemilius directed Nico to run them through all the regular exercises. They used the weighted practice shields, swords, and pilum. Nico gave no rebukes for missed attacks or for pila off target. He had little need for them; in general, the men fought the stakes like they marched, right on order, exactly in time.

Finally Aemilius nodded to Nico. "That is enough, Praefectus Castrorum."

Nico called the men into formation. Nico spoke quietly to the centurion for a few moments before taking his position beside the formation.

Aemilius paced slowly in front of them. "I am very pleased with the first part of your training. Nico knows better than anyone how to turn men into legionnaires. That is why he is the Praefectus Castrorum for the entire III Gallica. I have given Praefectus Castrorum Nico permission to start your armatura training. You will begin training with one another and eventually train against regular legionnaires. Continue at this rate, and I will award you your plumes before spring." He handed the training baton back to Nico, and Nico saluted him.

As soon as Aemilius left, Nico dismissed them.

Abenadar returned to the barracks. Portius, Lupus, and Euodus, as usual, rolled knucklebones. Abenadar sprawled on the cot next to them.

Portius looked up at him. "So the Praefectus Legionis passed you into the armatura." It was a statement.

"How did you know?"

"The whole camp knows. Took bets on it."

"Bets on the training."

"Yeah, but it's hard to get good odds anymore," said Lupus. "That is, since Nico was named Praefectus Castrorum. There hasn't been a group that didn't meet the standards of the Legionis. And Centurion Aemilius isn't easy to please."

"No one on barley either," said Euodus. "That's a welcome change. When the trainees go on barley, the centurions get picky. Half the centuries get a dose."

"Don't let it go to your head, Abenadar," said Lupus. "The armatura will be tougher than any training you've experienced yet."

"For myself," said Euodus with a smirk, "I hope I get the training stakes on the duty roster. I would love to show you how an expert handles a gladius."

Portius laughed. "You'll pull the pila and then Abenadar'll show you a thing or two."

Euodus just grumbled. His lack of skill with the pila was notorious.

"At least then you may be ready to practice with Abenadar. I heard our century is making an ambulatura tomorrow," said Portius.

Both Lupus and Euodus groaned.

Tomorrow, Abenadar and the trainees would begin to drill like full legionnaires.

Adonai, how my enemies have multiplied!
Many rise up against me,
many there are who say of me,
"Adonai will not bring him victory."
But thou, Adonai, art a shield to cover me:
Thou art my glory, and thou dost raise my head high.

PSALM 3:1-3

Seven

The air was frosty with a thick and icy feel. One of the infrequent rains that fall during the winter had saturated the ground, and the earth was frozen at the top and slushy underneath.

Abenadar's hands were still warm from holding his bowl of hot cibaria. Breakfast sat comfortably in his stomach. He took a practice gladius and hefted the too-heavy wooden blade in his hand. Overnight, a padded leather tip had been added to the sharpened end of the sword. He ran his finger along the dull edge of the blade; it would still cut a man if it were wielded with energy. The other trainees were arriving, so Abenadar took his gear and returned to the open side of the field.

Nico's cheeks were red with the cold, but his smile was large. He was very pleased with the men under his training. "Come on, you almost legionnaires. Get your gear and get in line." His baton sang smartly though the air.

Though sluggish from the day's chill, the men were in their positions as fast as the day before. The stink of success was on them; they now had a standard to beat, and they knew they would.

Today Nico loaded them down with a double-weight full field pack and took them on the ambulatura Aemilius should have. Nico didn't lead them into the hillsides, but he found plenty of rough ground, ditches, and brush. No one complained, but by the time they returned to the camp, the men staggered under the weight of their packs.

Following the afternoon meal, Abenadar's muscles protested the short walk back to the practice field. This was the first time in almost a month that his body perceived the strain of their training. Nico noticed the men's discomfort and made fun of them. "You'll have plenty of motivation when one of your friends comes after you with a blade."

While Nico demonstrated how they would now fight against a

man instead of a stake, the men gathered closely around him. "You know how to kill stakes. When you fight a stake, you don't pull your attacks. And you can't pull your attacks when you fight a man either. If you do, a man will kill you. The point is to learn how to fight, not how to die. If your training opponent is foolish enough to get in the way of your blade, teach him to stay out of the way. The single rule in this game is you may only attack with a padded tip. The idea isn't to *kill* legionnaires; it's to *train* legionnaires. If you wound your opponent with an uncovered tip, you will face lashes and my baton. Now pair off and let's see what you can do against a real opponent."

Nico matched Abenadar against Pallas, and they began the drill. Pallas was a huge man. He didn't hesitate but without warning lunged with his gladius at Abenadar. Pallas' attacks came fast and furious. Abenadar easily parried each of the blows with his practice scutum and gladius. At first, the feel of the blows against them was disconcerting, but Abenadar quickly became familiar with their response to Pallas' blade.

In all the flurry of Pallas' assault, Abenadar hadn't taken a single hit, and he was confident enough to try some attacks of his own. Pallas didn't fair as well as Abenadar had. When Pallas extended himself, Abenadar struck under Pallas' blade and poked him in the side. Pallas roared. He swung at Abenadar in a heavy overhand cut. Abenadar caught the sword with his shield and fell to a knee; then he thrust upward again, this time, under Pallas' shield.

When he felt the blow, Pallas became enraged. He threw down his scutum and gladius and made a dash to grasp Abenadar around the throat. Abenadar was too quick for him, and his gladius came between them, so Pallas only bruised himself once more on the tip of Abenadar's sword. Pallas howled in anger and grabbed at Abenadar again. His yell cut off when Nico struck him with the training baton. Once, Pallas turned toward his new attacker; twice, his fist came back in a rush, and thrice, he fell to the ground—out cold.

"Well, Abenadar, this is what happens during the armatura when you are matched unequally." So, in turn, Nico tried Abenadar against each of the other men. Abenadar had a natural inclination to the gladius and scutum—as though he were born to them. The other men sweated ineffectively under his well-planned assaults or grew wild with frustration. Eventually Nico pitted himself against Abenadar, and in Nico, Abenadar found a matched adversary. From Nico, Abenadar learned the finer points of swordplay. At Nico's hand, he received many bruises, but with each mark, he absorbed advanced skills and many ploys.

After a month of this kind of practice, Praefectus Legionis Aemilius Regulus visited them again. This time he came to observe a demonstration of their progress in the armatura. He was pleased with them and allowed them all to progress into training against men who were already legionnaires.

In this training, Abenadar finally found all the challenge he needed. Every day he faced more than one new opponent. Every day he observed new sword tricks and tried new attacks. He received plenty of welts to prove the feints that didn't work, but he found ways to ensure he would prevail against almost any foe. He knew he could triumph against any single soldier in the Galil or Y'hudah; they had almost no training at all. This was the hard-won secret of the Roman Legions—training: practice in the tools and techniques of war. Against any untrained army, they would always prevail. Against odds of two and three to one they could prevail, but only if they remained a professional and practiced force. The stupefying foolishness of poor leadership and lax discipline were the only flaws that could bring about their downfall and the eventual downfall of an empire.

The armatura training with the pila was similar to that with the gladius. The men used baited pila praepilata—double-weight practice pila with leather buttons on the tips and reinforced riveted seams. This was not as active a weapon as the gladius, and the men required less training with it.

Although the bulk of their morning exercise was still in marching and battle formations, Nico mixed up the training to incorporate the armatura into the march. The men also trained with ranged weapons like throwing stones, the bow, and sling. These weapons were never issued to them, and their familiarity was focused on protection from the projectiles, not proficiency in them. Using the wicker practice scutum, the trainees literally become the targets for their comrades firing the weapons. Luckily, no one was hurt during these exercises. The training achieved Nico's goal—protection and confidence under fire.

Nico increased the number of muli marinani; the field exercises now included both the ambulatura and armatura. They built camps all through the dry winter of the Galil. Once Nico inadvertently told them to build in a place where a camp was previously built. When one of the men pointed this out to him, he changed the location. "If the digging is years old, the ground is much too loose for you," grinned Nico. So they moved the camp, even though they already dug half the ditch.

Although the III Gallica saw only sporadic engagements in the last 10 years, during this time, both the Galil and Y'hudah simmered with rebellion. The sons of Herod were matched progeny with their cruel father, and the people knew their leaders controlled neither Yerushalayim nor the Temple. Herod Antipas held the Galil in an iron fist. And if he didn't respond with force, the Roman Procurator in Y'hudah certainly would.

Rome garrisoned legions in the Galil and Y'hudah to ensure the peace of the surrounding lands. The bridge between Africa, Europe, and Asia was the strategic underbelly for the entire Roman Empire, and the Emperor Augustus could not afford to have a revolt reduce his authority there.

Because the legion had no expectation of action, to Abenadar the promotion to full legionnaire was an anticlimax to the months of rigorous training. One day Praefectus Legionis Aemilius Regulus led their group on a muli marinani. After a day and a night in the field, they returned to a mock battle against the Decimus Pilus Posterior Century. Centurion Aemilius led them through the battle formations, and they fought the Pilus Posterior to a standstill.

Before tempers got too high, the Praefectus wisely called them back and reformed their columns. He turned to Nico, who fought on the trainee's side, and returned the training baton to him. "I am very pleased with the training of these legionnaires."

Nico saluted him. "Then they should be given back their plumes, Praefectus."

"Who has these legionnaires' plumes," called Aemilius, turning toward the Decimus Pilus Posterior.

The centurion of the Pilus Posterior came forward. "The Decimus Pilus Posterior Century has kept them safe. Come forward, legionnaires, and present your brothers with their plumes."

One by one, Nico called the name of each new legionnaire. When the man came forward, a legionnaire from the Pilus Posterior took a plume from his pack, and as he handed the plume to the centurion, he announced a name. The centurion repeated the name and handed the plume to Centurion Aemilius.

When Nico called Abenadar's name, Praefectus Aemilius handed a bedraggled plume to him. "Legionnaire Abenadar, this is the plume of the Legionnaire Titus. This plume is now yours, and you carry it for the name of Titus and for all the other legionnaires who carried this plume before him. Your brothers will tell you the names of all the men who with honor carried this plume."

Abenadar saluted the Praefectus and returned to his position in line.

That was all there was to the promotion to full legionnaire. Their initial formal training ended. Abenadar purchased a new plume in the forum from Varro, and put Titus' plume safely away in his wooden locker.

With the addition of the plume and the title Legionnaire, Abenadar found himself with new duties on the roster. Immediately, he learned how much work the librarius of a century had to do. He discovered he was one of the few true librarii in the Decimus Cohort. Only the first century, the Pilus Prior, also possessed a librarius who could both read and write.

Abenadar had been assigned to the Hastatus Posterior, the sixth and least of the cohort's centuries. That way, the other centurions could officially command his services. Abenadar was responsible first to Capilolinus, his centurion, and Tero, his optio, then at the mercy of every other official who needed a scribe or who was ready to put the next day's schedule on paper. All of the librarii could read the names and abbreviations on the schedules, but most couldn't write Latin and none knew Greek.

Because Abenadar understood both Latin and Greek, he was required to write out much of the correspondence between the Primus

Pilus and Herod's court. All of this was in Greek. Iulius Valens, the Primus Pilus, was an exacting taskmaster and Abenadar found, through constant use, his language skills increased quickly. When the Primus Pilus also discovered Abenadar could speak and understand the Greek dialect used in the Galil, Abenadar became a translator as well as a scribe. Anyone who was not familiar with the Greek used by the people of Syria, the Galil, and Y'hudah could not easily understand it.

As a consequence, Abenadar often found himself in the presence of the leaders of the Galil. The Primus Pilus, Legatus Legionis, Herod, and sometimes the Procurator of Y'hudah sat in the same room as Abenadar translated between the Romans and Herod. He reflected on their joint plans, and was asked many times to comment on how a decision might be viewed by the people of the Galil. Herod himself appreciated this information.

Abenadar had been a legionnaire for more than a year when the Emperor Augustus died and Tiberius was elevated to emperor in his place. Tiberius' new regime brought many changes to the Roman leaders in Syria, Y'hudah, and in the legions.

Burthus, one of Iulius Valens' guards, shook Abenadar awake in the middle of the night. "Abenadar. Abenadar. Get up, man."

"What is it, Burthus?" yawned Abenadar, rubbing the sleep out of his eyes.

"The Primus needs you."

"Now?"

"Yes, now. Put on your armor and get ready to travel."

"Where are we going?" asked Abenadar as he sleepily pulled his tunic over his head.

"How should I know? When you see the Primus, he will tell you everything you need to know."

In the dark, Abenadar put on his lorica hamata and his full kit. Burthus hovered over him, pushing him to hurry. When he was dressed and his pack ready, Burthus towed him to the officium and into the

Primus' quarters.

Iulius Valens leaned over a scroll on his desk, "There you are, Abenadar. Get your papyrus, ink, and quills. We must speak to the new Procurator, now."

"Yes, Primus," said Abenadar as he picked up the package of writing materials beside the desk.

The Primus rolled up the scroll and nodded to Burthus. They followed the Primus Pilus out toward the gate side of the officium. Before the gate, the Decurion Valerian was already mounted with a full turmae, 30 mounted cavalry of the III Gallica's auxiliary equitata. A fresh mount waited for the Primus.

The Decurion Valerian was a pensive and unambitious man of the equestrian rank. He was thin and slouched with an easy grace in his saddle. He was far too familiar and indecorous a leader to merit promotion to higher responsibility but known throughout the Roman Legions as a brave and intrepid commander. The proof of his leadership was evident in his authority in the III Gallica. The III Gallica possessed two turmae of cavalry in its auxiliary equitata. By rights, the legion should have two Decurion, one commanding each turmae of 30 mounted legionnaires. Instead, with the help of two principales, Valerian commanded both. He was, effectively, the commander of the III Gallica's entire auxiliary equitata.

A mounted legionnaire reached down to Abenadar and drew him up behind him on his horse. Abenadar was barely settled when Decurion Valerian ordered the turmae to ride. Abenadar held on for dear life as the horses started off in a walk, then eased into a cantor.

They were well away before Abenadar spoke to the legionnaire he rode behind. "Where are we going?"

"To Caesarea," said the horseman.

"What are we doing there?"

"I have no idea. You should ask the Primus."

In the moonlight, Abenadar glanced at the strained face of Iulius Valens and decided that the question wasn't worth asking. He would likely be ignored, possibly beaten, and when they got to Caesarea, Iulius Valens would explain everything to him anyway.

Their trip was uneventful. They arrived at the city just as the sun came up behind them. As they passed through the gates of Caesarea, Decurion Valerian slowed the turmae to a walk. They rode straight to the Procurator's headquarters.

When they reached the entrance, Iulius Valens dismounted, and with a word of thanks to the legionnaire who shared his mount, Abenadar slid off the back of the horse.

Abenadar rushed to catch up with the Primus. His bag of writing materials banged against his thigh as he slowed a step behind the head centurion.

"Abenadar," said the Primus, "be prepared to write for me in Greek and Latin. You will need to compose letters for both Herod and the legion."

"Yes, Primus."

The guards seemed ready to receive them and passed them immediately to the innermost court. The Procurator's court was almost empty of decoration, as though everything had been quickly removed. An old man sat in the only piece of furniture in the chamber, a decorated chair. Behind him stood an entourage of advisors and politicians.

The Primus went to one knee, and Abenadar imitated him.

The old man was dressed in a toga with a wide purple hem. He was balding and wore a golden wreath on his brow. His face was stern and wrinkled. "Ah, Iulius Valens, we are glad to see you again. As you know, the Emperor Tiberius has chosen us to rule as Procurator over Judea."

The Primus stood. "Procurator Valerius Gratus, I came when I received your letter. I hope you had a pleasant voyage from Rome."

"As pleasant as possible under the circumstances, yes."

The Primus bowed. "What do you require of the III Gallica, Procurator?"

"We require an immediate demonstration of our ascension to power. Since your Legatus Legionis has been recalled from Caesarea-

Philippi back to Rome, and we have yet no replacement; you are, for now, the head of the III Gallica. We now need your advice on how to proceed to assure our sovereignty over the lands the Emperor placed in our hands."

"Surely the VI Ferrata can provide this support."

"The VI Ferrata is already scouring Judea for rebels," snapped Valerius Gratus. "We require a more concentrated action that will convince the Emperor of our efficiency and loyalty."

"At the present, Procurator, the Galil is at peace and the Governor, Herod Antipas, is a friend of Rome."

"We realize that. What of the borders?"

"We have not had any altercations with the Arabians or the Parthians."

"The Parthians. They are still enemies of Rome?"

"Yes, Procurator, although we have not had any problems with them for many years."

"We would have some problems with them. Are there not some of their cities we can sack? They are not so strong that they can defeat any of our forces?"

"Our forces are spread thinly throughout these territories. In the main, we keep the peace by a balanced show of our force."

"Yes." Valerius Gratus nodded. "We understand that, but can we not make some limited incursions across our mutual boarder with them? We would have a show of real force to display to the Emperor and not a theoretical balance."

"Yes, Procurator. If it is your desire, there are a number of cities at the edge of our borders we can raid."

"How many would you suggest?"

"Out of 10 cohorts, I could safely send five of them to five different cities. The deployment of the Parthian forces in those cities is presently unknown, so there is some risk to our forces, but I would not hesitate to send a full cohort against them."

"That will be satisfactory."

"The ultimate risk, Procurator, is war with the Parthians."

"Do you believe they could mount a successful offensive against us?"

"Our forces are sufficient to match anything they can send against us, but following any action such as you propose, we will have to increase our patrols of the border."

"We are not concerned, at this point, with the far future, but rather with immediately pronouncing our Procuratorship. Let the Parthians know we are Judea and that we will rigorously defend the borders of the empire."

"I will need to inform Herod. Do you wish to confer with the Governor before you enact your policy?"

"No. We do not wish to confer with Herod Antipas nor with Herod Philip. You may tell them of our plans, but we will not seek their permission to act as we see fit."

"Very well, Procurator. I will have my librarius draw up your letters of instruction to the cohorts and to the Governors."

"Yes. That will do. You may go. We will review the letters when they are complete."

The Primus and Abenadar backed out of the court. The guards led them to an office within the Procurator's fortress.

"The man doesn't understand these lands nor their politics at all," Iulius Valens said. "He will bring both Herods and the Parthians down on our heads."

"What do you wish me to write, Primus," said Abenadar.

The Primus dictated the letters, and Abenadar wrote them carefully so he would not have to recopy them. Afterwards, he read them back to Iulius Valens.

"That will do. I cannot answer to Rome for Valerius Gratus' excesses, but perhaps the Herods will not be so offended they will decide to join against us. Perhaps our forays against the Parthians may bear some fruit—hopefully not a war."

As soon as Valerius Gratus approved the letters, Iulius Valens posted them to the cohorts and both Herodian Governors. In the morning, Abenadar and the Primus returned to Sepphoris with the turmae of their auxiliary equitata.

The Decimus Cohort marched out of Sepphoris the following day. Pilus Prior Turnus Rufus led the six centuries. Along the eastern road, they formed a long train in order of century precedence. The Lions of the Hastatus Posterior were last.

In the field, the centurion of the Pilus Prior Century was the head of the cohort. He led them and ensured the orders of the Primus Pilus and the Legatus Legionis were properly accomplished. The Legatus Legionis, a man of Roman senatorial rank, commanded the legion. In the field, the Primus Pilus fulfilled the Legatus Legionis plans and directions. The orders of the Legatus Legionis came directly from the Governor in Syria or sometimes, as was this case, through the Procurator of Y'hudah.

Turnus Rufus was the centurion of the Pilus Prior for the Decimus Cohort. A stolid unimaginative leader, he knew nothing of war except the few battles he participated in himself. Turnus Rufus was known as a great centurion, but he was a poor leader for a cohort. Because he thought only in terms of small units, he couldn't grasp the concepts of mass and economy of force. These ideas flitted at the edge of his understanding, but he never could fit them cohesively into his operations. To his account, as the cohort made its way to the east, each night Turnus Rufus ordered them to build a solid camp with ditches and stake-capped walls.

Iulius Valens expected Turnus Rufus to fight a short campaign, but the Pilus Prior did not want to be caught unprepared, nor without the common luxuries the camp afforded him. The Pilus Prior requisitioned sufficient supplies for more than three months and a supply train of carts and drivers. For the protection of the supply train, Turnus Rufus assigned it to march in the center of the centuries. In this position, the carts were an impediment to the entire cohort's movement. Primarily, because of the carts' slow speed, it separated the cohort into two sections.

By evening, the first three centuries and the last three centuries were nearly two miles apart. Worse, as they drove further from the fertile Galil, the carts began to bog down in the sandy soil of the Parthian plains.

Because the supply train held them back, they didn't cross into the territory of the Parthians until the fifth day of the march. The Primus Pilus warned Turnus Rufus that his mission was not to start a war but to remind the Parthians that the Roman Empire still watched at the boundaries and was willing to fight to maintain them. Abenadar knew all this too. He had written the orders from the Primus to Turnus Rufus. In the letters Abenadar wrote to Herod, the Primus assured the Governor that the III Gallica was firmly ensconced in the Galil and that this campaign would not lead to any reduction in Herod's lands or authority.

Turnus Rufus' objective was the large city of Ctesiphon, about 10 miles inside the Parthians' lands. He could harass settlements on the way, but nothing was to hinder the attainment of his objective: the sacking of the city of Ctesiphon.

By the time the Decimus Cohort reached the Parthian border, the lax conditioning of many of the legionnaires became obvious. Capilolinus had not kept his century in good training. The centurion was a good leader. He had made his way through the ranks, but the years in the Galil with little action made him soft. Capilolinus didn't see any reason to work harder than necessary, and he believed his men would bless him if he kept their workload low as well. The result was an under-trained century.

Abenadar noticed that many of his fellow legionnaires found the march difficult, but he was unconscious of the failings of his centurion. He had become used to the rigor of his initial training and learned to love it. He spent every free moment with Nico, refining the skills he mastered in the field and at the stakes.

Nico, for his part, was only too happy to tutor the trainee who with the gladius bested the most seasoned legionnaires. Abenadar kept in excellent shape and steadily improved his skills; on the whole, his century did not. But nothing Abenadar or the individual legionnaires in the century could do would build the esprit, formation, and military skills they collectively needed to succeed in battle. If Abenadar had been a more experienced legionnaire, he would have petitioned Optio Tero for more training. Unfortunately, these were symptoms, and all the training in the world would not be enough to wipe away the lack of energy of their centurion.

As the Decimus Cohort approached its objective, the Parthian city of Ctesiphon, Turnus Rufus separated the cohort into five forces. He placed the first three centuries at the center of the attack and marched them straight toward the city. He then ordered the Princeps Posterior and the Hastatus Prior Centuries to flank the main force. This could have been an outstanding plan, but the terrain on either side of the main valley of their travel was severe; both the Princeps Posterior and the Hastatus Prior could not keep up with the main force. Turnus Rufus then sent the Hastatus Posterior, the Lions, to quick-march in a wide arc around the city to block the Parthians' escape route. He did not want to allow the Parthian forces in the city any opportunity for reinforcement.

Turnus Rufus gave Capilolinus six hours' lead to get into position, but that still meant he had to march the century at night over extremely rough terrain. The Hastatus Posterior Century was soft from months of inactivity. They were not ready to make a forced march in darkness. Capilolinus was lucky he didn't get them all lost during the march. Tero, the optio, kept him on a good path, but by the time the century was in position in a valley behind the city of Ctesiphon, few of the men were in any condition to fight.

Foolishly Capilolinus didn't order them to build a camp. This decision contradicted every basic principle of Roman doctrine and training, but not even Tero dared tell the centurion any differently. The legionnaires fell where they stopped, and stragglers struggled in for more than two hours.

By the time the sun came up, the columns of the Hastatus Posterior Century stretched raggedly across the eastern road out of Ctesiphon. They manned a position in a hollow of the valley well out of sight of the city. The valley was a natural funnel that directed anyone fleeing the city right into the laps of the Hastatus Posterior. Around the century, except for the open valley, there was no place to retreat. Unencumbered and fresh, the legionnaires might flee up over the tops of the hills on either side of their position, but most of the men were already exhausted. To the rear lay only more flat and rising terrain with a twisting road weaving through it. Capilolinus could not have picked a worse place to meet the enemy. Here they had little cover and no clear view of the western approach.

Abenadar felt uncomfortable with the position, but he couldn't say why. To him, it just didn't feel right. He was lucky his column was stationed near the north side of the valley—near some avenue of escape and next to some cover. Abenadar took the stakes out of his pack and stuck them in the ground in front of his position. It wasn't much protection, but the stakes were better than nothing. The other men in his column followed his example and that small protective hedge began to show among the other columns.

When the sun rose, almost as an afterthought, Capilolinus sent scouts out forward to the west and out on the high ground in the center of the valley. The scouts were not far enough forward to observe the valley adequately. The valley made a slight turn to the north at a rise of ground about a half mile west of the Hastatus Posterior. Because of the shape of the valley, the visibility was sufficient to move the scouts out on the hilltops more than a full mile from the century and still be able to see both the western approach and the legionnaires' end of the valley. But this strategy didn't occur to Capilolinus.

When they sighted the front line of fleeing Parthians from the top of the rise in the valley, the scouts came running back to the thin lines of the Hastatus Posterior.

The men reported to Capilolinus and Tero. "The Parthians are as numerous as ants. They are rushing straight up the valley toward us," panted Lupus.

"So many?" Capilolinus turned his eyes slowly up to Lupus. "No 10 Parthians are a match for a single legionnaire. Tero, instruct the columns to hold their positions. Surely the cohort has taken care of most of the city's forces. I do not see any reason to move from here."

Not long after that, though the Parthians were still not visible, the noise of their retreating force filled the valley. The first sight of the swiftly moving army was an immense gout of dust.

The legionnaires showed alarm at the dark clouds that topped the rise in the center of the valley, but Tero, Stechus, and Rufus moved up and down the line of legionnaires. Their encouragement didn't reduce Abenadar's apprehension, but the men around him quieted.

Suddenly a vast dirty wave, the front lines of the Parthians, appeared over the rise at the lower end of the valley. There seemed to be thousands of them. Many rode on horseback, but they were unorganized. They hadn't expected to come up against legionnaires deployed across the valley.

"Ready, light pila," cried Capilolinus.

The line of Parthians stopped abruptly, and the pile-up of men and horses was evident from the position of the legionnaires. A full half-hour of indecision elapsed as the Parthian leaders organized and rallied their forces. To Capilolinus' credit, he didn't call for a rush on the Parthians' position. That might have caused a rout of the front line of Parthian troops, but with pressure from the rest of the army behind them, the Parthians would have turned and immediately crushed the Hastatus Posterior. As it was, the legionnaires were in a precarious position, and without any defensive breastworks, the men were barely protected behind their stakes and scutum.

Right before the eyes of the Hastatus Posterior, not a half-mile away from them, the front ranks of the Parthians arranged themselves and prepared to assault the single century ranged thinly across the valley. The Hastatus Posterior had no escape route. No place to go except up the sides of the valley, and those were steep and without cover. That would have been suicide because, as they knew, the Parthians invariably included mounted archers.

When the Parthians were ready, the front wave of soldiers started moving again. In the fore, a reinforced line of footmen advanced up the valley. Directly behind them pranced a mounted troop of archers. A smaller force of heavy cavalry assembled at the rear of the archers and began to cut around the flanks of both forward lines.

Tero suddenly realized one of the weaknesses of their position. The Parthians could flank them on the sides of the valley and send archers to fire into their ranks from the steep slopes. He didn't know if the Parthians were sending forces around them, but he spoke to Capilolinus. In response, Capilolinus sent the two scouts, Lupus and another man, up the slopes to watch from the peaks and lookout for flankers around the sides of the valley. These precautions came too late. Had the century been larger, and the Parthians any need of strategy, they might have determined the fate of the Hastatus Posterior. The leaders of the Parthians needed no plan. Although they approached the ragged line of legionnaires with caution, they didn't expect the fight to delay their passage for long.

The line of warriors stopped 200 feet from the legionnaires, and behind them, the mounted archers raised their bows.

"Scutum," cried Capilolinus.

A flurry of arrows soared through the air. At the same time, a great cry rolled through the front line of the Parthians. The horsemen held back at the flanks, but before the arrows reached the top of their flight, the footmen rushed toward the legionnaires.

The arrows fell randomly, without any real accuracy, among the legionnaires. Abenadar's scutum caught two, and more arrows pelted the ground around him. Before the arrows landed, the Parthian archers loosed another volley. Abenadar deflected those also, but by that time, the foremost warriors were nearing his position. During the charge, the Parthian line had broken up and was no longer continuous. At the same time, most of the running footmen converged toward the center of the valley and away from the sides.

"Light pila, now," cried Capilolinus.

Abenadar threw his pila into the fast-moving crowd of men. He barely aimed, and he didn't wait to see the result. As the legionnaires loosed their pilum, the ragged charge of Parthians increased speed.

"Heavy pila, ready gladius," commanded Capilolinus.

Abenadar hefted the heavy pila in his hand. He braced it in the earth at his feet and lowered the tip to chest height. The Parthian charge resolved into individual men. They were armed with scythe-like scimitars and long spears, and as they ran, they bellowed individual war cries. Fear gripped Abenadar, but he stood his ground.

The Parthians charged as though driven by a senseless lust for battle. The first warrior to Abenadar's position, without slowing, reached for Abenadar and ran full into the heavy pila. The Parthian gave a choked gasp and screamed. Hadn't he seen the spear? Abenadar watched in horror as the man, pierced through by the pila, curled up on the ground and shrieked his life away.

Abenadar shook his head in disbelief. His mind was in shock, but he recovered enough sense to counter the attack of the next Parthian who charged toward him. This man struck at Abenadar with a heavy scimitar. The slashing blow was aimed straight for Abenadar's head. Intuitively, Abenadar caught the curved sword with his scutum and thrust his gladius into the Parthian's chest. Abenadar leaped back. The Parthian's face was overcome with surprise. His mouth opened and a bloody froth foamed up out of it and choked him. He fell beside the other man, and both of them, mortally wounded, writhed and moaned on the ground.

Almost immediately, another Parthian rushed at Abenadar. The Parthian swung his sword menacingly around his head and stepped toward Abenadar with more caution than the others. He acted as if he waited for Abenadar to attack him. Abenadar crouched defensively and glanced around. The number of Parthians on every side dismayed him. Out of the corner of his eye, Abenadar saw nothing but swiftly moving Parthian warriors in their ragged leather tunics. He stood too far forward to make out any of the men in his century. When the Parthian pressed toward him, Abenadar moved back, and from there, the Roman line became evident. The sight of the fighting legionnaires heartened Abenadar; the Parthians hadn't broken the legion line—yet.

The Parthian, still swinging his scimitar in a wide deadly circle, followed Abenadar. Without another thought, Abenadar stuck his scutum into the arc of the blade and thrust his gladius upward. The scimitar clanged against the shield, and Abenadar felt his own blade go home. He aimed lower than before and the gladius sunk into the Parthian's abdomen, disemboweling him. With an earsplitting scream, the Parthian grasped at his outpouring intestines.

Abenadar stood back, watching for the next attack, and was horrified as the Parthian, still howling, tore at his organs. The man fell to his knees and gaped imploringly at Abenadar as though begging him to put an end to his suffering. But Abenadar was too busy. Already another Parthian had spotted him. This man was as poorly trained as the others, and less wary than the last. He attacked immediately and fell from Abenadar's single thrust to his neck. The blow almost took the man's head off, and the spray of blood covered Abenadar from head to foot. He had to pause to wipe the gore out of his eyes.

Abenadar was amazed so much blood could come from a human

body. The man died so quickly, Abenadar was astonished the spirit could leave that fast, especially since the others still writhed on the ground, screaming out their lives without hope of succor.

Abenadar wiped his face and took a quick look around. He found himself isolated on the battlefield. No Parthians were near him, and all the legionnaires of his column lay dead on the ground beside the pitiful line of stakes. The remaining Parthian foot soldiers converged near the center of the line where Capilolinus and the optio last stood. To Abenadar, it appeared like a mob of men in Parthian jerkins completely surrounded the remaining group of legionnaires. Abenadar could do nothing to stop them, and he saw no other legionnaire alive who could help.

Without another thought, Abenadar raised his gladius and ran at the backs of the yelling mob of Parthians. None of them appeared to notice him…until it was too late. With his sword, Abenadar struck one man after another. He left them gasping out their lives on the rocky ground.

Abenadar was covered with blood and flush with the lust of battle. He was a killing machine— so absorbed in his assault he didn't perceive the approach of his own doom.

The first indication was the heavy thud of a hoof on stone. Abenadar spun around. He had no time to move out of the path of the armored horseman bearing down on him. Instinctively, Abenadar threw up his scutum. The lance, aimed at his chest, glanced off the shield and caught under the brim of his helmet. At once, the helmet's chinstrap burst, and the force of the blow threw his helmet nearly a hundred feet away. The razor-sharp tip of the lance caught Abenadar on the side of his scalp and glanced off his head. The tip didn't pierce his skull, but the blow of the lance almost broke it.

Abenadar cried out and crumpled to the ground. His scutum fell halfway over him, and he knew nothing more.

The next day, the Decimus Cohort found the remains of the Hastatus Posterior Century. Lupus and the other scout led them directly to the killing ground at the east of the city of Ctesiphon. The heaped bodies of legionnaires and Parthians showed the fight had gone to the century; the battle had not. Capilolinus' predication was wrong: each legionnaire had not been able to best 10 Parthians. But it wouldn't have mattered if they had since there were more than 10 Parthians for each of the 76 legionnaires in the century. Mercifully, Capilolinus, Tero, Stechus, and Tiras, the men who had led them into this death trap, were themselves killed. They lay together, back to back with a heap of Parthians all around them. Capilolinus would not have to face censure for the loss of his century, nor would he know the accolades for its bravery against unassailable odds. The legionnaires had given up their lives dearly.

Lupus found Abenadar. He was coated with dried blood and appeared more dead than alive. His scutum still covered him and of the 74 legionnaires left on the battlefield, he was the only one still breathing.

Lupus removed the shield and gently took the gladius, still half in Abenadar's grasp. He shook Abenadar lightly to revive him and checked his wounds. When his eyes fluttered behind their lids and his lips began to move, Lupus sighed a prayer to Zeus. The gore-spattered legionnaire's eyes opened slowly.

Lupus' first words were, "How many did you kill?"

For a long time, Abenadar didn't say anything. Lupus just shrugged, placed his kit behind Abenadar's head and started to clean and bandage his wounds.

Abenadar couldn't remember where he was. His head hurt incredibly, and he couldn't think very well. Finally, oblivious to Lupus' protestations, he lifted his aching head and scanned around. The burial parties gathered the bodies of the legionnaires into an enormous pile. They layered bodies and wood into a giant pyre.

Abenadar lay back and gazed up at Lupus. "Ten, I think."

"What? Oh, 10 Parthians. With your gladius?"

"Eleven perhaps. If the pila found its mark. I lost count."

"Who got you in the head?"

"Horseman with a lance."

Lupus whistled. "You're lucky to be alive."

"Lucky?" Abenadar could only think, *Have I broken the law of God?* He'd killed more men than he could count. Was this murder? Not murder, but he had blood on his hands. This was a stain he could not wipe from his life or his memory, and those memories came flooding back to him. He could still hear the death cries of the men he'd struck with his gladius. They'd traded their lives to him, but for what purpose? They were less well-trained, but the century was neither manned nor able to fight such a large force. "What about the Lion Century?"

"The other scout and I survived. Capilolinus sent us out from the flanks to the tops of the hills on either side of the valley." Almost with embarrassment Lupus said, "We rushed to bring the rest of the cohort when the Parthians overran your lines. You are the only legionnaire alive who fought in this valley."

"The only one alive? They are all dead?"

"All of them. Capilolinus was a fool." Lupus' voice was full of anguish. "Yet tonight we will honor him, and our lost century."

They both lapsed into silence. Abenadar wondered about Portius and Euodus. His friends were dead.

Turnus Rufus, the Pilus Prior, strode up to where Abenadar lay on the ground. The first century's signifer and optio followed closely behind him. "There is a survivor after all? Who is it?" Turnus Rufus went down on one knee to get a closer look.

Lupus said, "This is Abenadar, the librarius of the Lion Century."

"The librarius?"

"Pilus," said Lupus, "this is Abenadar, the swordsman who can best Praefectus Castrorum Nico. Yesterday, he killed 20 Parthians by himself."

"Yes, I know of Abenadar. He is the man who speaks Latin, Greek, and the language of the Galil. Killed 20 Parthians, you say?"

"Look at the blood on him. When I found him, his sword was still grasped in his hand."

"How did he survive?"

"A horseman struck him with a lance, and the Parthians left him for dead."

"Lucky. Yes, very lucky." The Pilus Prior peered more closely at Abenadar. "The wound is on the front." He smiled. "Good, that will make an honorable scar. He is fortunate the gods spared him." Turnus Rufus stood and turned to his optio. "We have a man here who can accept the honors for the Hastatus Posterior Century." Turnus smiled broadly. "I must have this man in the Pilus Prior Century."

"Yes, Pilus Prior," said the optio.

"Put together a detail. We will carry him back to camp in honor."

Lupus found Abenadar a fresh tunic and wiped the blood and dirt off his armor. Lupus made him as comfortable as possible. Turnus Rufus sent Abenadar his own cape to wear.

That night the cohort built the camp Capilolinus should have. The pyre of the Lion Century burned brightly amid the glimmer of the small altars on every side. Each man honored the gods of Rome and of the Roman Empire. Amid the devout worship of the legionnaires, Abenadar remembered his promise to Yeshua. He didn't sacrifice to the gods but made a prayer to Adonai, trying to honor the bravery and faith of his friends and all the legionnaires in the Lion Century. Their deaths seemed senseless, and he sought some meaning in their loss.

Abenadar had witnessed much he never desired to see. He had met death—had dealt out death—yet Adonai spared him. It was a miracle. He knew there was a reason that he was alive and they were all dead.

In the morning, the cohort formed up and started back toward the Galil. Abenadar marched at the front, right behind the Pilus Prior's signifer. Around his shoulders he still wore the cape of the Pilus Prior himself and at his sides marched Lupus and the other scout from the Lion Century. Except for the men of the Lion Century, the cohort's only other loss was the tesserarius of the Pilus Prior Century. Lupus told Abenadar, a woman felled him in Ctesiphon with a well-thrown brick. Senseless, reflected Abenadar. As senseless as the loss of the Lion Century—of 76 men, only the three of them came back alive.

*My heart is stirred by a noble theme,
in a king's honor I utter the song I have made,
and my tongue runs like the pen of an expert scribe.*

Psalm 45:1

Eight

The Decimus Cohort entered Sepphoris to the blaring fanfare of their corniciis' horns. The men paraded in perfect formation. Their steps were measured and exact. Pilus Prior Turnus Rufus marched in the lead. At his side came his signifer and just behind him, the two cornicii. Abenadar marched between the cornicii and the Pilus Prior Century. On either side of him tramped Lupus and the other scout. Lupus carried the signum of the Hastatus Posterior, the Lion Century.

In the Pilus Prior Century, the optio stood in the centurion's position. Behind the first century marched only four others—the Hastatus Posterior was conspicuous by its absence. At the very end of the parade plodded cartloads of Parthian spoils: gold and jewelry, armor, clothing, weapons, rugs, silks, cattle, horses, sheep, goats, and a handful of pitiful slaves. They stumbled, confused and disorganized, while around them the centuries moved with perfect unity.

As it entered the legion camp, the Decimus Cohort was a powerful and barbaric sight. With marked precision, Turnus Rufus led the cohort twice around the inside of the wall. By the time they made their first tour, the Primus Pilus Iulius Valens and his Officium were lined up to receive the returning cohort. At the first sound of the horns in the city, the legionnaires of the Primus Cohort began to gather at the fringes of the parade ground. Almost the entire Primus Cohort stood in place when Turnus Rufus started the cohort's second pass.

Already, a growing murmur rose from the men of the Primus Cohort. The legionnaires were already asking, "Where is the Hastatus Posterior Century?" The signum of the sixth century was evident in front of the Pilus Prior Century, but there was no sign of the century itself.

After the second excursion of the Decimus Cohort, Turnus Rufus turned directly toward the front of the parade ground and headed for the Primus Pilus. On queue, the centuries of the Decimus Cohort marched into their usual muster positions. Turnus Rufus motioned for the carts of spoils to be brought forward.

When the cohort halted in position, Turnus Rufus smartly saluted Iulius Valens.

"You may report, Decimus Pilus Prior," said the Primus Pilus.

Turnus Rufus fell to one knee and saluted again. "Primus, I bring back the Decimus Cohort—victorious. In these carts are the riches of the Parthian city of Ctesiphon and the wealth of their garrison. The centuries, centurions, principales, and legionnaires of the Decimus Cohort proved themselves worthy on the field of battle." Turnus stood up. "I bring to you the weapons of more than 500 warriors."

Iulius Valens caught Turnus Rufus' eye. "Are all your centuries accounted for?"

"Primus, amid our victory, there is sorrow. The Decimus Cohort did not return without knowing loss. Capilolinus and the Hastatus Posterior Century fought the entire retreating Parthian garrison. They left the battlefield strewn with Parthian dead. Our brothers fell with the blood of the Parthians on their pilum and swords. Every man of them was accounted for; we brought back their plumes to pass on to their legion brothers."

"Did you lose the entire Hastatus Posterior Century?" growled Iulius Valens.

Turnus motioned for Abenadar and the scouts to come forward bearing the signum of the Lion Century. "Primus, these are the surviving heroes of the Hastatus Posterior." He gestured to Abenadar. "Here is the Librarius, Abenadar. You know him yourself, Primus. He alone killed 30 men. Beside him stand the century's scouts. They brought the cohort to relieve their friends and brothers, but we were too late."

The Primus stood silent for a long time, gripping his vitis with white knuckles. Abdenar could sense his anger, though the Primus kept it under control. What good were spoils and slaves when he had lost almost 80 trained legionnaires?

The Primus finally asked, "Turnus, how do you suggest we reward the Decimus Cohort?"

"I suggest the legionnaires receive a full share of the spoil. The principales a double share and the centurions a triple share."

"And for you." Iulius Valens glared at him.

"I will take no share at all, Primus. I am too saddened by the loss of one of my centuries."

"Very well spoken," replied the Primus Pilus. "Now, Turnus, how shall we reward the Hastatus Posterior?"

"Primus, their signum should carry a golden phalerae and their names should be added to the roll of honor."

"Good. They shall also not end. The Lions will roar again in battle. Do you understand me, Pilus Prior? We will work out the details of the reorganization tomorrow." Turnus Rufus flinched. He would bear the brunt of the transfers from his own century.

"Now," continued the Primus, "Turnus, how should we reward this courageous librarius and the scouts of the Hastatus Posterior?"

"Abenadar has earned the rank of tesserarius; his bravery and skill in battle are attested by his wounds and victories."

"He shall be the tesserarius for your century, Turnus."

Turnus bowed, concealing his smile.

"I shall also bestow on him a gold and three silver phalerae. The gold for his stand with his century against overwhelming odds, and the silver commemorating his victories in battle. To the scouts I also grant each a silver phalerae. You, Turnus, shall provide Abenadar with a silver torque and a golden armillae." Iulius Valens stared into the Pilus Prior's eyes. "These shall remind you of the bravery of the Hastatus Posterior and the strength of a single man—for good or ill."

Turnus bowed again.

"See your men well fed and give them two days of leave. I congratulate you on your victory." The Primus spun on his heel and marched off the field.

That night, with the wealth of a Parthian city in their pouches, but without the decorations of victory, the Decimus Cohort caroused the streets of Sepphoris. Abenadar was treated to drink after drink—he was immediately a celebrity in the cohort. Almost at once, the men discovered how well he could converse with the people of the Galil. After that, he spent his sober moments of the night negotiating for the other legionnaires with whores and bartering for the next round of drinks. Abenadar was not used to the strong wine they bought him. Before half the evening passed, the legionnaires of his new century carried him back to the camp and left him in his cot so they could return to their night in the city.

Abenadar awoke the next morning sick and with a headache worse than any affliction he had ever known. He swore to himself never to drink that much again. There was little pleasure in the drinking and none in the aftermath. After stumbling to and from the latrines, he tried to go back to sleep.

"Friend, Abenadar." Lupus' distorted and breathy voice came across the darkened room.

"That you, Lupus?"

"Yes. It's me. Abenadar, do you miss Euodus and Portius?"

"I miss them all."

"I wish I could have done what you did."

"You followed your orders. If you didn't, you would be dead like the rest of them."

Lupus remained silent for a while. "I would be dead. Everyone says the gods protected you."

"Adonai protected me," Abenadar said under his breath.

"Doesn't it make you wonder why you are alive, and they are all dead?"

"Lupus, our friends are dead because Capilolinus stationed them, without a defensive camp, right in the path of a thousand Parthians. The scouts were the only wise decision he made, and you are alive because of it. What I wonder about more is why the tesserarius of the Pilus Prior Century was the only man struck down in the attack on the city. The deaths of our friends were almost predictable; the death of this man is inscrutable."

"Especially if you imagine that you were the only man living from the attack on the Lions while you replaced the only man killed in the Century of the Sun."

"Lupus, have you ever earned a phalerae before?"

"No. We have seen so little action that no one has earned any honors since I have been here."

"What do you do with such a thing?"

"You wear them on your armor on the clasp chain at your left shoulder. You can see many of the older veterans with them."

"Nico has 10."

"He has more than any other principales. He also has many torques and armillae, but I have never heard how many."

"Now you have a phalerae. That makes you a veteran," said Abenadar.

"What does that make you? I have never heard of anyone earning four at once."

"The Primus was angry and wanted to punish Turnus."

"How could he punish Turnus by giving us phalerae?"

"The Primus awarded us the phalerae that should have gone to the centuries of a victorious cohort. He awarded one for each century and the cohort's phalerae he gave to the Lion Century."

"I see. He gave you Turnus' phalerae—the gold one."

"He also put me in Turnus' century—to remind him that the loss of one of his centuries cost him these honors."

"The Primus is a wise centurion."

"More likely, he is a worried centurion. Our cohort met its objectives against the Parthians, but Valerius Gratus, the new Procurator, did not expect to lose a century."

"How do you know all this, Abenadar?"

"I wrote the correspondence for the Primus and Procurator. I will have to pen the report to the new Legatus Legionis and the Procurator. I bet Fonteius comes looking for me tomorrow."

"I don't envy you. I was sent to school in Rhegium. I couldn't get very far in the teaching and finally my father sent me to the legion. It was that or into the marketplace."

"He would have sold you as a slave?"

Lupus laughed. "No, he would have made me a seller of his trade goods. My looks would have hurt his business. I think he was glad to be rid of me."

"You never told me this before."

"Euodus, the gods rest his soul, teased me enough as it was. I didn't tell any of them how I got here."

"I won't tell anyone either."

"I know you won't. Do you smell dinner?"

Abenadar raised his aching head a little and tested the air. "I can't smell anything in here except legionnaires."

Lupus laughed again. "I'm going to eat. Do you want me to take your bowl and cup and bring you something?"

"No, I'll go with you. I lost everything when I went to the latrine, and I need fresh air along with something to eat and drink."

The food was the same they ate every day, but after field rations for a month, cooked cibaria, watered beer, and a piece of cheese tasted like a temple meal of fresh meat.

With their bowls in their hands, Lupus and Abenadar sat in the sunlight against the forum and watched the other members of the Decimus obtain their rations. Most were hung over worse than Abenadar and some were still drunk.

Nico sat down beside Abenadar. "Hey there, Tesserarius Abenadar."

"Welcome, Optio Nico."

"With one more, I could be addressing the entire Hastatus Posterior." He didn't smile, and neither Lupus nor Abenadar responded. "The Primus will be reorganizing the centuries and rebuilding the Hastatus Posterior. I have been promised more recruits to train—perhaps as many as an entire century. I need a good principales, one who is proven in battle and who does not shirk the stakes. Tesserarius Abenadar, you are an excellent swordsman, and you have a scar, or you will have when you heal."

Abenadar unconsciously touched the thick scab on the side of his head.

"And phalerae to prove your bravery. I need some help at the stakes. What do you say? You could learn how to manage a century…"

"I would be honored, but what about Cornicularius Fonteius and the Pilus Prior? Already Fonteius and the Primus keep me busy in the headquarters. I don't know how I will have time to also serve as Turnus' tesserarius."

"I spoke with the Primus today and I think Turnus, for now, would rather forget you exist. You will go on the daily schedule as training tesserarius at the stakes. If Fonteius needs you, he will know where to look." Nico stuck out his big scarred hand. "Do you agree?"

Abenadar didn't have to think long. He liked the big veteran and he knew, firsthand, the effectiveness of Nico's training. He put his palm over the proffered hand. "I agree."

Nico wiped out his bowl with sand and leapt to his feet. "Thanks, Abenadar. I assure you, the Primus will be pleased."

Abenadar's prediction to Lupus was correct. The Cornicularius himself awakened Abenadar early the next morning. Inside the headquarters, the Primus dictated a report for the Procurator, and Abenadar made copies to dispatch and for the records. The Primus also worked with Nico on the duties of the two cohorts, and Abenadar recorded the resulting rosters and made six copies.

When Cornicularius Fonteius and the Primus were finished with him, it was too late in the day to eat in the camp. Nico took Abenadar by the arm. "Come on, Abenadar. You have one night of leave left, and I'm tired of cibaria."

"We're too late to get anything in the camp," Abenadar pointed out.

"True, true, but let me show you how a principales should eat—when he can."

Nico led Abenadar out of the camp and into Sepphoris. He didn't stop until he reached an inn near the center of the marketplace. Nico went right in the door, and Abenadar followed closely behind him.

The innkeeper was a fat man with an expansive smile. At the door, he greeted Nico and Abenadar with a handful of oil for their heads.

"Hello, Optio Nico," he said in barely understandable Latin.

Nico pulled Abenadar forward and said very slowly, "This is my friend Tesserarius Abenadar."

"Tesserarius Abenadar," repeated the innkeeper, slaughtering the title.

"Close enough," grinned Nico.

Abenadar spoke in the Aramaic of the Galil. "Thank you for your greeting, Innkeeper. May Adonai, blessed be He, keep your house safe from all want and unrighteousness."

The innkeeper stared at Abenadar for a long moment, then bowed very low and replied in the same language, "My inn is blessed by the presence of a righteous man."

Abenadar nodded in return.

The innkeeper showed them to a prominent table and almost ran into the kitchen.

Nico lay on the cushions beside the low table. "The food is good here, and the wine isn't watered before it gets to the table. What did you say to the innkeeper? He really brightened up in response to whatever you said."

Abenadar reclined at the other side of the table and propped his head on his hand. "I just greeted him with a blessing to his house. It is a common custom in the Galil. Do you come here often?"

"As often as I can afford to. I miss meat; only meat puts real muscle on a man's bones."

By this time, the door to the kitchen was crowded with the faces of everyone in the innkeeper's family. Abenadar thought he could count 10 people staring at them. The many children were cautious enough not to point. The crowd didn't last long. The innkeeper broke it up when he grabbed a boy of about 12 by the ear and towed him into the room. He told the boy, "Stop wasting the good masters' time and wash their feet." The faces at the doorway reappeared almost immediately.

As the boy began taking off Abenadar's caligae, the innkeeper implored Abenadar, "Please, young master, will you speak a little of the language of the Galil? They don't believe a Roman can speak our tongue so well."

"I am pleased to speak to you in the tongue of Father Avraham.

You have almost as many children as he did. You are already blessed more than I could ever bless you."

The faces at the doorway let out a collective, "Oh," and made no sign of moving.

The innkeeper turned to them. "You heard him. It is the voice of a man of the Galil, like I told you. Go on. Go on." He brushed them out of the door and back to their work.

Meanwhile, the boy removed Abenadar's caligae and gently washed his feet with water. He then took off Nico's sandals and washed his feet.

"Have they never seen a Roman who can speak their tongue?" Abenadar asked Nico in Latin.

"Not like you can," said Nico. "As a legionnaire, in every place you are stationed, you learn how to order wine, beer, food, and hire a woman. That is usually enough, but I can see your skill has promise. If I were not so thick in the head for learning, I might pick up more. Here comes the innkeeper. Order us a lamb stew and bread."

Abenadar ordered the stew, bread, and wine.

The innkeeper brought them a large pitcher of wine and a smaller one of water. He carried these himself. Behind him came a young woman with a large round loaf of bread and a bowl of olive oil. A boy, older than the one who washed their feet carried a large pot full of a thick lamb stew. The smell was rich and intoxicating. Abenadar and Nico dug right into the hot food in the pot. They used the bread as napkins and to absorb the last bit of gravy in the pot. In his whole life, Abenadar had never seen so much food for just two people.

Nico smirked at him. "You probably think the camp's cibaria is good."

When they were finished, the innkeeper gave the price of the meal in kodrantes and Abenadar paid him.

"Abenadar, what did you give him for the food?" said Nico.

"I gave him what he asked, four kodrantes."

"How much is that?"

"About a copper as."

"A copper as? I always gave him an obol just for one meal, the old thief. I could eat here every day for that price."

"The old thief may understand the obol as well as you do the kodrant."

When they were ready to leave, Abenadar placed another kodrant in the innkeeper's hand. The innkeeper tried to give it back to Abenadar, but he pressed the coin more firmly in his hand. "Your food and inn have given us pleasure tonight. Let us share our pleasure with you."

The man bowed. "Please come back, Roman who speaks like a man of the Galil. You and your friend are always welcome here."

As Abenadar and Nico made their way back to the camp, Nico said, "That was a better meal than I have eaten there before, and that is the best house in the city…at least the best house that will feed Romans."

"When do we get new recruits to train?" said Abenadar.

"They are here already. They arrived from Egypt and Tyre last week. We already have four columns and the new Legatus told the Primus to expect 16 more men. That will make six columns in all."

"Why all the recruits? Did the Procurator expect us to take so many losses against the Parthians?"

"He expected more losses than that, but no one thought we would lose an entire century. By the way, I haven't heard the whole of what happened to the Lions. Did you really kill 30 Parthians by yourself?"

"I put my gladius in at least 10, but then, I lost count. My light pila may have slain one, and another ran against my heavy pila. When Turnus Rufus announced 30, I didn't think that was the right time or place to correct him."

"Very wise of you. Twelve is still an impressive number. Few have killed so many by themselves."

"The Parthian attack was not well organized, and the leaders distributed their forces piecemeal. They wasted their soldiers. If they had been better led, they could have overwhelmed us without losing a man."

"I gather you didn't think much of Capilolinus' leadership, either?"

"He murdered his century. He didn't build a camp or instruct the men to prepare defensive positions. He chose an impossible place to defend."

"It's one way to make Imperial heroes."

"An extreme method."

"I didn't think much of the Lion's training, either," said Nico.

"There wasn't much."

"I thought so. Don't discuss this with anyone else and only with the Primus if he asks you. It is enough that you absorb and remember the lesson taught to you by the blood of 74 legionnaires."

"I learned something else."

"What's that?"

"I don't like to kill."

"Few enjoy killing other men. I have known some who liked to kill, but most of them are dead. The battle lust steals their sense from them, and they become easy targets. Or worse, their enthusiasm leads them to take risks, and the enemy overwhelms them. The century must be a cohesive fighting force. Only as a single force can it succeed. Killing is an unpleasant side of our profession. It is necessary, but I avoid it, when possible. Remember this also, Abenadar. A man can be a great soldier. He can become a great centurion. But there is also the cohort and the legion. Observe all you can of the different levels of command. Learn them all. I myself will never become a centurion. I haven't the education or the status for it. Yet, the Primus relies on my judgment and knowledge. For the Primus Pilus Century, the Primus Cohort, and the III Gallica, I provide counsel to the Primus. But Abenadar, you could become a centurion. The way is already open to you and you haven't been a legionnaire longer than three years. Remember your optio, signifer, and tesserarius. The principales are your life, your success, and your conscience."

"Why do you say the way is open to me to become a centurion? I have no status. I am only a bastard son of a Roman official."

"You are blessed with an exceptional skill in the gladius. Already it has earned you a reputation in this legion, and it has won you a torque, armillae, four phalerae, and a promotion. You will accomplish even more. I will see to it."

"Why do you care what happens to me?"

"I am your friend, am I not? But, more than that, I have served under both wise and foolish centurions. Like the Praefectus Castrorum before me, I try to raise up men who can lead. You won't disappoint me, Abenadar."

"I won't. Not if I am able."

The guard passed them through the gate. Nico paused before he turned toward his room. "Tomorrow we begin the training of our new legionnaires and your new training as well."

They shook hands and headed for their quarters.

Who makes me swift as a hind
and sets me secure on the mountains;
who trains my hands for battle,
and my arms aim an arrow tipped with bronze?
Thou hast given me the shield of thy salvation,
Thy hand sustains me, thy providence makes me great.

Psalm 18:33-35

Nine

The next morning's muster was a different experience for Abenadar. As tesserarius, instead of being wakened himself, he helped rouse the men of his new century. Before the muster, the optio of the Pilus Prior Century presented Abenadar with the wooden badge of his rank—an ornamental leather necklace with a small wooden plaque like the larger tessera used to track the sentries. With the optio and signifer, Abenadar inspected the men and helped form them up. He took the position of the first column leader beside the signifer.

During the morning muster, another unexpected event occurred. The Primus Pilus ordered Abenadar and Turnus Rufus forward. Abenadar marched behind his new centurion to the Primus and the headquarters group. The Primus motioned Abenadar to stand directly before him and called, "Post the orders."

Fonteius marched to his usual position between the cohorts and bellowed, "By order of Iulius Valens, Primus Pilus of the III Gallica, Tesserarius Abenadar, Decimus Pilus Prior Century is awarded a golden and three silver phalerae for exceptional valor in the service of the republic of Rome.

The Primus attached the phalerae on the left shoulder of Abenadar's lorica hamata. At the same time, he said quietly to Abenadar, "You have made me very proud, Tesserarius Abenadar."

Abenadar saluted the Primus and stepped back behind Turnus.

Fonteius continued, "By order of Iulius Valens, Primus Pilus of the III Gallica Legion, Turnus Rufus, Decimus Pilus Prior of the III Gallica Legion awards Tesserarius Abenadar, Decimus Pilus Prior Century, a torque for bravery and an armillae for military prowess in the service of the republic of Rome."

Turnus Rufus turned to face Abenadar. He hung a silver torque around Abenadar's neck and placed a golden armillae on his right arm. "You have brought honor to my cohort. I am grateful."

Abenadar saluted Turnus. Turnus faced the Primus again. Then Turnus and Abenadar marched back to the Pilus Prior Century.

Cornicularius Fonteius now called the Hastatus Posterior Century forward. The Lion Century's new centurion, the optio from the Primus Cohort's third century, came forward with a new signifer and the two scouts. Fonteius posted the orders, and the scouts and the Lion's signum received their new phalerae. That was the end of the muster, and the Primus released the cohorts to their duties.

Just as Praefectus Castrorum Nico and he discussed last night, Abenadar was assigned to duty at the stakes. In the practice field, Nico greeted him. "Abenadar, are you ready to turn some boys into legionnaires?"

"I'm ready. You just tell me what to do."

Nico sounded disappointed. "We train them the same way I trained you. That method seemed to work before. But you'll need a special instruction tool." Nico handed Abenadar a training baton. It was similar to the baton Nico carried. "Don't spare it," Nico warned.

Nico and Abenadar gathered the trainees together and started them with the basics of the formations and marches.

Nico did not vary his training formula of morning marching followed by a hard afternoon at the stakes. After years of refinement, for Nico, this course of training built up legionnaires more quickly than any other. Abenadar found the practice exactly like the training Nico put him through. But now Abenadar had to work harder. He, like Nico, acted as though the labor they expected of the men was nothing to him. This was easy at the beginning, but it became more and more difficult as the year's training approached its end. Eventually Abenadar gave up any impression of invulnerability. Abenadar was surprised to discover the men respected and trusted him more when they knew he worked as hard as they did.

Throughout the year, Abenadar didn't have to use the baton as much as he originally thought. He could have been mistaken, but—when he was a trainee, he thought the rod was ready at every moment to come down on his head. As an instructor, he used it seldom and only when absolutely necessary. He discovered it was a better goad when used infrequently. That way the trainees didn't become used to it.

All through the training, Nico let Abenadar lead the small "almost century" Nico commanded. In all, they received 62 men to train. The Legatus Legionis furnished the original four columns of 30 men with another 32. Nico and Abenadar put together a training century of ten columns with six each. This allowed a more complete curriculum than when Abenadar was trained. In addition, they could split the century into two parts and maneuver them against each other.

Following the first training evaluation, Praefectus Legionis Aemilius Regulus praised the recruits' proficiency to both Nico and the Primus. Aemilius was equally impressed with the skill Abenadar demonstrated as a leader. He also passed this private assessment to the Primus.

All the trainees advanced into the armatura without a punishment ration of barley. This was unheard of for so large a group, and all the legionnaires of both cohorts were happy to share the good news.

The muli marinani training went equally well. Abenadar routinely ran the men through their paces. When Abenadar led, Nico acted as optio and tesserarius for Abenadar, who took the centurion's position.

With his large force, Nico was willing to venture further afield than before. He always kept their ambulatura in Roman territory, but frequently he led them into the verges of the rebel-held mountains.

When the skill of his force allowed them to complete a full muli marinani, Nico routinely took them across the great plain of the Esdraelon into the mountains that overlooked the Yarden River valley.

Nico was not looking for trouble. He was certain the presence of a Roman century would discourage any rebel force. They started one of their last muli marinani on a bright morning that promised to turn into a scorching afternoon. Abenadar took the centurion's position while Nico stood near the rear, ever watchful to correct his troops with his baton.

Abenadar led them out the caravan road from Sepphoris. At the quick-march, they passed Natzeret in about an hour. The many familiar landmarks made Abenadar think about his mother and friends as he hadn't for a long time. He hadn't seen his mother during the four years he had been a legionnaire. A Roman soldier could not travel alone in safety anywhere in Syria, the Galil, or Y'hudah.

When they passed the trail that led to Natzeret, Abenadar almost stumbled as he strained to look back and catch a glimpse of his mother's house. He knew it was invisible from the road, but he wanted to see it. He wanted to know if she was still alive, and he wanted to see her again. Perhaps she could visit him. When he got back to the camp, he would send a message to her. He had saved almost all of his salary for three years. Certainly, that amount would allow her to live comfortably. He could bring her to Sepphoris and rent a house for her. He wondered: would she be proud of him or still disappointed with his choice to join the legion?

Yeshua was right. The legion was his calling. Adonai, blessed be He, gave him success and honor. Abenadar was alive, while most of his early legionnaire friends were dead. Abenadar had not bowed to other gods. He was resolute to keep that part of his mother's heritage. Had not Yeshua warned him?

When they reached the town of Nain, Abenadar let the troop rest for half an hour, and that gave him an idea. On their return, he would keep the men at a quick-march and rest them at Natzeret. That would allow him at least half an hour to stop at his mother's house. Natzeret was far behind them before Abenadar stopped thinking about his childhood and put his mind completely on the task at hand.

Out of Nain, they continued at a slower pace down into the pass from Esdraelon to the Yarden River Valley and up the sides of Mount Gilboa. After another hour, during a break, Nico told Abenadar to find a place to build a camp for the night. Abenadar knew what he was looking for—an area easily protected but not an easy place to build a camp. This was virgin territory for Nico's training; they had no chance of stumbling into an old training camp.

The sides of Mount Gilboa stretched to the left of the columns. Over the high ground to the east lay the depths of the Yarden River Valley. Scythopolis and Pella would be directly across from the mount.

The mountainsides rose precipitously, and the way became harder to traverse. Abenadar halted the columns and walked back to speak with Nico.

"I think we should reorder the century."

"Because of the ground?"

"Yes, I don't think we can make it through the next group of valleys in six columns."

"I agree," said Nico. "How would you split us up?"

"Three groups of two columns each would be the best division for the terrain, but there are only the two of us to lead."

"Two of three then."

"I'll put the men in rout step and we'll take the high track on the ridge."

"Keep close enough to see me," warned Nico.

Abenadar nodded.

They divided the training century into two groups of three columns. Abenadar took the first group and ordered them up the ridge and into rout step. Nico took the other group lower on the ridge and did the same. They traveled for a couple of miles in this formation. At first, they were always within sight of each other, but Abenadar's columns stretched out ahead by about a quarter of a mile, and the terrain sometimes came between them.

The ground was very rough, packed with boulders and a heavy cover of wood and shrub. The well-watered sides of the mountain provided a satisfactory foundation for the vegetation. To the west, at times they could see the fertile ground of the Esdrealon miles below them.

Abenadar's columns crested a high ridge and started down the far side. There a fast stream tore down the mountain and through a ravine. Below them, Abenadar spotted a perfect site for a camp. In the place Abenadar had in mind, the ravine opened up and the stream cascaded into a wide pool. To the north of the pool, the ground was reasonably flat and raised. The camp would be a challenge to build there, but the ground would be easy to defend.

Abenadar ordered the men to a quick step and led them along the side of the ravine. As they marched closer to the pool, the ground beside it looked better and better for a camp—just the place he was seeking. Unexpectedly, Abenadar called out, "Halt!"

At the abrupt command, the men stopped raggedly, but Abenadar, staring ahead, didn't notice. "Quiet," he said without taking his eyes off the ground beside the pool. The foliage at the edge of the water was trampled and broken down. The footprints of many men crisscrossed the ground beside the pool. Abenadar scanned to see if anyone hid in the tall grass still standing around the pool. He couldn't see anyone, but at least five fires still smoldered in the cleared area. As Abenadar guessed, it was a perfect place for a camp and someone was already using it. It couldn't be a Roman camp; he saw no ditch or breastworks. Because Abenadar noted no tents or other enclosures, the fires wouldn't likely be a work group or a group with women and children. The place was too isolated and too far from the roads or from any village. Abenadar could come to no other conclusion; this had to be a military camp or at least a rebel bivouac.

Abenadar waved the men to get down and slowly worked his way into the clearing. He silently scouted the area. No one else was near. He examined the fire pits, the fires were put out less than an hour ago. Because of the wooded terrain, he had not noticed the smoke before. The footprints around the pool all appeared to be men's. This was a strong defensive position. He signaled his men forward. They approached him with questions.

Abenadar cut them off. "Be quiet. Single line, behind me."

Without another word, the men ranged out behind him across the clearing.

"Close it in. Swords ready," said Abenadar as he pulled out his own gladius. "You may get a chance to see some real fighting. Follow me!"

Abenadar saw no signs that the men from the camp escaped up the ravine. He would have noticed them on their approach, and the ground on the ravine side of the camp would have shown signs of their passage. As he led his men toward the northwest side of the camp, he saw evidence that many men recently passed that way. The trail of trampled grass and broken shrub crossed the rough side of the valley and headed in the direction from which Abenadar and his columns had just come. The trail was unmistakable, and it was much lower down the slopes—almost aligned with Nico's line of march.

"Columns," Abenadar ordered, "Quick step, h'arch." Nico hadn't been very far behind them. If Abenadar's formation followed the trail from the camp, they should be able to catch anyone from behind who tried to intercept the other group of legionnaires. If not, then Abenadar could rendezvous with Nico, and they could decide whether to track down whoever made the camp.

His men had barely come up over the ridge when, ahead of them, Abenadar heard the scattered whine of sling-launched stones. The sling was a signature weapon of the Zealots. Before them, Abenadar saw the slingers crouching behind boulders and trees readying their weapons to fire a second salvo. Pila would do no good in this terrain, and his men held swords already in their hands. Surprise was with them. "Prepare for combat," Abenadar ordered as he led his men in a rush toward the slingers. He heard his men drop their heavy field packs. He loosed his own and let it fall behind him. When they had covered half the distance to the enemy Abenadar cried, "Attack!"

They increased their speed to a run. Almost as an afterthought, Abenadar tucked his training baton in his belt and pulled his shield into position. His preparations came none too soon; a rear guard popped out of the grass ahead of him and stood wavering for a moment. The man was dressed in a short warrior's tunic and held a long knife in front of him. In the face of the legionnaires' onslaught, the guard quickly made his decision: he turned to run. But he was too late. Abenadar's hurried thrust pierced the man through the lungs and left him screeching in the grass. That wasn't enough noise to alert the slingers ahead of them. Abenadar's three columns hit the slingers like a brick wall. The first slinger Abenadar came to stood ready to fire. Abenadar ran full into him with his shield and thrust his sword home. He felt the blade pierce flesh and grate on bone.

From the slinger's position, Abenadar observed the man's target: Nico's columns crouched behind their shields in a field of boulders and sparse shrubs. They couldn't retaliate against the stones without making themselves targets. Nico lay full length in the open. He wasn't moving. Beyond the pinned columns, Abenadar noticed a large body of men creeping toward them on the slope below. The attention of the legionnaires was on the slingers and not toward any attack from their rear.

Abenadar scanned around him. His surprise attack had significantly decreased the slinger's numbers. He had not heard a stone fly for almost a minute. "Finish the slingers and follow me," he called back at his own men. Without looking to see if they followed, he leapt down the mountainside toward the other columns.

Abenadar ran to where they were grounded and lifted up his baton, "Up! Up you dogs. The enemy is almost upon you." Most of the men stood up. With his baton, Abenadar struck one or two who still crouched, and they scrambled to their feet.

The ground here was clear enough to use pila. "Prepare for attack. Shields and pila, out." He heard their packs falling, and ran to the edge of the scree. "Double line. Nico's columns forward, my columns in back."

The men formed a double line. They held their pila ready.

"Throwing pila, ready."

From below, the enemy started to run toward them. The rebels wore the same short tunics as the slingers, but they were armed with scimitars and spears. They carried no shields.

Abenadar glanced around. The lines of his men looked strong and they were ready to throw. He yelled back to the man at his end of the second line, "Fadus, take three men and scout our rear quadrants with two groups of two. Report immediately if you observe anyone coming toward us."

"Yes sir." Fadus saluted and moved off.

"Fill in," shouted Abenadar. Adonai help me, these men were green, he thought. They should have closed ranks without his command.

The rushing mob closed quickly on them.

"Ready...ready," ordered Abenadar, raising his arm. "Pila, throw," Abenadar lowered his arm. "Gladius," he roared before the first pila reached its target. "Second line, heavy pila," he said as the light spears found their targets. The rushing line of rebels gave out a chorus of groans and almost broke. Men tripped over the fallen, but their leader rallied them. As the rebels ran the final 30 feet toward the waiting legionnaires, their leader called in Aramaic for spears, and the rebels let them fly. Most of the heavy spears fell short. A few lodged in the scutum of the legionnaires.

"Men without shields exchange with the second line," Abenadar shouted. He marked the leader. The ragged rank of rebels, winded by their rush, finally reached the double line of legionnaires. Abenadar called out, "Second line, forward. Spread out." The second line struck forward with their heavy pila and left many of the rebels unable to return any attack. At Abenadar's order, the second line readied their swords and all along the now single line, the rebels discovered firsthand and finally the skills that made the Roman Legions largely undefeated in Y'hudah.

The fight was Abenadar's from the beginning. Although the rebels were easily double their numbers, they didn't stand a chance as long as the Romans' discipline held.

Abenadar signaled the right end of the line to turn with him. They bore around the flank of the beleaguered foe and cut off any retreat. Since his first rush against the slingers, Abenadar had not engaged anyone himself. He struck now right and left and forced his way through the press toward the leader of the band. His men followed him. They protected his back and sides and made the lethality of his quick gladius attacks certain. In moments, Abenadar came face to face with the leader. He was burly and dirty with a Zealot's blue rag wound around his head.

"Are you ready to surrender or die?" Abenadar called in Aramaic. The Zealot was taken aback. With an oath, he stepped menacingly toward Abenadar and attacked with his scimitar. The man was fast. Abenadar took the cut on his shield and stabbed at the leader's sword arm. His point went home and the rebel gasped, but the wound wasn't enough to disable him. The leader took a couple of steps backward, but the press of battling men didn't allow him to retreat any further.

"Now will you surrender?"

The man spat, "No, you will die." He leapt at Abenadar and cut fiercely at his head.

Abenadar caught the blow partially with his shield, but the scimitar struck his helmet a glancing blow that almost sent him reeling. After more than a year, the injury on the side of his skull was still sensitive, and his ears rang with the force of the blow. Abenadar ignored the pain. His riposte was already moving.

The rebel stayed extended and left himself open to attack. Abenadar thrust his blade savagely through the man's upper thigh and twisted. The rebel screamed and jumped back in shock. Abenadar almost lost his grip on his gladius, but instead of pulling against the moving man, he followed him, working the blade in and thrusting his shield against him. The blade pulled out with a jerk, and a fountain of bright red blood followed it. The rebel stared down at his mangled leg and the blood pumping from it. His face turned ashen, and without another sound, he dropped his sword. The rebel leader slumped, gasping to the ground as his life fled from him.

Around them, almost as shocked as their leader, the remaining rebels stood still. Abenadar called out in Aramaic, "Surrender or die." The rebels kept up a few scattered points of resistance, but his legionnaires quickly took care of them. The rest of the rebels threw down their swords and stared fearfully at Abenadar.

"Halt your attack," Abenadar shouted in Latin. "On the ground," he ordered the rebels in Aramaic. Almost as one, the remaining rebels dropped to the earth and lay quiet.

The legionnaires pulled back and watched the Zealots cautiously. Immediately, a cheer went up from Abenadar's soldiers. The men erupted in a frenzy of relief and delight. More than one legionnaire exultantly pounded Abenadar on the back. "Tie them up and tend to the wounded. Don't let any of them escape. We don't want to have to deal with another attack tonight."

He set the men to work tending their men and the rebels. They tied the captured men hand to foot in three long chains.

When Abenadar was sure of his men, he went to check on Nico. He found him, helmetless, unconscious, and lying in a pool of his own blood, but thankfully, still breathing. Abenadar propped Nico up and tied a cloth around his head. A large bump under a stone cut traced the side of Nico's skull. Nico's helmet strap was broken, as though the stone had caught him on the brow and lifted the helmet right off his head.

Abenadar wet a rag and wiped Nico's face. He poured water on his lips.

After a while, sputtering, Nico's eyes opened and he shook his head. He was sick and cursed himself for wasting the little food he had left in his stomach. "What happened, Abenadar?"

"We just beat a hundred rebels."

"The last thing I remember was the slingers...I must have taken a stone."

Abenadar nodded. "A stone took you, alright."

"Help me up. I want to see what happened."

Abenadar helped him to his feet, and they walked to where their men were putting the finishing touches on the prisoners' bonds.

"Bless Zeus and Mithras." Nico spat on the ground. "You did it, Abenadar."

"I'm happy to pull your rear out of the fire."

"Where is the leader?" said Nico.

"I killed one of them. I went to check on you. I haven't had time to look for more."

"How many men did we lose?" Nico asked the legionnaires who stood around them.

No one could answer him. He and Abenadar surveyed the battle scene. They found two dead legionnaires and 54 dead rebels. None of their men were severely wounded and all of them could march. The rebels were not so lucky. Many of the prisoners were wounded, and some wouldn't be alive tomorrow, no matter how they were treated today. Abenadar and Nico instructed their men to tend to the injuries of the rebels the best they could. Then they moved them all to the camp in the ravine. There the legionnaires and rebels who could work were put to use building a Roman night camp.

Abenadar and Nico couldn't identify another leader among the remaining group of rebels. At the beginning of the night, they guarded 66 prisoners. In the morning, 59 were left alive.

After a quick breakfast, the legionnaires refilled their trenches and smoothed the soil. Then they began the long march back to Sepphoris. To guard the prisoners, they put them in the center between two groups of three columns. The legionnaires bound the prisoners in three lines and connected them from hand to foot to one another by short ropes. They connected the first rebel by his right wrist to the right ankle of the rebel behind him, who was bound by his left wrist to the left ankle of the prisoner behind him, and so on down the line. Because of the wounded prisoners, the return trip took twice as long. They built another camp that night and slept on the north edge of the great plain of the Esdrealon. They lost another five prisoners on the march and during the night.

In the morning, they limped back toward Sepphoris the same way they had come. About noon, they came within sight of Natzeret and Abenadar spoke to Nico, "Natzeret has a well. We should let the men drink."

"Good, I'm parched too."

"Let's rest the men. We only have a couple of hours to Sepphoris, and I want to speak to someone."

"Should I send a guard with you?"

"Not necessary."

When they spotted the approach of the legionnaires and their prisoners, the women and children of Natzeret ran screaming from the well. The Romans had the well to themselves.

Abenadar walked toward the lone hut where his mother lived. He thought he should have seen it earlier. He walked back and forth across the place for a while before he realized the small house was gone.

Then he sat down with his head in his hands.

"Abenadar." A lean man in a robe approached him from the path.

"Who are you?"

"Don't you recognize me?"

Abenadar stood up. "Yeshua?"

"Yes." Yeshua grabbed Abenadar around the shoulders. "Would you like to see your mother?"

"Yes. Where is she?"

"She is in my house. Wait here. I'll bring her."

Yeshua ran off down the path, and Abenadar sat down again. He took off his helmet and laid it on the ground. Why was his mother at Yeshua's house? Would Yeshua truly bring her to see him? Or would he bring the village malcontents to stone him? Not likely with almost a century at the well.

After a short time, Abenadar saw two people walking up the path. He knew the first was Yeshua, but the second was bowed over. Could this be his mother, Naomi? Abenadar stood up and rushed down the path toward them. He didn't hesitate but grabbed her up in his arms. "Mother, mother. It has been a long time."

"Abenadar, my son. Are you a Roman?"

"I am still your son, mother."

Naomi was crying. "I thank Adonai for bringing you back to me." She brushed back his hair. "You are scared." She examined his arms and head. "You have been wounded many times. Can you stay—for a while?"

"He cannot stay, Mother Naomi," said Yeshua. "His men expect him back soon."

"Is this so? Are those your men at the well?" she said.

"My men." Abenadar was almost overcome. "I wanted to see you for so long."

"And, I you."

"Mother, will you come to Sepphoris to live? There, as a son, I can care for you and watch over you." Abenadar blurted out the words. Somehow he knew she would not come.

Naomi answered immediately. "No, I would like to return with you, but I have friends here now. Friends who no longer care what I was or what I did—or what you are." She put her hand on his arm. "Yeshua and Miryam care for me. Yosef tolerates me. He is a friend, of sorts, also."

"Thank you, Yeshua." Abenadar studied his friend.

"Kiss your son, Naomi. I want to speak to him."

Making a lie of her words, Naomi clung to Abenadar, but she kissed him and let him go. She turned and walked back down the path a few steps.

Yeshua stepped toward Abenadar. "I know you must go soon."

Abenadar nodded.

"Your mother is safe in my house. I told you I would take care of her."

"Thank you, Yeshua. Do you need anything?"

"Only that you remember Adonai."

"I have not forgotten Him."

"I know this. But you come from the wilderness with blood on your hands."

"Yes."

"David always did the same. I told you before: you will win glory as a Roman soldier. Adonai watches over you, Abenadar."

"He has so far."

"And He will continue to do so as long as you remember Him." Yeshua's face took on an added concentration. "Your men are ready to leave. It is time for you to go to them."

"Yes. It is time." Abenadar went to his mother and held her again. He caught Yeshua's gaze. "Keep my mother safe, friend."

"I shall," said Yeshua. He and Naomi began to walk back down the path.

"Yeshua."

Yeshua turned to Abenadar.

"Take this." Abenadar placed a golden aurie in Yeshua's hand. "If you need more, send a message to me."

Yeshua took the coin. "This is more than enough." He put the coin in Naomi's hand.

She stared at it. "You put such a coin in my hand before, Abenadar. Then, as now, it meant you were leaving me."

Yeshua said. "Your son has earned honor in the legions of Rome. This is a gift. It is not as great a gift as a son, but it is a gift nonetheless. Take it, Mother Naomi."

Naomi stared longingly at Abenadar. "Thank you, my son."

"You should go. Your men wait for you," said Yeshua.

Abenadar picked up his helmet and reluctantly started back down the track. Before he was out of sight, he turned to take a final glimpse of them. They both waved.

Abenadar continued to the well.

*Thou didst go up to thy lofty home with captives in thy train,
having received tribute from men;
in the presence of Adonai no rebel could live.
Blessed is Adonai; he carries us day by day,
Adonai our salvation.*

Psalm 68:18-19

Ten

In the late afternoon, Nico, Abenadar, their training century, and 54 rebel prisoners marched into the legion camp in Sepphoris. The moment the guards spotted them from the walls they started a call taken up by every man in the camp. By the time, the strange procession marched through the postern legionnaires lined the walls. The bulwark of soldiers inside the camp gate peeled open for them, and Nico led his training century to the parade ground. In the field, Nico assigned guards for the prisoners and dismissed the rest of the men.

As soon as Nico cleared off the trainees, the legionnaires, full of questions, descended on them. Before nightfall, the whole camp knew what happened in the mountains of Y'hudah. The legionnaires gazed in amazement at the crestfallen Zealots tied together in the center of the camp. Within their knowledge, no Zealot had ever allowed himself to be captured by the Romans. But they reasoned, before Abenadar no legionnaire spoke the language of Y'hudah with authority.

The men of the cohorts hounded Abenadar until he told them the story himself. He had to recite it so many times, he wondered that the entire camp had not heard it at least once from his lips, and he knew the recruits were not silent. When the men knew the facts, Abenadar could not escape notoriety.

Before Nico could report to the officium, the Primus called for him. After Nico told his tale, the Primus had to hear it from Abenadar's lips too.

"Let me get this straight," he said to Nico and Abenadar as they stood at attention in his quarters, "Nico was unconscious, and you, Abenadar, fought 110 armed rebels with 64 trainees and not only defeated them, you took more than half prisoner."

"Yes, sir," said Nico and Abenadar in unison.

"I also understand, Abenadar, you killed the leader in single combat?" The Primus pounded his hand with his vitus.

"Yes, sir. I had to defeat him to get the rest to surrender," said Abenadar.

The Primus shook his head. "I am not happy, Nico, that you took the men so far into threatening territory."

"Yes, sir," barked Nico.

"That does not mean you should not do so next time."

"Thank you, sir," said Nico.

"Get that grin off your face, Optio."

"Sir?" Nico's features returned to blandness.

"I also understand, that you, Abenadar, disobeyed your commander by losing sight of him."

"Yes, sir," said Abenadar mechanically.

"Make sure you train the troops to obey better than you did."

"Yes, sir," said Abenadar.

"In the main, however, I am pleased with your performance." Iulius Valens smiled broadly. "I can't imagine a more outstanding exhibition of leadership. I can only thank you, Nico, for training the men so well, and to you, Abenadar, for commanding them."

"Yes, sir," said Nico and Abenadar together.

"Now get out of here and send in the Praefectus Legionis. I want to speak with him."

Sporting grave expressions, Abenadar and Nico withdrew from the officium. When they stepped outside, they slapped each other on the back and returned to their barracks laughing together.

In the morning muster, the Primus called Abenadar forward. While Abenadar stood before him, Iulius Valens addressed the cohorts, "Tesserarius Abenadar saved the life of Optio Nico. For this act, I award him a corona civica. I will have the wreath made of silver and bronze from my own treasury. The Tesserarius Abenadar also bested a rebel leader in single combat. For his bravery, I award him a golden torque.

Finally, his leadership resulted in the capture of 66 and the death of 54 rebels, all members of the Zealot party of the Judeans. For this magnificent display of skill as a principales I present him this golden phalerae."

Because he knew he truly earned them, Abenadar wore these decorations with more pride than all the other awards he had been given.

Abenadar returned to his place with the Pilus Prior Century, but the Primus was not finished. He turned to Cornicularius Fonteius and said, "Post the orders."

Fonteius took his position and called out, "By order of Iulius Valens, Primus Pilus of the III Gallica, due to the skill and bravery shown during battle, the legionnaires in training are awarded their plumes and granted full stature as legionnaires. The Decimus Hastatus Posterior Century has kept the plumes of these legionnaires safe until they were ready to wear them. Legionnaires, come forward and receive your badges of rank."

One by one, with the same ceremony when Abenadar graduated to a full legionnaire, the men marched forward. This time, the Primus Pilus himself handed each of them the plume of a dead legionnaire. Abenadar was pleased to hear the names of Portius and Euodus passed on with their plumes. The midnight blessings of the Praefectus Legionis advanced the men early. Both the Primus and Aemilius Regulus saw no reason to keep them in training when they already demonstrated the combat skills necessary to be full legionnaires.

Following the day's muster, every man in the camp wanted to talk to Abenadar, and he found himself compelled to repeat the story over and over again.

Over the protestations of Turnus Rufus, during the next month, the Primus Pilus moved Abenadar to the position of tesserarius of the Hastatus Century of the Primus Cohort. The promotion to the third century of the first cohort was considered a significant advance.

Praefectus Legionis Aemilius Regulus, the centurion of the Hastatus, had long coveted Abenadar in his century.

Abenadar, in his new position, continued to act as Nico's aid in the training, but he also became the III Gallica's official instructor in the gladius. In order to carry out his new duties, Abenadar traveled with the Praefectus Legionis to all the forts of the III Gallica. In coordination with the legion's training cycle, they visited Capernaum, Caesarea-Philippi, Tiberius, and Julias. During their stays, Abenadar evaluated, primarily, the armatura training of the legionnaires while Aemilius Regulus appraised the ambulatura and the men's overall skill level. Each time they entered the legionary outposts, Aemilius Regulus insisted that Abenadar wear all his decorations. With little active warfare in the eastern territories of the Roman Empire, few men had the opportunity to earn awards. Abenadar became a symbol of encouragement and an example to the men. With each of these contacts, the stories of Abenadar's exploits reached the common soldier, and he gained a measure of fame throughout the Galil and the III Gallica.

Primus Pilus Iulius Valens sent the prisoners Abenadar had captured in the mountain battle to Vittilius, the Roman Governor of Syria in Ptolemais. There, Vittilius assigned them as slaves on his galleys.

In his travels, Abenadar had the opportunity to see the extensive investure of Rome throughout the Eastern end of the Mediterranean, but because of the threat of rebellion, that investure was always conditional. For safety, Aemilius Regulus regularly traveled with an escort of Roman cavalry, the auxiliary equitata. In addition to the protection of the Praefectus Legionis, the mounted legionnaires carried diplomatic and military messages all across the Galil, Y'hudah, and Syria. The decurion in charge of the cavalry took at least a full turmae of 30 mounted legionnaires to ensure their protection on the roads. The III Gallica was assigned four turmae under a single decurion. The camp at Sepphoris boasted two turmae and the decurion. The Legatus Legionis stationed the two other turmae in Caesarea-Philippi and Tiberius. To aid in his travels, Abenadar learned to ride a horse, and though he never became expert, he was reasonably proficient.

Abenadar's skills in Latin and Greek grew with his expanded exposure, and that, along with his knowledge of Aramaic, served him well. He became adept at working the taverns of five different cultures in three languages. If Aemilius Regulus had not put down his foot to stop it, the legionnaires of the auxiliary equitata would have taken Abenadar on every trip.

On the behalf of the legionnaires, Abenadar bargained for the services of many women. In his dealings, he saw many pitiful and ugly women and on rare occasions some who were beautiful. He was too steeped in the teachings of his culture to participate in these sexual liaisons himself, but he longed to know the love of a woman. Not the lust of the flesh, but the full devotion he had witnessed when he'd lived in Natzeret.

His options were few. He could never hope to win a bride from any household in Y'hudah or the Galil. If he found a family willing to let him pay the bride price, the woman's relatives would likely have him and his bride killed. The Samaritans were no different. Their hatred for Rome was little less than that of the people of Y'hudah. He could buy a slave, but, in his mind, that was no different than purchasing the use of a whore. The other cultures might provide the source for a bride, but he knew little about them, and their women were so few in number he didn't think he had any hope with them. The Romans with children in the Galil and surrounding provinces were mostly wealthy and highly placed. They sought the same for their marriageable daughters and that left out anyone such as Abenadar. Except in the cities of the Decapolis, the Greeks were in less evidence, and they wanted nothing to do with the people of Y'hudah or the Romans.

The regulations of the legion were also a problem. The legion did not officially allow legionnaires of any rank to marry. Though it was forbidden to marry, most of the centurions kept at least a slave or found a local woman to cook and pleasure them. These local women were whores or some order of courtesan. Some of the regular legionnaires also maintained households and women. In the Galil, these women were all either whores or slaves. The Romans stood less a chance than Abenadar of building a familial relationship with a free woman of

Y'hudah or the Galil.

Still, Abenadar's father found an honorable bride, or so Abenadar wanted to think. He reminded himself that his father was a highly placed Roman and a member of Herod's court. Most of his mother's family was dead. To keep from paying a dowry, they were probably happy to part with Naomi in spite of Abenadar Iustus' origin.

Abenadar didn't want a slave or a whore. He wasn't looking for a temporary relationship or a pleasure woman. Abenadar wanted someone to love and who would love him. When they spoke on this subject, Nico said to him, "Any slave will love you if you feed her well." Abenadar rejected his friend's advice. He didn't want a slave, he wanted a helpmate—an Eve. He wanted to find a woman like those he knew in Natzeret. There, they were pretty and kind. Sometimes they spoke to him though their fathers had forbidden them. He remembered their long black tresses and deep almond eyes. Their skin was as soft as their voices. He missed his friends as well. He had a few—and Yeshua. With almost 1200 legionnaires fighting for his friendship and attention, he longed for the simple relationships of his youth.

Abenadar wasn't looking for just any friend, but someone who shared his beliefs and his needs. His closest friend, Nico, was a military man and knew little of languages, reading, or writing. The other legionnaires were brave and some were good, but a tankard of local beer, a meat stew, and a cheap woman satisfied their needs. Abenadar aspired to more. He couldn't fully articulate what he meant by more, but he knew he wanted someone who would make a home for him like the home he lived in as a child. He wanted a woman of Y'hudah. Not a woman who was drawn to him for money, or because he owned her. He wanted someone who would love him in spite of who he was. He realized, though he had cut himself off from his people by joining the legion, he wanted in some ways to return to them.

When they parted, Yeshua had told him that Adonai wanted Abenadar to be a legionnaire. At that time, Abenadar had no idea what that success and later fame would bring him. He couldn't know it would separate him absolutely from his home and his people. If he had stayed in Natzeret, he would have gained a profession and a chance at a family. Although the people of the village looked down on him, he knew of others, like him, who were accepted by the community. His own mother was now almost a full person in Natzeret.

Abenadar had made his own choice long ago. For many reasons, at the beginning, his choice had appeared to be a good one. But if he could not establish a home and family, Abenadar reasoned, he would not succeed in an important part of life—an element of living critical to him and his future.

For almost five years, Abenadar worked as the aid to Aemilius Regulus and the tesserarius of the Primus Hastatus Century, III Gallica Legion. Abenadar knew Aemilius Regulus wanted to promote him to signifer and then optio, but in all that time, there were no openings to move the current optio, Poplas, to another century or up to the centurionate. Abenadar learned from Nico, that the Primus and Aemilius Regulus did not want to move Abenadar to signifer because they didn't want to lose his fighting strength as a swordsman.

"When they can," said Nico, "they will make you an optio and put signifer in your records as an honorarium. You would have been a signifer already if there were a position, and except for your skill."

The job of the signifer was to carry the signum and to guide the century in following the orders of the centurion. Because Abenadar was already doing much more than this, actually acting in the position of centurion and optio in training, he didn't need more experience in guiding a century.

Aemilius Regulus did not show favoritism to Abenadar nor did he denigrate the signifer or Optio Poplas. And the circumstances did not seem to bother Poplas either. Poplas was certain of being promoted to centurion. He waited for an opening just as Abenadar did, but Abenadar was concerned Aemilius Regulus gave him much responsibility that should rightly have been Poplas'. This happened first when Aemilius Regulus put Abenadar in charge of training the century. That same day, Abenadar sought out Poplas after they both received their dinner rations.

"Poplas, let's sit over here behind the forum." Abenadar led the older man by the arm.

When they both sat on the ground, Poplas said, "I take it you want a private conversation with me. I suppose you don't need advice on how to train a century?" Poplas jeered.

"As a matter of fact, that is just what I need."

"Really?" His eyebrows raised.

"I did not ask Aemilius Regulus to let me train the Hastatus," said Abenadar.

"I understand his motivations," snapped Poplas. "What do you propose to do about it?"

"We could ask Aemilius Regulus to let you train."

"He won't, and I wouldn't want him to. The training of the century is more important than my desires."

"You could take on other duties while the training is going on."

Poplas smiled. "What, and let you take over without any opposition? I need to train as much as the others. Tell you what. You don't worry about my acquiescence. When we start, I'll make a big show of letting you have the responsibility for the training. How would that be? Then I don't lose credibility, and that legitimatizes your authority."

"That would be perfect. As long as you agree."

"It doesn't matter if I like it or not. Aemilius Regulus is not going to change his mind, and he expects us to work out the details."

They shook on it, and that is how they managed the training of the Hastatus Century.

Abenadar and Poplas never became fast friends, but they supported each other, and they kept the balance of leadership at an amiable level. The men respected them both. However, they never got to test either the training or their combined leadership in battle.

In that year, because of losses in the Rhineland, the Emperor moved many centurions to Rome to be assigned to other legions. In response, Vittilius, the Roman Governor of Syria, reassigned his centurions to better balance his forces. He promoted Poplas to centurion and moved him to the Ferrata VI Legion in Y'hudah. Primus Pilus Iulius Valens promoted Abenadar to optio, but much to Aemilius

Regulus' chagrin, Abenadar did not become the optio of the Primus Hastatus. Iulius Valens moved Nico into the officium and gave him the duties of Aquilifer. As the Aquilifer, Nico became the bearer of the aquila, the eagle signum of the legion. This position was just below centurion and was usually reserved for the most decorated and acclaimed veteran principalis in the legion. Nico retained his position as Praefectus Castrorum and aid to Praefectus Legionis Aemilius Regulus. As the Praefectus Castrorum, Nico continued to be the official trainer for the entire III Gallica Legion. This arrangement pleased both Aemilius Regulus and Nico. The move recognized the importance of the duty Nico accomplished for many years, and his rank, and it gave Aemilius Regulus a principalis in the officium.

Abenadar took Nico's place as the optio of the Primus Pilus Century. Primus Pilus Iulius Valens had desired this for a long time. He had seasoned Abenadar as a leader and watched him closely in the Hastatus. He listened to Nico's reports of Abenadar's progress, and as a result, embraced Nico's recommendations. But in addition to prowess in the skills of battle, Iulius Valens rated Abenadar the most knowledgeable Roman in the provinces of the Galil, Syria, and Y'hudah concerning the people, language, and cultures. The Primus didn't overlook Abenadar's popularity and his military skill; he wanted Abenadar as both his aid and optio. He couldn't imagine a more powerful combination in diplomacy or war.

With the blessings of Nico and Iulius Valens, Abenadar took over as optio of the Primus Pilus Century. This caused a greater change in Abenadar's life: the Primus Pilus shared his scrolls with Abenadar. To Abenadar, this was a completely new thing. In the past, he dealt only with official reports and simple letters. Scrolls of philosophy and poetry were something altogether different. This was a circumstance the Primus could never exploit with Nico. Nico knew little of reading and less of writing. He was an extraordinary trainer and a respected leader. He was not a potential centurion though he was the best principalis in the legion. Nico didn't have the necessary diplomatic skills or education. Abenadar did.

Iulius Valens saw in Abenadar a protégé to the centurionate and a potential Primus. He was the kind of man Iulius Valens would like to leave in charge of a legion. But unlike Iulius Valens, Abenadar had little hope of a higher rank. Abenadar wasn't a full Roman. In spite of his father's standing, he wasn't highborn. Caesar would never make a man like Abenadar a Tribune, much less the Legatus Legionis. But a man like Abenadar could fill the rank of Primus Pilus. He could train, equip, lead, and bring great honor to a legion, and this was the kind of man Iulius Valens would like to leave in command. Who knows, thought Iulius Valens, he might live to see such a thing come to pass. Though he had no illusion that it might be in his legion or during his service.

Iulius Valens planned to give his Optio, Abenadar, the skills to be both a centurion and a Primus Pilus. The rest would be up to Abenadar and the gods.

*Thou hast rebuked the nations
and overwhelmed the ungodly,
thou hast blotted out their name for all time.
The strongholds of the enemy
are thrown down forevermore;
thou hast laid their cities in ruins,
all memory of them is lost.*

PSALM 9:5-6

Eleven

Procurator Valerius Gratus's tribute to Rome decreased in proportion to the rising rebellion in Y'hudah. Unlike Y'hudah under Valerius Gratus's Procuratorship, the lands of the Galil were stable and prosperous. The Galil, though poorly managed by Herod Antipas, was fertile and well watered. While the mountains of Y'hudah were, in the best of times, mostly barren and, in these days, especially dry. As a result of drought, food was scarce, and local famines tested both the patience of the people of Y'hudah and the Roman Procurator.

During this time, Valerius Gratus called on the III Gallica and primarily the Primus and Decimus Cohorts to march throughout the Galil as a show of force and to keep the borders clear.

In Y'hudah, the immigration of Jews from Babylon and the pressure of Zealots and other rebels kept Valerius Gratus' own forces constantly busy. Unfortunately, the Procurator's abilities were not up to the job, and he fought a battle that his diplomatic and military skills could not win. This fact had become obvious even to the Emperor Tiberius.

Iulius Valens found out about the installment of a new Procurator in Y'hudah before the word came to Valerius Gratus. In the Primus' mind, the change was long overdue. He had been tasked to transfer too many good legionnaires to the Ferrata VI in the past year. He could little spare the loss of manpower.

Abenadar read much of the Primus Pilus' correspondence and realized from his own experience what a new Procurator meant. During the last change of Procurators in Judea, the III Gallica lost the Hastatus Posterior Century, and Abenadar almost lost his life. He hoped for a more tranquil change, but knowing the past appointments of

Tiberius, he wouldn't hold his breath. When Iulius Valens showed Abenadar the official letter announcing the assignment of the new Procurator, Abenadar knew the transition would not be pleasant.

"Optio Abenadar," said the Primus as he entered into his own office in the officium.

Abenadar saluted him from the desk.

Iulius Valens sat heavily in his chair and waved his guards out of the room. When they were alone, he put his hand on his chin. "As I feared, Pontius Pilate will be the new Procurator of Judea."

"Pontius Pilate!"

"Yes. You know of him?"

"How could I not know of him," said Abenadar.

"You think he is a bad choice?"

"No, not for Rome, but bad for the people of Judea."

The corners of the Primus' lips twitched. "What about for the III Gallica?"

"I see action in Judea, but can that be bad?"

Iulius Valens' expression became very serious. "If we lose another century, yes. The recruits appointed to us are already few, and with the fighting on the Isle of Britain and the Rhineland, we certainly won't get many more."

"Primus, what do you know of this man, Pontius Pilate?"

"He is a hard taskmaster and harder on his legions."

"He has been successful before?" asked Abenadar.

"Yes. But he climbed to Procurator on the backs of his legionnaires. Everywhere he was assigned, he left them victorious but broken."

"What do you propose we do?"

"Pilate will have too much to do in Judea quelling the Zealots and the people. I suspect we will be called on to provide a show of force. With the situation in the provinces of Judea as it is, we will have to go to battle for the VI Ferrata. I will not send out the Decimus this time. Tell Nico, but no one else. I will inform the centurions myself. I need to put our cohort into training...as well as the Decimus. We will be ready for this one—" He sighed and stared thoughtfully at Abenadar. "Draft a letter to Herod. I will need to tell him in diplomatic terms why both the Primus Cohort and the Primus Pilus will be away from Sepphoris."

"Herod will not be pleased."

"Write the letter in Greek so he can understand it without translation. I don't want to be misunderstood on any account. We will bring it to him ourselves."

"How much time do we have?"

"A month, maybe two. Valerius Gratus started his small war as soon as he stepped ashore at Caesarea."

Abenadar saluted and left for his own quarters in the officium.

Three months later, under the orders of Pontius Pilate, Procurator of Y'hudah, the Primus Cohort moved out toward the Yarden River Valley. Abenadar marched in the van, at the centurion's position alongside the Primus Pilus Century. Nico carried the III Gallica's signum with the bull at its peak and not the aquila. By tradition, the aquila did not leave the legion's winter quarters unless the whole legion was in the field. Nico proudly marched with the bull signum at the head of the cohort. Iulius Valens walked just behind him. They traveled fast and without a supply train: Iulius Valens was a wise and experienced leader.

By this time, Pilate had chased the Zealots out of the major cities in Y'hudah. He lost many legionnaires and angered the people of Y'hudah, but he was intent on holding on to his victories. Emperor Tiberius was pleased. The tribute Pilate took from Y'hudah already made up for everything Valerius Gratus had neglected during the years of his rule.

Abenadar was surprised that all of Y'hudah was not up in arms. The leaders of the people of Y'hudah in Yerushalayim convinced the people and themselves that the Zealots were the enemy and not the Romans. But Pilate could only keep this balance of power through a continual show of Roman force.

The Primus Cohort of the III Gallica was the force Pilate intended to flush out and destroy the Zealots; in his mind, the III Gallica would bear the loss and not his own legion. Iulius Valens did not covet this job, but he did not trust anyone else to tackle the problem. Unlike Valerius Gratus's attack against the Parthians, the Zealots fought with their backs to a corner. This would not be a simple campaign but an invasion against a numerous and dedicated foe. When the the Primus Cohort met the enemy, the Zealots could not retreat; they had no place to go. And their own brand of religious fervor made them, if anything, more dangerous. The Zealots would fight like furies and take no prisoners—not on either side. The Zealots wanted to clean the land of Romans, and Pilate decided instead to wash Y'hudah in their blood. Already a thousand of their brothers lined the roads of Y'hudah, crucified and left to rot as a warning to the others.

Abenadar knew all this. He and the Primus made careful plans. Abenadar hoped they could limit the bloodshed, but he didn't hold to any false notions.

When the cohort marched past Natzeret, Abenadar gazed wistfully toward his old home. Natzeret held nothing for him now. His mother had died a year ago. Yeshua had sent a message to him. He wrote that she died peacefully and with little warning. Yeshua said Natzeret mourned her, and Adonai surely blessed her death as well as her life. Abenadar hoped this was true. He had not forgotten Adonai, but by now his youth was only a hazy memory. The business of the legion and his responsibilities left him little time for personal reflection. He mourned his mother by sending an aurie to Yeshua with a note of thanks.

The seasons were in change, and as they marched toward Y'hudah, the day stayed cool. The night would be very cold. Abenadar deployed scouts ahead, behind, and to the sides of the long column of legionnaires. He trusted this would keep their march safe from the Zealots' hit-and-run guerrilla tactics. Ahead of them, the legion's two turmae of cavalry scoured the major roadways.

As the afternoon wore on, Iulius Valens was unwilling to immediately leave the boarders of the Galil. He halted the cohort just outside of the city of Agrippina. Abenadar set the cohort to build a cold camp for the night; within the camp, he did not allow any fires. The men, not yet used to extended time in the field, were uncomfortable but wise enough not to complain. The Primus didn't want to overly discomfort his legionnaires, but both Abenadar and Nico insisted they not broadcast their movements to the enemy. They had worked the men much harder than this already, and deprivation would be easier on them if it was constant. Stealth, security, and surprise were their main weapons against the Zealots.

Before the end of the day, a cloud of dust announced the cavalry's return. Their orders were to encamp with the cohort for the night, so Abenadar anticipated them, but unexpectedly, less than a turmae, only 15 horsemen, entered the encampment. Valerian, the decurion of the auxiliary equitata drove his horse straight into the center of the camp and came to a quick stop in front of the Primus Pilus. He saluted, and without a pause, blurted out, "Primus, the rebels have taken Scythopolis."

The Primus took the news calmly. "The city is no more than five miles from here. How many rebels are there? Did you see them for yourself?"

"We heard the news from some merchants and from the farmers in the valley. The Zealots overwhelmed the city this morning; they are as numerous as locusts. They took the city for their god and put many of the Greeks to the sword."

"What of the defenses of the city?"

"I took a scouting party all around the walls. The walls are low and not well defended. The rebels are on a raid. They don't realize we are anywhere near."

"How many do you think there are?"

"From the evidence we found from their attack on the city, I would guess around a thousand."

"Abenadar, what do you think?"

"There could be more than a thousand. The reports from the new Procurator are somewhat cryptic. I think we could easily encounter as many as a thousand and not more than 1500 rebels organized into a single force. They will not be well trained or well armed."

"How would you catch them?" He looked at Abenadar.

"That would be for the Primes Ordines of your centurions to determine, but I suggest we prepare scaling ladders and move close to the walls during the night. We could attack at dawn and surprise the Zealots before they wake."

"Why not go through the gates?"

"The rebels will think to guard the gates. They will expect an assault to the city front, from the direction of Judea."

"Would you send a century to guard their retreat?"

"Not in the center of the retreat. I would put a century to the east and west on either side of the southern part of the city and order them and the auxiliary equitata to harry the rebels when they withdraw."

"Valerian, gather the Primes Ordines. In the morning, we will see whether these rebels can stand up against a Primus Cohort."

"Yes, sir!" the decurion saluted.

"Abenadar, How long would it take you to make the scaling ladders we need?"

"One hour. The material is at hand and the men have practiced this more than once."

"Can they do it in the dark?"

"Yes, Primus."

"Very well. Set the men to work and return to me as quickly as you can. I will talk to the Primes Ordines. I am sure their plan will be similar to yours."

When Abenadar returned, the centurions were bent over a map Decurion Valerian had scratched on the ground. Iulius Valens stuck wooden markers on the map to represent each of the centuries in their battle positions. The markers depicting the Primus Pilus, Princeps, and Hastatus centuries were placed beside the back wall of the city, while the Princeps Posterior, and Hastatus Posterior centuries lay near the front of the city to the east and west. Two small, carved horses in the hills to the south of the city marked the turmae of the auxiliary equitata.

The Primus stood up and gazed around the circle of men. "We will move to the back of the city and wait until dawn. When I give the signal, the Primus Pilus, Princeps, and the Hastatus Centuries will climb the wall and seek out the Zealots in the city."

Aemilius Regulus interrupted, "Primus, how will we know the Zealots from every other man in the city?"

"Go house to house and round them up. The men with swords are rebels—they will fight." The Primus noticed Abenadar. "You know the people, Abenadar; what do you think?"

"I don't think we will need to go house to house. If the tales of those who escaped are true, the rebels will fear the people of the city more than any external attack. I think we will find them encamped together in the marketplace," said Abenadar.

"How do we know the rebels are still in the city?" said Aemilius Regulus.

"I left a small scouting party to watch the main gate," said Valerian. "They will inform me when the rebels withdraw."

"Warn your men. I don't want the Zealots to have any idea we are near—not until we attack. Do you all understand?"

The men nodded all around.

"What do we do if we cannot overcome them in the city?"

"Valerian will stay near the back wall with some riders. If we are separated and anyone gets in a bind, send a runner to me. I will signal through Valerian for the Princeps Posterior or the Hastatus Posterior to attack. The Princeps Posterior and Hastatus Posterior will provide our reserve." Iulius Valens pointed at the map on the ground. "If we can't get over the city wall or we are discovered before dawn, retreat to the western hills and reform there. But don't retreat without my orders. Centurions, are you ready?"

The centurions nodded.

"I have already started the men on the scaling ladders. We will move out in an hour. Abenadar, is there anything else you can tell us about the city?"

"I would only caution you against harming any of the people of Scythopolis. They are all under the protection of Rome. They already believe they have few reasons for not joining the rebels. The rebels made the mistake of attacking these people. We cannot."

"I second your words, Abenadar," said the Primus. "Gentlemen, caution your men. A thousand rebels we can handle, two thousand angry men are beyond the strength of our cohort."

An hour later the Primus Cohort broke camp. Each column carried a siege ladder. The men made the ladders from camp stakes and rope.

To help make a stealthier approach to Scythopolis, the legionnaires padded their armor and equipment. Before they crossed the Jezreel River, they discarded their packs and were ready for battle.

Thankfully, the moon was only a thin slice in the sky. The Primus Pilus, Princeps, and Hastatus centuries made the last mile of their movement alternately on their bellies or, when they could find cover in the sparse fields around the city, rushing in a crouch.

Scythopolis was not well prepared for defense. In the wane light of the night sky, Abenadar saw the walls were very low and appeared unpatrolled. The cultivated fields marched right up to the city walls without a break. During their approach to the city, the legionnaires saw no one; neither guards nor the farmers whose huts dotted the fields. Abenadar guessed, when the rebels entered the city, the farmers escaped into the hills with their families. The legionnaires were prepared to handle guards, but fortunately, they didn't encounter any.

With some luck and because of careful planning and caution, their advance came off without incident. As dawn neared, the first three centuries of the Primus Cohort, a force of almost 500 legionnaires sat quietly at the bottom of the walls of Scythopolis. Abenadar detected no sign they were under observation from the city. The Princeps Posterior and Hastatus Posterior Centuries would likely find it easier to position themselves to the east and west of the city.

At the walls, the men poised, silent and motionless. They were still wet from crossing the cold Jezreel, but the fire of battle was alight in their bellies. Abenadar crawled down the line of his legionnaires to check each man. No one spoke. They barely moved, but he could feel the excitement...and fear in them. This, he knew, was warfare: the expectation of victory, the dread of death.

Abenadar returned to his place beside the Primus. Iulius Valens caught his eye and raised his hand.

Abenadar nodded the affirmative. The men were ready. He sat down beside the Primus to await the sun. To Abenadar, this seemed the longest night of his life. No one dared sleep. At each sound, Abenadar and Iulius Valens started up, fearful they had been discovered. Their fears were unfounded, and the night unfolded slowly but without any disturbance. Abenadar began to wonder if they would enter the city to find the rebels gone.

When the first gray of dawn shone across the Yarden River Valley, the Primus stood up. He was chilled and sluggish but knew that would soon wear off. Abenadar stood beside him. He signaled Abenadar to move to the other end of the line and alert the centurion of the Princeps Century while he notified Aemilius Regulus himself. The signals were unnecessary; all three centuries were already on their feet and ready for the attack. Iulius Valens motioned the men to raise the scaling ladders. Almost as one, the legionnaires lifted the ladders, which bumped quietly against the top of the wall. The Primus waited a single heartbeat, then gave the signal—up and over. Along the line, the legionnaires repeated the gesture. Silently, the men swarmed over the walls. They made it to the top unopposed.

Abenadar was the first man over the wall. Right behind him came the last column of the Primus Pilus Century. At the top of the wall, he squinted down for a moment into the dark shadowed street on the other side. Then, sure no one hid in the darkness below, he let himself down by his hands, swung a moment, and dropped to the dirt street. He drew his gladius, and held it out before him as he ran toward the center of the city. Abenadar didn't stop to see if his men followed—the sounds of scrambling and the rattle of their unsheathed weapons told him they were right on his heels.

Abenadar ran in a crouch. He headed straight for the marketplace. Around him, the streets were empty, but he could feel the pressure of the men behind. He turned at a corner of the main thoroughfare, and the market stood before him. Sleeping men packed the whole open space. In the dim predawn light, Abenadar saw they wore the dark headbands and turbans of the Zealots, and not a single sentry stood among them. Then the slaughter started.

Stabbing and slashing with his sword, Abenadar led the legionnaires as he waded into the sea of men. The groans and screams of the dying filled the marketplace behind the quickly advancing line of legionnaires. The blood of the Zealots splattered the attackers and their gore covered the ground. As the morning sun rose, the blood turned from black to bright red, and the dark turbans of the Zealots became blue. But only for a moment—blood soaked the garish turbans and turned them a sickly purple. Ahead of the line of legionnaires, the rebels shamelessly clawed over their own brothers trying to get out of the reach of the Roman scythe. More than five full minutes went by before the Zealots put up any active opposition to the legionnaires. At scattered points, rebels tried to take a stand, but from behind, their own pushed them into the Roman swords.

The slaughter sickened Abenadar, but he could not stop—they could not stop. If they lost the momentum of the attack, the Zealots would turn on them and destroy them. As the sun rose, Abenadar noted their three centuries were outnumbered by more than three to one. The refugees from Scythopolis had been right. The Zealots were like locusts—at least 1500 were encamped in the city. The legionnaires moved forward, mechanically, unwavering. Any falter would portend their own death and defeat.

Abenadar called out both encouragement and orders; his men followed him like automatons. Some were tense and obviously disturbed by the slaughter, others moved like unrestrained dogs after their prey. Whatever their feelings, they flawlessly performed with the discipline Abenadar had daily hammered into them. They followed his commands without hesitation. Abenadar doubted any of his men realized their true danger. Abenadar knew that soon the Primus Pilus must signal either the Princeps Posterior or the Hastatus Posterior Centuries to reinforce them. Without the full strength of the Primus Cohort supporting the legionnaires, the Zealots would eventually find their courage and rally behind their leaders. When that happened, the current slaughter would turn into a frantic legion defense.

Abenadar spotted Iulius Valens leading from the other side of the Primus Pilus Century and moved toward him. The men fanned around Abenadar, but they kept their line. Abenadar waded through the dead and dying, sometimes using his gladius to cut clutching hands from his legs and feet. When he reached the Primus, Abenadar was careful not to slow the advance. His sword still slashing, he said, "Primus, if the rebels turn on us, we are done for. There are too many of them."

"What should we do? Should I call on the Princeps Posterior and Hastatus Posterior now?"

"I think one century would be enough; keep the other in reserve.

But they should not come in by the front gate. Have the Hastatus Posterior, near the river, scale the walls behind the Zealots and take them from the rear."

"See to it, Abenadar."

"Yes, Primus." Abenadar didn't turn. He called his instructions back to two of the men near him, and the legionnaires took off running. They dashed back through the dead and dying and the maze of lightening streets to deliver the orders to Valerian.

For a long time Abenadar felt sure the small relief would not come. His arm ached from the effort of killing. The rebels fought back now. The cohort's operation turned from an offense to a defense—the rebels fell less often and their leaders were trying to rally them. Abenadar knew that unless the Hastatus Posterior could quickly get into position behind the Zealots, the whole battle would turn against them.

The reversal happened in a moment. The Zealots regained their morale. They were threatened from one side by their own leaders and on the other by bloodthirsty legionnaires. Enough of the rebels decided if they didn't do something soon, they all might die. Though hundreds of their comrades lay motionless at their feet, they began to inexorably push the legionnaires back across the blood-soaked ground.

"Double line," yelled the Primus.

The centurions and optios for the three centuries passed the command along. The single line collapsed into a double line and the legionnaires in the back readied their heavy pila.

A murderous defense began. In the initial assault, the rebels were backed to the end of the marketplace. Their only escape was the main street to the city gate, and they had no intention of leaving. Caught between the buildings lining the square and the double line of legionnaires, the rebels found very little room to maneuver. Frenzied with fear and encouraged by their leaders, the Zealots threw themselves at the double line of troops. The swords cut the men in the front to pieces while the pila impaled those at the back. When a screaming rebel could not be removed from a pila, the swordsmen in the front row cut him loose. At first, the rebels could make no inroad against the centuries; their bodies just stacked higher and higher before the line of Romans. Desperation showed in their ranks. When they backed off, Iulius Valens ordered the legionnaires forward. When they attacked, the Primus pulled his lines back.

The press of Zealots finally made a wise tactical move. Their leaders got behind them and, cursing and beating them with the flats of their swords, they pressed the mob forward. Under this constant barrage, little by little, the centuries fell back. Iulius Valens and Abenadar knew the ultimate result of this action. Right now, the rebels were contained and unable to maneuver. If they could force the line of legionnaires back to the point where the marketplace opened up and the streets allowed access behind the Roman lines, the centuries would have to give up the open ground in the square and fight a retreat through the narrow streets. Abenadar was confident they could eventually prevail against the Zealots, but he would prefer not to fight them with his back against the walls of the city. Escape from the marketplace would be difficult, and he was certain they would lose a good number of their men.

"Primus," said Abenadar, "to provide security for our flanks, we should separate out the columns as necessary and have them back down the side streets."

"Yes," the Primus reluctantly agreed. "Pass the order to the centurions."

Abenadar sent runners from the back of the line.

For now, the legion's lines appeared complete. Abenadar didn't see any yawning gaps in them. Although many of the men had taken injuries, and he was himself cut more than once on his arms and legs, Abenadar had not seen any of his men fall and not get up again. Their discipline was unbroken. They fought like a machine, synchronized and mostly silent. The rebels, on the other hand, threw themselves yelling against the line of iron points as though by numbers and momentum alone they could breach it.

As the Primus ordered, when the line of legionnaires backed as far as the first side street, a column broke off from the line and moved to cover the breach. With the rebels in front of them, they backed down the narrow street. When this happened, the rebels let out a collective groan and thrust themselves with a greater vigor against this smaller group. The retreating legionnaires pulled back a little faster to prevent their front lines from being overrun, and the Primus pressed his main group momentarily forward to take some of the pressure off them.

As the main group of legionnaires still in the square moved back, the need to cover the side streets slowly ate away at their force. The number of men in the main lines dwindled. They fragmented their force to maintain their security. The Primus Pilus realized this and protested to Abenadar, "If they back us all the way to the end of the square, we'll lose any chance of forcing them out of the town. Any ideas?"

Abenadar pointed, at that moment, three side streets to the left and behind the Zealots erupted with legionnaires. At their head ran the signifer of the Hastatus Posterior Century.

"There's my idea." A grim smile skewed Abenadar's features.

Iulius Valens laughed out loud and ordered, "Single line, gladius, attack."

The line of legionnaires leapt forward. In this new onslaught, as many rebels were knocked down by the legionnaires' scutum and crushed underfoot as were thrust through with the sword.

The Zealots wavered a moment, then broke ranks and rushed for the city gates. The rout trampled many of their leaders. The leaders who were still alive joined the routed mob and tried to outrun the surging line of legionnaires.

Abenadar sent columns from the Primus Pilus Century down the liberated side streets to break the rebels between groups of legionnaires.

At the city gate, the legionnaires crushed the desperate press of rebels against the barred gate. The disciplined line of legionnaires struck the back of the rebel forces and hewed them down like practice stakes. When the gate burst open, the rebels stampeded into the fields. On the other side of the gate, the Princeps Posterior Century ambushed the retreating Zealots from the right and forced them down toward the river. In full chase, the front lines of the Primus Pilus, Princeps, Hastatus, and Hastatus Posterior centuries dashed through the gates into the open fields. The Primus halted them in front of the city.

The rebels were at a full run away from the city of Scythopolis. Scattered groups of Zealots, rallied by their leaders, stopped for a moment and were overrun by the still pursuing Princeps Posterior

Century.

When the auxiliary equitata took up the chase, the legionnaires at the gate let out a loud cheer.

"Call back the Princeps Posterior," said the Primus to Abenadar.

Abenadar signaled the cornicen, and he let out a blast on his horn. The Princeps Posterior stopped their pursuit and marched jubilantly back toward the city. The two turmae of the auxiliary equitata continued to harass the rebels until they were out of sight.

Iulius Valens peered out of his helmet triumphantly at Abenadar. "Set guards, and let's clean out the rest of the town."

They reentered the city and, in an expanding single line, made their way through the streets. When they arrived at the marketplace, the people of the city were already making sure of their rebel tormenters. Greek men, women, slaves, and children worked through the carnage with knives and baskets. With kitchen knives, they killed any rebel who was still alive. They gathered the valuables and clothing stripped from the dead men in their baskets.

When they noticed the returning legionnaires, the people stopped their plunder and stared fearfully at them.

"Abenadar," said the Primus Pilus, "warn the people not to harm any Romans, and tell them that they may take anything that is not metal or weapon."

Abenadar passed this message to the people, and they bowed and lustily continued their looting.

The Primus broke the centuries into three columns each under a centurion, optio, or tesserarius, and set them to comb the streets. As they made their way through the midmorning city, it came alive with people. Shops and taverns opened; men and women came out into the streets. At each street, people bowed to Abenadar and showed him where they last saw rebels trying to escape the Roman onslaught. They tried to give his men gifts of food and trinkets, but Abenadar begged them off. By the afternoon, Abenadar was certain the city was empty of living rebels.

When Abenadar returned to the marketplace, it was entirely cleared of bodies. The blood was already covered with fresh sand and the weapons and metal implements, money and jewelry of the Zealots was carefully arranged in finely woven baskets at the center of the square.

The Primus sat on his chair near the rebel's plunder, and all of the legionnaires' packs that they left in the fields to the north of the city were stacked neatly near him. Behind Iulius Valens, Nico held the legion's signum, and the Primus' guards were stationed on either side. A group of old men stood in front of the Primus, and one of the elders and he were trying to have a conversation.

When Abenadar and his columns marched into the square, Iulius Valens motioned to him. "They speak Greek, but I can barely understand them."

"It is the dialect of the Decapolis," said Abenadar. He had spoken this dialect for most of his life and interpreted for the shopkeepers in Natzeret. "He is thanking you for running the Zealots out."

"Is that all?"

"More or less. He wants to know what you are going to do now."

"Tell him we will stay the night and leave in the morning."

"He is relieved."

Iulius Valens grinned and rubbed his chin. "Ask him if we may stay in the city."

"Good idea," Abenadar responded in Latin. To the city leader, he said in Greek, "With your permission we will stay the night in Scythopolis."

The leader bowed and answered yes, but he was not pleased.

When the man left, Abenadar said, "Primus, of soldiers, lately the city has only known the rebels out of Judea. I suggest we keep the men under a tight reign while we are here. If we do, Rome is certain to make some fast friends."

"Very well. Put out the orders. But I think with this city's reputation, the people would be more pleased by the money the men will spend in their brothels."

"You are probably right. I'll have the signifers limit the funds available to each man and put them on a midnight curfew."

'That should do the trick. Let them blow off some steam, but keep them fit for the morrow. How many men did we lose?"

"The reports from the centurions say 26 dead and 53 wounded too badly to fight."

"Ten dead from our century." The Primus gripped his vitis until his knuckles turned white.

"Our men bore the brunt of the fighting."

"The city is secure?"

"Yes, Primus."

"It was a necessary question, Abenadar. I know you wouldn't be here if the defense of the city wasn't assured. How many of the enemy did we kill?"

"The full count is not in, but over 600 bodies were in the city alone. There are no wounded; the people of Scythopolis made sure of that."

"When we march, I want to leave our wounded here."

"I would also advise that. You will need to leave a guard."

"Five responsible men and enough money to ensure they and the wounded are fed and housed."

"I will make sure your orders are accomplished."

"Good. One other thing: I want to be out of the city by dawn."

Abenadar saluted and left to carry out the Primus' orders.

*The nations have plunged into a pit of their own making;
their own feet are entangled in the net which they hid.
Now Adonai makes himself known. Justice is done:
the wicked man is trapped in his own devices.*

PSALM 9:15-16

Twelve

Before the sun rose in the eastern cradle of the mountains, the Primus Cohort of the III Gallica marched proudly out of the city of Scythopolis. As the victorious legionnaires passed through the gates, atop the walls of the city, the people of Scythopolis waved and cheered. Abenadar was amazed the people roused so early to see the cohort off. He hadn't fully realized the atrocities of the Zealots against the Greeks in the city.

As soon as the cohort lost sight of the city, a turmae of their auxiliary equitata rode up to the Primus. Lucius, a principalis, and not the Decurion, led the turmae. He dismounted and handed the reigns to one of his men. Then he saluted the Primus. Iulius Valens didn't bother to stop the moving cohort.

"Go ahead, Lucius. What's your message?" said the Primus Pilus.

"Primus, we have been harassing the retreating rebels through the night. The Zealots camped about five miles from here and left a half an hour ago. About a thousand of them remain, and they have no supplies."

"How successful have you been?"

"We attacked their stragglers and killed perhaps fifty."

"Any losses?"

"No, Primus."

"Good." Iulius Valens turned his head, "Abenadar, quick-march."

"Quickstep, h'arch," called Abenadar and almost as one, the entire cohort came to the faster pace. "Scouts, out." The scouts broke out of the century and ran forward and to the sides of the marching legionnaires. The rest of the centuries followed the example of the Primus Pilus Century.

The Primus turned back to Lucius. "Lead us to the camp and then on to the rebel force. I want to catch them before sunset."

"Yes, Primus." The principalis saluted again and remounted. The turmae of cavalry moved forward and to the left side of the roadway about a hundred yards in front of the cohort.

The camp was a killing field. The Zealots did not leave their wounded to die—they simply murdered any that could not march that morning. At least a hundred bodies littered the ground.

Iulius Valens didn't take time to scout the place; he saw no need. The path of the fleeing Zealot army was obvious in and about the road. Without stopping, he led the cohort around the impromptu camp and headed south behind Lucius' turmae of auxiliary equitata. As the cohort advanced, the many wounded in the ranks of the Zealots became evident from the cast-off bloodied rags and occasional dead or dying man left on the roadside.

The Primus called a stop at a muddy wadi a few miles south of the village of Aenon. Abenadar saw to the men, then stepped to where the Primus sat at the edge of the stream.

"The Zealots are moving slowly," the Primus said. "I suspect they have no idea we are following them. What would you do if you were a rebel leader with a wounded army?"

"I would disperse into the hills and lick my wounds. There will always be another chance to attack," replied Abenadar.

"I would too." The Primus tapped his teeth with his vitis. "Why has this Zealot leader not done that?"

"Could we have killed their main leaders in Scythopolis?"

"No, we are still following a cohesive force." He leaned forward a little. "And they are held together with barbarous methods. The dead men we found on the roadway prove that. Without strong leadership, the whole of them would have dispersed on their own."

"I agree. They think they are safe. Pilate's forces have been unwilling to pursue them after a battle. They are used to being the hunter and not the hare."

Iulius Valens smiled. "I believe you are right, but surely our auxiliary equitata on their heels tells them they are being watched."

"They may expect other forces to join with them, or perhaps they have a safe haven where they can supply so large a group."

The Primus reclined slightly. "Where would you shelter an army of rebels?"

"The mountains of Judea have always been their favorite hiding place."

"But only for small groups." The Primus stared at Abenadar. "Where could a force this size expect to hide?"

Abenadar thought for a moment before he answered. "Few live in the wilderness of Judea at the edge of the Salt Sea. If they could be supplied, an army ten times the size of this one could loose itself."

"If they reach the Salt Sea, do we stand a chance of fighting them?"

"The hare could turn again into the hunter. I don't think we could beat them in the mountains. Not if they knew we were coming. Our only hope is to cut them off before they are reinforced or before they reach their refuge."

"How would you cut them off?" The Primus cocked his head toward Abenadar, as though he expected an entirely thought-out answer to this simple query.

Abenadar was ready to answer his question. "Right now the rebels are moving slowly enough that we could cross the river and pass them. I would set up an ambush in their path with a century to the west to prevent them from dispersing into the mountains and one to the east to keep them from crossing the river into Perea."

"You think three centuries in the open can overcome a thousand Zealots?"

"They are unsupplied and already half beaten. The two other centuries can flank them when we engage."

"Where would you meet them?" Iulius Valens' voice grew excited.

Abenadar caught his enthusiasm. "I walked this way many times as a child on the way to Yerushalayim. The ground rises when it approaches Yericho and becomes a wide plain. We should meet them before that point. North of Yericho, just before the village of Archelais, the ground is hilly with plenty of wadis for cover. We could hide all our men in this terrain and still be able to observe the rebels' approach."

"Abenadar—" the Primus Pilus' eyes twinkled—"gather the Primes Ordines and their optios. Let's see if they will agree to this battle plan."

An hour later, the cohort crossed the Yarden River and headed deep into the uplands to the east of the river. Although Decurion Valerian reported the rebels were out of sight of the river, Iulius Valens wanted to make sure they couldn't spot the swiftly moving cohort from the other side. And swift they were. The centuries moved in a double-time rout step. Abenadar kept the centuries well spread out to hold down the dust of their passage. The Primus sent the cavalry turmae ahead to inform the rest of the auxiliary equitata of their plans. Iulius Valens ordered the auxiliary equitata to keep pressure on the rebels and to report immediately if their line of march changed.

At noon, the reports from the decurion told them the Zealots still moved along the west side of the valley on the main road. The rebels had not sent out scouts or changed their formation. By Abenadar's calculations the cohort passed the rebels just after the sun dropped past zenith, and when the sun went down, they were well ahead of them.

Not long after, Valerian reported the rebels had stopped for the night. Iulius Valens made a night stop too. The cohort built a camp in the eastern foothills just south of the Jabbok River. They made no fires, and Abenadar doubled the guards during the night.

Before the sun rose, the Primus Cohort was on the move again. The cohort crossed the Yarden River before noon and dug into the hills and wadis north of the village of Archelais.

About a half-mile north of the rest of the cohort, the Primus placed the fourth century, Princeps Posterior, to the west and the fifth century, Hastatus Posterior, to the east. He gave their centurions strict orders not to attack until they received a signal by runner or from the auxiliary equitata. Now the hunter's trap was laid. They need only wait for the beaters to force the hare into it.

When the rebels had not shown by nightfall, Abenadar worried the Zealots had cut across the Yarden or dispersed into the mountains. The principales' turmae of cavalry brought them news.

The Principalis Lucius dismounted right before the Primus. "Primus, the Zealots have slowed their march. They are making camp for the night. They are five miles north at the village of Phasaelis."

The Primus swore. "Instead of an exhausted army, we will meet a rested one." He turned to Abenadar. "What about a night attack?"

"Phasaelis is on a plain. We won't be able to take them by surprise, and many will escape in the darkness."

"Principalis, what do their plans seem to be?"

"They have continued straight along the road. The decurion thinks they are certain the main body of our troops have not followed them. They pillaged the village of Phasaelis and are eating for the first time in two days."

"A choice target." Iulias Valens eyed Abenadar expectantly.

"I would not advise it."

"Very well. Tell the decurion to keep a watch, but stay out of sight. Let them think we have entirely given up on them. Bring me a report when they decamp."

The principalis saluted and rode back out into the night.

Iulius Valens stared straight at Abenadar. "I hope you are right."

"I do too. Primus, what should we do if they do not continue into our ambush?"

"What would you suggest, Abenadar?"

"If they flee into the mountains, I would have read them incorrectly and led you astray. You may give my position to a more worthy man. We will not be able to stop them if they disperse and escape in that direction anyway. If they continue into your trap, they will be rested, but surprise will be complete. We have almost 700 men, all legionnaires. They are now less than 900. In our last fight, they lost more than 20 men to every one of ours. I think you will annihilate them."

"Very well. My mind is made up. We need not call the Primes Ordines together. Send runners to their positions and alert them to the location of the enemy. We will wait for them here." As Abenadar left, the Primus took his arm. "Optio if you are right, I will give you a corona aurea. But if you are wrong, I will let you write the letter to the Governor yourself."

Abenadar smiled at Iulius Valens, saluted him, and left to send out the runners. He did not feel as confident as he'd sounded before the Primus. If they defeated the rebels and lost half the cohort, Iulius Valens would be a hero before the Roman Senate. If Abenadar let them slip through the Primus' fingers, Iulius Valens might not remain the Primus Pilus of the III Gallica for much longer.

The morning sun slowly lighted the positions of the Primus Cohort. The dawn came without the usual camp bustle. The men lay silent and almost unmoving in their positions. Abenadar made his rounds from column to column to check on the men and ensure their vigilance and quiet. He examined the scouts in their positions and finally settled with Iulius Valens and Nico at the center of the trap. On either side of the Primus Pilus Century, the Princeps and Hastatus lay invisible in their positions. They all waited for the sign of the raised bull *signum* to announce the ambush.

An hour after dawn, unmounted, Lucius, the Principalis of the auxiliary equitata, strode up to their position. He had crossed the river twice and walked on foot to their hiding place. "Primus, the rebels are moving out of Phasaelis…straight down the road."

"How long?"

"An hour, maybe two. They are moving slowly."

"Do they suspect anything?"

"No, and they are loaded down with the pillage of Phesaelis."

"Take your position with your turmae. Best of luck to the Decurion Valerian, and tell him I am pleased with his work."

"Yes, Primus."

When the man had gone, the Primus clapped Abenadar on the shoulder. "You have half the corona aurea in your hand already. Let us see if you live long enough for me to put it on your brow."

Abenadar smiled back at him and thought, *I will live if Adonai, blessed be He, wills it.*

The Zealots moved slowly indeed. By the time they came within sight of Abenadar's position, they trudged down the road with no order at all. Their force spread out for almost a full mile down the dusty track and more closely resembled a group of farmers headed for market than an army. At the end, interspersed with animals and hobbled together by ropes, they led some of the inhabitants of Phasaelis. On the rebels' backs and in their hands was all the wealth of the village: grain, vegetables, clothing, rugs, mats, and cooking pots.

When Abenadar saw them, any compassion at their plight washed out of his heart. The Zealots had left the people of Phasaelis with nothing…not even the ability to furnish themselves a single meal. A whole season's food stuffed the Zealots' sated bellies. Like locusts, they had stolen the livelihood of their brothers—and taken their own brothers and sisters as slaves.

"Primus," whispered Abenadar, "they are so strung out we won't be able to surround them all."

Iulius Valens replied, "I will let them come as close as I dare before I give the signal."

Abenadar judged the movement of the Zealots. "If they come right up to us, half of them will be beyond the Princeps Posterior and the Hastatus Posterior Centuries."

"What do you propose?"

"Don't signal the Princeps Posterior or Hastatus Posterior until the rebels at the end move up to attack us."

"And if they don't move to the attack?"

"We will lose some into the mountains or they could possibly flank us."

"It is too late for us to do anything else now. Watch them, and tell me when to give the signal."

The head of the ragged group moved closer and closer to their position. Abenadar lay still and unmoving. Around him, the men were restless. He motioned for quiet. On the ground in front of Abenadar lay his pila and gladius.

Nico moved to gather his feet under himself. Abenadar laid a hand on his shoulder.

Abenadar could see one of their leaders. He plodded at the front of the long line of men. His face was strained but did not seem alarmed or cautious. The rebels had no scouts out and moved forward as though they expected no opposition.

Abenadar let the leader come within five yards of his position before he tapped Nico on the back. "Attack!"

The signum came up immediately. All around Abenadar the legionnaires rose and launched their light pila. Abenadar's own pila caught the surprised leader in the chest and pierced him completely through. Abenadar threw his heavy pila after the light. He caught a man behind the fallen leader in the leg and pinned him to the ground.

The Primus shouted, "Single line, forward!"

Beside him, Nico and Abenadar advanced and encouraged the men. They didn't need much encouragement. They rushed against the awestruck rebels and cut down those not already impaled by their pila.

Abenadar waded into the mass of men. His gladius thrust again and again into men now running away from them. The rebels bunched onto one another and ran over the men behind. The fight was a slaughter until the Zealots threw down their plunder and pulled out their weapons. Throughout the mass of screaming and fleeing men, Abenadar heard the rebel leaders as they encouraged their men to fight—fight, or they would certainly be butchered by the Romans. Opposition built from the back of the army of Zealots while the rebels in the center formed a meager defense. They moved quickly to fill in their front lines. Many of the rebels, still driven by hysteria, ran unrestrained into the legionnaires and their own troops, but most were disciplined enough to form around their leaders.

The Zealots at the rear had not turned and run yet. Evidently they still nurtured some hope of opposition. They clambered forward to bring their weapons to bear against the legionnaires in the front of their lines.

When the back line of Zealots came nearly even with the still-hidden legionnaires of the Princeps Posterior and Hastatus Posterior Centuries, the Primus Pilus gave the signal. The Princeps Posterior and Hastatus Posterior leapt from their hiding places and surrounded the back lines of the rebels. Now the legionnaires cut off all avenues of escape, and the rebels collectively realized their only hope was to fight.

Some still tried to run. The auxiliary equitata, patrolling the periphery of the battle, struck them down. Concerted groups tried vainly to break through the legionnaires—they died quickly. Finally, when the rebels had been beaten down to less than a hundred standing men, Abenadar said to Iulius Valens, "This has gone on long enough. They are defeated. Let me try to encourage them to surrender."

Iulius Valens shrugged, and Abenadar, taking that to be an affirmative, shouted to the Zealots in Aramaic, "You will all die. Throw down your weapons and surrender."

The rebels simply stood in shocked silence.

The Primus called out, "All legionnaires, to the defense, now."

The centurions and optios took up the call, and the legionnaires stood back in their single lines waiting for the rebels' response.

From the center of the bunch of blood-splattered Zealots came a desperate voice. "You will kill us anyway. Why should we not let our lives be given at the highest cost?"

"We are tired of killing. Put down your weapons now, or you will be slaughtered, and no one in Y'hudah will mourn your deaths."

Slowly, one by one, the Zealots let their swords fall.

"Pilate will crucify them," remarked the Primus beside Abenadar.

"They know that, but they believe they will achieve martyrdom on a cross. Here they will die and no one will care."

"Is that best for Pilate or for their cause?"

"Pilate will think he is doing himself a favor. I have no compassion for them—I don't want to lose any more of our men."

"Spoken like a legionnaire." The Primus nodded slowly. He called to the legionnaires, "Tie them in a hobble chain."

The centuries saw to their injured and dead. They lost 18 men with only a few badly wounded. The legionnaires released the captured men from Phasaelis and, at Abenadar's insistence, left all the pillage the rebels had taken from the village. The people blessed the Primus again and again. The citizens of Archelais came up to help the people of Phasaelis and to gaze in amazement at the masses of dead and dying men.

The legionnaires reformed their centuries and, with the rebels in the rear, marched to Yericho for the night and then on to Yerushalayim.

The Primus Cohort made a triumphant entry into Yerushalayim. The city shined with whitewash under the late afternoon sun. It lay bright and beautiful with sparkles of gold, the tops of gilt towers, and blue, the clear pools scattered throughout the city. The Temple and the Fortress of Antonia rose high above the other buildings. The fortress served as Pontius Pilate's Praetorium when he dwelt in the city.

Iulius Valens led the cohort along the road down the Mount of Olives and through the Fish Gate directly in front of the Praetorium. The people scattered from the streets when they saw the Roman cohort enter the city. In the lead marched Nico and the Primus Pilus. Behind them came the centuries in their carefully dressed columns and at the end stumbled their bedraggled prisoners. The Primus ordered the cornicens to sound their horns. By the time they stopped before the doors of the Praetorium, Pilate, the Legatus Legionis, and the other leaders of the Ferrata VI Legion lined its outer walls.

The Fortress of Antonia was a massive crenellated fortification near the eastern side of Yerushalayim. Three stairways protected the main entrances to the fortress. It shared one wall with the Temple and possessed two towers that peered down into the Temple's Court of Gentiles and Court of Women. The fortress was separated into two parts: the Pavement and the main fortress. The Pavement was a large open court connected to the southern end of the fortress. The people of Y'hudah would attend the Procurator on the Pavement, but, under the Romans, they believed the fortress a dwelling place of pagan gods. They considered anyone defiled who set a foot inside. The fort itself reached high above the city, while inside it, deep below, rotted the Procurator's political prisoners.

The Primus halted the cohort before the main inner gate to the Pavement, and his legionnaires waited in silence. Finally, Pilate came to the gate, and the guards opened it before him.

Pilate was a tall and lean man. His face was angular and strong with a perpetual thin smile as though he was accustomed to holding his thoughts to himself. Although his shoulders were straight, he stood with a slight slouch, and his eyes examined the Primus and his men with the steady gaze of a soldier. Like a man accustomed to the wear of a legionnaire's helmet, his head was balding only on the crown. His sparse dark hair lay flat on his head covered by a thin sheen of fine oil. He wore a legate's gold crown entwined with the enameled wreath of a Procurator.

Pilate addressed Iulius Valens with a strong and steady voice. "We recognize your signum. Are you Iulius Valens, Primus Pilus of the III Gallica?"

"Yes, Procurator, I am Iulius Valens."

"Why are you here, Primus?"

"Vittilius, Governor of Syria, at your request sent me to quell the rebels at the border of the Galil and Judea. I found a force of 1600 Zealots pillaging the city of Scythopolis and attacked them. Almost 1000 escaped from me, so I pursued and conquered them. All that is left of their army are these hundred prisoners…and their weapons." He turned to Abenadar. "Optio, present the rebels' weapons to the Procurator."

Abenadar saluted and signaled the men. Each legionnaire walked by the portico where Pilate stood, and laid two weapons at his feet. This continued until every man in the cohort passed by. The pile of swords grew before Pilate until they almost covered the portico. After that, the legionnaires led the captured Zealots before the Procurator. As they hobbled to the front, Pilate took a step forward, then turned and gesticulated to the Legatus Legionis behind him. The prisoners were sullen, and Abenadar kept them well back from the Procurator.

"A brave and glorious victory, Primus. How did you accomplish it?"

"My Primus Cohort and the advice of the…"

"A single cohort?"

"Yes, Procurator."

Pilate glared at the Legatus Legionis behind him, and they

whispered animatedly for a few moments. He turned back to the Primus. "Go on."

"My Primes Ordines and the officium were my primary advisors on military tactics. Their strategies ensured our success."

"Well spoken, Iulius Valens. But how did you capture these rebels? Normally, they would rather die than fall into our hands."

"I have a principalis, my optio, who himself convinced these and has persuaded other Zealots to be taken prisoner. He knows the language of the Zealots and the people of these lands."

Pilate rubbed his chin. "Such a man would be invaluable. We want to meet him and hear more about this battle. We invite you and your Primes Ordines to a banquet tonight in honor of your victory. We thank you and your men for the triumph our legion could not deliver to us."

Iulius Valens saluted Pilate. "Now, if I may, Procurator, where can I house my cohort?"

"They are welcome in the Praetorium. They may stay as our guests on the Pavement within."

Again Iulius Valens saluted.

Pilate nodded to him, a grand gesture to a Primus Pilus, and stepped back into the fortress. The guards opened the large doors to their full width and, with horns blaring, the Primus Cohort of the III Gallica entered, the guests of Procurator Pontius Pilate.

After the legionnaires were settled, Iulius Valens found Abenadar. "You must accompany me to Pilate's banquet. Your advice, after all, allowed us this victory."

"I offered you only what I have been taught. My thanks go to you, Primus."

"You have certainly earned the corona aurea I promised you. Your offer of surrender to the rebels was also well thought. Pilate seemed more impressed by the capture of a few dirty Zealots than by our victory. Come with me now. Pilate made his baths available to us to clean off the grime of battle, and he will provide us clothing for his feast."

Abenadar washed in the fortress baths, and a slave handed him a toga to wear. Abenadar had never worn a toga. By Roman law, only citizens of Rome could wear the garment, and although he was a citizen, he never had a reason to own one. He was given one with a fine blue hem. The slave showed him how to don and tie it.

Two of Pilate's guards led Abenadar, Iulius Valens, and the centurions of the Primus Cohort high up into the rooms of the main part of the fortress. The guards opened the door to Pilate's private quarters and gestured them in. They entered into a beautiful and barbaric room. The walls were covered with patterned tapestries. Swords and shields hung against the hangings with no thought to the colors or designs beneath them. A long thin wooden table filled the center of the room and around this table stood couches arranged for eating.

The table was already covered with cold foods and Pilate and his chief officers lay on the couches around it. When the Primus Pilus entered, the Procurator and his officials stood up.

"Welcome, Iulius Valens and the Primes Ordines of the Primus Cohort of the III Gallica Legion. Come forward and be recognized. You have brought great joy to us today. Let us return some of that joy to you."

Iulius Valens introduced each of his centurions, and one by one, Pilate graciously welcomed them to a place at his end of the table. When the Primus came to Abenadar, he said, "This is my Optio, Abenadar. He is the son of Abenadar Iustus and the man I told you about. He is the man who captured the Zealots for you."

"Yes, this is a man I would like to know better. Here, Iulius Valens, sit beside me, and, you, Abenadar, beside your Primus. I want to hear how you convinced these men to accept my crucifixion instead of your swords. But, first—" he clapped his hands—"wine and food. Let the symposium begin."

Slaves brought out cups and pitchers of unwatered wine. They poured the cups full and, even if only a single sip had been taken from them, refilled them whenever they were placed back on the table. The slaves were young women, all beautiful, and represented every nationality Abenadar had ever heard of and some he could not place. They wore short tunics. Some strutted like whores while others tried to not call attention to themselves. Among them were women as white as alabaster, with yellow hair; Abenadar guessed they must have been taken from the wilds of the Rhineland. There were also maidens soft and slight with a cast of yellow in their skins. Abenadar could only imagine they had come from the Persian slave markets. The slaves brought him hot bread and meat of all kinds. He had never seen such rich and varied food nor such beautiful and sensual women. The other men ignored them, and he tried to also.

The wine was clear and fine, better than any Abenadar had ever tasted. After a while Pilate turned to Iulius Valens and spoke to both him and Abenadar. "Iulius, is this Abenadar the son of the Abenadar Iustus who was our ambassador to Herod?"

"Yes, Procurator, the same. He was born to a woman of the Galil and vouched as a citizen by his father."

"You, Optio Abenadar, the son of my friend, you were raised in the Galil."

"Yes, Procurator. My mother taught me Latin and Greek."

"You speak Latin and Greek and the language of the people of these lands as well?"

Iulius Valens interrupted before Abenadar could answer. "He not only speaks to them, he can read and write their languages. I examined him, and his first posting was as the librarius for one of my centuries. He is my official translator and even now writes much of my correspondence."

"But he is also an optio, so his skills are not just those of the pen."

"He is the gladius trainer for the III Gallica. He has never been bested in combat and wears two gold and three silver phalerae, one armillae and two torques. I will award him a corona aurea for his leadership in this last battle."

Pilate stoked his chin. "You trust his advice and his leadership that much? Such a man should be a centurion."

"Next to my Primes Ordines, I value him as the best legionnaire in the III Gallica."

"He is more than a soldier. I need such men in Judea. I have constant problems with these people. Abenadar, what would you do to quell their rebelliousness?"

Abenadar took a drawn-out sip of wine to conceal his surprise at the unexpected question. He thought for a long moment. "Procurator, I would not want to give you any advice without knowing the full situation here."

"You know the people. What would bring us peace and make them productive? You may speak freely. We are asking the opinion of one who has earned the right to speak. No one has brought so many Zealots to us before."

Abenadar took a deep breath. "The Judeans' desires are not completely at odds with ours. They desire the freedom to worship according to their beliefs and to uphold their law."

"This is a simple thing for me to grant. But what of the Zealots who plague me? I have killed enough of them, but even then, they will not let me be."

"The Judeans want two simple things: their law and their worship. If you were to grant it to them, they would oppose the Zealots for you. They desire to worship their God. To do this requires security of the land and the freedom of their Temple. They will not oppose you in this. With that, the Zealots will have little cause to oppose the priests and leaders of the people. And the people will not support their opposition. They may oppose you; they will not oppose the priests and their leaders. "

"That is wise advice. It is perhaps a course worth trying." Pilate turned to Iulius Valens. "Iulius, is your optio usually right about these things?"

"For the legionnaires in the III Gallica, at half the asking price, he procures women and wine from the taverns throughout these lands and both the legionnaires and the tavern owners thank him for it," said the Primus, laughing.

Pilate's smile widened. "This is a resourceful man. I will think on this. The gladius has gained little for me...other than dead subjects. But, enough of this. Let us speak about your battle with the Zealots. I want to know the whole of it—from the beginning."

Iulius Valens gave a complete report of their excursion. Pilate leaned forward throughout the whole account. He asked questions about points on which he was not clear and made the Primus repeat the description of the battles twice. Iulius Valens did not leave out Abenadar's role either as leader or as strategist, and Pilate made Abenadar clarify how he came to his conclusions and plans. Lit by the flickering oil lamps, their conversation continued far into the night.

When the tale was finally told and retold to his satisfaction, Pilate sat back and stretched. "I have kept you up much too late. When do you plan to leave Jerusalem?"

"I think a week of rest will be sufficient for my legionnaires. I may have to leave some of the badly wounded with your legion."

"If a week is enough, you may remain in the Pavement. I will supply your needs. You may billet your cavalry in my camp next to the Praetorium."

"Thank you, Procurator."

"I know you wish to be with your troops, but tonight you may soothe your desires with any of my slaves you fancy." He glanced up. "I think your centurions have already taken their prizes." With that Pilate left the room.

The Primus immediately stood up and grasped the slave standing next to his seat by the hand. She giggled nervously and led him out of the room.

Abenadar didn't know what to do. His head was befuddled with too much wine and food. One of the slaves, a girl of ravishing beauty and a light northern complexion, came to him and sat on the couch beside him. Some other slaves removed the lamps, and in a moment, Abenadar lay alone in the darkness with her. He could smell her closeness. Her body breathed a scent of fresh flowers and sweet-smelling grapes. A musty fragrance—one Abenadar had never noticed before—underlay her perfume.

The girl caressed him and gently kissed his lips. At first he didn't respond. She lay next to him and moved sensually against him. As though driven by an unquenchable force, Abenadar's lips tasted hers, and his body reached for her. In moments he became one with her and groaned out his abrupt passion. He lay still for a moment while she tried to take some little pleasure in him. But he had no thought for the slave. A wave of shame flooded over him that immediately cleared his befuddled mind.

Abenadar tried to get up, but the girl held him fast, moving futilely against him. He pushed away from her and stood up. She cried out as they separated and cursed him first in a foreign tongue and then in broken Latin.

Abenadar had nothing to say to her. He understood her anger, but he could think of nothing but what he had done. He pulled his toga from under her and threw it around his shoulders. By that time, the slave lay crying in a heap with her tunic bunched around her waist. She begged him, "No tell master. No tell master."

Abenadar said something, a guttural sound without meaning, and left her and the room. This was just the thing he did not want. He now knew his greatest personal shame in the moment of his finest public victory. He had betrayed himself and Adonai...and he betrayed this girl. What a fool he had been. He'd let his body rule him.

Abenadar determined then to rule his own body; no one and nothing else would. He had seldom prayed since he'd lived in his mother's home, but he prayed now for forgiveness. He promised Adonai he would not be weak again. When and if he ever knew a woman intimately again, the time and place would be his choice—and her choice. The commitment of a lifetime—a choice of mind, heart, and soul...not a foolish moment of weakness.

Abenadar found the baths and, by a flickering lamp, scrubbed himself as though that action would clean away his memories of the night. He traded the toga for his helmet, tunic, and armor. Out on the Pavement, Abenadar wrapped himself in his blanket and lay down in the midst of his men. His eyes did not close for the entire night, and the sun seemed to be late returning the day.

*I rejoiced when they said to me,
"Let us go to the house of Adonai."
Now we stand within your gates,
O Yerushalayim.*

PSALM 122:1-2

Thirteen

The Primus Cohort of the III Gallica entered Sepphoris with horns blaring. Iulius Valens marched the entire cohort through the city streets and into the camp. He did not review the troops with a march around the inner perimeter of the camp, though the new Legatus Legionis and Vittilius, the Governor of Syria were present. He did order Nico to bring out the III Gallica's Aquila, and by century, he had the men salute the Governor. In perfect order, the men formed up in their usual positions with the Primus Cohort in the front and the Decimus Cohort to the rear.

When the men were lined up in their centuries, the Legatus Legionis and Governor Vittilius walked up to Iulius Valens. Vittilius accepted Iulius Valens' salute and said, "Iulius Valens Primus Pilus of the III Gallica Legion, you have much to be proud of. Pontius Pilate sent word of your victory before your Decurion reached us. We came to praise you and reward your cohort."

The Primus saluted again.

The Legatus Legionis said, "As the senatorial head of the III Gallica, I am pleased to present each of the men of the Primus Cohort, III Gallica with two gold phalerae, one for each of the battles you fought. I further award your cohort two gold phalerae to be mounted on each of the signum of your centuries. To the principales of the Primus Cohort, I award a gold torque and to the centurions a gold armillae. To you, Primus, I present a vexillum of the III Gallica." The Legatus took a miniature of the standard of the III Gallica mounted on a silver disk and handed it with true pride to the Primus.

Governor Vittilius waved the Legatus back and stepped forward. "I have more honors to present. Until ratified by the senate, by my command and the recommendation of Pontius Pilate, your Primus Pilus

Iulius Valens has been named Legatus Legionis of the Ferrata VI Legion."

Unconcealed surprise washed momentarily over Iulius Valens' features.

Vittilius continued, "Step forward, Optio Abenadar." The Governor gazed out over the cohorts.

Abenadar marched to a position by the Primus and in front of the Governor. Vittilius placed a corona aurea on his head and handed him a golden vitis with silver decorations. "Until ratified by the Emperor, by my command and the recommendation of Pontius Pilate, Optio Abenadar is promoted and installed as the centurion of the Decimus Hastatus Posterior Century VI Ferrata Legion."

Iulius Valens and Abenadar rode to Yerushalayim with a turmae of the auxiliary equitata. The auxiliary equitata was under orders to deliver correspondence from Sepphoris to the garrison in Shomron and to officials in Neapolis, so instead of the Yarden River route, they took the caravan road through the mountains. Since Pilate became Procurator, this road had been safe for travel. The trip took three days because protocol forced the legionnaires to stay a night in both cities.

The new Legatus Legionis and centurion had much to talk about together, and Iulius Valens had plenty of information to pass on to his protégé.

"Abenadar, I am moving from a soldier to a politician," said Iulius Valens as they rode.

"Isn't Legatus Legionis a position you desired?" asked Abenadar, pulling up beside him.

"I desired it, but days ago the honor seemed far away. A week ago I was responsible for a cohort and commanded a legion. Soon I will be responsible for a legion and command neither legion, nor cohort, nor century. I envy you, young friend."

"And I envy you also, but surely it is too late for regrets now. You can only march forward and not back."

"You say some insightful things for a young man."

"For a centurion, Legatus?"

Iulius Valens chuckled. "Yes, even for a centurion."

"What will you do when we reach Jerusalem?"

"Pilate will billet me in the Praetorium," Iulius Valens said. "He will keep me at his beck and call. I will review the cohorts. I would like to move Aemilius Regulus and Nico into the VI Ferrata to help me train the legion. You will be available to help instruct, but as you will soon discover, you must always rebuild your credibility and reputation when you move to a new legion. It will be as if you never earned your awards or rank. I have been in four legions, and for me, it has always been the same. I will help you." He paused. "You will certainly help me."

"What should I do when I take over the Decimus Hastatus Posterior Century?"

Iulius Valens smiled. "You must do the same thing you did when you took over as optio of my century: train the weakness out of them. I admit, before you became my optio, I let my century's combat skills deteriorate. A lot depends on your principales."

"What can I do if my principales are not competent or capable?"

"You train them or replace them. A good battle always gives you the opportunity to remove a poor principalis. You can always petition me, but you must work through the chain of command. We have both had the opportunity to benefit from the other's skills. I count you a friend, Abenadar, and a great warrior. I will ensure you have what you need to succeed. But let me warn you, I may not be able to provide you the best. I assure you, you will get material you can work with."

"Thank you, Primu…Legatus."

They topped the Hill of Scopus north of the city of Yerushalayim, and before them, the city unfolded in the bright afternoon.

"Stop," called out Iulius Valens. "Decurion Valerian, halt your turmae for a few moments."

Valerian raised his hand and the auxiliary interrupted their march. "Yes, Legatus."

Iulius Valens dismounted and motioned to Abenadar. "We must enter the city and our new roles as befits our rank and honor."

The new Legatus Legionis took off his armor and put on the

clothing that displayed his semi-senatorial rank. He wore a white wool toga with a wide purple hem. On his head, he placed the enameled wreath of a Legatus Legionis. Over his left shoulder, Iulius Valens hung the chains that held the phalerae he'd earned and on his arm, the rows of armillae. Around his neck he placed his torques. He gingerly unwrapped his personal signum, itself a hasta pura, a silver spear shaft that bore the shining vexillum, and handed it to one of the auxiliary troops to carry.

Abenadar already wore the armor of his new rank. Pilate had sent him a generous viaticum of six aurei. Abenadar used a full aurei from this to buy new tunics and equipment. He wore a centurion's helmet and plumes. Abenadar likewise put on his phalerae, armillae, and torques. He held onto a soldier's private vanity that he had more decorations than Iulius Valens but reminded himself that most of these had been awarded to him by the new Legatus.

When the two men had prepared themselves by donning their finest, they remounted and Iulius Valens motioned for Decurion Valerian to proceed.

From their vantage point, Abenadar could view the entire city. The Hill of Scopus descended into a line of four hills marked by white sepulchers—the tombs of the kings and with many smaller gardens and tombs. Past these hills, the ground became a plain marked, at first, by fields and infrequent buildings. The buildings increased in number and size until they reached the walls of the city. The walls of Yerushalayim rose above this plain and set the city apart from the rest of the terrain. It was, literally, a city on a hilltop; a beautiful city set apart from the rest of the world.

The Procurator's Praetorium in the Fortress of Antonia and the Temple both rose above the city just as the city rose above the rest of the land. The Temple was especially conspicuous. Even at this distance, the beauty of the courts and brilliance of the decorations were obvious.

From the north, the city was shaped like a thick inverted *L* with an extended serif at the toe, or as the rabbis liked to remark, like the Hebrew letter *he,* the first and last consonant in the true name of God. The caravan road went straight to the heel of the *L* and entered the city at Efrayim's Gate.

The people kept out of their way as the soldiers rode across the plain toward the gate. They seemed more cautious and fearful of the Romans than were the people of the Galil. As the turmae approached the city, Abenadar caught sight of one of the reasons for their fear. Outside the city, along both sides of the road to Yafo, stood lines of crucified men. Some of the crosses bore only bones, but at least 100 held whole bodies, the Zealots their cohort had brought to Pilate's justice. Some of the crucified men might still be alive. The thought of such suffering made Abenadar shiver. The stench of rotting flesh flooded across the lower reaches of the plain to him.

Efrayim's Gate was a large crenellated structure with a thick multiple door, and a gate with twin towers on either side. Like the rest of the walls, it was built with large, well-set, and mortared limestone blocks. The column of legionnaires at the gate saluted the Legatus Legionis and waved the turmae into the city. Before they entered, the principalis of the guard sent two runners to announce the arrival of the new Legatus and centurion.

As they passed through the walls, Abenadar noted they were very thick and appeared secure. There would be no chance of scaling these walls easily as the Primus Cohort had at Scythopolis. Two regular centuries would be required to guard the city walls, and a full cohort to man them during a siege. Abenadar could see the legionnaires at each tower. The closer ones craned their necks to catch a glimpse of the new officers.

The principalis of the gate sent two legionnaires to escort them through the city. These two walked before them and warned the people of their approach. When they entered the upper market, their escort didn't have to clear the way for them. Here too, although the streets from the gate were wide enough for a century to march, the people kept carefully out of their way. The streets that ran away from the main thoroughfare were narrow and dark. They were crowded with the curious who lined them to see this unusual parade.

Until they entered it, the market was vibrant and packed with activity. At the legionnaires' approach, the buyers and sellers quieted and moved well out of the way. They watched the Romans surreptitiously from their tents and stalls. Abenadar could mark Greeks,

Syrians, those from the Galil, Persians, Babylonians, and Romans, all side by side with the people of Y'hudah. Of the people of Y'hudah, Abenadar observed Tz'dukim and Essenes along with many of the common people and laborers. He saw no P'rushim. He learned later that this market was considered a neutral ground for Goyim and the people of Y'hudah, and therefore labeled unclean by the P'rushim. The market of the P'rushim was in the part of the city called Zion, and the P'rushim did not allow the Goyim and unauthorized people of Y'hudah to buy or sell goods there.

Abenadar noted many taverns that gave the impression they might offer a good meal and drink. Already he missed the camaraderie of his friend Nico.

Abenadar understood the words of the people who crowded the sides of the street. He already began to search his mind for the different inflections and intonations. He knew he wouldn't get far in Yerushalayim speaking with the accent of the Galil. The people of Y'hudah held the Galil in almost as much contempt as they did the people of Shomron and the Romans.

At the edge of the market, their small parade passed through a second gate, and in front of them, stood the main portico of the Praetorium. To the right, over a six-foot wall, Abenadar marked the barracks of the two cohorts stationed in the city; like Sepphoris, they were the Primus and the Decimus Cohorts. Pilate himself did not greet them at the portico as he had when their cohort arrived there in victory. Instead, an honor guard that consisted of a column of the Primus Century along with Cecilius Bassus, the Primus Pilus, and the Primes Ordines stood at the entrance. They had quickly donned their arms and decorations. Abenadar was again secretly pleased that his complement of honors was greater than any of theirs.

Cecilius Bassus stood at the head of the group and glanced nervously at Iulius Valens. Abenadar guessed the large man was concerned that his position, like that of the last Legatus Legionis, would abruptly evaporate at Pilate's whim. Primus Pilus Cecilius Bassus was a rough-looking centurion. He had a classically heavy Roman face with a strength about it, in spite of his uneasiness. Abenadar felt immediately that he could work with the man; Cecilius Bassus possessed an obvious openness in his speech and actions that became unmistakable as Abenadar learned to know him.

As Abenadar dismounted, the men saluted Iulius Valens and surrounded him.

Iulius Valens said, "Thank you for your reception. Let me also reintroduce to you Abenadar. As you know, he is our new Decimus Hastatus Posterior Centurion."

"Welcome, Abenadar," said the Primus Pilus of the VI Ferrata, his eyes flickering over Abenadar's armor, "I will introduce you to your century during tomorrow's morning muster. Your fame is not unknown to me nor to your men. Come now." His gesture included Abenadar. "Legatus Legionis Iulius Valens, Pilate awaits your arrival."

They all entered the Praetorium and the door closed behind them. This time, instead of climbing up into the higher levels of the fortress, Cecilius Bassus took them straight down the long corridor that led to the outer portico. At its end, the corridor opened into a very large vaulted chamber. This was Pilate's court. It wasn't much different than many of the courts Abenadar had seen. A row of columns stood four feet from every wall and supported the vault of the ceiling. The columns marked five-foot intervals except at the front, where a 10-foot opening fronted the doors to the corridor.

Pilate sat in a portable, interlocking field-chair covered with purple cloth. In spite of this finery and unlike the barbaric dining hall on the floors above, there was no other evidence of Pilate's personality in the room.

As soon as they entered the court, Pilate motioned them forward. "We hope your journey was satisfactory."

Iulius Valens and Abenadar saluted, and Iulius Valens stepped forward. "Our trip was very agreeable, Procurator."

"We are pleased to see you. When we spoke last, there was mention of a new approach to taming the people of Judea. We would like to put this plan into practice. Legatus—"

Iulius Valens bowed slightly.

"We want you, along with Abenadar, to prepare a letter to the Sanhedrin, the Judean rulers. In this letter, you will spell out their responsibilities and rights and mine. In the main, they shall be allowed to govern themselves by their own laws. They may try anyone who is not a Roman citizen, but they shall not pronounce any capital or corporeal punishment—that shall remain our providence. Also, their laws shall not govern any Roman citizen, but we will endeavor to protect and support their Temple and religious events. When this proclamation is complete, we will bring the Sanhedrin together to formalize the agreement. For their part, you will write that we expect them to discourage the rebellion of the people and to actively encourage their cooperation." Pilate glanced at Iulius Valens to see that his words were understood, then continued, "We want to make it clear to them, we desire their cooperation both in our collection of tribute and in the apprehension of the rebels."

Pilate then stared directly at Abenadar. "Do you think they will agree to this?"

Abenadar glanced at the Legatus and, with his nod of approval spoke. "I believe the people are as tired of the rebels as are we. I think they will yield to your conditions so long as they see your willingness to uphold their autonomy."

"Centurion Abenadar, how would you ensure this?"

"At this moment, I am not certain. I have been in the city for only an hour, but I suspect the easiest action is to provide a benign presence that keeps the peace."

"Do you mean we should keep a close reign on the legionnaires, while at the same time allowing them, in their official capacity, to protect the people of Judea?"

"Yes, Procurator, that is just what I mean."

"Legatus Legionis, do you agree with your new centurion's appraisal?"

"I cannot find fault with it. He knows the people."

"Very well. We shall attempt these specific actions. If they prove fruitful, they shall be the model for our realm. Legatus Legionis, instruct your centurions to train and control your legionnaires in this manner. We do not want the people to be abused." Pilate paused. "Against the Zealots, rebels of any type, and criminals you may use any force necessary to quell and capture; however, we will hold any man and his leaders responsible for unjustified actions against the people of this land. We retain the ability to punish, and the rulers of the people of Judea shall hold the ability to judge their own. Is this clear?"

The men bowed.

"In honor of our new Legatus, I am happy to provide a feast for you." Pilate clapped for his slaves. "Refresh and dress these two officers. They are a very desirable addition to our forces." With those words, Pilate rose and left the court.

In the morning, Abenadar formed up in the officium of the VI Ferrata. Cecilius Bassus introduced Iulius Valens. Iulius Valens gave a long speech in which he encouraged the men to hold firm to the training and honor of Rome. When he was done, Cecilius Bassus called Abenadar to stand in the front of the formation, "VI Ferrata, many of you have heard of the Legionnaire Abenadar. He is now appointed the Centurion of the Decimus Hastatus Posterior. I am certain he will bring great honor to our legion." With that, he led Abenadar to the centurion's position of the Decimus Hastatus Posterior Century and gave him their charge.

When they fell out, the men gathered to hear the postings from the librarius. The optio came directly up to Abenadar and saluted. "Centurion, I am Gaius Flaccus, your optio and the legion's Quaestionaris and executioner."

Gaius was an enormous, muscled man. A veteran's battle scars marked his armor and limbs, and he held himself stiffly erect with a poise that made him stand out among the other principales of the cohort. The man's presence was palpable.

"Well met, Gaius. The crosses on the road to Yafo are your handiwork?"

Gaius bowed with some pride but without any of the evident cruelty that usually marked the Quaestionarii of a legion.

Abenadar didn't let his distaste flavor his words. "Who are the other principales in our century?"

"This is Eurycles the Signifer." Gaius indicated the man beside him.

"Tiras there is your tesserarius, and the librarius." He pointed. "Over there is Antonius."

Each of them were fine-looking legionnaires. Abenadar knew he had been honored with some of the best in the VI Ferrata.

"Come with me, Gaius. I want you to show me my quarters and brief me on each of the men."

Abenadar's room was a small one in the headquarters. It was almost square and barely contained a raised cot and an ancient writing table. A thick reed mat covered the floor. Abenadar's meager belongings had already been conveyed to the room.

Abenadar and Gaius sat on the mat.

"What is the training of our century like," began Abenadar.

"It is low, Centurion. We spend every fourth day on the walls, and there are no training grounds in the camp."

"I want our century up to the peak of training in a month. Optio Gaius, are you capable of doing this?"

"I…yes, I can do that."

"You plan and lead the training. If you require help, I can tell you what needs to be done. In the main, however, I will train with you."

"Sir?"

"I will not ask anything from the men that I would not ask from myself. Tomorrow, what is the schedule?"

"The men are not assigned to the walls, that was yesterday. They will be given their common work."

"Then tomorrow the duty roster will read *Training* for all the men who are not already occupied. In the cohort's scheduling, I will ask for all the men once a week. Get the librarius—who is he? Antonius?—to work out the schedule with the rest of the librarii."

"What kind of training do you want tomorrow?"

"Marching and the stakes."

Gaius appeared incredulous but kept his thoughts to himself. "Where would you like to hold this training?"

"Is there no place in the city with enough space?"

"Beside the Ophel, just to the south is a barren space within the walls. It is large enough to march and train at the stakes."

"Good. We will drill there tomorrow. Prepare the century."

Abenadar spent the rest of the day with Iulius Valens. Together they wrote the letter to the Sanhedrin that Pilate directed the night before. When the letter was finished, the Legatus wouldn't let Abenadar leave until he had copied it twice in Latin, Greek, and Aramaic. Abenadar returned to his quarters late that evening.

The next morning, Abenadar led the Decimus Hastatus Posterior Century through the city and into the open area beside the Ophel. It was a dirt and grass field at least 500 yards long by 250 yards wide. On one side was the inner wall of the old city. On the other side stood the earliest portions of the City of David and the most ancient part of Yerushalayim.

Without moving from the centurion's position, Abenadar called out, "Optio Gaius, you may train the century."

Gaius reformed the columns and started the march. He worked the men though the basic marching steps and turns. Before they crossed the green twice, a crowd formed. By the time they made their fifth circuit, people lined the walls all around the open area.

The legionnaires threw their shoulders back at the people's attention and kept their march perfect. Abenadar didn't have to upbraid a single man. As the day progressed, the people came and went, and as the sun crept toward noon, many of the adults departed, but a host of children lingered to watch. Wide-eyed, they observed the soldiers intricate maneuvers. Gaius performed credibly as he led the men through the steps and battle formations. By noon, the legionnaires were exhausted, but they knew enough not to complain. Gaius was not in the best training himself. Abenadar would have pushed the men harder, but for the first day, he didn't think it was a bad workout.

Abenadar called a halt and gave the men time to put up their stakes. He could see their relief as they shrugged off their packs and started digging the holes. They had carried the stakes from the camp and had marched the entire morning with them on their backs.

Abenadar was glad to see that, without his prodding, Gaius made some of the men move their stakes to put more space between them. There was no reason to risk injury during this kind of training.

After his men positioned the stakes, Abenadar gave them a full hour of rest. Then he motioned for Gaius to call them to weapon's practice. Along with their regular weapons, the men had carried weighted practice swords. As soon as the legionnaires pulled out their weapons, the boys along the wall rushed to get their friends. Shortly a larger crowd of children stood watching their practice, and adults rejoined the spectators throughout the afternoon.

Encouraged by the audience, the legionnaires gave a good accounting of themselves. Gaius was an unremarkable trainer, but Abenadar would ensure he and his men came up to the required level.

At the end of the watch, the century marched back to the camp for the second meal of the day. While Abenadar planned the next day's training with Gaius, a messenger from the Legatus Legionis entered Abenadar's quarters.

"Centurion, the Legatus Legionas and Procurator require your presence."

Abenadar followed the messenger back to the Praetorium. The guard led him directly into Pilate's court, not in the great hall but at the Pavement.

"Centurion." Pilate sat up in his chair. "There you are. The letter is exactly what we desired. The three languages will make the perfect impression. We have asked the leaders of the Sanhedrin to come to hear our pronouncement. We will have the letter read in Greek to them. We want you to translate any comments they make in their own tongue for us.

"Now, Centurion Abenadar, before we call the Sanhedrin to enter our court, you have had a full day to evaluate the city and its people. Do you have anything to add to your appraisal?"

"I have been training my century in the green of the Ophel. The people came all day to watch. They were curious and didn't seem hostile."

"And you gathered from this?" Pilate stretched forward.

"I will continue to train my century, and see what else I can learn from the people. Right now this presence among them appears positive."

"Very good." Pilate thought for a moment. "That is sufficient for now. Come stand beside me. We can hear the Judeans at the portico."

The leaders of the Sanhedrin walked solemnly into Pilate's presence. Their leader was Anan, appointed by Pilate the high priest for that year. Anan was a striking man, tall and spare with a long and angular face. His lips split his features in a remarkably straight line. Abenadar noticed the Praetorium was distasteful to Anan, but whether Anan disliked the Romans or the place alone Abenadar could not tell.

The ten leaders of the Sanhedrin stood in a silent and sullen group, unwilling to move closer to Pilate than necessary.

Pilate signaled the Cornicularius. "Read the proclamation."

The men of the Sanhedrin cringed as though they were only too used to Pilate's proclamations and their aftermath.

As the Cornicularius began to read the letter, the men stared first at the principalis and then at Pilate. To catch every word and to assure themselves they had not heard wrong, they discarded their usual caution and stepped a little closer. Anan's face registered incredulity.

The Cornicularius finished reading the letter and rerolled the papyrus. Pilate pointed at the copies, and the Cornicularius picked up the ones in Greek and Aramaic and handed them to Anan.

"There, Anan," said Pilate. "Those are copies for you. You see, we have signed them ourself. Will you add your mark to the bottom along with ours?"

Anan opened the first scroll handed to him. He started visibly when he unrolled it. The men crowded behind to see what had surprised him. When they recognized the Aramaic writing, they began to whisper among themselves. Anan signaled for their silence. "Procurator, this is indeed a great honor. Your suggestions are very pleasing to me. You know, I must have time to confer with the full Sanhedrin before I give you an answer, but I believe they will accept your recommendations."

"Good. We will look forward to hearing from you soon. You see, we can be accommodating when you are. We do not want a repeat of the events in Caesarea. It is too easy for us to mistake such displays as rebellion."

Abenadar knew Pilate referred to the event when the imagines, the signum bearing the portraits of the deified and reigning emperors of Rome were brought into Yerushalayim by night. The people of Y'hudah thought the images were pagan idols, forbidden by their law. They believed the imagines desecrated the holy city. The people protested vigorously in Caesarea, and Pilate killed many of them. The slaughter did not halt the insurrection, and Pilate, as quietly as he had brought in the hated imagines, removed them back to Caesarea.

"Procurator—" the word was obviously distasteful on Anan's tongue—"the offending items are no longer in the holy city. That is pleasing to us and to the people. The event was unfortunate, but necessary to show you our concern."

"Bring us back your answer soon." Pilate waved his hand to signal the interview was at an end.

"Yes, Procurator." Anan nodded only slightly so the motion could not be considered a bow. Then he and the men backed out of the court.

After they left, Pilate sat staring out across the Pavement. At last he stroked his face and turned his gaze first to Abenadar, then to Iulius Valens. "That went very well. They were startled and pleased by our suggestions. Centurion Abenadar, will they try to negotiate for more concessions from us?"

"No. I don't think so. Your reminder to them of your power and the lengths to which you will go to honor the Emperor will ensure they insist on no other conditions."

Pilate stared at Abenadar. "Your observations are very astute. We did indeed remind Anan for that reason. Continue to train your century in the city and bring us back your impressions of Jerusalem and its people." He eyed the court. "Gentlemen we have started well." Then he stood up and returned to his quarters.

But thou hast given a warning to those who fear thee,
to make their escape before the sentence falls.
Deliver those who are dear to thee;
save them with thy right hand, and answer.

PSALM 60:4-5

Fourteen

Abenadar found much to please him in the city of Yerushalayim. The city was vibrant and jammed with a myriad of peoples from the lands all around Y'hudah. The upper market was as cosmopolitan as the cities of Sepphoris, Caesarea, or Tiberias. And the prices in the upper market were always lower than the closed market in the ancient part of the city. The people in the upper city respected the Romans without hating them. Abenadar didn't find this to be the case in the areas that catered mainly to the P'rushim, Sanhedrin, and Temple castes.

The Sanhedrin hated the Romans just because they were Goyim. They needed no other reason. Their plans were simple: with the help of the Procurator, they would maintain control of Y'hudah until they could foment a successful revolution. At the moment, without the Roman authority, they held no real power, but no one knew what the future might bring.

The Sanhedrin accepted Pilate's offer, and, without fanfare, returned a copy of the letter with their marks upon it. From that moment, Yerushalayim fell into an uneasy peace. Pilate was very pleased with this turn of events and felt secure enough to restore his court to Caesarea. The Primus Cohort escorted him back to the coastal city and then returned. For the few days they were gone, the Decimus Cohort was stuck with the duty of guarding the walls.

Gaius' skill as a drillmaster increased, and this allowed Abenadar to bring his century to an intense level of training. Every day, except the days they spent on the walls, Abenadar led them to the green in the lower city. Surprisingly, the crowds of spectators didn't decrease, and on some days, the exercise of the Decimus Hastatus Posterior Century was almost as popular as the shows in the arena.

The only time Abenadar encountered problems with the people was when he unintentionally took his century to train on the seventh day of the week. That day was the Shabbat and sacred to the people of Y'hudah. Abenadar should have known better. Unlike the other days, when they left the area of the Praetorium, no one followed to watch their drill on the green. Instead, the people cursed the legionnaires as they marched through the streets. The old men and women wagged their heads at the Romans, and others made a sign warding the evil eye. These ominous portents gave enough warning to Abenadar that he turned his men around and returned to the camp.

That day Abenadar spoke to Primus Pilus Cecilius Bassus in his office. When Abenadar entered, the Primus was working busily at his desk. With little success, Cecilius Bassus gamely labored at a report and welcomed Abenadar with a grunt. Abenadar stood a yard inside the door and waited while the Primus finished the last of the line.

"There," announced Cecilius. He seemed happy for the interruption. "What do you need, Centurion Abenadar?"

"There was some commotion in the city today…"

The Primus broke in, "A disturbance that requires my immediate attention?"

"No, Primus," said Abenadar, "It is not an immediate problem, but a recurring one."

"Go on," said Cecilius with some impatience.

"The people of Judah celebrate every seventh day as a holy day. They do no work and have many rules and laws that govern their conduct during that time. Today is that seventh day. On the way to training my century today, I noted that our activities encouraged an intense degree of hostility from the people."

"You returned to the camp early. I noticed that myself," said Cecilius.

"Yes, Primus. I have a suggestion that may improve our overall relations with the people of the city. Out of deference to the people of Jerusalem, our legionnaires should do no work outside the camp on the Sabbath except to man the walls."

Cecilius Bassus chewed on the end of his brush. "You really think this will help?"

"Have you noticed problems with the people on certain days and not others?"

"I am not sure...but now that you mention it, on the days the Temple is most active, we have the greatest difficulties. I thought it was the nature of their religion."

"I assure you, it is not."

"Well, whether or not it is the religion, it would make sense to keep the legionnaires apart from the people, especially during those times when contact will result in friction." The Primus leaned back and glanced up. "How would you suggest we go about this new policy, and what should we do when some action is required in the city?"

"The people are offended by obvious work on the Sabbath; they will not be opposed to defensive actions. Such are even allowed by their law." The Primus nodded, and Abenadar continued, "All that is required is a letter to the centurions, followed by a slight revision to the schedules. I will write the letter and work out the schedules, if that is your desire."

Cecilius Bassus seemed relieved. "Very good, Abenadar. You handle the writing and the schedules. I will check them, of course, before they become official policy. What do you think Pilate's reaction will be?"

"I think he will praise your wisdom. Anything that ensures the city is quiet and the people continue to pay the tribute is what he most desires."

"You are right in that. Go to it then."

After the Primus signed the letter, Abenadar ensured the new policy was proclaimed throughout the city. When the order became common knowledge, both the legionnaires and the people of Yerushalayim praised the policy. The former for a day free of patrol, and the latter because they could celebrate Shabbat without seeing it defiled by actions not allowed by their law.

In his own way, Abenadar kept the Shabbat. He never tried to worship, as did the people of Y'hudah, but he participated by hearing and seeing their devotion. Although the Law patently excluded him from the worship of Adonai in the Temple, the constant devotion forcefully affected him. In his spirit, he felt a measure of expanding faith—faith that came welling up from the memories of his mother and childhood. He became convinced that Adonai made him for some purpose. For now, it was enough to know he lived in the spiritual center of the people of Adonai. In the city of Yerushalayim the blessing of Adonai was lifted up on thousands of lips every day.

In the upper marketplace, Abenadar found more than goods to purchase. He also discovered an atmosphere of acceptance. Many taverns gladly served Romans. When the men in his cohort heard of his near mythic ability to communicate with the tavern owners and whores, they made immediate use of his capabilities. Although he wanted none of it, quickly enough, through them, he found the places with women for sale and cheap drinks.

On his own, he discovered an inn much like the one in Sepphoris that served both good food, wine, and tolerance in reasonably abundant amounts. The owner was a fat jolly man of Y'hudah named Yotam, who didn't mind feeding a Roman centurion in his house.

Yotam's Inn stood near the Praetorium at the far end of the upper marketplace. It was convenient to the legion camp, but the inn was small and did not traffic in whores, so it was not a favorite with the legionnaires.

Abenadar knew Yotam's household included his wife and a daughter. Except that Yotam's daughter routinely washed his feet when he patronized the inn, he rarely saw them and never remembered hearing their names. To Abenadar, his acquaintance with Yotam was only casual, and he didn't realize the status his presence conferred to Yotam's Inn.

The existence of a Roman who could speak the tongue of Y'hudah like a native was unique enough. When that Roman was also a centurion and was said to stand up for the people of Y'hudah in the court of Pilate, Yotam counted it a blessing to have Abenadar under his roof. Abenadar drew much more attention from the people of the marketplace than he realized.

In Yotam's Inn, Abenadar heard many of the rumors circulating the city, and it became his primary point for gathering information. While Yotam's regulars knew Abenadar, most of the patrons were unaware the Roman at a corner table could understand their every word.

Even if Yotam didn't follow every jot of the Sanhedrin's law, his inn was a respectable place. He did not allow rabble-rousers in his house, but he gladly accommodated the Goyim. He did not allow prostitutes to sell themselves under his roof, but if a man brought one in with him, Yotam would serve them both. Yotam was a businessman and counted himself a respectable one. So his business was respectable. Because of this, Abenadar learned little he could use directly to counter the rebels and Zealots, but in Yotam's Inn, as Pilate desired, Abenadar could measure the temper of the city.

The holy city of Yerushalayim, like all cities, had a dark underbelly. The stain on the city of Yerushalayim came from its most ancient part, the quarter called the Ophel. The original City of David had been built on the Ophel, but that was long ago. From the Temple, the Horse Gate and Water Gate exited into the Ophel, and the Fountain Gate and Valley Gate pierced its outer walls, but the Ophel's chief fame was that its south wall held the Dung Gate, also called the Refuse Gate and the Garbage Gate. So if not in actuality, then according to tradition, all the refuse of Yerushalayim went first into the Ophel before it was carried through the Dung Gate and cast into the Valley of Gey-Hinnom to the south of the city.

The people of the Ophel lived out a similar theme; they were the refuse of Yerushalayim. They came into the Ophel in many ways: by birth, disease, law-breaking, the death of a husband or a father. In some way or other, each person in the Ophel was damaged physically or morally. To the people of Yerushalayim, the occupants of the Ophel were refuse, and the Ophel itself a dung heap. It held on to its inhabitants until, in death, they could be carried though the Garbage Gate, and their bodies, with the rest of the rubbish, cast into the Valley of Gey-Hinnom.

The Ophel was the source of the beggars in front of Yotam's Inn. It was where the whores lived when they weren't plying their trade. It was a place for men who knew no trade, and who lived off the gleanings of the fields when they couldn't find a day's work.

The Ophel was also a place with a long history of redemption. David's ancient palace once sat there. The Pool of Shiloach rested at its southern end. Chizkiyahu's long forgotten tunnel fed it with an ever-churning flow of cold clear water. The waters of the Pool of Shiloach had saved the people of Yerushalayim more than once during siege and drought. Every day the sick and lame lay around it, waiting for an angel to stir its waters: the first to touch it, they believed, would be healed. The Pool of Shiloach was the source of the eternal water poured during the festival of Sukkot on the altar in the Temple. Every year, a priest caught the sparkling deep mountain spring water in a golden ewer and carried it through the Ophel, through the Water Gate, and into the Temple. One day a year, the contents of the Ophel was not refuse on its way to Gey-Hinnom, and because the run-off from the altar entered the Valley of Y'hoshafat to the east of the city, its initial destination was not that cursed valley. But, all the Temple run-off eventually merged with the refuse of the Gey-Hinnom, so the difference was only cosmetic.

Abenadar served in the city of Yerushalayim for about two years before he finally had more to offer Pilate to help keep the peace of the city. Pilate held his court in the city for a month during the festivals the people of Y'hudah called Sukkot and Pesach. During these visits, he ordered Abenadar to his court to report on the mood of the people.

On the day of his arrival in Yerushalayim for the Pesach visit, as was his custom, Pilate called for the Primus Pilus and Abenadar. When they entered the familiar court, Pilate rested on his purple-covered chair. Behind him, as usual, stood Iulius Valens, who was still the Legatus Legionis of the VI Ferrata. Iulius Valens had proven a much more able leader than his predecessor.

Pilate sat slumped with his head on his hand. This did not usually show weakness, but as Abenadar learned, indicated the Procurator was deep in thought. When Abenadar entered the court, Pilate glanced up at him and brightened. Abenadar thought he noted some weariness in the man's features. Abenadar and Cecilius Bassus saluted the Procurator.

"There you are, Primus Pilus and Centurion Abenadar," said Pilate. "We congratulate you. Jerusalem is still quiet even as the traditional season of these people's rebellion begins."

Cecilius Bassus stepped forward. "The city is at peace, and I don't expect any problems during your stay."

"Good. We have had three profitable years in Judea, and as a result, we expect the Senate to ask a larger tribute. What will be the reaction of the Sanhedrin?"

"I don't foresee any problem with the Sanhedrin, Procurator. The people will not be pleased. Their Temple tax and our tribute already squeeze them from both sides," said the Primus.

"No hope of procuring a portion of the Temple's goods?"

"I would recommend against it, Procurator. The priests chafe against our restrictions, and they form a large portion of the Sanhedrin."

"Our restrictions, their restrictions, surely they fear us more than their god." Pilate smiled through tight lips. "But enough of this. We will heed your warnings. Yet there may be little we can do to ease the burden on the people of Judea."

The Primus bowed.

Pilate eased back in his chair. "Our main concern is the city itself. There have been few incidents in its walls this year. For that we commend you, Primus Pilus. We heard that your legionnaires practice some of the traditions of these people." Pilate held up his hand when the Primus started to speak. "We praise you, Cecilius Bassus. It is wise to accommodate the people on such a simple thing as a day of rest. Following your example, we have initiated similar policies among our legion in the rest of Judea."

"Thank you, Procurator. Centurion Abenadar recommended these policies."

"Ah, yes, Abenadar. We are pleased to hear you trust his advice, Cecilius Bassus. Although we are certain the—shall we say...lack of action—vexes him. Centurion Abenadar, we have impatiently awaited your report for six months. Do you have anything new to tell us?"

Abenadar turned his gaze to the Primus, then at Pilate. "Yes, Procurator, I do have new information. The greatest problems I have encountered in this city have not been with rebels, but outright theft and murder against the people."

"Surely not by legionnaires," said Pilate.

"No, Procurator, your cohorts are well disciplined. Whether rebel, Zealot, or outlaw, the people's greatest threat is from their own. The people do not blame us, but they blame our policy that restricts the Temple guards to the Temple when they bear weapons. This policy leaves the people unprotected from common predators."

"Are you asking us to allow the Temple guard free reign?" Pilate's eyes took on a dangerous glint.

"No, Procurator, not at all. I have a better plan. I recommend your centuries daily send columns to patrol the city. In this way, we can protect the people, and at the same time, we can keep an eye on them and the rebellious factions in the city."

Pilate stroked his chin. "Your idea has merit. Where would you start this show of force, and could the people find greater offense by our expanded presence?"

"The Ophel is the most dangerous quarter of the city. With your permission, I will lead two columns of my legionnaires through those streets each day. The measure of our success will be a decrease in the daily incidents there. But, I warn you, the result may be more action for our legionnaires and not less."

Pilate nodded. "We knew Abenadar would discover a way to find a fight even while in garrison." He raised his hand again when the Primus started to protest.

"Yes, Primus Pilus, we know you discussed this idea with the Centurion. We like his approach. It could bring us more support from the common people and blunt the pain of an increase in tribute. But it could also make the people less inclined to bear our yoke." Pilate sat in thought a moment. "We approve a test of this type of patrol. Confine your show of force to the Ophel, and we shall hear from you again in six months—that is, unless the Sanhedrin complains to us or the people rise up against it. What do you say to that, Iulius Valens?"

"I agree with the proposal."

Abenadar bowed. "Thank you, Procurator. I have heard rumors that the Blue Shawls of the Zealot party are occasionally in the city. If so, I will deliver some to you."

Pilate smiled again, "You bring us a good report, Primus. We will take our rest now. Tomorrow, expect us at the muster. Then we will review your cohorts."

The Primus and Abenadar saluted the Procurator and backed out of the chamber.

As they crossed the portico on their way back to the camp, the Primus laughed. "I didn't think he would go for your idea. Now you have the Procurator's blessings to protect the people of Jerusalem." He laughed again. "But be careful not to let the people return your head to Pilate...wrapped in a blue turban."

The spring sun had just risen. Dust and people and little children running underfoot already crowded the streets of Yerushalayim when Abenadar led two columns of his century into the Ophel quarter. He had been at his patrol for almost a month already, and the Pesach had come and gone without incident. Pilate still called Abenadar's forays a show of force, but they had become a regular reassurance to the people.

Gaius Flaccus, Abenadar's optio, walked at his left and a little behind him. Gaius called their daily forays a temptation. "Those blasted rebels will ambush us one day," he said as they passed through the Water Gate.

Abenadar responded, "We haven't harmed these people. Our patrols have decreased the assaults in the Ophel. Don't you think the people give us some credit for that?"

"They hate us more than their own criminals," Gaius spat.

A child scurried between the marching soldiers.

Abenadar looked ahead and stopped. "What's that?"

"Columns, halt." Gaius checked the legionnaires and followed Abenadar's pointing finger. Taking in the incident at a glance, he shook his head. "Blasted Judeans, fighting over a woman."

As if in response to Gaius' words, a woman screamed, and a flurry of curses rose from the courtyard ahead of them.

"Clear the street," Abenadar shouted in Aramaic. "Single line," he ordered, more quietly in Latin to Gaius.

"Single line, now," called Gaius, immediately all business.

In the wide street, the legionnaires quickly formed a perfect line.

"Forward," said Abenadar to the columns. He stared at Gaius. "Back me up."

"Forward, h'arch," ordered Gaius.

Abenadar strode ahead of the moving line of legionnaires and confidently toward the disturbance. Now more than one woman was crying, and the wails of small children began to fill the air.

"They're Blue Shawls," hissed Gaius, still right beside Abenadar's left arm.

Indeed, Zealots or maybe a group of mountain rebels themselves. About thirty men in elaborate blue turbans crowded into the courtyard. They outnumbered Abenadar and his columns of legionnaires two to one. The air crackled with nervous energy.

The Blue Shawls hadn't spotted the Romans yet. As Abenadar came closer, he saw the men's attention was focused on a very large man and a young woman. The man was massive, scarred, and ugly. His rough and heavy features were screwed up into an uglier scowl. A huge scimitar hung at his waist, and his arms were as big around as water jugs—they almost burst the sleeves of his robe. The man held the woman tightly by her wrist and was about to strike her a second time. Blood already ran down the side of her face, but she was not cowed. The cries had not come from her but from the clump of women behind her. Five women of all ages and a dozen children stood clustered fearfully in a doorway at the end of the courtyard.

"You are the most piteous prostitute I have ever desired." The man jerked the young woman from side to side. Then, while he aimed another heavy blow at her, he spat in her face.

"Stop!" ordered Abenadar in Aramaic.

"Stop?" The man half-turned toward Abenadar, dragging the woman in his grasp at the same time. "Who dares challenge Balim?"

Abenadar pushed his way through the crowd of Blue Shawls. He stood with his arms crossed. "I said stop! Let the girl go!"

"She won't take me to her bed. And I have good money," protested

Balim, patting his heavy pouch.

"Maybe she isn't a prostitute."

"Ask her." Balim sneered. He threw the girl to the ground.

She dropped into a heap at Abenadar's feet, then raised herself to her knees. "I am a prostitute, but please help me, my lord. I can choose who I will sleep with even if I am a woman of the streets."

Abenadar examined the pile of robes at his feet, and still in Aramaic, said, "She's not worth the trouble, Balim. There are many women for you to choose from." He motioned to the group at the back of the courtyard. "Why not let this one go?"

Gaius, at Abenadar's side, whispered in Latin, "All these men are armed."

In response to Abenadar, Balim didn't say a word. As he glanced over the small number of legionnaires fronting him, the right side of his face twitched uncontrollably.

Abenadar held out his hands. "Balim, take your men out of the city—now! You may return, if you wish, after the Shabbat, but I will not allow you to harm the people of Yerushalayim."

"Centurion," Gaius hissed, "a large crowd is gathering behind us."

Abenadar turned his head. "I can't back down now. We'd never make it out of the court alive."

Balim watched the crowd gather. His eyes glinted in anticipation. As soon as Abenadar turned his head to speak in the abominable tongue, without warning, he pulled the long scimitar from his belt. Balim gave a battle cry and slashed at Abenadar. The scimitar sang a flat tone coming out of the belt and then a high-pitched whine as it cut through the air.

Gaius anticipated Balim's attack. He cried out an oath, and thrust his scutum to block the blow. The scimitar struck with a clank and glanced off Gaius' shield. Abenadar grabbed his gladius as he called to Gaius, "I'll take this one. Go for the Blue Shawls but don't attack anyone else unless you're attacked first."

Abenadar cleared his gladius from its scabbard and struck at Balim. To forestall any threat from the crowd, he cried out in Aramaic, "Go for the Zealots but don't harm the people of the city."

Balim moved his huge scimitar to easily block the thrust, but that was Abenadar's desire. He wanted the large man on the defensive. Abenadar wasn't carrying a shield—he had to take the offense immediately. Against Balim's powerful weapon wielded by a trained swordsman, Abenadar would stand little chance in a defensive fight. Luckily, Abenadar quickly discovered Balim wasn't a trained swordsman. As Balim's men clambered behind him and tried to strike at Abenadar around both Gaius's scutum and Balim's bulk, Abenadar effortlessly blocked Balim's wild cuts, then lunged forward and pierced the large man cleanly through the chest. Balim gave a surprised bellow half choked off and took a step backwards. A bloody froth rose to his lips. Without a word, he tossed down his heavy sword and threw himself at Abenadar.

Abenadar put up his sword. This time he aimed for Balim's heart, but his sword tip was low, and Balim rose up as he rushed toward Abenadar. The point slid across Balim's ribs and sunk to the hilt in his belly. Balim gave a howling grunt and grasped Abenadar around the throat. Two Blue Shawls rushed right behind him. They slashed around both sides of the large man and tried to strike Abenadar. Gaius stood on the left side, fending the blades from Abenadar, but on the right, Abenadar was unprotected. Abenadar yanked his blade out of Balim's gut. A gout of blood and offal followed the length of iron. Balim's eyes bulged in pain and rage, and he reflexively tightened his grip on Abenadar's neck. Abenadar chopped upwards with his gladius and struck Balim's arms. The man was dying and had little fight left in him. The blow knocked his hands loose from their death grip around Abenadar's neck. Balim took a jerky step backwards and fell gasping to the ground.

Abenadar called out to Gaius, "See to the columns! I'll handle these."

Gaius stared at Abenadar as though he did not want to leave, but at the order, he rushed over to the line of fighting legionnaires at the far edge of the court.

Now alone, Abenadar faced the two remaining Blue Shawls who sought his blood. They were wild swordsmen—they chopped and hacked without any understanding of the craft. He thanked Nico for his training as he caught one blade and slipped under another.

Unbelievably, Balim still grasped at Abenadar's legs with his mangled arms. Abenadar kicked the flailing limbs back, and from the side, he caught a savage cut on his armor. The blow was glancing, but it bloodied his upper leg. Like a snake, Abenadar struck back. He pushed the point of his sword into the side of the man who slashed him and was satisfied to see the rebel fall. The attacker scrambled on his hands and knees into the crowd and left a long trail of blood behind him.

Now only one man faced Abenadar. The other Blue Shawls were not faring well. Gaius and the legionnaires had chased them as far as the street and there slowly reduced them all to bleeding corpses. Facing a centurion, even one wounded and bleeding, alone was more than the rebel's courage could bear. Without a word, he turned and ran.

Abenadar grunted with pain as he lunged at the rebel and caught some flesh, but the blow wasn't enough to halt the man. Already, at the street, Gaius led the legionnaires in an organized rush against the last of the blue-turbaned band.

Abenadar caught his breath and propped himself heavily on his sword. Balim lay in a growing pool of blood. He was finally silent and likely dead. Amid the scene of the battle, the crowd still stood in the street, and people hung out of every window within sight. They watched the fight intently but showed no outward menace toward the legionnaires. For that Abenadar gave thanks to—in Yerushalayim, who else should he thank?—"Thank Adonai, blessed be He," he intoned under his breath.

A small cry rose near him. The prostitute Balim had beaten sat on the ground about a yard from Abenadar. She squinted at him in amazement. "Who are you? You are a Roman, but you speak like the people of Yerushalayim, and you give thanks to Adonai, blessed be He."

Under her bruises, the girl was very pretty. She couldn't be much more than twenty. Her face, now smeared with blood and partially covered with caked strands of her long dark hair, was small and angular. Her eyes were large and defiant, and her features full of intelligence. She had a dark complexion, and that, along with her accent, branded her a woman of the Galil. She wore a patchwork robe without a veil; she was obviously a whore.

"Who am I to speak of Adonai? Who are you to speak of Him? You are only a whore."

She turned her face away from him, and Abenadar was suddenly ashamed. The girl didn't deserve his anger. She displayed dignity and great bravery, though she should rightly possess little of either. Abenadar had risked his life for that spark of dignity. He ruefully shook his head.

From across the courtyard, Gaius waved his gladius in victory and called out to Abenadar, "All is well."

Abenadar turned back to the woman. He reached out to pull her up to her feet, but she refused his touch. "I only want to help you stand. Are you injured?"

The woman peeked up into his face. "I am wounded in my heart, and I certainly cannot touch a Goyim."

"My mother was a woman of Y'hudah," he said.

She appeared startled again.

He reached out to her once more, and this time she grasped his hand. On her feet, she stood as tall as his shoulder.

"What is your name?" said Abenadar.

"I am called Ruth."

"You are a beautiful woman. I am not surprised Balim desired you."

She wrinkled her nose and pushed the bloodied hair out of her eyes. The strands were stuck in the drying blood on her face. "You are an unusual Roman," she said with a haughty tilt of her shoulders.

"I am only half a Roman."

"Half a man of Y'hudah then?"

"Wholly a man, more than Roman and more than a man of Y'hudah."

She made a depreciating sound.

Abenadar said, "I would like to speak to you again—later."

"Business?" she asked him. "I do not bed the Goyim."

"A pity." Abenadar touched the unbloodied side of her face. She tossed her head away from his hand. He said, "You are from the Galil."

"Yes," she stammered, amazed at the observation of this half Roman. "Who are you?"

"I am the Centurion Abenadar from Natzeret."

She said nothing, and supported by his sword, Abenadar began to limp away.

"Thank you, Centurion." She paused. "I may speak to you again, Abenadar, but I will not bed you."

Abenadar smiled back at her, but Ruth had already turned to the door of the house and was walking toward it. The women there greeted her with sympathetic murmurs.

Abenadar limped to Balim's body. The man was very dead. Abenadar unwrapped the blood-splattered turban from Balim's head. Then, he reached down, picked up the large scimitar, and put it in his own belt.

Gaius waited for him at the entrance to the courtyard. The legionnaires were exuberant with their victory. They stood in even rows in the street. Abenadar counted all of them. Many were covered with blood, but they were all standing and none seemed more injured than he.

"The crowd is gone, Gaius."

"The people wandered off. Perhaps you are right—they may have some respect for us, Romans though we are. At least they didn't attack us."

"Perhaps they despise the Blue Shawls more than they despise us," countered Abenadar with a laugh. "Let's get back to the camp. I need to report this encounter to the Primus Pilus. He will want to inform Pilate immediately."

"Yes, Centurion," Gaius saluted him.

"Did you take the Zealots' weapons and turbans?"

"Yes, Centurion, we have them all. The legionnaires are fit and ready to march, but you're not. Before we leave, I need to dress your wound."

Abenadar let Gaius cover the slash across his leg with a clean folded piece of cloth. Gaius wrapped it around with another length of material and tied that over the wound.

"Good," said Abenadar. "That will last me until I get to the camp. Hand me a pila." Leaning on a heavy pila, he started off through the streets, and the columns automatically took their place behind him.

The people crowding the streets were jovial in spite of the fighting, or maybe because of it. They showed his small force much more respect than when they had started out that day.

Not long after Abenadar reported to the Primus Pilus, Pilate called for them. The word from the street already reached the Procurator. Cecilius Bassus walked beside Abenadar when they entered Pilate's court. The Legatus Legionis Iulius Valens stood at Pilate's side. Abenadar and Cecilius Bassus both saluted and knelt.

"Rise," said Pilate. "So, Abenadar, the Roman who knows the people of Judea, what words do you bring concerning the Ophel quarter, today?"

"Only a few hours ago, my century fought a band of blue-turbaned Zealots in the city."

Pilate bent forward eagerly. "So we heard. How large a band?"

"As many as 30 men."

"They attacked your century. What fools."

"No, Procurator. In accordance with your orders, I had only two columns with me."

Pilate was astounded. "Only 16 men, how did you fare?"

"We killed over half and set the rest to flight. We wounded many more."

"How many men did you lose?" Pilate covered his face with his hand.

"Not one. Except for a few scrapes, I was the only man wounded."

"You were wounded? Step closer."

Abenadar walked up to the chair and turned his leg so the bloody bandage over the slash was more visible.

"None of your men were harmed?"

"They fought well. If Gaius Flaccus had not been at my side, we would have fared much worse."

"And did the people riot?"

"No, Procurator. The people kept well out of our way."

"So much the better. What about the leaders of the Zealots?"

"The leader of the band is dead. I killed him myself."

The Primus spoke up. "Centurion Abenadar slayed three men himself in single combat. Or so my men tell me."

"Three!"

Abenadar said, "I killed Balim, their leader, and mortally wounded another. I stabbed a third man as he ran away, but I don't think I pierced him in a vital spot."

"We are still impressed, Abenadar." Pilate turned to whisper to Iulius Valens. After a quiet discussion, Pilate turned back to the men before him. "Primus, I grant, for this action, in the name of the Emperor, to Centurion Abenadar a golden torque and three golden phalerae. To the Optio Gaius one golden phalerae and to every man who distinguished himself, you may award one silver phalerae."

Abenadar bowed. "I am honored. Thank you, Procurator."

"You may mint these awards from my own treasury, Primus," said Pilate.

"Thank you, Procurator." The Primus bowed.

"Procurator…," started Abenadar.

"Yes, Centurion Abenadar."

"I am grateful for your praise, but I came to you not to tell of my own triumph but to report my observations of what this incident portends. May I speak?"

"We are greatly pleased, Centurion. You may speak as you like."

"Very well. As I have already reported to you, the people did not rise up against us when we fought the Blue Turbans. I think your plan of daily patrols is working well. The people trust us, and we have reduced the violence in the city."

"We are mindful it was with your advice we began this plan."

"Yes, Procurator. You foresaw its success. I am grateful for your trust, but 30 rebels in the city is something to think about."

"What would you have us do?"

"I suggest the other centuries begin daily marches of two columns through the other quarters of the city. They must be cautious and not offend the people overmuch, but we can then keep a watch on the streets for these bands of rebels within our gates. Except on the days we man the walls, my century and I will continue to keep our watch in the

Ophel quarter."

"We agree with your suggestion. Primus, can your other centuries man a patrol without inciting the people?"

"I believe so, Procurator, but the other centurions may not want to make the circuit with only two columns."

Pilate turned to Abenadar. "Abenadar, what do you say to this?"

"More than two columns are difficult to maneuver through the city streets. I think two columns are sufficient, but it is possible to send four columns if they trail each other. The centurion can command one set and his optio the other."

Pilate stroked his chin. "Primus, work with Centurion Abenadar. His plan is acceptable to us if it is to you."

The Primus bowed.

"As before, we will try your plan for six months, and we will keep the ear of the Sanhedrin. If they make little complaint, we will continue this course as long as necessary."

"Thank you, Procurator," said Abenadar.

"We are very pleased with your accomplishments, Abenadar. Primus, we praise your leadership of your men. You are dismissed."

Iulius Valens nodded to Abenadar and smiled.

The Primus and Abenadar saluted and left the court.

When they passed through the portico, Cecilius Bassus clapped Abenadar on the shoulder, "Good work. You placated both the people and Pilate. I knew bringing you here was a good idea."

Abenadar walked slowly beside him. "Thank you Primus. I will speak with Gaius and tell you tomorrow how many silver phalerae will be necessary."

"Very good," said the Primus. "Stay off that leg the rest of the day. I'll tell Gaius to take care of your century, and I'll instruct my slave to bring up your evening meal."

They parted at the entrance to the camp, and Abenadar returned to his quarters. The wound in his leg throbbed continually; he had been on it too long. On his bed he lay restless. Between the pain in his thigh and his thoughts, Abenadar could not ease himself into sleep. He could not get the image of the girl—what was her name? Ruth—from his mind. She was nothing but a whore, a common woman of the streets, yet his intuition told him his initial appraisal was wrong. Her carriage and the fact that she rejected a customer with money told him something was different about this woman. Still he couldn't imagine why her face and voice stuck so obsessively in his thoughts.

After he ate, he finally fell into a fitful slumber, but the morning dawned much too early for the little sleep he attained. And when he awoke, Ruth was the first thought in his mind.

He brought me up out of the muddy pit,
out of the mire and the clay;
he set my feet on a rock and gave me a firm footing;
and on my lips he put a new song,
a song of praise to Adonai.
Many when they see will be filled with awe
and will learn to trust in Adonai.

Psalm 40:2-3

Fifteen

Abenadar's leg was stiff in the morning, but fortunately, he could walk on it. After the muster of the troops, Abenadar drew Gaius aside. "Gaius, put together a list of the most valiant legionnaires in the fight yesterday. Pilate granted them each a phalerae for their courage."

Gaius' mouth twisted into a large grin. "Good. They were very proud of their work. The word has already gone around the cohorts about your fight."

"My fight?"

"Don't be surprised if you killed half a dozen Zealots and rescued the most beautiful woman in the city of Jerusalem."

"They think that highly of our little operation?"

"They think little of the operation and much of you. Abenadar, every man in the cohort would transfer to the Decimus Hastatus Posterior Century if he could. If only every one of the legion's operations could end so cleanly."

That day the schedule assigned the decimus Hastatus Posterior to duty on the walls. Abenadar spent the day in his office working with reports and schedules. He knew the wound on his leg needed at least another full day of rest. More likely a week, but he didn't want to let it get stiff.

The next morning Abenadar limped through the day's patrol. For him, this patrol was luckily more quiet than the last. The people seemed more acquiescent than usual, and that pleased Abenadar. The calm, hopefully, would mean an extended period of peace in the city.

When they passed the place where his men had fought the Blue Shawls two days before, Abenadar watched discretely for the girl, Ruth, but didn't see anyone who looked like her.

In a week, the Primus presented the phalerae to Abenadar and his century. His legionnaires were ecstatic. They wouldn't dare say anything directly to Abenadar's face, but Gaius told him over and over that his century held him in the highest esteem of any commander he ever knew. His men now gladly volunteered for the daily patrols. Before this, Abenadar had to almost order them to serve. As Gaius prophesied, his popularity didn't stop at his century. Now an embarrassment of volunteers from the other centuries in the cohort wanted to transfer to the Hastatus Posterior—an unheard-of situation. The men usually considered transfer from a lower-numbered century to a higher a demotion.

Abenadar was just happy to see his men wearing their awards. For many of them, these were the first and possibly the only decorations they would receive during their service. As much as his men thought of him, he could not guarantee them more. In spite of his reputation with Pilate, his own personal desire was to see as little bloodshed as possible.

In moments of quiet the girl, Ruth, preyed upon his thoughts. In his mind, he could picture her youthful features. She reminded him of the beautiful, dark-eyed women of Natzeret. With little prompting, Abenadar recalled the remnants of beauty in his mother's features, and, in his mind's eye, he saw this same beauty in Ruth. He wondered what he would say to her if he ever saw her again. He wondered if his imagination made her something that she wasn't and could never be.

More than once, Abenadar counted himself a fool for thinking of her at all. He had never wasted time with thoughts about any woman.

Abenadar realized, with embarrassment, he had not thought as much about his mother when she was alive. Surely, he had not honored his parents as much as he honored his memory of a whore. He couldn't help himself. Daily he wondered what Ruth was doing, and if she was selling herself for food, and if her latest customer was like Balim. Had she been killed or injured? That train of thought disturbed him, and he tried to block it out immediately. He was foolish to let his imagination run away with him; jealousy over a whore who probably thought less of him than she thought about her next meal was the highest degree of absurdity.

Over time, Abenadar's musings about Ruth moved from annoying thoughts to an obsession. His speculations led him to seek her out. One afternoon, about ten days after the incident in the streets, his leg was almost completely healed. He dressed in a plain tunic and walked through the Water Gate out into the Ophel. With each step away from the Praetorium, he became more and more convinced of the folly of his quest. He felt naked without the usual guard of legionnaires; the Ophel was the poorest and most dangerous part of the city. If he found Ruth, he was certain her answer would be the same as the day he first spoke to her. She didn't consort with the Goyim. In at least this part, she followed the Law. He knew he had no hope of socializing with her, and he was suddenly unsure why he wanted to. With that thought, Abenadar sighed mightily and turned around. He returned to the camp with a heavier heart, and with each step tried, unsuccessfully, to put the girl out of his mind.

When Abenadar reentered the camp, he discovered his optio searching for him. Gaius met him by chance in the officium and appeared surprised to find Abenadar sporting a melancholy appearance and not dressed in his usual apparel. The optio studied Abenadar, as if his disappearance, features, and attire was a mystery and required some explanation. When Abenadar offered no information, Gaius took the hint and didn't say a word about it.

Over the next few hours, Abenadar helped Gaius put together the duty schedule for the next day. By the time they finished, the horn announcing the last daylight watch had already sounded. Gaius left, and Abenadar stretched out on his bed to await the final watch. He was dozing when a rap came to his door.

"Enter." He rose and dashed the sleep out of his eyes.

A legionnaire opened the door. "Guard of the watch, Centurion. A woman is at the gate asking for you. Should I send her away?"

"For me?" he asked. Then he thought of the girl, Ruth and he smiled. Could it be her? He said to the legionnaire, "Don't send her away. I will speak to her myself."

At the gate, Abenadar peeped through the bolt hole at his visitor.

The woman was Ruth all right. She stood before the gate in the best of her bedraggled clothing. Out of deference for the part of the city she was in, she wore a headpiece and veil. She was more beautiful than he remembered. The shawl over her head mostly covered her black hair, but loose strands framed her face and tickled the edges of the veil. Her eyes were dark brown, almost black, and the portion of her face that he could see was scrubbed and clean...and more ravishing than he had imagined it. She appeared nervous and danced from one foot to the other as though, at any moment, she might run back into the streets.

The guard let Abenadar out of the small door in the gate. The portal closed behind him with a thud, and he stood in the street towering over the girl. She stepped back from him.

"I'm glad you came," he said.

"I am hungry," she responded. "And I did not want to sell myself for only a few coins."

"Are you a righteous woman now?" He flipped her veil.

"No," she said as she drew the veil from her face, but she left the shawl covering her hair.

"Where would you like to eat?" said Abenadar.

"I have never eaten in this part of the city."

"Have you ever eaten in any inn in the city?"

"I have been in many of them, but to have eaten, no. I have better things to do with my lepton."

"Then I will take you to a place you will like, and since you know no better, it will be very fine dining for you."

She smiled slyly at him but said nothing in response.

Abenadar led her through the darkening streets of the foreign quarter. Pilgrims and Goyim of every description passed them on the way. The market was just closing up as the last rays of the sun disappeared from the pavement. Abenadar stopped at Yotam's small inn at the edge of the upper market. The lamps inside were already lit and they fanned a bright glow throughout the ground floor.

Ruth and Abenadar were the only customers. When they walked in, Yotam eagerly rushed up to them, and in his rough accent, said, "Centurion Abenadar, welcome, welcome. May I serve one or two tonight?" He patently ignored Ruth.

"Two, Yotam."

Yotam led them to a small table at the back of the common room. The table was private with curtains on either side. Abenadar pointed to the cushions and Ruth sat down. He sat beside her and then lay propped on his elbow. She remained sitting.

"Yotam," said Abenadar, "bring us wine and bread."

"Yes, my lord."

After a moment, Yotam's daughter approached them. She took off Abenadar's sandals and washed his feet. Then she gave him a handful of fragrant oil. She did the same for a surprised Ruth. Ruth sat with the oil in her hands unsure what to do with it until Abenadar told her, "Put it on your hair and face."

Ruth daubed the oil gently over her hair and cheeks. Unused to any sweet fragrance, she sniffed her hands over and over.

Abenadar laughed at her. "Haven't you had oil before?"

"Only to eat," she replied.

Yotam brought the wine and bread himself. He sprinkled a piece of a small flat loaf with salt and took a bite, then he presented the rest to Abenadar. Abenadar took a bite and handed the salted bread to Ruth, who ate the rest.

Yotam and Abenadar chuckled until Ruth became indignant, but she didn't speak.

Finally, as Yotam walked away, Abenadar said, "There is plenty of fresh bread and oil. You don't have to eat all of the peace bread."

She shrugged. "I have never had enough. It would be a crime to waste it."

In answer, Abenadar dipped a piece of bread liberally in the garlic-flavored olive oil and gave it to her. Ruth wolfed it down.

"There is plenty. Don't make yourself sick." He poured a cup of wine and mixed in a bit of water, then handed it to her.

She took a gulp and choked. When she caught her breath, she said, "What is that?"

"It is only wine." Abenadar took a drink from the same cup and passed it back to her. "What did you do the other times you were in an inn?"

"I watched them eat and drink. Sometimes they would throw me scraps until they were ready for me…"

"How could your life make such degradation necessary?"

Ruth cocked her head as if thinking about something far off and in another place. Then, as though she abruptly made up her mind, she said in a quiet but merciless voice, "My father and mother came to Yerushalayim from the Galil to repair the walls and towers. They brought me with them. I was their only living child. All my brothers and sisters died in infancy. My father was working on the tower near the Pool of Shiloach when it fell."

Ruth stared out across the low table. "My mother died too. When she tried to dig him out, a stone fell on her." Ruth's throat visibly tightened. "I wish a stone had fallen on me. I was only sixteen at the time. I had no family—no place to go."

She turned her head away. "The first was a man of Y'hudah who promised me a place to stay. He used me for a while and left me on the street. I was ashamed—it was terrible. After that, the women in the Ophel let me stay in their house, but their acceptance wasn't free. It came with a price, a high price. There was nothing else I could do."

Ruth glanced up at Abenadar. "Those women are not so horrible. They are just hungry themselves—they and their children. As I grew older, I took as few…customers as I could. I hate them. They don't care for me. They wanted nothing more than my body, and I am a poor lover—only a sack for them to vent their lusts." She stopped, out of breath. Then she glared at Abenadar. "Do you want me to leave now?" she asked, her eyes defiant and at the same time strangely afraid.

"No…no. I think you are a beautiful woman, but I did not ask you to come with me because you are a prostitute." He smiled.

"What other reason could there be?" She stared at him in

amazement.

"I have seen many prostitutes. I assure you, I didn't want to speak to you because you were one of them. I wanted to know you better because of the strength I saw in you. You are not like the others. You are a brave woman with dignity."

"The dignity of a whore, you mean. That is very little."

"What other woman could I aspire to know?"

"Surely a Roman woman or one from the Greeks."

"The stink of the Galil is on me." He smiled wistfully. "I am a man of Y'hudah, but rejected—even by you. No family of the Galil or Y'hudah would let me look on their daughters. I am a Roman, but any Roman family would laugh at me if I sought out their daughters. The Greeks think the Romans and people of Y'hudah are savages. How far do you think that would get me?"

She tossed her hair back. "So what does that make me?"

"That makes you a woman I can approach."

"Like all the other whores you have known."

"I have never known a whore. Except for some shameful indiscretions, I have tried to keep the Law."

Her jaw dropped. Ruth consciously closed her mouth, and she stared sadly at the bread, oil, and wine. Her voice became a whisper. "Perhaps I should leave. I shame you by being with you."

"Have you not tried to keep the Law?"

"I try...have tried." Ruth threw back her shoulders. "It is a question of survival for me and not of faith."

"My failures have not been a question of survival at all. Perhaps I shame you."

She put her hand on his arm. "I think I begin to understand you, Centurion Abenadar."

He studied her with a smile, and she quickly took her hand off his arm.

"You may call me Abenadar. That was my name before I was anything but a boy from the Galil." He dipped a piece of the bread in the oil and offered it to her.

She took the bread from him without touching his fingers and chewed it thoughtfully. Then she asked, "What do you want from me?"

"For the moment, company, companionship. When I lived in Sepphoris, I used to eat in an inn like this with my friend Nico. He trained me to be a legionnaire. He didn't care if I came from the Galil or from the ends of the earth. All that mattered to him was that I was a warrior and a friend. In Yerushalayim, in the camp, I have many friends, but I have no friends like Nico. They don't enjoy the city or the people. They enjoy whoring and drinking. They don't spend their time and money on conversation and a companionable dinner. The centurions come mainly from Rome. They consider me an interloper. Some outwardly hate me; most ignore me."

"Yes, yes," Ruth interrupted, "It is much the same for me. The women wonder why I do not bring them more money. They look down on my accent and my ancestry. They are all from Y'hudah; I am only from the Galil."

"Perhaps you are as alone as I am, Ruth." He turned his face from her. "You needn't look at me that way. I grew up a lonely child in Natzeret in the Galil."

"But you are a Roman centurion."

"My mother made the mistake—or had the fortune...however you want to look at it—to be the concubine of a Roman ambassador. She was a beautiful woman who foolishly thought a Roman could love her, and that her life with him would continue forever."

Ruth settled herself on her elbows and stared at him in the lamplight. "What happened?"

Abenadar forced a sad smile. "The ambassador, as is the way of things, was recalled to Rome. You see, he already had a wife and family there. My mother knew that. She was a fool. He left her with me. I was his gift. She is dead now, dead and still an outcast in Natzeret. I hardly saw her after the legion accepted me."

"You didn't visit her? She didn't live in your house?" Ruth burst out.

"If I had visited her, her life would be even more unpleasant. I chose not to burden her with my presence or memory."

"No, Abenadar. No." moaned Ruth. "She would certainly have wanted to see her only son."

"She would have paid a thousand times for the outrage. I

remember the cruelty of the children toward me. Her life could not have been much better. I reminded the people of her sin and her shame, and my mother paid over and over for it."

"It is a sin to forget your parents."

"A sin?" His smile broadened.

Ruth sat up and stared down at her hands.

Abenadar shook himself, then called, "Yotam, what do you serve tonight?"

The fat innkeeper came out of the shadows of the back room. "My lord, I have a stew of lamb, lentils, and leeks. There is also some hummus with garlic and fine oil." He bowed. "What do you wish?"

"Bring us the stew and more bread. We are famished, and you see the girl needs something more substantial than hummus."

"Yes, my lord." Yotam bowed his way back through the doorway.

Very shortly Yotam returned with a large bowl of stew. It was steaming and thick with a good portion of meat.

Abenadar nodded approval, and Yotam disappeared into the back room again.

Ruth gazed at the bowl with both apprehension and desire. She bit at her lip again and again.

"You may eat. If you wish, Ruth." When she still didn't put her hands in the bowl, Abenadar said, "It is kosher, I am sure of it. That is, until I put my hands in it."

She didn't look at him. "I haven't eaten meat in many years."

"Eat, Ruth. Eat. It is my pleasure to serve you."

"To serve me? A woman of the streets? You would get more worth from me by buying my body."

"You said yourself, it was not for sale to me."

"I am a whore, my lord. I am afraid I will be obligated to you, and I have nothing to give you that is worth the price of this meal—not even a bite of this meal."

"I promise you—no, I swear to you—I will accept nothing from you but your company. Don't you believe that?"

"No. Will you swear, by Adonai, blessed be He?"

"By Adonai, blessed be He."

"You know I would gladly give you my body for this bowl." She

215

trembled.

Abenadar was taken aback. "I should have known. That wasn't my intention."

She stared at him. "You are a strange man."

"I have never been called that to my face, but it is probably true. Please eat, Ruth. Just eat. That's all."

She gingerly reached into the bowl. In spite of scalded fingers, she took a large scoop with her right hand and put it in her mouth. Intense pleasure spread across her face and her eyes sparkled with the tears she vainly tried to hide from him. They were not tears from the heat of the food, Abenadar knew. "Thank you," she garbled through a mouthful of the hot stew.

Abenadar took a bite, and together they quietly devoured the large bowl. Ruth wiped it clean with the last of the bread. Abenadar handed the cup of wine to her, and she lay on her elbow to drink.

"My belly has not been full for a long time. I have not been willing to give myself as often as my stomach desired." She gazed at him expectantly.

"Do you wish more?"

"No. That was enough and more than enough. I wanted you to finish telling me why you are alone."

"Ah, yes. I am not alone for these past few hours."

She waited for him to continue.

"I was a lonely child. The other children in Natzeret rejected me just as the people rejected my mother. I am a child of the Galil. I had one friend. Other than Nico, he was the only person who has ever been a real friend. He was Yeshua, another bastard. A bastard of Y'hudah with a father who was willing to take him in. Everyone accepted and loved him, but not me. He accepted me. Since then, I have had friends, acquaintances, but no one who spoke our language. As I told you before, I am only partially accepted by the legionnaires."

"But they made you a centurion."

"Which is all I will be. I am a Roman citizen, but a half-Roman. They will not forget that. I cannot forget that. I am respected for what I do…not who I am."

"What does that have to do with me?"

"When I saw you being beaten by Balim in the courtyard, your courage and your beauty astonished me. To me, you are beautiful. The most beautiful woman I have seen in Yerushalayim."

Ruth's face took on a knowing smile. "So it is my services you want. I am not beautiful. Abenadar, I am a whore."

"Haven't I said, it was not? I don't care what you are. When I saw your face, I guessed you were a woman of the Galil. When you spoke, there was no doubt. I knew you were a prostitute. I am a prostitute. I am a whore for Rome." His voice rose a notch. "Who among my own people in the Galil or in Yerushalayim would speak to me without spitting on the ground? The only reason Yotam lets me in his inn is that he serves the Goyim. He serves them all, but he hates them. He hates them as much as you hate your customers. When I saw you, Ruth, I saw a person like myself. I saw someone who hates what they do, who is rejected by their people. They spit on the ground I walk on—they spit in your shadow too. Don't you see? You are like me. I can speak to you, and I hoped you would want to be my friend. At least I can trade food for your companionship. I cannot do that for just anyone else in Yerushalayim."

"Any whore would do."

"Are you any whore?"

"No," she said, then appeared startled, as if she surprised herself with the answer.

They sat in silence for a moment. Ruth handed him back the cup, and he drained it.

Yotam appeared from nowhere and refilled the cup with wine, then disappeared again.

"What are you thinking, Ruth?"

"Do you intend to speak with me tonight, and then wave me off back into the streets where you found me? I came ready to sell myself to you at a much lower price than you have already paid."

"What do you want?" Abenadar asked.

Her eyes widened, then she turned away from him. When she finally spoke, it was with great intensity. "No one has ever asked me that. No one. Do you ask that to tempt me? Or do you intend to listen to me and answer my desires?"

"I have little. I own more goods and money than many men, but it is little. I cannot offer you a kingdom or a city, but I want to know what you desire. Isn't that the way with friends?"

"I want. I want—" she became animated—"I long for someone to care for me. Could you do that? I want a house and a table and a Shabbat lamp with oil for every Shabbat." Tears welled in her eyes and streamed down her face. "Could you give me that?" She buried her face in her arms. "Or, at the first call of Rome, would you leave me like your father left your mother?"

Abenadar began to speak, but, placing her hand over his mouth, she cut him off. "You could buy any whore in Yerushalayim. You could buy slaves of any nation and rest in the bosom of any woman you wish. I know. I have seen the centurions come to the houses in Yerushalayim. Why do you want me? I am a ruined stone—a polluted woman. Surely the women in the palace desire you."

"The women of the palace despise me. They might bed me, but they would not, they *could not* be a friend to me."

"What makes you think I could be a friend to you?"

"Have I not told you? I have found the precious pearl. Perhaps you are my pearl."

"I want love."

"I desire the same."

"Would you love me?"

"I think I could. I think I do. I think I am a fool." Abenadar drew his hand through his close-cropped hair.

"Would you let me have a house and the table and a lamp?"

"All those things."

"And from me?"

"What do you mean?"

"What do you want from me?"

"I will take whatever you can give me. I want you off the streets and in a veil."

"No more than that?" Her voice softened, and she gazed into his eyes. "If you took me from the streets, I would give you anything. My lord, I would make you a home. I would light the Shabbat lamp for you. Don't you see that? No man has offered me so much. No one has ever given me anything but the dregs of the cup."

Abenadar stared straight back into her eyes. "We are agreed then?"

She sat back. "Just like that?"

"Yes, if you agree."

"I agree. If you are serious, my lord, I agree."

"Where will you go tonight?"

"Where will you take me?"

"You are too trusting, Ruth. Tonight you may stay here. Yotam will give me a room and watch over you for me. In the morning, we will find a place."

"Can't I go to the camp with you?"

"Only whores can enter the camp, and no whore of Y'hudah will defile herself that way."

She trembled again. "You will not leave me?"

"I must leave you tonight."

"I mean, you will not leave and then never come back?"

"Can you trust me?"

"You are my trust." She gazed piteously into his face. "Abenadar, you have become my only hope in this world. Please come back for me."

"Yotam," called Abenadar.

The fat innkeeper came running.

Abenadar placed a couple of coins in his hand, and Yotam bowed in gratitude, "Yotam, I need a room for the lady. Keep her safe; she is under my protection. In the morning, feed her whatever she wants. I will fetch her then."

"Yes, my lord." Yotam bowed.

Yotam led them both to a room on the second floor. It was a guestroom well swept and the linens freshly turned. "The lady may sleep here. Will you be staying, my lord?"

"No, Yotam. I must tend to my century in the camp. I will be back in the morning."

"Very well." He turned back the coverlet and put a small, lighted lamp on the low table beside the bed. Then he left the room.

In the lamplight, Ruth looked up into Abenadar's face. "I would never have believed that Adonai, blessed be He, would have made this happen. I have not deserved this. I never thought to ask Him for such a thing. I am yours, Abenadar. From this moment, I am yours." She put her arms around him. "You will not leave me like all the others?" It was half a question.

"My promise to you will last as long as my life. But I will not stay tonight with you. My part of the bargain is not complete."

"Bargain? There needs to be no bargain."

"Tomorrow we shall see."

"You must go?"

"I must go." He let her kiss him. Her kiss was clumsy and innocent. He would not have expected this kind of kiss from a whore.

She seemed to read his thoughts. "I am not experienced in this kind of love. I have never kissed a man; they have always kissed me—when they kissed me."

"I guessed." Reluctantly, he released her, but she would not let him go. "I must go," he said. "I will come for you tomorrow in the morning—I promise." She finally released him and watched him as he climbed down the narrow steps and made his way to the street.

Ruth stared out into the dark until she lost sight of him. When Abenadar was well on his way, she whispered under her breath, "I cannot believe you will come back for me—Abenadar."

*Your robes are all fragrant with myrrh and powder of aloes,
and the music of strings greets you
from a palace panelled with ivory.
A princess takes her place
among the noblest of your women,
a royal lady at your side in gold of Ophir.*

Psalm 45:8-9

Sixteen

Abenadar arose early the next day. The first thought in his waking mind was a vision of Ruth. He couldn't believe the events of the night before. When he returned to Yotam's Inn, would he actually find Ruth waiting? The idea that she might not be there was too painful for him to contemplate.

Following the muster of the troops, Abenadar drew Gaius aside. "I want you to take the patrol yourself today."

"By myself? I'm sure I could. But won't you be with us?"

"I have business in the city."

"That is a new one for you. What's up?" Gaius gave Abenadar the same questioning look he had the day before.

"I have things I must take care of," Abenadar said.

Gaius caught the hint and didn't ask any more questions.

"If there is a problem with the men, tell them the wound in my leg still aches and I need to let it heal a little longer."

"I understand," said Gaius, but the tone of his voice said he didn't. He let it go with a salute and turned back to the century now gathered around the librarius to hear their duties for the day.

Abenadar went straight to the camp forum. There he bought a printed shawl, a veil, and two dresses, one white and one blue. Abenadar knew little about women's clothing, but he had seen the women of the palace wear similar robes. He thought Ruth would like them. Her clothing was so threadbare, anything would be an improvement.

Without another word to his men, Abenadar left the camp and headed into the foreign quarter of the city. By the time he entered the marketplace, the sun was already well up in the sky and the first watch was almost at its end. He had dressed in his blue tunic with a white cape. He had filled his money pouch with leptons, kodrantes, a few asses, and two denarii. The air was cool and invigorating. A lilt Abenadar had never known before marked his steps. He wanted to see Ruth as he had never wanted anything before.

The marketplace was full of people. The shops had been open for a while. As Abenadar approached Yotam's Inn, he was surprised to spy a small group sitting in the stoop of the door. Fat Yotam, his wife, Sela, and Ruth crowded into the wide doorway. Like a lookout Yotam's daughter squatted in the dirt at the side of the inn nearest the marketplace. They all watched intently toward the street and into the marketplace.

As Abenadar pushed his way through the crowd, Yotam's daughter spotted him first and jumped to her feet. She pointed at him and raised her hands in a child's dance. Ruth immediately leapt to her feet and the others soon followed. Fat Yotam last.

Ruth ran to him and put her arms around his neck. She kissed his face and tears streamed down her cheeks.

"See, I told you he would come for you," said Yotam with a laugh.

As Abenadar and Ruth walked toward the family, Yotam's wife stepped forward and put her arms around Ruth's shoulders. Their daughter continued to dance up and down in the dust.

Abenadar was taken aback. He hadn't expected Yotam and his family to accept Ruth so readily. He acted as if nothing was unusual. "Yotam, do I owe you anything more for the night?"

"No, my lord. Come in. Come in! Have you eaten? Do you need anything?"

"Nothing," said Abenadar as he entered the inn. "Ruth, I have something for you." He flipped open the bundle of clothing he held under his arm. "Do you like these?"

All three women gasped. Ruth took the blue dress and held it close to her slight form. Her eyes, already glistening with tears, threatened to overflow. Yotam's wife and daughter made appreciative sounds and took the rest of the clothing from Abenadar.

"Come, Ruth," said Sela. "We'll help you put on this finery." Sela grasped Ruth by the arm, and with her daughter on one side and Ruth between them, they entered the room at the back of the inn.

"You were all waiting for me…?" asked Abenadar.

"Waiting since the cock crowed. She was certain you had forgotten her. I said you would come as soon as you could. And here you are."

"What do you know of this, Yotam?"

"Nothing," he lied. "Oh, the lady told me nothing about it. She came and sat in the doorway. The least we could do was wait with her."

"I need a room, Yotam. Do you know anyplace I could rent?"

"My brother has a room not a quarter of a Roman mile from here."

"And he would rent it to me?"

"To any friend of mine."

"Is it safe?"

"It is in this quarter and right across the courtyard from his house, my lord." He grinned broadly.

Abenadar grinned right along with him. "May I speak with your brother?"

"Wait here, my lord. I will get him myself."

Yotam, as quickly as his bulk could move, left the inn and walked down the street away from the marketplace.

In a few moments, Ruth and the other women returned. Abenadar almost didn't recognize her. She wore the blue robe, the shawl, and the veil. She looked like a woman of the court. The fine linen enhanced her delicate features, and she seemed to stand taller than before. Beside her, Sela and her daughter in their plain brown robes appeared like her servants. Ruth was radiant. A smile larger than he had yet seen stretched across her features and belied the tears that still welled in her eyes.

"I have never had anything so fine," she said finally. Yotam's wife and daughter shot admiring glances at her and at Abenadar.

"You like it? I know nothing of women's clothing."

"It is perfect," said Sela.

"Beautiful," murmured her daughter.

Ruth stepped close to Abenadar, and he smelled the rich oil on her face and hair.

"You are beautiful," said Abenadar.

At that moment, Yotam's brother rushed into the inn, and in spite of his size, Yotam trailed him by only a few yards.

"This is my brother, Ya'akov," puffed Yotam. "Ya'akov, this is Abenadar, the Centurion. He is a great soldier in the legions of Rome, but he is like us, a man of the Galil."

Ya'akov bent his gray head. "Well met, my lord. What do you require of me?"

"You have a room for rent?"

"Yes, my lord, a house. Would you like to see it?"

"Yes," said Abenadar.

They left the inn as a group. Ruth linked her arm in Abenadar's, and they followed Ya'akov. Yotam and his family trailed them at a discrete distance.

Ya'akov conducted Ruth and Abenadar down the wide market street. As if they were royalty, he opened the crowds for them. A block down he turned into a narrow but airy alley. This led to a small, wide courtyard. On either side of the courtyard stood a modest house. Each had a single door. When they entered the courtyard, Ya'akov opened the door to the smaller house on the right.

"I live in the house yonder," said Ya'akov, pointing at the building across the courtyard.

Ruth and Abenadar stepped through the door into the front room. The room was about 15 feet square and sported a cloth-covered door in the back at the left and a shuttered window at the front. Ya'akov threw open the shutters and the room glowed with the morning sun.

The house was empty, but clean. The front door was made of strong wood with a wooden and leather catch at the back. The floor was stone and not dirt, and under a smoke-marked chimney hole, a blackened hearth stood at the right side of the room.

Ya'akov pulled open the cloth curtain at the back. Behind it was a second room about ten feet square. It had its own wooden shuttered window. Ya'akov opened the window and the morning breeze immediately rushed through both rooms. When both windows were opened, the whole house overflowed with light and air. In spite of the morning warmth, the house was not stuffy.

"What do you think, Ruth? Could you live here? Is this the house you desired?"

Ruth stepped to each corner of the room. She touched the hearth and scuffed her foot on the floor. Her eyes were brilliant when she turned back toward Abenadar. "Yes, my lord." She barely restrained her excitement.

"Ya'akov," said Abenadar, "how much do you want for the house?"

Before Ya'akov could say a word, Yotam took him by the arm, and they began speaking in whispers. Finally, Yotam turned to Abenadar and bowed. "Let us all return to my inn where we may discuss this together over something to drink."

"Of course," said Abenadar.

In the same formation, this time with Yotam in the lead, they all retraced their steps back to the inn.

At the inn, Ruth and Sela retired to the back room. Yotam's daughter washed all three men's feet and withdrew to the back too. Yotam brought out a jug of his sweet beer and poured a cup for each of them. From the same cupboard, he removed a loaf of flat bread and passed around a piece with salt. For a while, the men sat drinking and eating the bread before Ya'akov brought up the subject of the house again.

"My lord, I have spoken with my brother, and since you are a friend of his and a good man besides. I will let you rent my house for two leptons per day." Before Abenadar could respond, he went on, "I know that may seem like a lot, but I live just on the other side of the courtyard. I will watch your house, and when you are away, your lady will be safe with my family. Not only that, you may eat a meal with Yotam's family once each week. This he has promised me. I will give you such things as you need to furnish the house. I have a bed and a table." He was about to continue, but Abenadar stopped him with a light touch on his arm.

"Ya'akov, your offer is acceptable to me. I thank you for your kindness." Abenadar took out his purse and opened it. He handed a denarius to Ya'akov. "This should be enough for about two months. I will pay you this much in another 60 days. Is that acceptable?"

Ya'akov took the silver coin and put out his hand. "Your courage and generosity is spoken of in the marketplace. We are in agreement."

Abenadar took the hand and clenched it.

Ya'akov took out a small piece of linen. "Let this signify our agreement."

"And mine also," said Yotam.

Abenadar took the square of linen.

Yotam, Ya'akov, and Abenadar lifted their cups and toasted their arrangement.

"Adonai, blessed be He, shall see that we keep faith between us," said Ya'akov.

"Adonai, blessed be He," repeated Yotam and Abenadar.

"A centurion and a man of the Galil for a neighbor," said Ya'akov. "Adonai, blesses the poor and the righteous." They lifted another toast.

"We would keep you drinking all day, but your lady would like to find the things she needs for her house. I am sure of this," guffawed Yotam. "I see them watching us from the doorway."

"Take her to the marketplace, my lord," said Ya'akov. "She surely wants to settle you in your house."

"Ruth," called Abenadar.

Ruth almost ran from the back room. "Yes, my lord."

"Yotam says you need things from the market to make our house livable."

"Yes, my lord."

"Let's go then. The century can wait only a day and then my optio will wonder where I have gone."

Abenadar thanked Yotam and Ya'akov, and he and Ruth left the inn.

The sun was past its zenith when they walked into the marketplace. People made way for them as they strolled by the stalls. They had not made so much room for him when he passed by alone, thought Abenadar with some chagrin. He had to admit: Ruth in her new clothing made a striking picture. She was slight, but her steps were sure and firm. Her face was beautiful with a natural look of distinction. In her new clothing, he would have guessed she was a princess of Syria. The common people certainly thought so. Who would have thought not a day ago, she had been less than a beggar on the street? What a change new clothing and a measure of hope made in her.

Ruth herself was radiant in her beauty, a captive set free, a soul redeemed from certain doom. She seemed on the outside like Abenadar felt inside, alive and liberated. He wanted to be alone with her and speak to her privately again. For once in his life, he was not alone. He was bound with some certainty to her, and he wanted to cement this moment so it would last forever.

They strolled through the market, barely speaking. Their gestures were enough. She indicated what she needed—they were so few things—and he purchased them and anything he thought would please her: a rug for the floor, a bowl, a metal cup, a cooking pot, lamps, wicks, and oil for the Shabbat. For her he bought wool and linen covers for the bed, cushions to sit and lay on at the table, and a small vase of fragrant oil. He did not buy the usual oil of the inns, but a costly oil for her body. Ruth was concerned by his extravagance and amazed at his generosity, but he told her, "Ruth, I have never had any reason to purchase these kinds of things. I own now more than I have ever owned in my life."

She scoffed at him but accepted his answer. She was too full of joy to do anything else.

With a small boy behind them carrying all their things, in the late afternoon they made their way back to the little house.

Abenadar paid the boy a whole kodrant and sent him on his way. Inside the house, Ya'akov had already placed the things he said he would. Ruth was amazed at the transformation. She walked from one piece of furniture to the other, and touched each as if to assure herself of their reality. Then she returned to all of them again and placed all her purchases where they should go.

Abenadar sat on the floor without speaking. He watched her put the covers on the bed and spread the rug on the floor, just so. She arranged the cooking and eating vessels on the hearth. She laid her new clothing—the things she wasn't wearing—under the bed. He realized he needed to bring her a chest from the camp to store her things.

Ruth placed the cushions at the table and bid him sit on them. Then she finally sat down herself.

She closed her eyes. "My lord, it seems that if I were to open my eyes, all this would immediately fade into the only world I once knew."

"Ruth," he said putting his hand on her arm, "call me Abenadar. You are my friend and not my servant."

She opened her eyes and breathed out. "Abenadar. Yes, I should call you Abenadar." She sat closer to him and put her arms around his shoulders. "I cannot thank you enough."

Abenadar put his finger to her lips. "There is no need to thank me. I should thank you."

She shook her head and took a deep breath, "You do not know."

"I know. Oh, how I know."

"Put your arms around me, Abenadar."

Awkwardly, he circled her waist. "I am a man who has known only sacks."

She glanced down for a moment and then up into his eyes. She shook her head slowly. "Never again. I'm willing to learn how to love you."

She kissed him, and he returned her kiss. Their lips parted after a moment and she lay her head against his chest. She began to cry and her slight body trembled against him.

"Why do you cry?" he asked.

"I am so afraid this will suddenly end. I am so afraid I will awake and find it is only a dream."

Abenadar lifted her face to his. "I will not leave you. I made up my mind a while ago to have you—a friend, a woman I could love, and whom I hoped could love me. Is there anything else you want that you need?"

"Nothing. Nothing." She breathed into his tunic.

He held her tighter. "You cannot know what it has been like—a man of the Galil, a Roman, a man apart from other men. I have already found a comfort in you that is like nothing I knew before."

As the sun set, the room began to darken. Abenadar gently released her. "Are you hungry? Would you like to eat?"

She nodded.

Abenadar stood up and lifted her to her feet. They walked the short distance to Yotam's Inn and ate his stew again. Yotam plied them about how they liked the house until Sela chastised him.

After their meal, Yotam would not take Abenadar's money. "Just tonight, you see, you are my guests."

In the dark, Abenadar and Ruth made their way back to the house.

Their arms were wrapped about each other. Inside, he and Ruth undressed, and without speaking, slipped under the new covers on the bed. Her body was soft and warm against his rough skin. She was like a faun, lean, dark, and lithe beside him. She put her arms around his neck, and he felt her small breasts press against him. With a laugh, she pulled his face close to hers, and he kissed her and kissed her and kissed her. With many kisses and great tenderness, as though they had never known another, they melted into each other's embrace. For the first time in both their lives, they knew they weren't alone.

Abenadar awoke well before the sun came up. He sat up groggily, and a moment passed before he remembered where he was. Ruth lay warm beside him. When he slipped out of the covers, she did too.

Deftly, Ruth struck flint and steel to light their oil lamp. It flared brightly until she trimmed the wick. A pensive smile flooded her features as she examined his scarred body. Outlined by the blackness, her slight form glowed like a dark coal in the lamplight.

She is so beautiful, thought Abenadar.

In the fitful light, he put on his tunic and cape. Ruth nimbly helped him, and before long he was ready to go.

Gently stroking his arm, Ruth said, "Do you have to leave now?"

"Yes." He stared possessively at her in the dim light. "I must be at the daily muster."

"Will you come back soon?"

"I cannot come home until late in the afternoon. I left my century for the whole day yesterday. I cannot do that often."

Ruth put her hand to the side of her face. "I have no food for you, my lord." Her voice grew sad.

"It doesn't matter. I will eat with my century. But you must have something." He emptied his purse on the table. "Here is enough for many days, perhaps a year. Buy whatever you need. When we need more, tell me. I have plenty of money."

"Thank you, my lord…Abenadar. I will have everything ready for you when you return tonight." Her soft voice was wistful.

He took her in his arms. "Just to have you is enough. I need nothing more."

She smiled at that. A deep and petulant smile as if to say it wasn't enough for her. As he held her, she kissed him, then kissed him again. Abenadar unwrapped her arms from around his neck, "I must go now."

Ruth's arms still gripped him as he disentangled himself and opened the door. In the courtyard, Abenadar looked back at her one more time. She stood like a spark in the black room. The lamp on the table at her feet lit her gentle curves like ocean waves blanketed in the last rays of the sun. He could not stand to go, but he knew he must. He quickly shut the door behind him, but the memory of that last sight of her would sweeten his thoughts throughout the long day.

The morning chilled him as Abenadar made his way through the empty streets and marketplace to the camp beside the Praetorium. The guards were alert and didn't seem surprised to see him. They immediately opened the postern for him to enter. He just had time to put on his uniform and armor before the cornicen called the muster.

As soon as the centuries were dismissed, Gaius came to Abenadar, "Well, Centurion, will you tell me where you were yesterday, or is it still some great secret?"

"It is a great secret. But you do need to tell me how things went for you."

"The men were moody and uncooperative. They did not want me alone leading them. They are not comfortable in the Ophel without you."

"I wouldn't have thought that."

"It is the truth. We made the rounds well enough, and no one attacked us."

"That is good." Abenadar slapped Gaius on the shoulder. "Well, for you, I am here today. What is this? This is a training day. So let's get the men fed and into formation. I want to see again if my legionnaires were hardened by the combat they encountered."

Gaius pursed his lips. "Now that sounds like the centurion I know." He rounded the men up with a single curse and sent them off to breakfast. He and Abenadar followed more leisurely behind them.

Abenadar worked his legionnaires especially hard that day. Gaius' comments concerned him that the men were too dependent on his leadership. If he fell in battle, he was worried that they would not be able to continue the fight. He deemed it necessary to build their confidence in themselves and in Gaius. He let Gaius run every part of the training that day and only advised him during the rests.

The daylight was fast slipping away from the sky by the time Abenadar finally returned to Ruth. As he approached the courtyard, a thin stream of smoke rose from the chimney of their house. When Abenadar opened the door, Ruth turned from the hearth and ran to him. She kissed him again and again. After a while, she helped him take off his cape and sat him down on the cushions by the table.

She returned to the table carrying an earthenware crock and a loaf of bread. Her face was beaming. When she took off the lid, the small room was permeated with the rich scent of spices and lamb. Ruth's eyes sparkled. "Sela told me how to make her lamb stew. I let it cook all day long. She says it is a sure way to a man's heart."

Abenadar reached for the pot, but Ruth put her hand on his arm. "Bless it first, my lord. Say a prayer of thanksgiving to Adonai, blessed be He. One like my father would have said." Her head nodded up and down and her eyes were a thousand miles, or perhaps, years away.

Abenadar searched his memory. The blessing was ancient words in his mind, sentences so long unused he stumbled over them. "Blessed are You Adonai, Ruler of the Universe, who draws bread from the earth."

Ruth didn't care. She smiled at him as though the words he said were as resounding as a cohen's, one of the Temple priests.

"Thank you, Adonai, blessed be He," she said under her breath.

Abenadar took a generous fingerful of the stew and closed his eyes. It was better than anything he had tasted, even better than Yotam's stew. "It is the best I've eaten," he said.

Ruth frowned as though she didn't believe him. He took her hand in his and said, "Here you have some."

"No, not until you've finished."

"You fixed it; you must also share in it. Come now."

Finally, at his prompting, she ate with him. Together they devoured every bite. He let her finish off the broth with a piece of bread.

※※※

In the morning, Ruth fed Abenadar bread and honey with thick slices of goat's cheese. When he arrived at breakfast in the camp, Gaius wondered aloud why Abenadar didn't eat the morning meal of cibaria.

Abenadar worked his men twice as hard that day. He didn't return to the small house until after the sun was well down. The streets were emptier than he was used to. When he came through the door, the hearth was cold and Ruth did not greet him. She sat at the table and, as he stepped into the room, she straightened her shoulders. "My lord, it is Shabbat."

"Shabbat?" said Abenadar.

"Yes, Shabbat. You should have been home before the sunset."

"I didn't realize."

"I waited for you." The Shabbat lamps were already lit on the table before her.

Abenadar sat beside her, and she said the blessing over the lamps. Ruth swept her hands three times over the flames, and covered her eyes with her hands. "Blessed are you, Adonai, Ruler of the Universe, who has sanctified us with commandments and who has commanded us to kindle the light of Shabbat." Abenadar remembered his own mother blessing the light of Shabbat, and he sadly realized how late Ruth's blessing came.

On the table stood their two cups of wine and a meal of challot bread and hummus. Abenadar remembered the Kiddush. The words were rough on his lips, but he knew them; his mother had made him learn it by heart when he was only a small child: "And it was evening, and it was morning... the sixth day. And the Heavens and the earth and all that was in them were completed. And Adonai completed on the seventh day all the work that He had done. And Adonai rested on the seventh day from all the work that He had done. And Adonai blessed the seventh day and sanctified it, for on that day Adonai rested from all his work, which He had created. Blessed are You, Adonai, Ruler of the

Universe, Creator of the Fruit of the vine."

Abenadar put his hand over the cups and Ruth said, "Amen."

Abenadar continued more strongly, "Blessed are You, Adonai, Ruler of the Universe, who sanctified us with Your commandments. Lovingly You have favored us with the gift of Your holy Shabbat as our inheritance, a reminder of creation, first among the sacred days which recall the exodus from Egypt. You have chosen us for Your service, and given us a sacred purpose in life. In loving favor, You have given us Your holy Shabbat as a heritage. Praised are you, Adonai, who sanctifies the Shabbat."

Abenadar and Ruth together said, "Amen."

Abenadar picked up the challot loaves and held them together, "Blessed are You, Adonai, Ruler of the Universe, who draws bread from the earth."

Abenadar broke one of the loaves and handed it to Ruth. They ate in silence as the oil in the lamps slowly burned lower and lower. Ruth didn't say anything to him, but Abenadar knew she was pleased he remembered the blessings.

After a while, Abenadar said, "I will work the schedule so I can keep Shabbat with you, but this time I cannot."

"You cannot? But you will break the Law." She turned her face away from him.

"I may break the Law. I am not used to keeping Shabbat. In the camp, I barely know one day from another."

Ruth held her hands together in her lap and stared into the flickering flame of the lamps.

"I'm sorry, Ruth. I will keep the next Shabbat and every one I can, but tomorrow morning I must be in the camp for the muster."

She did not speak to him. Abenadar said the blessing at the end of the meal, and they went to bed.

In the morning, Ruth got up early and helped Abenadar dress. She fed him bread left over from the challot loaves and honey, but he could see the displeasure in her eyes.

The next week, Abenadar worked the schedule with all the centurions in the camp. He arranged his duties so his century was assigned to the walls every seventh day in addition to their usual fourth. That way he wouldn't have to make the muster on the Shabbat. This pleased Ruth, but his men were not so happy. They thought he had put them on an extra tour to toughen them up. The guard duty on the walls was easy, but boring. Abenadar knew it wouldn't hurt them.

Ruth and Abenadar settled into a very pleasant routine. During the evening, night, and Shabbat, he dwelt in the little house close to the marketplace. While he was with Ruth, he lived like a man of Y'hudah. During the day, Abenadar acted the part of a Roman centurion. Gaius wondered, but no one asked Abenadar about his evenings. They assumed Abenadar spent them in the taverns and inns in the marketplace.

Ruth and Abenadar spent almost every moment they could with each other, and though that was never enough, their life was pleasant and they both felt whole. They spent their time together alone, except the one night a week when Yotam entertained them as part of his family in his inn. Eventually, Ruth and Abenadar ate two and sometimes three nights a week with Yotam's whole family. Those were pleasant evenings, and afterward, they returned to their house dog-tired and sunk almost immediately into slumber.

Abenadar was happier than he had ever been. The Primus Pilus, Legatus Legionis, and Pilate were all pleased with his leadership. The city of Yerushalayim was at peace.

Abenadar could not imagine how this serene existence could suddenly change....

*Keep me like the apple of thine eye;
hide me in the shadow of thy wings
from the wicked who obstruct me,
from deadly foes who throng around me.*

PSALM 17:8-9

Seventeen

The city's heat roared over Abenadar as he led his century through the crowded avenues. The orderly rows of legionnaires marched at a quick-time pace that cleared the streets. But his century's rapid progress could not ease Abenadar's impatience.

The news came to them first during the afternoon meal, and the camp was in an uproar. Fabius, the Centurion of the Primus Hastatus, the third century in the Primus Cohort and his columns ran into an ambush at the Pool of Shiloach. A runner brought the message: a band of rebels attacked Fabius and his men as they made their turn at the lowest point of the city. Abenadar knew the area well. It was the southern point of the Tyropoeon Valley that divided the city of Yerushalayim. The Pool of Shiloach was the furthest point in the city from the Praetorium and right beside the Refuse Gate. An attacker could easily escape through the gate. For those reasons, it was the most vulnerable place in the city to an ambush.

Abenadar cursed himself, then cursed Fabius. Fabius was a fool. He allowed his men to abuse the people. Likely, the people of Yerushalayim themselves had set upon his columns.

Abenadar led his men through the Valley Gate and to the top of the Ophel, the hill on which David's city had been built and the bad quarter of the city. They marched quick-time along the back streets near the top of the ridge that overlooked the valley. As they approached the area of the Fountain Gate, Abenadar signaled Gaius to slow the men to a normal march. The Pool of Shiloach was close—not more than fifty yards down the narrow streets from the Fountain Gate.

"Quiet the men," Abenadar told Gaius. "Send out two scouts."

Gaius signaled, and two men from the tenth column left their scutum with their companions. The two rushed quietly through the alleyways toward the pool.

Abenadar's century approached the Pool of Shiloach from the southeast. Whoever commanded the force that attacked Fabius at the pool, Abenadar hoped the enemy leader expected Fabius to be reinforced from the north, the direction of the Praetorium, and not from the southeast.

The scouts returned quickly and signaled that all was clear. Abenadar left Gaius with the century and crept up with the scouts to a position overlooking the pool. They crouched in the shadows at the edge of a street that entered into the large court near the southern end of the Pool of Shiloach. On the other side of the pool, about 100 men in both blue turbans and common city headgear stood shoulder to shoulder and three ranks deep guarding the narrow streets to the north and west. They carried knives, sickles, and staves, and all of them craned their necks, nervously watching the approach to the north. If Fabius and his columns were on the other side of the buildings, reasoned Abenadar, the rebels were trapped, and if his century attacked from the south and east, the rebels could not escape.

Abenadar crept back to his century and explained the situation to Gaius. Then he gave his orders to the columns. "I want a double line. Gladius at the front, heavy pilum behind. Block the rebels in the alleyways and give them no place to escape; then wash the streets with their blood."

Quietly he and Gaius marched the men into the streets below the pool. When they were in position, he signaled Gaius, and almost soundlessly, the men advanced toward the rebels.

As the legionnaires rounded the pool in the center of the courtyard, Abenadar raised his arm and sounded the charge. "Attack." His men rushed toward the unsuspecting Zealots.

As the double lines of the century met the back row of the blue turbans, a few scattered screams announced the assault. The rebels' surprise turned almost immediately to dismay when they recognized their attackers. Many of the rebels in the back row threw down their weapons and ran from the legionnaires without putting up a fight. Their companions didn't have time to turn and defend themselves. Before the front rows could turn the back row trampled them under foot. In the confusion, rebel fought rebel, and much of the blood spilled was not drawn by Abenadar's men.

As the lopsided battle progressed, groups of the rebels dropped their weapons and fell groveling at the legionnaires' feet. When Abenadar could, he stopped the slaughter of unarmed rebels. His men captured them and bound them with the rebel's own head gear. Knowing Pilate, capture meant a fate worse than clean death on the battlefield, but the immediate fear of the sword was a powerful inducement to surrender. After a few minutes, the paving stones were already slippery with blood.

As the legionnaires chased the Blue Shawls down the narrow streets, the fighting moved out of the large court around the Pool of Shiloach. At first Abenadar and Gaius followed closely behind their men, then Abenadar put his hand on Gaius' arm. "Did you notice any leadership among the men we are fighting?"

"None. They act as if they have no direction at all."

"But they required some very bright commanders to plan this ambush and catch Fabius off guard. I didn't see anyone try to rally or lead them."

"Where do you think the leaders are?"

"Where would you position yourself to watch for legionnaires?"

They both glanced up at the same time.

"Myself, I'd watch from the rooftops," said Gaius.

"You want to bet they're still there?"

"They have to be up there, and the only way down is the stairs on this side of the court," said Gaius.

"Why don't we wait until they come down and greet them?"

"They may not appreciate our greeting?"

Abenadar smiled. "That's their problem, not ours."

Abenadar and Gaius hid in the shadowed alleyway at the edge of the pool's court. Abenadar was certain the leaders of the Zealots kept watch from the rooftops accessible only from this side of the pool. He knew they would try to make their escape as soon as the court cleared.

He and Gaius weren't disappointed. As soon as his legionnaires disappeared down the side streets, six men stole down the outer steps of a building close to the street where Gaius and Abenadar hid.

Abenadar hefted Gaius' light pila in his hand. They waited until the men stood about five steps from the pool before they attacked. Surprise was with them and the lust of battle engulfed them.

With a precise throw, Abenadar drove Gaius' light pila through one of the men. He fell screaming to the ground and lay heaving against the spear. Gaius threw his heavy pila and pinned another. He made a cleaner attack than Abenadar, and it killed the rebel immediately.

With a savage yell, Abenadar leapt among the four remaining men. He struck one in the chest with his vitis while his gladius bit deeply into another. Both men dropped, groaning, to the paving stones. The Blue Shawls hadn't raised their swords.

Gaius struck with both his gladius and scutum. He blocked for Abenadar on his left, and at the same time attacked the two remaining men. Gaius knocked the first to the ground with his scutum, and he ran the second through the chest with his gladius.

Within a minute, only Gaius and Abenadar were left standing, and at their feet, all six of the rebel leaders lay either dead or wounded. At least three were alive and incapacitated while the others were obviously dead or near death.

Abenadar immediately marked the foremost man in the group. He was tall and finely dressed in a blue mantle and a blue turban. He wore a full beard and carried a Roman gladius instead of the long knife used by most of the rebels. He was still alive, but a large gash creased his skull, and he gasped for each breath as though some of his ribs were broken.

"This man looks like he might be their commander," remarked Abenadar to Gaius.

Gaius growled. "Then he shall be the first to be bound."

Starting with the leader, while Abenadar guarded them with his gladius, Gaius bound the three living men with their turbans and shawls. After they laid the three out like trussed pigeons, Gaius watched over the captives while Abenadar raced through the streets to catch up with his men. He passed two small groups of legionnaires guarding wounded and bound rebels. His men directed him further up the street. The battle was well over when he found the main part of his century.

About 70 of his men stood before a lone stone house at the edge of the street. They surrounded a frightened group of unarmed rebels and menaced them with their pilum and swords. The legionnaires cheered Abenadar's appearance. Although the rebels had wounded some of Abenadar's legionnaires, through the wild fight, not a single one of his legionnaires was killed.

"Where are the columns of the Primus Hastatus Century and their centurion?" Abenadar asked them.

The men pointed to the stone house before them. The door teetered on its hinges.

As if on cue, Fabius, the Centurion of the Primus Hastatus stumbled out of the doorway. Fabius grasped the door and spat. "The rebels trapped us between their forces and the old west wall. Before they wiped us out, we luckily found refuge in this house." He bowed his head. Only about eight men limped behind him out of the building.

Fabius was a man of equestrian rank—born into a good family in Rome. He was an adequate centurion but with a reputation for limited courage and initiative. Fabius was a foppish man who wore his hair long and unbound. His uniform was covered with gold and silver ornaments but no phalerae, armillae, or torques. Fabius raised his head. When he finally noticed he spoke to Abenadar, his face turned red and he shrieked, "Put all these rabble to death."

"Oh no, friend Centurion, I intend to present them as a gift to Pilate."

"Curse you, Abenadar. It was your stupid idea that caused this."

"I doubt it, Fabius. I told you before what would happen if you abused these people. Maybe now you will make sure your men keep their hands off the women of this city. Then they may live to see their next battle."

"Paugh," sneered Fabius. "We'll see what the Primus and Pilate have to say about this."

"Use care, Fabius. I advise you, as a friend, do not antagonize the Procurator."

Fabius cursed again. He swung his vitis and signaled his remaining men. They began gathering their injured and dead.

Another century approached from the northwest. By its size,

Abenadar could tell it was part of the Primus Cohort. As it neared, he identified the signum as the Princeps Century, the second century. At its side, ready for battle, marched its centurion, Valerius Regulus. Valerius and his men spoiled for a fight. Their march was tightly controlled, but they moved with a forward posture like a horse champing at the bit. Valerius halted his century only a few yards away and rushed up to Abenadar. His eyes flashed and he held his gladius unsheathed in his hand. "Where are the rioters?"

Abenadar swept out his hand and pointed to the sad-looking clump of men surrounded by a guard of his legionnaires. "That's about all that are left."

"Have you beaten them all?" Valerius said as he shoved the gladius back into its sheath.

"Every one of them."

"What about the leaders?" Valerius crossed his arms.

"My Optio, Gaius, should be bringing what's left of them up in a minute."

Down the street, Gaius waved his arm and called a greeting. Before him, a column of legionnaires half carried, half dragged the large man in blue and the two others Abenadar and Gaius had subdued. They dropped them all in front of the centurions.

"Dead?" remarked Valerius.

"No, they should still be alive," said Abenadar. "They are? Aren't they?" He turned to Gaius.

Gaius nodded.

"Who are they?" said Valerius.

"I don't know." He signaled Gaius.

Gaius reached down and grasped the leader's long locks of hair. He hauled the man's face up to eye level. "Who are you?"

The Zealot stared at them blindly.

"He won't understand Latin—or Greek. Let me try." Abenadar barked Aramaic in the man's face. "What's your name?"

The man was somewhat conscious. His mouth worked unproductively for a few moments, then he croaked out, "Jesus—Jesus bar-Abba."

Abenadar waved at him, and Gaius let the man's head drop heavily back to the flagstones."

"Jesus, 'son of the Father,' " Abenadar translated the surname. "Another messiah of the 'hammer.' They would be better off with a messiah of the sword. We would be better off if they claimed no messiahs at all."

"Come, Abenadar, where's the glory in that?" said Valerius.

"There is better glory in a long life and old age."

They all laughed.

"Any legionnaires killed?" asked Valerius.

"None from the Decimus Hastatus Posterior. I don't know about the Primus Hastatus. You'll have to ask Fabius."

"Where is Fabius?"

"Behind you, Valerius." Fabius wiped off his gladius with a bloodstained rag as he came up to them.

"How did you fare?"

"Not well. The Zealots ambushed us when we entered the court by the pool. There were over a hundred of them. They chased us into that house and tried to batter down the door."

"That's when Abenadar fortuitously rescued you?" asked Valerius.

"Rescued?" Fabius' eyes bulged. "His stupid idea to patrol the streets caused the riot."

"Pontius Pilate would not appreciate hearing his orders described as stupid," said Valerius. "The patrols have kept the peace—that is, until today."

"They didn't work this time. Pilate needs to know what his orders have achieved."

"Your patrol flushed out a hundred rebels," said Abenadar. "That sounds like a significant achievement to me."

"Not when you are under the knife, Centurion." Fabius gritted his teeth. Then he nodded to Valerius and patently ignored Abenadar. Without another word, Fabius turned on his heel and led the remnants of his columns limping back toward camp.

"A centurion unhappy with a battle he caused and then lost." Valerius grunted. "Why am I not surprised?" He clapped Abenadar on the shoulder. "If this is the kind of reception you can expect in the Ophel, I think I will have to take some of the patrols here myself."

"You will have to lead your men using Fabius' style, I think," Abenadar returned.

Valerius stroked his chin reflectively. "That would certainly not do." He nodded to Abenadar. "See you back in camp." He turned and walked back to his century.

Gaius saluted Valerius while Abenadar nodded in return.

"Gaius, form up the men. Let them march back in honor."

"Look," Gaius said, "Valarius is moving his Primus Princeps Century out of the way so we may precede him."

"Move quickly enough and we will pass Fabius." Abenadar grinned.

With a couple of instructions, Gaius formed the century and Abenadar took his place at the front. When Abenadar began to move forward, Gaius called, "Forward, h'arch." As one, the century started. Each footfall sounded like one. Behind them, bound with their turbans and shawls and tied to each other by their own robes, the Zealot prisoners hopped and shuffled to keep up. At the rear, two legionnaires prodded the prisoners with their pila so they wouldn't lag too far behind the century ahead of them.

Behind them, Abenadar heard the Primus Princeps begin their march. They matched the Hastatus Posterior step for step. The march of the two centuries sounded like a mighty roar, a reverberating drum, the beat of a single gigantic pulse. Each step announced their approach and warned any opposition to beware. Abenadar raised his vitis, and Gaius bellowed, "Quickstep." When Abenadar brought it down, Gaius roared, "H'arch." The men accelerated like a single entity. The drumbeat of the footfalls increased. The march sounded like the passage of a great wind. With his pila in hand, Gaius guarded over the men's steps, ready to correct any who were not in perfect sync. Not a single man faltered.

The prisoners stumbled at this faster pace, but their tormenters made certain they kept up. Behind them, the Primus Princeps took up their pace. In the streets, the people of Yerushalayim heard the approach of both centuries and hurried out of the way. Ahead of them, small boys ran to warn everyone off the streets. The legionnaires were like a force of nature, unstoppable, powerful, and unrelenting. At one point, Abenadar noticed Fabius and his luckless columns at the side in an alley. The glare of the foppish centurion followed Abenadar long after he was lost to sight.

Abenadar was unaware of Fabius' gaze. He felt at that moment nothing could stop them. Nothing could stop his century, and he led the charge.

As the camp came into sight, the guards at the gate opened the large doors to their full width. They had also heard the centuries' approach. Abenadar held up four fingers and Gaius gave the signal to reform the columns. While still at the march, the century collapsed into four columns and swept through the gates. Inside, Abenadar signaled them to expand back to the regular formation. Then he led the century around the walls of the camp. As they marched, all the legionnaires in the camp gathered to watch them. They had heard of the riot in the streets and they knew this display only accompanied a great victory.

Finally, directly before the officium, Abenadar commanded the century to halt. In perfect formation, his men silently waited for the Primus Pilus to appear.

Wearing his war helmet, Cecilius Bassus finally exited the officium.

Abenadar and the Hastatus Posterior saluted.

"What do you have to report, Centurion Abenadar?" asked the Primus.

"Primus Pilus, the Hastatus Posterior Century of your Decimus Cohort relieved columns of the Hastatus Century of your Primus Cohort near the Pool of Shiloach. We have taken 34 men and three of their leaders captive while killing 52. We accomplished this without a single loss from our century."

"Excellent, Centurion Abenadar. I prescribe extra rations and beer for the Decimus Hastatus Posterior Century. You may release your men, but you must come with me now. We will bring this report directly to Pilate."

Abenadar saluted and swung around. "Optio Gaius, you have command of the century."

"By your leave, Centurion," called Gaius.

The Primus continued to Abenadar, "Bring the leaders of this rabble with us. I'm sure Pilate will want to interrogate them."

Abenadar spoke with Gaius, and the Primus' guards removed the three leaders from the group of prisoners. Gaius took the rest to the dungeon under the Praetorium.

Pilate did not make Abenadar and the Primus Pilus wait. As soon as Abenadar and Cecilius Bassus went to a knee before him, Pilate ordered, "Get up. What is this news of a riot in the city?"

"A short-lived one, Procurator," said the Primus.

"Short-lived? Better never to have been."

"Procurator," said the Primus, "it is better to hobble the rebels and kill their men whenever we can."

"Yes, yes. How many men did you lose this time?"

"Half a column with about as many wounded, but Centurion Abenadar lost no one from his century."

"What does this mean? How many centuries were fighting?"

"Two columns of the Primus Hastatus Century were on patrol when they were ambushed by a band of the Zealots."

"How many Zealots?"

"At least a hundred. Possibly more."

"And from these columns…?"

"From these columns we lost five men with four wounded severely."

"We take it these two columns didn't fight off the rioters alone."

"No, Procurator. Abenadar marched the Decimus Hastatus Posterior as soon as the word came to us about the battle."

"Abenadar? Our Centurion from the Galil." Pilate settled back, a little more at ease.

"Yes, Procurator."

"Abenadar, you took no casualties, and there were as many as a hundred rebels? How many did you have to let get away?"

Cecilius Bassus waved at Abenadar to speak.

"Procurator," said Abenadar, "few escaped death or capture. I brought my men through the Ophel and around the back of the courtyard at the Pool of Siloam. The Zealots did not expect an attack from the rear. They were all armed with swords and knives. My men counted 52 dead after our attack. We captured 34 and brought them back to you."

"Thirty-four of those Zealot monsters, and you say you killed over 50 of them. Herod will be impressed; he has never caught so many at once." Pilate repeated to himself, "Herod has certainly never been able to take so many." Then he spoke out loud to Abenadar, "What of the commanders? Did you kill, or better yet, capture any of their leaders?"

"Procurator," said the Primus, "Abenadar apprehended three of their leaders, and we brought them here for you to question, yourself."

"Marvelous. Bring them to me. We would like to see these men."

The Primus gave a signal and his guards brought the three men forward. They were a sorry-looking lot. All of them were wounded, and their wounds had not been tended. Abenadar's men had shorn them of their robes, blue and otherwise, and they stood, almost naked, before the court. Their bodies were sinewy and undernourished, and they glared at Pilate with a sullen defiance. Forged within their eyes was hatred.

"Who is the leader of this group?" asked Pilate.

Abenadar indicated the large man slightly to the rear.

"Bring him forward," ordered Pilate, tapping his chair with his baton.

One of the guards roughly separated the man from the group and pushed him forward.

"So you are a commander of these pitiful Zealots who disturb the peace of Judea," said Pilate.

"I doubt he understands you, Procurator," said Abenadar. "Should I translate for you?"

"Yes, yes. Insult him a bit. Then ask him what he expects to achieve by attacking us."

Abenadar did as Pilate commanded, then reported the man's response. "He has told me before he is called Jesus bar-Abba, which means 'Jesus, son of the father.' Jesus means 'Adonai saves.' That is one of their names for God. 'Son of the father' is a title and implies he is a messiah. Jesus bar-Abba told me that he and his people will not stop fighting until they have driven all of us back to Rome."

"Ask him what he will do about the priests and the leaders of his people. They have supported us since we came to this forsaken place. Will he oppose them?"

"He says they are no true priests or leaders if they bow to Rome, which he calls 'the abomination.' "

Pilate snorted. "We, an abomination. We can show him an abomination. How many of his men did you say were prisoners?"

"Thirty-four, Procurator."

"That will do nicely. Crucify them before him and these others. Arrange the execution-stakes along the road to the Pool of Shiloach, just outside the gates. Place above each stake the sign, 'friend of bar-Abba.' Then beat these with the cat and put them in the dungeons below the Praetorium. If they want to see an abomination, we will show them one. Take them away."

The guards led the three men out of the court.

"Now, what about you, Centurion Abenadar? We are pleased with your success. Would that you were fully Roman. We have need of such men as you, but you are cursed with only half the noble blood. How did we honor you before?"

The Legatus Legionis, Iulius Valens, who stood behind Pilate whispered in his ear.

"Ah, we remember. We presented you with a golden torque and three golden phalerae. Your current victory is a much greater achievement and requires a greater reward. Primus."

"Yes, Procurator."

"Two columns of the Primus Hastatus, you said, were ambushed. Is that not so?" Pilate continued without waiting for an answer, "Fabius is the centurion."

"Yes, Procurator."

"Find Fabius a position in your staff—worthy of his rank, of course. Place Abenadar at the head of the Primus Hastatus. In the name of the Emperor, we grant you, Abenadar a golden armillae, five golden phalerae, and for saving Fabius, a corona civicae aurea. Mint these from my treasury. Also from my treasury, you may mint a golden phalerae and a torque for the optio and one phalerae for yourself, Primus. Mint a further 34 gold and 52 silver phalerae. Abenadar, you may present them to your men as you desire. Your optio is Gaius Flaccus. Is that not so?"

"Yes, Procurator," answered Abenadar.

"The Optio Gaius Flaccus shall be the new centurion of the Hastatus Posterior Century of the Decimus Cohort. Does this please you, Primus?"

"Yes, Procurator."

"Does it please you, Abenadar?"

"I am honored," said Abenadar, "But I don't wish to take advantage of another centurion's misfortune. Anyone in Fabius' position would have had a difficult time pitting only two columns against over 100 men."

Pilate put off Abenadar's objection with a wave of his hand, "Fabius has caused us problems before. He will not lose his rank, only his position. We need peace in Judea, not discord. Continue the patrols, Primus. Let us see if we can tempt more rats into the open."

"Yes, Procurator." Both Abenadar and the Primus dropped to one knee and Pilate dismissed them.

As they left the Praetorium, the Primus continued to match steps with Abenadar. "Your actions continue to gratify Pilate. That is good for both you and for me. But you must tread carefully—Fabius is a vindictive man. He will not misinterpret Pilate's promotion."

"I don't want his place."

"That doesn't matter. The Procurator has spoken, and it will be, but I warn you, as a friend, be cautious of Fabius."

"Thank you, Primus," said Abenadar.

*My enemy is like a lion eager for prey,
like a young lion crouching in ambush.
Arise, Adonai, meet him face to face and bring him down.
Save my life from the wicked.*

Psalm 17:12-13

Eighteen

Abenadar should have been exuberant as he made his way back to the small house he shared with Ruth. Instead, he was unhappy he would have to leave the Decimus Hastatus Posterior Century. He had worked so hard to train them, and he admired their dedication and strength. They were the best century in the Decimus Cohort, and he would put them up against any other century in the VI Ferrata. His mind brimmed with the unhappy thought: tomorrow he would have to break the news to them that he was no longer their centurion. He consoled himself with the knowledge that Gaius would now lead them. Gaius, Abenadar knew, would watch after them and keep them fit for battle.

The afternoon sun lingered in the sky as Abenadar turned down the narrow street to his house. Shadows covered the small courtyard in front of it.

The moment Abenadar opened the door, Ruth rushed at him and fell at his feet. "Dear Adonai," she cried, raising her hands above her bowed head. "Thank Adonai, blessed be He, you are alive."

Yotam's wife, Sela, sat on the floor of the kitchen. She quietly got up and left the house.

Abenadar lifted Ruth to her feet, but tears streamed down her face. She still clung to him. "What's wrong, Ruth?"

"Nothing is wrong," she said between sobs. "I heard Romans were killed in the streets today, and I feared for your life."

"No." He shook his head. "It was not me." He kissed her face, and she dried her tears in her veil. She would not smile at him. She finally released him and stepped to the hearth. She knelt down and ladled some food into a bowl. She mixed some wine and brought the bowl and cup to him. Abenadar lay on the cushions beside the table as she served him. He recited the blessings over the wine and food.

"Aren't you going to eat?" he asked her.

She looked away from him. "I'm not hungry."

As he ate, Ruth knelt at his feet and unlaced his caligae. She pulled off the heavy sandals and toyed with the folds of his tunic.

Abenadar took a bite. "Shall I tell you what happened today?"

"If you wish. I am just glad to have you here with me."

"The Zealots attacked a patrol today…"

"Not yours?" she interrupted.

"No, not mine. When the news came, I marched my century before anyone else. We approached the Zealots—they were Blue Shawls—from behind and caught them by surprise. There were more than 100 of them. My men killed almost two thirds and captured the rest. They are to be crucified tomorrow."

"A horrible way to die."

"They killed five legionnaires."

"They didn't kill you and that, for me, is the important thing."

"I have been awarded five golden phalerae, a golden armillae, and a corona civicae aurea."

"Five?"

"Yes, five for the leaders and men Gaius and I captured. Their chief called himself Jesus bar-Abba; he probably thinks himself a prophet. Can there ever be any more prophets in Y'hudah?"

"I have heard of a prophet in Y'hudah," said Ruth, laying her head against his leg.

Abenadar stopped eating, "A prophet. Really?"

"Yes, he is called Yochanan the Immerser."

"The Immerser. What kind of prophet is that?"

"He immerses people in the Yarden River to cleanse them of their sin."

"A dirty river, the Yarden. It wouldn't wash away dirt; it might as well wash away sin." Abenadar sighed. "That sounds like the kind of prophet I could like. At least he isn't trying to kill my legionnaires."

"Half the city has gone out to see him," said Ruth.

"He is here?"

"Yes, near Biet-Anyah."

"That is quite a ways from Yerushalayim."

"The roads are full of travelers this time of year, and the countryside has been safe since Pilate has been Procurator." Her words sounded practiced.

"The Zealots hide in the Wilderness of Y'hudah. They hurt their cause when they attack the people," said Abenadar.

"I don't know." Ruth tugged at his clothing. "Will you take me out to Beit-Anyah to see the Immerser?"

Abenadar paused and glanced down at her. Ruth lay against his legs, a faraway look on her face.

"Why?" Abenadar asked.

"I want to see the prophet."

"I cannot take you tomorrow. Pilate assigned me the third century in the Primus Cohort as my command. The Hastatus Century."

Ruth stared up at him with her large dark eyes. "I know little of the legion, but from what you told me, doesn't that mean you advanced nine cohorts?"

"Yes, nine, by Pilate's decree. I am now a Primes Ordines Centurion."

"It is a great honor."

"It is a considerable honor, and a way to make a great many enemies."

"My lord!"

"You needn't fear for me. I have the ear of Pilate and the blessing of the Primus."

She gazed down again. "I always fear for you. I don't trust the Romans."

"I am a Roman."

She peered at him from under her veil but found no anger in his expression.

"I must take command of the Hastatus Century tomorrow and give my old command to Gaius. I have few friends in the legion but still fewer enemies than friends."

"Will you take me to see the Immerser after that?"

"A few days after or perhaps a week. I am intrigued myself. I would like to see this peaceful prophet."

"Thank you, my lord." Ruth almost bowed at his feet.

The next morning, the Primus Pilus did not release the cohorts following the muster. The men stood at attention as he walked with the men in his staff to the Hastatus Posterior Century of the Decimus Cohort and called, "Post the orders."

The legion's Cornicularius read from his scroll, "By order of Pontius Pilate the Procurator of Judea, Abenadar of the Galil, the Centurion of the Decimus Hastatus Posterior Century of the VI Ferrata Legion of Rome is relieved of command. Optio Gaius Flaccus, come forward."

Gaius marched to the front of the century and stood to the right of Abenadar.

The Cornicularius continued, "Gaius Flaccus, you are ordered to assume command as Centurion of the Decimus Hastatus Posterior of the VI Ferrata Legion of Rome."

Abenadar and Gaius turned to face one another. At Abenadar's signal, the signifer, at first slow with astonishment, marched between the men and the century. He handed the signum to Abenadar. Abenadar passed the signum to Gaius with the words, "I relinquish the command."

Gaius took the signum and said, "I assume the command." Then he handed the signum back to the signifer.

Gaius saluted Abenadar, and Abenadar grasped his former optio by the shoulders. "Welcome, my friend, to the brotherhood of centurions."

Then Abenadar turned and marched to stand at the right side of the Primus. As they left, the entire century saluted Abenadar—a salute taken up by the rest of the cohort.

They marched to the third century in the Primus Cohort. Fabius had not heard the orders read to the Decimus Cohort, because the Primus was too far away. By the time the Primus and his staff stopped in front of the Primus Hastatus Century, sweat already poured down the sides of his face.

"Post the orders," said the Primus.

"By order of Pontius Pilate the Procurator of Judea, Fabius of Rome, the Centurion of the Hastatus Century of the Primus Cohort of the VI Ferrata Legion of Rome is relieved of command. You are promoted to Officium Princeps. Centurion Abenadar of the Galil, step forward."

Abenadar walked to stand to the right of Fabius. Fabius' face reddened, as if barely containing his anger.

The Cornicularius continued, "Abenadar of the Galil, you are ordered to assume command of the Hastatus Century of the Primus Cohort of the VI Ferrata Legion of Rome."

Abenadar faced Fabius. Fabius turned slowly. The century's signifer quickly marched between the centurions and the century. Fabius almost ripped the signum from his hands. He threw the signum at Abenadar and spat out, "I relinquish the command."

Abenadar grasped the signum tightly. "I assume the command." Then he handed the signum back to the signifer.

Abenadar saluted Fabius. Fabius did not return his salute, and still seething, took his place in the Primus' staff. The Primus returned Abenadar's salute and released the cohorts.

Abenadar did not dismiss his new troops. He stood in front and addressed them. "Legionnaires, I am very proud to be given command of this century. You perhaps have heard of the successes of the Decimus Hastatus Posterior Century. Without the loss of a single life, almost every man in that century has earned phalerae." Abenadar paused to let his words sink in. "The Optio, Gaius Flaccus, earned two golden phalerae and is now a centurion. I trained these legionnaires myself. Their training and discipline made them exemplary, and I expect you to be as great as they are. Optio Cerus, prepare the men for inspection."

"Open ranks, h'arch."

The ranks of the century stepped forward a prescribed number of steps to make room for Abenadar and Cerus to walk between them. Abenadar made a very slow and deliberate inspection of each man. He started with the optio and ended with the tesserarius. At the end of the inspection, he held the men in their ranks while the librarius read the duty roster. When the librarius finished reading the roster, Abenadar took the rest of the men, more than half of the century, to his impromptu training field at the west of the Ophel. There they practiced marching and maneuvering, changes of facing, and formation. Following Nico's example, and just like Abenadar trained his last century, he had the men practice with the weighted practice weapons against the stakes and against each other.

That night, when Abenadar dismissed them to the barracks, they were weary and sore, but quietly, he was pleased with them. Their performance was better than he expected.

Abenadar kept them in this training regime for a month before he was fully satisfied with them. On the whole, the men enjoyed the activity. They complained, but it was the complaint of contented soldiers. Now that he brought them to a fevered pitch of readiness, they wanted nothing more than to use their skills against a worthy foe.

Abenadar was so busy that he forgot his promise to Ruth. During the month, he kept very late and very early hours at the camp, even during Shabbat. Though Ruth never said anything to him about it, he knew this displeased her. During Shabbat, on Friday evening, he came home well after dark to find Ruth waiting. She waited expectantly for him, sitting at their table with her lighted lamps, challot loaves, and a cooling pot of soup. The hearth was always swept clean and burned with the bright fire she left untouched until the next evening. When he left her early on Saturday morning, at the door, she called out to him, "Shabbat Shalom," but he could not stop. Automatically, he repeated the words back to her—in his mind, Abenadar already trained his men and that was far more important to him.

Almost a month later, Abenadar came home in the early afternoon and took Ruth in his arms. "The Primus Hastatus Century is proficient, now."

She kissed him and said with a sly smile, "Then can we go see the Immerser?"

"Is he still around?"

"Yes and still at Beit-Anyah."

"Very well," said Abenadar. "Tomorrow, in the afternoon, we will leave for Yericho."

With unrestrained joy, Ruth clasped her hands together, and

Abenadar had to smile at her.

Abenadar left the house early the next morning. As usual, the day was still dark and the streets almost empty. He planned to work out the duty schedules right after the muster so he could leave his century in the charge of his optio, Cerus for the next couple of days. Tomorrow was the day before Shabbat, and he would surprise Ruth by staying the entire Shabbat with her. As Abenadar entered the main street, he heard some movement behind him, but he dismissed it from his thoughts. In his mind, he was already working out each of the men's duties. He wanted to give the men a well-deserved break.

Abenadar came almost in sight of the wide street before the camp when, without warning, a dark clad figure stepped out of an alley and stood before him. Abenadar was about to say something when a blow to the back of his head sent him reeling. A writhing mass of heavy arms and legs leapt on top of him. Abenadar held himself on his feet for a while, but when he felt the hot stab of a blade into his thigh, his leg collapsed under him, and he fell to the pavement of the street. Blows rained down on him. Abenadar heaved himself up and tried to strike back, but another knife slash struck his chest and slid across his ribs. He rolled away from the blade and spied the shadow of a cudgel aimed for his face. He twisted again, away from it, and the heavy club caught the side of his head. Abenadar's brain burst with flashes of light and a red glow, and he lost consciousness.

A merchant found Abenadar half-dead in the street and told the guards at the camp gate. The legionnaires followed quickly after the merchant. The two of them lifted Abenadar between them and brought him into the camp.

"Send for the Primus. The Centurion Abenadar is injured."

Cecilius Bassus came immediately. Caught in his preparations for the morning muster, he was only half-dressed. "Take the centurion to his quarters and call for the surgeon."

A guard ran from the gate to find the ancient principalis who took care of the legionnaires' wounds.

With the call for the surgeon, the word of Abenadar's injuries went around the camp. Not long after the surgeon arrived, both Gaius and Cerus came running from the barracks.

The camp physician shook his head at Abenadar's injuries, and without a word started to wash and bandage them.

Gaius and Cerus burst into the room. "Primus," they spoke at once. Gaius continued for them both, "Is he—"

"No, not dead. What do you say, Rubrius?" Cecilius Bassus asked the surgeon.

"They cracked his skull and sliced up his chest and leg. Lots of bruises as well. The knife cuts don't look deep enough to kill...not right away. If he coughs up blood, he's probably as good as dead."

"Who did this to him?" said Cerus.

The Primus pursed his lips in dismay. "The guards found him just minutes ago." Then Cecilius Bassus turned decisively to Gaius, "Centurion Gaius, take the Decimus Hastatus Posterior into the streets. Try to find the men who attacked him. I suspect Abenadar's assailants are long gone, but see if you can capture them. Go. Now."

Gaius took a last look at Abenadar and ran out of the building to muster his century.

"Primus?" said Cerus.

"Yes, Optio Cerus."

"I would like to mount a guard here."

"Permission granted. Ensure the Decimus Hastatus Posterior is also included in your roster. I am sure that will please Gaius and his men."

Cerus left to cobble together a guard from the current roster.

Cecilius Bassus hovered over Abenadar as the old principalis

Rubrius washed the Abenadar's wounds and bound them up. What would Pilate think when he found that one of his favorites had been attacked so close to the Praetorium?

Luckily Pilate had left earlier in the month to return to Caesarea. Cecilius Bassus wouldn't have to answer directly to the Procurator for at least four months. But what if Abenadar should die? If the man died, Bassus could never acceptably explain this lapse of security to Pilate.

Before the old man finished dressing Abenadar's wounds, Cerus himself returned to the room and installed a guard at the door.

"Optio Cerus, I give Centurion Abenadar to your charge. Ensure no additional harm comes to him. I don't want you to neglect your duties, either. The men of the Primus Hastatus must not lose their training or overlook their responsibilities."

"Yes sir." Cerus saluted as the Primus left the room.

Gaius found no sign of the men who attacked Abenadar. Crestfallen, he and his century returned to the camp in the late afternoon. With few words, he relieved Cerus. They began a day and night watch, and ensured one of them stayed beside Abenadar all the time. They both tended his wounds, and legionnaires from the two centuries gladly guarded him. Legionnaires volunteered from across the centuries of both cohorts. The men worried that they would lose their lucky charm—the only leader who had seen action in Yerushalayim and not lost a single legionnaire.

In the afternoon, when Abenadar did not return, Ruth was, at first, unconcerned. Abenadar seldom came early to their home, but, then again, he usually kept his promises. He said he would take her to see the Immerser. Dressed in traveling clothes, she paced back and forth in the small house and then later in the courtyard before their door.

When the sun went down and Shabbat came, Ruth's heart was overwhelmed with fear. She debated whether she should go look for him.

That evening, though it was Shabbat, Yotam's wife, Sela, came to Ruth. Sela carried a lamp from her own table, and like Ruth, her face was creased with worry. As Ruth stood in the dark before her door, Sela called out, "Ruth. Ruth! Shabbat Shalom."

"Shabbat Shalom," said Ruth and fear made her voice tremble.

Sela continued, "I heard in the marketplace—the word is whispered—that bandits killed a Roman centurion in the streets."

A wild and distraught look wrenched Ruth's features under the warm golden glow of the lamp. Sela reached out for the younger woman and folded her into her arms like her own child.

But Ruth's weakness lasted only a moment. Then she stood up straight and threw back her thin shoulders. She immediately made up her mind. Abenadar told her she could never enter the camp, but she could not wait for him any longer.

Sela stepped back at Ruth's abrupt change. "What will you do, child?"

"I must find him. I must know if he is dead, or if he needs my help. Sela, you go back to your family. It is Shabbat. You are needed there. I know what I must do."

Ruth had to convince Sela to leave, but after a few words, Sela took her Shabbat lamp with its comforting glow and returned to her home.

When Sela was out of sight, Ruth's nerve left her. After a couple of false starts, she finally screwed up enough courage to disobey Abenadar. With burdened steps, Ruth trudged to the large gate that fronted the legion camp. When she reached the camp, for a while, she couldn't bring herself to approach the entrance. Finally she crept over and knocked on the massive portal.

Ruth trembled with fear and uncertainty. The small door opened slightly, and a large, scarred veteran in full armor stood before her.

"I must see Abenadar the Centurion," she said with her eyes cast toward the ground.

"Centurion Abenadar?" the man repeated and then went on in Latin.

She couldn't understand another word the man said. She reached out to the man with one hand. "Abenadar, please. I must see Abenadar. Is he still alive?"

The legionnaire shrugged and called to another guard. A flurry of voices sounded behind the gate. The man stood in front of her and blocked her entrance. Ruth hadn't come this far to be turned away.

"Abenadar, please. I must see him," she cried out.

The soldier shrugged again, but he didn't close the gate. After a while another legionnaire came up behind him. The guard saluted him and stepped back.

Ruth stared pitifully up at the new legionnaire and again tried to make herself understood. "I must see Abenadar the Centurion." Tears streaked her face. Although she didn't know it, the resolution in her voice and face spoke more strongly than her words. "Where is Abenadar?" she repeated, and hysteria tinged her question.

The man was not dressed in armor, but Ruth recognized he was likely a centurion. He held himself much like Abenadar—a surety that spoke his rank as loudly as any uniform.

In pidgin Aramaic, the man said, "I am Gaius."

Ruth knew the name. He was one of Abenadar's friends, Abenadar's old optio. "Please, Centurion Gaius. You don't know me. I am Abenadar's..." She did not know what to call herself.

"You are Abenadar's whore," he said, and a look of understanding flooded his features.

"I am no whore," she cried, then realized he had fewer words than she to express their relationship. "Is he alive?"

He shook his head, but she couldn't tell if he didn't understand her or....

"I must see him. Please, let me see Abenadar."

He stood unmoving, yet she could detect uncertainty in his stance.

"I know who you are, Centurion Gaius. Please let me go to him."

With an immediate decision, Gaius reached out and took her arm. She was startled and resisted a moment, then let him draw her into the camp. The small gate closed behind her, and she was trapped. The legionnaires stared at her with unguarded expressions. She was nothing to them. Nothing more, in their eyes, than a woman of the streets, and though protected by her veil and shawl, she was afraid for a new reason. Gaius did not release her. He spoke quietly to the guards and drew her further into the camp.

Ruth stared wide-eyed around her. Guards stood all around. She walked through a gauntlet of men and their stares, but their gaze was more curious than threatening. Gaius said something to her, but Ruth shook her head—she could not understand him. He gently led her through the camp, and Ruth wondered if he thought her a new prostitute for the legion. Surely they recognized her veil and head covering. Surely they knew those marked her an unavailable woman.

In the dark, Ruth couldn't make out much of her surroundings. She perceived walls and buildings and everywhere the smell of men, fires, and metal. Gaius pulled her into the large building just behind the gate. Inside, another compliment of guards stood before a plain door. Gaius spoke to them and they parted before him. He opened the door for her and tugged her in behind him.

A charcoal brazier and an oil lamp partially lit the room, which was spartanly furnished with a cot, a writing desk, and some chests. On the cot lay Abenadar. A heavy Roman wool blanket covered him to the neck, and blood-soaked rags bound his head. He breathed with a rasping sound. Ruth let out a cry and tried to run to him, but Gaius held her fast. He was uncertain whether to let her approach closer.

"Let me go." She tried to pry her arm out of his grasp. She stared beseechingly up at Gaius. "Let me see him. Please, let me go to him."

Gaius made up his mind, and slowly he released her. She ran to the cot and knelt at its side. It was Abenadar, but she could hardly recognize him. His face was swollen and bruised. Ruth lightly stroked his hair. She feared he was near death. She said a prayer to Adonai and pulled back the blanket. Gaius reached forward to stop her, then thought better of it and stood back.

Bloody bandages covered Abenadar's chest and leg. Ruth covered him again and kissed his face. Then she bowed her head against him and leaned on the edge of the cot. Silent prayers flooded her heart and mind.

Gaius sat on the only chair in the room and watched her cautiously.

In the morning, Cerus entered the room. Ruth didn't look up. The legionnaire spoke with Gaius. They traded places and Gaius left. After a while, Gaius returned with a couple of bowls of wheat gruel. He handed one to Cerus and tried to give the other to Ruth. She raised herself up and shook her head. The men stared at one another. Then Gaius left the untouched gruel on the floor beside her and went out.

Ruth hadn't slept. In the new Shabbat's light, she inspected Abenadar's bandages again and saw they needed to be changed. She turned to the man in the chair and demanded, "I need bandages and clean water."

Cerus could not understand her so she touched the bandage at Abenadar's head and pulled on it. She mimed unwinding it and wrapping it back up again.

Cerus nodded and stepped to the door. He brought her back some clean rags. Ruth tried to make him understand she wanted water. She made more signs, and he went back to the doorway and returned shortly with a full bowl.

Gently, under Cerus' scrutiny, Ruth removed one bandage after another and washed Abenadar's wounds. The gashes were deep and ugly, and more than once, she wondered that he still lived. Ruth rebandaged his wounds, and afterward Cerus, with a sound of approval, sat back in the chair.

So began Ruth's watch. Cerus and Gaius kept it with her, but from the first day, they realized it was hers alone, and she was in control. They could only participate in it with her. Cerus and Gaius coaxed her to eat some of the wheat gruel and brought her a blanket to sleep on the floor beside the cot. She would not move farther from him than that. They provided her bandages and water and some weak wine to drink. Others came and left the room, but they did not attempt to speak to her. Ruth was cognizant of the very well accoutered men, centurions and the Primus, she guessed, who daily came to check on her injured Abenadar.

After three days Abenadar finally awoke. He called in Aramaic for a drink, and Ruth held the cup to his lips. He drank a little and fell again into a dazed slumber. That day, along with the water, her tears washed his wounds. With mumbled prayers and unheard encouragement, she kissed his face over and over.

Over time, Ruth learned some Latin—enough words to ask for water, the bandages, food and drink. Except to encourage her to sleep and eat, the legionnaires didn't bother her. She cared nothing for her own needs and spent almost every moment at Abenadar's side.

On the fifth morning, Abenadar startled all of them. He awoke and sat up. For a while, he gazed around the room as if trying to determine where he was.

In fear and excitement, Ruth peered intently up at him from the floor. She was torn between joy and how he would view her presence. More than once he had told her to never come to the camp.

Abenadar glanced around without recognition until his gaze rested on Ruth. His eyes widened, and he stared at her. His lips parted as though he were about to speak. Then he grabbed his head and his eyes squinted in pain. After a moment, he croaked in Aramaic, "Ruth…" His voice trailed off and he tried again. "Ruth, why are you here?"

She reached up and put her arms around him. In half an answer and half a prayer she cried, "Oh, Abenadar, I was so afraid you would not live."

"Of course I live. Let me rest a little and then we will go to Beit-Anyah."

"Beit-Anyah? Oh, Abenadar, you cannot leave for a while yet." She was near tears.

"Why not, Ruth?"

"You have lain almost unmoving for five days."

He touched his head again. "Five days?"

Gaius stepped to the side of the cot. "Abenadar what do you desire? How are you feeling?"

"Gaius, Gaius, are you there too? What has happened? Ruth says I have been asleep for five days. Is she right?"

"Yes, you were attacked in the street. They left you for dead."

"Who?"

"We don't know, but Fabius is dead and by his own hand. You know, he had been mouthing threats against you since he passed you his century. Whoever attacked you didn't take your money."

"So, Fabius?"

"That is what the Primus believes."

"Why is Ruth here?"

"Who is Ruth?"

"This woman. My woman."

"She came looking for you the evening after we found you. She has taken care of you ever since then. We couldn't separate her from you if we tried."

"I'm glad you didn't try." Abenadar turned to Ruth and said in Aramaic, "Why are you here? I told you to never come to the camp."

She put her lips close to his ear. "I love you more than myself. I could not leave you when I knew you were hurt."

Abenadar stroked her hair. "Thank you, Ruth. I needed you." He kissed her lips.

Ruth drew back and hid her face. "My lord, you embarrass me."

"I'm sorry. I show my approval of you." He lay back on the cot. "I am weak."

"Can you take food? Drink?" said Gaius.

"Yes, I am hungry."

"Centurion Gaius," said Ruth, "wheat gruel. Wine. Water." She used the only Latin words she knew.

As if obeying her commands, both Gaius and Cerus left the room.

Abenadar laughed and reached again for his head. "You have charmed them, Ruth."

"Tush," she said, "be quiet. You tax yourself."

Abenadar said nothing and obeyed her orders without a compliant.

The next morning, a guard wearing a tessera of the gate came to the door of Abenadar's quarters. He saluted the men and waited for them to speak.

"What is it?" asked Gaius.

"Centurions, a Judean family stands at the gate and asks to see Centurion Abenadar and a Ruth."

"Let them come in," said Abenadar with a smile.

The guard left and a few moments later Yotam, Sela, their daughter, and Yotam's brother, Ya'akov, entered the small room. Ruth, Sela, and her daughter hugged and kissed one another. Yotam bowed to the men. "My lord, Centurion Abenadar, when Ruth did not return to your house, we came to find you. We thought she had been kidnapped, but you are hurt, my lord?"

"I am recovering. Thanks be to Him."

"Thanks be to Him. And Ruth is safe?"

"Yes, she is safe. I will come back home with her in a couple of days. You needn't worry."

The family stayed half an hour longer. Ruth and Sela caught up on gossip, and Yotam told Abenadar of the news of the marketplace. When they left, Ruth appeared happier than she had since she had come to the camp. "You see," she said to Abenadar, "they care about you. They were worried and wanted to see if you were safe."

"No, Ruth," he said, "they were worried about you. They were afraid I left you on the streets or that you had been taken away while I was in the camp. They care little for me."

"They care for you, my lord."

Abenadar said nothing more.

A few days later, an unusual amount of martial noise from the gate of the camp roused Abenadar from his fitful afternoon slumber. Within minutes, outside his door came the sound of legionnaires as they snapped to attention. The door burst open, and the Legatus Legionis Iulius Valens entered the room. His tribunes and the Primus Pilus trailed closely behind him.

Gaius and Ruth stood. Abenadar tried to get up, but Ruth pushed him back down on the cot.

Iulius Valens said, "That is right, girl. Don't let him get up. Lay back, Abenadar. Pilate sent me to find out how you are recovering. The Primus dispatched word to us only a few days ago." He glanced disapprovingly at Cecilius Bassus. "I came from Caesarea as soon as I could. Pilate was worried that he had lost the most valiant centurion in Judea." He gave his hand to Abenadar. "I was afraid I had lost a friend. When will you be back on your feet, Abenadar?"

"I would be today, if they would let me, Legatus."

The Primus spoke. "Legatus, I don't know what you have been told about Centurion Abenadar's injuries, but they are grave. I want to keep him in his quarters a month before he takes the field again."

"Surely not a month," said Abenadar.

"Your Primus is wise," said Iulius Valens. "I also advise a long convalescence. Pilate and I require your continued service in Yerushalayim. Primus."

"Yes, Legatus."

"Ensure Centurion Abenadar is well cared for. Pilate and I hold you personally responsible for his full recovery."

"Yes, Legatus."

Iulius Valens put his hand on Abenadar's shoulder. "I know I have taxed your strength. I can see the strain in your face, friend. Right now, I am retiring to the Praetorium, but I will be here for the next month. I will visit you and we shall speak about our days in the III Gallica."

"Thank you, Legatus." Abenadar put his hand on Iulius Valens'.

"Get well soon." The Legatus took a long look around the room as if seeing it for the first time. He noted Gaius, then his gaze dwelt on Ruth in her veil and shawl and stayed there. He didn't say anything, but surprise passed across his face. He turned back to Abenadar and nodded to him, then stepped out of the room. Abenadar could hear his progress through the gates and on to the Praetorium.

After Iulius Valens departed, only Gaius and Ruth were left in the room. Abenadar spoke to Gaius. His voice was weak and he lay back with his eyes closed, "Gaius, I want to move back to my house in the city—especially if I have to recuperate for a month."

"It would be easier to take care of you here."

"I would rather have Ruth take care of me, and I don't care much for your stares."

Ruth tried to follow their conversation from her usual place beside the cot. Although she could not understand most of the words, she cocked her head when her name was mentioned.

"Any man would rather have Ruth care for him. She is a beautiful whore."

"She is no whore," snapped Abenadar.

Gaius still grinned. "She is beautiful and your relationship peculiar. Do you lead a double life? A family from the marketplace and the Legatus Legionis visits you. The highest of the high and the lowest of the low." Gaius shook his head. "Were you foolish enough to marry the girl?"

"No. We have an agreement."

"That's good. I thought you were getting soft."

"Say that in a month and I will humble you with the gladius, pila, and scutum."

"Ha, we shall see."

"Back to my main problem; how do I get out of here? I want to go to my house."

"The Primus would have to agree."

"Well then, ask him for me. You can leave me for a little while."

"My men would never forgive me. And you might take advantage of this young woman."

"Send for the Primus, then."

"All in good time. All in good time."

After a few days of Abenadar's complaints Gaius and Cerus together obtained the Primus' permission to let Abenadar convalesce in his home. "There are conditions," said Gaius, counting them off on his fingers, "First, the legion will provide a guard for you wherever you go. Second, for at least a month, you must stay away from the duties of the camp. And third, so they can report on your condition to the Primus, at least once a day, you must check with the guards in front of your house."

Abenadar only protested a little.

Gaius said, "Your century and mine would have provided guards if the Primus hadn't ordered it. After the pronouncement of the Legatus, you can expect to be escorted in the city until he leaves or you are transferred."

They made an interesting procession through the marketplace. On Abenadar's right and left walked Gaius and Cerus. Ruth followed just behind him. In front and behind marched two sets of guards. Abenadar needed little help to make the short walk, but Gaius and Cerus held his elbows to ensure he didn't take a misstep.

The procession finally arrived at the small house across from Ya'akov's. At the house awaited another surprise. Yotam, Ya'akov, and their families all waited at the entrance to greet him. Sela had kindled a hearty fire on the hearth. Yotam provided beer, hummus, and bread for everyone, including the Roman soldiers. Half the men retired to Yotam's Inn, where the old man made back more than double his slight investment. The others returned to the camp. Cerus and Gaius laid Abenadar like an old woman on his bed, and in front of the house, they stationed a guard of four legionnaires.

Gaius and Cerus saw that Ruth had everything she needed—bandages, food, wine—then, in a cheerful mood, they also retired to Yotam's Inn.

Abenadar stretched out on the bed. He glanced possessively at Ruth as she busily put her house in order, and he smiled.

Ascribe to Adonai the glory due his name;
bow down to Adonai in the splendor of holiness.
Adonai of glory thunders:
the voice of Adonai echoes over the waters,
Adonai is over the mighty waters.

Psalm 29:2-3

Nineteen

For days, until Abenadar regained enough strength to get out into the marketplace, he stumbled around the house like a caged bear. After he could get out, leaning on Ruth's arm and with his guard in tow, he trudged restlessly through the foreign quarter. But the crowded city didn't give Abenadar the freedom and exercise he desired. When he finally felt strong enough to travel for a distance, he said to Ruth, "Is the Immerser still at Beit-Anyah beyond Yarden?"

"Yes, my lord. Sela told me, yesterday, he still waits by the river."

"Then let's go today." Abenadar sat up at the table.

"Are you well enough?" Ruth came over to him. "The Yarden is over 15 miles away."

"Yes, I can make it. If I get tired, I'll lean on you."

"Where will we stay the night?"

"In Yericho on this side of the Yarden."

"What about the legionnaires?" she said.

"I don't think I can keep them from following. I'm sure they'll come to guard us. They won't be very good conversationalists, but they are excellent companions. Now, no more discussion." Abenadar smiled. "I want to stretch my muscles, and I want to see this peaceful prophet."

Still not fully convinced of the wisdom of traveling all the way to Biet-Aynah with a convalescing centurion, Ruth just nodded. She put on her fine blue robe, shawl, and a veil. Abenadar wore a simple Roman tunic and belt. Around his neck, he placed a golden torque of rank. When they were ready to leave the house, Abenadar spoke to the principalis in charge of the guard. "We are going to Yericho and then on to Bethany beyond the Jordan River. Give our itinerary to Centurion Gaius and draw a ration for your men. I will feed you during the days we are gone so you needn't worry about carrying a full kit." The principalis left immediately and, after about half an hour, returned with Gaius beside him.

"Come in, Gaius," called Abenadar through the open door.

Gaius stepped into the house. "Where do you think you are going, Abenadar?"

"We are going to see a prophet."

"A prophet? And where is this prophet?"

"In Bethany on the other side of the Jordan River."

"Will you be safe there?"

"We have a cohort at Cyprus by Yericho. We will lodge in Yericho. It's a walled city, and the land is quiet. You needn't worry about us. Or if you like, you can come with us. Come see the prophet for yourself."

"I cannot come with you, or I would. But I have no desire to see another prophet. I have seen enough of these Judean prophets," he spat.

"This is supposed to be a different kind of prophet."

"For your sake, and mine, I hope he is. Cecilius Bassus will have my head if you don't return as healthy as when you left."

"We will be back in a few days, and I promise, I will return healthier than when I left."

"If you don't, be sure I will come looking for you. You still haven't made good on your promise to best me in 'gladius, pila, and scutum.'"

"Soon, soon," said Abenadar as he stood. Abenadar motioned to Ruth, and she followed him through the door.

In the courtyard, Abenadar took Ruth's arm and the guards immediately fell into step behind them. Gaius paced beside Ruth and Abenadar as far as the Praetorium. When Gaius turned onto the street that fronted the camp, he saluted Abenadar, and with a rueful shake of his head, returned to his duties.

Ruth, Abenadar, and the legionnaires continued straight toward the fish gate. With more caution than he thought necessary, Abenadar kept to the main streets and the major thoroughfares of the city. Yerushalayim had been quiet a long time, but for Ruth's sake, he didn't want to tempt either his enemies or those of Rome. He still wondered about the attack against him. Fabius' suicide seemed to end the matter, but the men who'd attacked him were never captured. And Fabius' death may have been unrelated to the attack. Abenadar could imagine his many enemies among the Blue Shawls and other Zealots. Any of them would fight for the honor of leaving him dead in the street.

The small group exited the city through the Fish Gate. To the east, the road crossed the Valley of Kidron and ascended the Mount of Olives. On this side of the valley, the olive trees were in full bloom; they covered the hillsides with a bright green and white carpet. The morning air was still chilly. Ruth shivered under the shade of the trees until they topped the mount and came out into the full light of the sun. As soon as they crossed the Mount of Olives, the road began its decline through the mountains into the valley of the Yarden River.

Not many people traveled the roads with them. Today was neither the day before Shabbat nor the day after. It was not a market day, and the farmers had only begun cultivating their crops. Ruth pranced next to Abenadar. In her excitement to get to Beit-Anyah, she almost pulled him along. The legionnaires marched stolidly behind them. In the presence of the Centurion Abenadar, they kept their silent decorum as though that were an honor itself. The few people that passed them stared at the strange group on its way to Beit-Anyah: a finely dressed woman of Y'hudah in a veil and shawl, a richly dressed Roman centurion, and four Roman Legionnaires. But for the veil, they might have guessed Ruth a slave or a concubine.

As the day wore on, the sun rose warmly, and the miles seemed to melt underfoot. After weeks of inactivity, Abenadar reveled in the freedom and exercise. He felt elation as the sun and wind caressed his new scars. He strode out once more with the confidence of a free man.

Ruth was the first to show any weariness. Her ardor was undiminished, but she wasn't used to long journeys. After midday, they rested about every hour, but they still reached Yericho early in the afternoon. Far below them, dotted with forest, spread the Valley of the Yarden. In its center, a solid line of trees and greenery outlined the slovenly track of the river.

Abenadar led them into the city and almost immediately found an inn that would accept them. The atmosphere of the whole city seemed more like Sepphoris than Yerushalayim.

Ruth was amazed; in the inn, the legionnaires broke their bread on the bare floor while she and Abenadar sat on cushions and ate at a table. She and Abenadar slept in a private room on a soft bed; the legionnaires kept a vigilant guard outside. Ruth guessed they took turns sleeping—keeping a pair on guard throughout the night.

In the morning, from the innkeeper, Abenadar obtained directions to Beit-Anyah beyond Yarden. They left the city by the Yarden Gate and continued down into the valley.

The way to Beit-Anyah was easy. Not long after they entered the valley, they came within sight of the Yarden River. Past the second turn in the road, the village of Beit-Anyah appeared on the other side of the water. Ruth leaned forward in her eagerness.

Almost as a guess, Abenadar asked her, "Have you been outside the walls of Yerushalayim?"

She stared out across the valley. "Not since I came there with my family."

"Where do you think we will find Yochanan the Immerser?"

"Sela says he stays where the Yarden joins with a wadi and a stream. The bed of the Yarden flattens out there. He makes his camp on the banks on the other side of the Yarden River."

As they approached the river, the trees and undergrowth thickened on either side of the thin road. Here, the thoroughfare was barely clear of brush, and ahead of them, the road turned sharply to the north. As they made the bend, the trees fell away, and before them flowed the Yarden River, golden and sparkling in the morning sun. Along the bank, marked by hundreds of footprints, the dusty road became a quagmire of drying and sodden mud. The ground was so torn up they could no longer determine the boundaries of the road. The fan of muddy soil stretched straight down the bank to the water's edge. It sliced through a thick hedge of reeds and formed a clear a wide spot on the closer bank of the river. The Yarden was deep here—at least now. At this place, it carved a partial pool about 30 feet wide and, because of the muddy water, an indeterminate depth. North of the pool, the river spread out into a shallow ford about fifty feet wide, where the water flowed less than a yard deep.

A large flat rock stood in the center of the pool. Its top reached nearly two feet above the water's surface, and on the rock sat a very unusual man. He wore an undressed camel hair tunic with a thick leather belt. His hair reached to his waist, and a leather headband pulled it away from his forehead. He kept nothing else with him, neither a staff nor a bag, and he appeared to be asleep or praying.

"Do you think that is Yochanan the Immerser?" Abenadar whispered to Ruth.

"I don't know, but he certainly looks like a prophet."

"Shall I ask him?" Without waiting for her answer, Abenadar stepped to the bank and called to the man, "Are you Yochanan the Immerser?"

The man on the rock opened his eyes and searched around. His gaze settled on Abenadar. He didn't seem surprised that a well-dressed Roman spoke to him in Aramaic. "I am Yochanan Ben-Z'kharyah, sometimes called the Immerser."

On either side of the pool, men as raggedly dressed as Yochanan stood up in the high grass. At the sight of the legionnaires, a couple of them immediately began to run. They splashed noisily across the ford and scurried up the eastern bank toward the village on the other side. They were quickly lost to sight among the brush and trees,

A few of the men stared with resigned expressions at Abenadar, Ruth, and the legionnaires. Four others waded into the pool and, with arms linked, formed a ragged wall in front of the Immerser. One of their number called out, "Are you soldiers from Herod? Have you come to take our rabbi?"

Another man on the bank said to him, "Look at them, Andrew. They are Romans. Since when does Pilate carry out Herod's bidding?"

"All the same...," said Andrew.

Yochanan interrupted them. "Draw aside, you foolish talmidim. The man speaks to us in the tongue of Y'hudah. He cannot harm me unless Adonai, blessed be He, allows it. Step aside, Andrew. Step aside, all of you."

Then he spoke directly to Ruth and Abenadar. "Come forward,

friends of Y'hudah. Who are you? What do you wish from me?"

At the prophet's rebuke, his talmidim slunk off like beaten curs and disappeared again into the brush at the far side of the stream. From the reeds, Abenadar still felt their steady gaze on him. The legionnaires remained relaxed but alert. Abenadar's guard was made up of good soldiers, cautious and ready. They understood none of the discussion, but they read the threat of Yochanan's talmidim.

"I am Abenadar, Centurion of the Primus Hastatus Century, VI Ferrata Legion."

"And the woman?"

Abenadar stared at Yochanan in confusion for a moment. He saw no harm in telling the prophet her name. "She is called Ruth."

"Come closer." Yochanan motioned with his finger.

Abenadar and Ruth stepped to the edge of the water. Yochanan sat motionless on the rock. He wasn't an ugly man, or malformed. He did not look insane or foolish. His appearance was nothing like the rebel leaders Abenadar had killed or captured. The Zealots were defiant and full of their own boasting. Still…Abenadar felt uncomfortable under the man's gaze. Yochanan didn't seem to weigh them with his look, but rather, Abenadar sensed a presence greater than any of them.

"So you are a prophet, Yochanan?"

"Perhaps I am a prophet. I have been called a prophet. I am not sure myself. I know I am a Nazerite—" he fingered his long locks—"I do not cut my hair. My lips do not touch wine. I proclaim a great proclamation…"

"What do you proclaim?"

Yochanan's voice took on an increased intensity. His eyes seemed to bore into them. "I am the voice of someone crying out: In the desert prepare the way for Adonai! Make the paths straight for Him!"

"That is all?"

Yochanan roared out a hearty laugh. "No, not all. I proclaim that to prepare yourself for the coming of Adonai, you must confess your sins, turn to Adonai, blessed be He, and be cleansed from your sins by this sign: immersion in water."

"You believe this?"

"Believe it? I know it. It is the Word of Adonai, blessed be He."

"Look at him, Abenadar."

Abenadar studied the Immerser more closely. "What do you see, Ruth?"

"In his eyes, his face, he has the Ruach HaKodesh upon him."

"The Ruach HaKodesh, what is that?"

"The Spirit of Adonai, blessed be He."

Yochanan said, "You are very wise, Ruth. For truly it has been said that the Ruach HaKodesh is upon me. Now, tell me, Ruth, who are you?"

Abenadar realized the direction of Yochanan's words and said more fiercely than he meant to, "You needn't answer him, Ruth."

She glanced up at Abenadar. "I know, but I want to."

"Then, if you will answer," said the Immerser, "who are you, Ruth?"

She looked around her. The legionnaires and Yochanan's talmidim stood too far away to hear. "I am a woman of the streets. I live with Abenadar."

"You are true to him, I see."

"I am bound to him."

"You are both from the Galil and of our people. Confess your sins, turn to Adonai, blessed be He, and I will immerse you. You will then be ready for the coming of Adonai."

"How did you know we are from the Galil?" said Abenadar.

"It doesn't take a prophet to know when a man speaks with the accent of his country. I am myself from the Galil. Your accents are slight, but not imperceptible. Ruth, my sister, will you confess, repent, and be immersed?"

"I wish to be...that is, if Abenadar will permit it."

"If that is your desire, Ruth."

"Will you also prepare yourself, Abenadar?" said Yochanan.

"I don't think so. Not now."

"Very well." The Immerser stepped into the river. The muddy water rose above his waist. He reached his hand out to Ruth. She grasped his outstretched fingers and stepped into the water beside him. "Are you confessing your sins, and have you turned your heart toward Adonai, blessed be He?"

"Yes," answered Ruth, trembling.

"I immerse you as a sign; make straight the way for Adonai." With these words, Yochanan gently submerged Ruth for a moment and then brought her back up out of the water.

Ruth rose out of the Yarden sodden, but exuberant. A large smile enveloped her features with a light as bright as the sun.

As Abenadar reached down to help Ruth back onto the bank, he asked Yochanan, "What does it mean?"

Yochanan turned his face toward Abenadar. "When a man decides to join our people, he is immersed at the temple as a sign that he is cleansed. With this sign, he becomes one of us. My immersion initiates you into a new relationship with Adonai, blessed be He. This symbol reminds the Children of Avraham where they come from and where they are going. Are you sure, Abenadar, that you do not want to join with Ruth?"

"Not now." Abenadar cast his eyes across the river. "There doesn't seem to be a great demand for your services today."

"Adonai, blessed be He, granted me the opportunity to proclaim my message to you, but you are right. The pilgrims do not favor this day. The days before and after Shabbat are the most popular. And the crowds have become less, but I cannot move on yet."

"Why not?"

"Adonai, blessed be He, directs my steps and my days. He has not told me to go yet."

Ruth carefully wrung out the dripping ends of her dress.

"Are you ready to leave, Ruth?" asked Abenadar.

"Yes, my lord. I have seen what we came to see. Thank you, Yochanan the Immerser."

"You are welcome, Ruth, the blessed." He turned to Abenadar, "Will you come again?"

Abenadar glanced again over the banks of the Yarden. People began to gather near the ford. "I think your crowds have finally made their way here."

Yochanan turned his head. "Yes, they are coming."

Abenadar gazed at Ruth. She smiled back at him, then spoke again to the prophet. "One last thing, sir. What should I do now?"

As though his thoughts were suddenly preoccupied, Yochanan said, "Do not go back to your previous life. Do not sin. Hold to your companion, Abenadar. Share with those who have needs. This is an easy saying…but difficult to put into practice."

Yochanan's words were mesmerizing. Abenadar read the truth in them. He said almost without thinking, "What should I do?"

"If you will not be immersed, my injunction is the same. Do not sin. Hold to Ruth, it is only right. Share with those who need. You are a soldier. Don't unnecessarily intimidate anyone, don't accuse anyone falsely, and be satisfied with your pay. Don't threaten others to take money from them."

"I can and have done this."

"Follow the Law, my friend. Perhaps you are not as far from repentance as you believe."

"Perhaps not."

Abenadar grasped Ruth's hand and drew her back to the road. When he turned back, many people flocked toward Yochanan. They fought for his and for his talmidim's attention.

Yochanan shook his head and jumped back on his stone. He called out to the people, "Listen, listen to the Word of Adonai. I am the voice of one crying out: in the desert make the way of Adonai straight! Confess your sins, repent, and be immersed. Be cleansed. Be prepared for the coming of Adonai." Yochanan stopped speaking. He stared intently through the crowd. Everyone, including Ruth and Abenadar, followed his gaze. Then Yochanan stretched out his hands. His eyes reflected an inner light. "The one I told you about yesterday." Yochanan pointed into the throng. "Among you stands someone you don't know. He is the one coming after me. I'm not good enough even to untie his sandals."

A man separated himself from the crowd.

"Look!" Yochanan said. "Look! Adonai's lamb! The one who is taking away the sin of the world! This is the man I was talking about when I said after me is coming someone who has come to rank above me, because he existed even before me."

The man walked slowly toward Yochanan. He was of middle height with the coloring of a man of the Galil. His beard was full and as dark as his hair. He appeared mature, but not old. His shoulders were wide and his hands gnarled as though he worked with them. Abenadar thought he recognized the man, but he couldn't remember where he might have seen him. He was too far away to know for sure.

A smile played across the man's features, not as if to dispute Yochanan's appraisal but as though there was nothing else to say.

Yochanan jumped down from the rock and ran to meet the man. Yochanan would have gone to his knees, but the water was too deep. Instead he bowed, and his face almost touched the surface of the river.

The man put his hands on Yochanan's shoulders and lifted him up.

Yochanan held his eyes downcast. "You are coming to me? I ought to be immersed by you!"

The man spoke to Yochanan. His voice sounded deep and resonant. "Let it be this way now, because we should all do everything righteousness requires."

With Yochanan, the man waded into the deeper water. Yochanan immersed him as he had Ruth.

As the man came up out of the water, the sun blazed, and at the same time the clouds tore open. Yochanan stepped to the side and stood staring—dumbfounded. The sunlight illuminated the man alone. Abenadar covered his eyes because of the brilliance.

Ruth pointed excitedly up into the sky. In the shaft of sunlight, a flickering, white creature flitted down toward them. It fell fluttering like a falling bird. As the creature approached the man in the water, it slowed and landed gently on his head.

The place swirled with a panoply of sounds. The noise reverberated like thunder, but it clearly formed words. In the language of Y'hudah, Ruth and Abenadar heard, "This is my Son, whom I love; I am well pleased with him."

A burst of light flashed from the head of the man.

Abenadar's face was struck with amazement. He clung to Ruth's arms. "Who is this man?"

Ruth smiled broadly. "Could he be the one we have been looking for? Could he be the messiah?"

Abenadar stood straighter. "Nothing more than a trick of the sunlight—the sound of the river." He said more loudly, "Another messiah. He is nothing more than another bar-Abba to quell. Let's go, Ruth."

Abenadar turned around. The legionnaires cowered at the edge of the brush. Their eyes whirled with fear. Under Abenadar's scrutiny, with chagrin, they came to attention. Abenadar walked past them and headed back up the road to Yericho. Ruth rushed to catch up with him.

Ruth slowly dried out as they made their way back up the road to Yericho. Her clothing was splattered with mud, and her hair saturated with it, but she didn't seem to notice. She ignored the stares of the passersby as they made their way back through the city. Some of the stares were full of understanding—many recognized the immersion of Yochanan.

When they returned to the inn, Ruth changed into a borrowed robe, and Abenadar sent out her dress, shawl, and veil for the innkeeper to clean. A woman from the inn brought a large bowl and pitcher of water. As Ruth scrubbed her hair, the woman poured clear water over it. Ruth kept her eyes open while the water poured in a second immersion over her head. The mud drained in clearing rivulets from her locks. *Just like my sin when I turned toward my heart toward Adonai, blessed be He,* she thought.

As Ruth fell asleep that night, cradled in Abenadar's arms, she said to him, "Thank you, my lord, for taking us to see Yochanan the Immerser. I am well pleased."

In the darkness, she could hear the mirth in his voice. "I was also pleased. Pleased to see a prophet in Y'hudah who didn't wield a sword." The expression in his voice changed. "Yochanan's words made sense to me. But who is this man he called the Lamb of Adonai?"

The next day Ruth and Abenadar spoke little on the journey back to

Yerushalayim. Their thoughts revolved around the events at the Yarden River.

When they arrived back at their house, Ya'akov, Yotam, and their families waited to greet them. Any pilgrimage was a great blessing. They were full of questions about what had happened, and what Ruth and Abenadar had heard and seen.

"Come to my inn," said Yotam. "You shall eat and drink with my family and we will hear about everything you saw."

All of them were astonished when Abenadar told what happened at the banks of the Yarden. They compelled him to tell the story more than once. Everyone wanted to hear, over and over again, about Yochanan the Immerser and the man he called the Lamb of Adonai.

"Who was this man, this Lamb of Adonai, blessed be He? Could he be the messiah we are expecting?" Yotam asked.

"I am not in favor of messiahs, especially ones with swords," said Abenadar. "I have killed too many of them."

"Then may he be a messiah without a sword." Yotam raised his cup. "Then we can all be happy."

The next day Abenadar returned to his duty as the Centurion of the Primus Hastatus Century. At muster, the men greeted him enthusiastically. He only limped a little; the wound in his thigh had not healed as quickly as his head and chest. The injury had damaged the same thigh he'd wounded in the fight with Balim. Abenadar expected his leg to improve with exercise.

Optio Cerus trained the century well. When Abenadar put them through their paces, he rejoiced with their progress. They were almost the force he expected them to be.

Even in the camp, Abenadar couldn't shake his guards. Like hovering wraiths, they followed him from one place to another. Eventually, every night, they ended up outside his house in the city.

That night Ruth lit the Shabbat lamps just as Abenadar entered their house. His dinner was still warm in the pot by the hearth. Except for the constant ache in his thigh, his life was the same as it had been before the riot in the city, before the morning ambush, before their pilgrimage to see the Immerser.

Then Abenadar caught sight of the look in Ruth's eyes. Something was not the same. A joy infused her that he did not share. He realized that in his success as a man and a legionnaire, an element was missing. Something he knew he could not discover by himself, and Ruth had found it before him. Perhaps he was too hardened by his life as a soldier of Rome, but surely Ruth knew more of life's harshness than he.

Tonight Abenadar said the blessings and the Kiddush with more feeling than he had in the past, and in Ruth's face, he saw she was pleased.

Thou hast no delight in sacrifice;
if I brought thee an offering,
thou wouldst not accept it.
My sacrifice, O Adonai, is a broken spirit;
a wounded heart, O Adonai,
thou wilt not despise.

Psalm 51:16-17

Twenty

Ruth's face, outlined by the firelight, turned expectantly toward Abenadar. "Have you heard, my lord, he is here in the city?" Ruth raised to one knee.

"Who is in the city?"

"The Lamb of Adonai. He has come for the Pesach. I even heard his name."

Abenadar lay on the cushions beside their table. "How do you know all this?"

"The man came to the Temple when I went with Yotam and Sela to buy the lamb for Pesach."

"How did you know he was the one we saw at the Yarden?"

"I recognized his face. He stood not more than a few yards from me. He is just one man." Ruth grinned. "One man, and his talmidim stood back as if he embarrassed them. He chased the merchants out of the market in the Temple. He shooed them out like you would shoo chickens from a house. The very lamb Yotam bargained for rushed ahead of its master from the Temple. They all did. You should have seen the merchants. They all chased their animals or scrambled for their money. And the cohanim and P'rushim couldn't do a thing about it. The people were already angry at the price of an approved Pesach lamb this year." Ruth brought Abenadar a bowl of thick stew and a couple of flat pieces of bread. "I already discarded the leaven," she said.

Ruth ate at the hearth while Abenadar lay at the table. After a moment, he said to her, "Come sit by me, Ruth, and tell me more about what you saw today."

Ruth moved to the table. She was pleased. She sat cross-legged on a cushion at Abenadar's side. "His name is Yeshua."

"Another Yeshua." Abenadar shook his head. "What is the rest of his name?"

"I don't know. I never heard it spoken. They just called him Yeshua."

"Did he carry a knife—or his talmidim?"

"No, my lord, they had nothing. Even their clothing was threadbare."

"Good. That is the best kind of prophet: no weapons and no money." He waved a piece of the unleavened bread at her. "Lack of bread keeps a man weak, and he won't fight. Give him bread and he won't think of anything else. Did Yotam get his lamb?"

"Oh yes, my lord, a fine one, just large enough. There will be plenty for all of us and nothing left over."

"Tomorrow, Ruth, I want to see this man, Yeshua. Where do you think I will find him?"

"Surely near the Temple. He came to the court of the Goyim today."

"Then tomorrow I will seek for him there."

Ruth stared up at Abenadar with fearful awareness. "You will not arrest him, will you?"

"No. No, I don't think so. That depends on this Yeshua. If he plays the hammer, I will show him a Roman gladius."

The next morning Abenadar took two columns from his century to the Temple. He didn't have to worry about seeking anywhere else in the city for Yeshua. To Abenadar, it seemed like half the city gathered in the Temple to see the man. Across the court of the Goyim, both the sick and the whole watched expectantly for the prophet, Yeshua, to appear. When Abenadar and his legionnaires entered the court, the crowd became so agitated that Abenadar took his men up into the tower of Antonia.

Abenadar watched from the top of the tower until he observed a large commotion in the crowd. The people moved in a wave toward the massive doors of the Temple. Like a single being, they reached out to the entrance. By the response of the crowd, Abenadar could mark the movements of the man as he traveled through the throng. When the motion stopped near the center of the court, Abenadar took four men and left the rest with Cerus.

This time, in the Court of the Goyim, the people ignored Abenadar and his men. They were too interested in seeing the prophet, Yeshua. Abenadar pushed his way closer and closer to the center of the crowd. The people were expectant and excited. After about half an hour, Abenadar advanced nearly within sight of the man. Soon Abenadar swept through the last row of people and came almost face to face with him.

This was obviously the Yeshua Ruth spoke about. He was, without a doubt, the one they saw at the Yarden River. Yeshua was dressed in a coarse wool robe that was bleached a dirty white. His face, hands, and speech all branded him a man of the Galil. Behind him bunched a dirty assortment of talmidim. They seemed harmless, and there were few of them. But external appearances did not prepare Abenadar for the presence of Yeshua. What the man did told Abenadar that he indeed watched Yeshua, the man the people called the Lamb of Adonai.

In front of Yeshua stood a man with an arm so withered it resembled a knotted stick.

"Reach out your arm," invited Yeshua. It was the same voice Abenadar remembered at the Yarden. Even the voice seemed familiar to Abenadar.

The man stretched his crumpled claw toward Yeshua. Yeshua took the hand between his own. He said some words so quietly they were lost in the din of the crowd. As Abenadar watched, the arm became whole. This was like nothing Abenadar had ever seen before. Right before his eyes, the man's arm began to fill out into a more natural shape. The flesh turned pink with life. The man, now healed, stared at his arm in disbelief. He opened and closed the fist and spread out the fingers. He raised his open hand toward the Holy Place and shouted, "Adonai be praised, blessed be He." Then he fell to the ground in front of Yeshua.

Yeshua gently raised the man to his feet. "Go, my friend. Adonai has given you the gift of a whole arm. Use it to lift up others."

Abenadar's attention focused completely on the events before him. He didn't immediately perceive the discomfort of his men. They bunched directly behind him, but Abenadar didn't feel any threat in the crowd. The people were here to see this Yeshua; they didn't notice the legionnaires. Abenadar realized the power of Yeshua disturbed his men.

As Abenadar watched, Yeshua healed one person after another. He spoke encouragement to everyone. Abenadar lingered for almost an hour, but he didn't see another healing as astounding as the stick-like arm that became whole. All the while Yeshua told the people, "The Kingdom of Adonai is at hand."

Abenadar had seen enough. This Yeshua and his talmidim did not seem like threats to him. They might threaten the cohanim and the P'rushim but not the authority of Rome. Abenadar motioned to his men and turned to make his way back to the tower. Perversely, he cast back for a last glimpse of the prophet.

At that moment, Yeshua glanced up at Abenadar and their eyes met. Yeshua smiled. Recognition enveloped his expression, and Abenadar thought, for a moment, he knew the man. But no, he rejected the notion. He didn't have any idea who Yeshua could be. With an arrogant tip of his chin, Abenadar followed his men through the crowd and back to the tower of Antonia.

That evening, at Yotam's Inn, Ruth and Abenadar ate the Pesach with Yotam and Ya'akov's families. The blood of the lamb marked all three of their doorways. As they lay at the table, Yotam said to Abenadar, "My lord, what do you think of this new prophet in Yerushalayim?"

"You mean Yeshua? The man who infuriated the cohanim and Tz'dukim by throwing the merchants out of the court of the Temple?"

"Yes, the same."

"I saw him myself today. He is as disheveled as Yochanan the Immerser. He and a good many of his talmidim look and speak like they come from the Galil."

"From the Galil. Who ever heard of a prophet from the Galil?" Yotam raised his arms, then lowered them. "Yet I heard that he healed people."

"He did heal them." Abenadar's throat was dry. "I saw him heal many."

"Another charlatan."

Abenadar took a drink of wine to moisten his throat. "No, whatever he is, I don't think he is a fraud. I saw a man's arm turn from a stick to be as whole as his other arm."

"You saw this?"

"Today, in the Temple. I saw it myself."

"Could this man be the messiah, the Lamb of Adonai?" Yotam wondered aloud.

"I don't know. Yochanan the Immerser said he was. This Yeshua heals the sick and chases the merchants out of the Temple. What else would a prophet do?"

No one spoke.

Abenadar glared around the table. "Yes. Yes, I know what you are thinking. The Lamb of Adonai will drive the Romans out of Y'hudah, but that is not possible for this prophet or any prophet. He would be crushed like meal between the stones."

"But," said Yotam, "what if he were the Lamb of Adonai? He could do anything."

"He doesn't seem like a warlike prophet," said Abenadar.

"What else could a prophet do?"

"He could save his people," said Abenadar. "But the problem for every man is, what is salvation?"

"For the people of Y'hudah, it is written: salvation is the land," said Yotam.

"But, for all men, including the Goyim, salvation is shalom."

"You speak wisely, friend. Salvation is shalom."

"Shalom," said each of them, even the children.

They passed the evening together. Ruth and Abenadar didn't leave until the sun of the Shabbat illuminated the small courtyard between their houses.

Ruth and Abenadar slept until the sun was well up in the marketplace. The streets were very quiet; many stayed late at their Pesach feast.

Ruth and Abenadar lay close to one another on the small cot until the persistent sunlight, dancing across their eyes, made it too uncomfortable to rest there. The room was still warm, though the usual Shabbat brassier did not heat the hearth.

Ruth rolled from under the covers before him and slipped into her light robe. Abenadar stretched and followed her. He wrapped the blanket around his shoulders and sat on the cushions at the table. Abenadar said a blessing and broke off a piece of the unleavened loaf that still sat there.

"I have figs and cheese," said Ruth from the hearth.

"I am not hungry." Abenadar took another piece of bread.

Ruth peered at Abenadar, pursed her lips in a pensive smile, then turned back to the hearth. "Shoshanah is pregnant again. She was showing last night."

"I didn't notice. Tell her and Ya'akov shalom for me."

Ruth's expression grew serious. She came over to the table and sat across from him. "You and I have been together for more than a year." She gazed down at her slim body. "I would have hoped...that I would have conceived by now."

"You would like a child?"

"Yes! A child." She reached toward him. "Wouldn't you like a child?"

Abenadar did not know what to say.

She stared disapprovingly into his face.

"I have not thought about it," he said.

"How could you have never thought about it? The very thought has been on my mind from the first day we—"

Abenadar cupped her chin with his hand. "Have you never conceived before?"

Ruth jerked her head back and slapped away his hand. "I traded my body for money. Not my womb."

"I'm sorry," he said. "I didn't mean to insult you."

She held her head in her hands. "Should I have starved in the street or sold myself into slavery?"

"I'm sorry, Ruth. Because of who you were, I am with you. I praise Adonai everyday, blessed be He, that you are here in my house. I wish you had never faced the life you did. But if you hadn't, I would never have known you."

She softened slightly. "I thank Adonai also… Oh, I am a fool. I have been given so much, but it never seems like enough. It is a sin to want a child when I have everything I ever desired before. But I cannot stop thinking about this. It is a curse on me."

He shrugged. "If it is a curse, it is a curse on us."

Ruth went back to sit by the hearth—as if that was now the warmest place in the suddenly cool house.

Abenadar took another bite of bread. "I did not want to tell you yesterday, but you will hear of it in the marketplace soon. Yochanan the Immerser was arrested a few days ago."

"Surely not by the Romans?"

"No, Herod sent his soldiers."

Ruth's voice, already harsh with angry introspection, dripped with bitterness. "Was the Immerser's message too defiant?"

"No, Yochanan the Immerser told Herod the truth. He advised him that by living with Herodias, the wife of his brother Philip, Herod violated the Torah."

"For that, Herod put the prophet in prison? Because a servant of Adonai said Herod broke the Law of Adonai, Herod bound the servant in chains. If Herod worried so much about Adonai, he would be more afraid of putting His prophet in prison."

"Herod fears no man or god. Herod fears the people. Insurrection is his worry and the people his greatest dread. The people respect the Law and the words of the Immerser. Herod believes that by locking the prophet away, he can make the people forget both his indiscretions and Yochanan's words. But he will find that the people have long memories and that peaceful prophets with hard words are always more desirable than warlike messiahs with iron knives."

Ruth came back to the table. "I'm glad you told me this. It saddens me, but it is better than hearing half the story in the marketplace and wondering all day long. Will Herod also take away the prophet, Yeshua?"

"If I were Yeshua, I would not mention Herod's name aloud, and I would stay well away from the Galil."

"What do you really think about this man, Yeshua?"

Abenadar took her hands in his. "I don't know what to think. Is he a prophet? I think he may be, but I don't know what a prophet really is."

"What would you do, my lord, if he were a prophet?"

"Are you asking me if I would follow him? I don't think I would. If that meant being a dirty talmidim sneaking behind him in the streets, the answer is no."

"David was a king and a warrior, yet he followed Adonai, blessed be He."

"I follow Adonai also. I am not always sure what that means, but I follow Him. I believe He led me to you."

"If this Yeshua is the Lamb of Adonai, what then?"

"Who is the Lamb of Adonai? I don't know. I don't know what it means."

"Maybe that is enough for now," said Ruth.

Abenadar drew her down beside him. He wrapped the blanket around her as they lay beside the table. They stayed there for a long time, both lost in their own thoughts and each comforted by the closeness of the other.

Blessed is he who comes in the name of Adonai;
we bless you from the house of Adonai.
Adonai has given light to us,
the ordered line of pilgrims by the horns of the altar.

Psalm 118:26-27

Twenty-one

"Ruth," Abenadar greeted her with a smile, "why did you leave your booth for the house?"

All of Y'hudah celebrated the Sukkot, the Feast of Booths. Ruth was living in the small booth Abenadar built for her on the flat roof of their house. He didn't expect to see her inside the house for another day. Abenadar did not celebrate the festival with her, though he slept with her on the roof—for her protection. So he said.

Ruth knelt beside the table. "My lord, the prophet, Yeshua, has returned to the city. Sela told me he is in the Temple now."

"I know. They already tried to arrest him twice during Sukkot."

"Have you?"

"No, Ruth." He chuckled. "The Temple guards. If I went to arrest him, I wouldn't need a second try."

"They haven't arrested him?"

"No, the cohanim and the Temple guards are afraid of the people. Though he speaks to them in riddles, they half believe the man."

"In riddles? His words always seem clear to me. Have you heard, my lord? Does he still work miracles?"

Abenadar stared into space. "Incredible miracles. That's the main reason he cannot be arrested."

"Why do they seek to arrest him anyway?"

"This Yeshua called himself a prophet and a son of the Most High, blessed be He."

"So what is that?" Ruth tossed her head. "He performs more miracles than any prophet I ever heard of."

"I suspect the P'rushim, cohanim, and the Tz'dukim hate him because his wisdom and miracles make them look like fools in comparison."

Ruth nodded. "Will you take me to the Temple now? Today is Hoshana Rabbah, the Day of the Great Hosannah. You haven't celebrated the festival, but I want you to join me when our Covenant with Adonai is restored for the year. And I would also like to see Yeshua again."

"Why not? Surely the man is marvelous to watch."

Ruth leapt up and pulled Abenadar up with her. "Come on then."

Ruth and Abenadar paused only long enough to grab a couple of branches from the booth on the top of their house, then they joined the growing throng of worshipers that headed toward the Temple.

As the crowds made their way to the Temple, they were exuberant. They sang and waved the fresh green branches over their heads. At the Temple, Ruth and Abenadar joined the many who did not or could not enter into the Court of Women. They stood in the Court of the Goyim as close to the entrance to the Court of Women as possible. From there, through the wide spaces between the columns, they could see the Altar and the enclosed Holy Place.

At the Altar, the cohanim beat the last of the leaves from their willow branches. The crowd was exultant. The people moved aside for the cohen who carried the golden ewer filled with water from the Pool of Shiloach. With great dignity, he made his way toward the Altar. The crowd parted before him and reformed behind him. He passed close enough to Ruth and Abenadar that they could see the clear water from the spring in the ewer.

The cohen climbed the Altar and, with majestic formality, poured out the ewer at its base. The people automatically began to sing the Hallel, and almost as an afterthought, the L'vi'im musicians joined them on their flutes.

"Hallelu Yah," sang the L'vi'im.

"Hallelu Yah," repeated the crowd.

"Hallelu, O ye servants of Y'hovah."

"Hallelu Yah."

The Hallel went on and on, and as the crowd recited each stanza of the Psalm, their response swelled louder and louder. At the end, the crowd's reply became a vast roar: "Save now, we beseech Thee, Y'hovah. Hallelu Yah. O Y'hovah, we beseech Thee, send us prosperity.

Hallelu Yah. Blessed be He that comes in the name of Y'hovah. Hallelu Yah."

As the last echo of the words of the Hallel reverberated through the Temple, the people fell on their faces, and the cohanim blew three great trumpet blasts. Compared to the roar of the worshipers, the noise of the trumpets sounded almost muted. The musical blast was the counterpoint that ushered in an unnatural silence. No one moved or said a word. They all waited Adonai's response to the Hallel. In the past, the response always came as the blessing of the Cohen Hagadol, the high priest.

Before the Cohen Hagadol could speak, in that silence, a man stood at the base of the Altar and turned to face the people. He cried out to the crowd. "If anyone thirsts, let him come to me and drink! Whoever puts his trust in me will truly become like the Pool of Shiloach and rivers of living water will flow from his inmost being."

The cohanim at the Altar stood dumbfounded, and with the people, they hung on every word. Everyone in the Temple could clearly hear the voice. The speaker was Yeshua. Abenadar recognized him immediately.

At first, the people were paralyzed. Then as Yeshua stood with his arms outstretched, they spoke to one another in whispers. "Surely this man is the prophet."

"This is the messiah," asserted others.

The cohanim's words were subdued. Almost unheard, they said, "How can the Messiah come from the Galil? Listen to the man's accent. Doesn't the Tanakh say that the Messiah is from the seed of David and comes from Beit-Lechem, the village where David lived?"

But the voice of the people drowned them out. To them the words of Yeshua needed no other explanation. The covenant ceremony focused on Yeshua's words and their import of Adonai's salvation. Without the Cohen Hagadol's blessing, the festival was over, but the people began to leave for their own homes expressing a greater joy that, in their own time, they had witnessed Adonai's revelation.

"Why are you laughing?" said Ruth with a frown at Abenadar.

He grabbed her shoulders and faced her toward the Altar. "Look at the Temple guards and the cohanim."

"They are arguing," she said unfazed.

"Yes, see, while Yeshua leaves with the rest of us, the Temple guards and the cohanim argue about what they should do."

Ruth laughed along with him. "I think the cohanim are arguing among themselves now."

"Come—let's go home or we will be left alone with the cohanim."

As they walked home together, Ruth said, "What do you think Yeshua meant?"

Abenadar thought for a moment. "During Sukkot, the water of Shiloach is the spirit of Adonai poured out on the Altar. Does Yeshua mean he will give this to anyone who asks?"

"That spirit is the Ruach HaKodesh," said Ruth, "the joy of the festival bubbling up like the water in the Pool of Shiloach. Is that what he means—joy? Or is he Adonai? Can he give away the Ruach HaKodesh?"

"I don't know. Perhaps you should ask him yourself," said Abenadar.

"Maybe I will. I will look for him in the Temple tomorrow."

"Take Sela with you. You should not go alone even to the Temple."

"Sundown today is Shabbat. You could take me tomorrow."

"I forgot the days. I will take you."

Abenadar could not keep his promise. Before the next morning was half over, a courier came from the Primus Pilus with a message that ordered him to report to the court in the Praetorium. Iulius Valens presided over the city while Pilate was still in Caesarea.

When Abenadar arrived, the Legatus Legionis was already questioning the Primus. Abenadar joined Cecilius Bassus near the center of the court and saluted Iulius Valens.

"Ah, good," said Cecilius Bassus, "Abenadar is here now. Centurion, the Legatus Legionis wanted some news from the city. Last night marked the end of the festival, right?"

"Yes, Sukkot ended yesterday, Primus," said Abenadar.

Iulius Valens stepped toward the two men. "The Sanhedrin brought word to me that a gross disturbance in the Temple incited the people. They said a rebellious group of Essenes from the Galil caused the disturbance. Abenadar, did you hear anything of this?"

Abenadar laughed out loud. "I was there. I saw it myself."

The Primus and Legatus stared at him in astonishment. "The people didn't attack you during the riot?" said Iulius Valens.

"Anan, the high priest, greatly distorted the matter to you. A single man inspired Anan's complaint. The man made an innocuous statement, then left the Temple. The people appeared neither antagonized nor upset by the proclamation. On the contrary, they seemed to welcome the man's words. But the incident greatly agitated the high priest, the priests, and the Sanhedrin."

"That is an entirely different story than the one Anan conveyed to us."

"What did Anan ask you to do?" said Abenadar.

"He demanded that I arrest a man of the Galil called Yeshua. I told him to arrest the man himself. I advised him that he should have arrested the man himself while he was still in the Temple. After all, Pilate allowed them the Temple guard for just that purpose."

"Because of the people, Anan and the Sanhedrin are afraid to arrest this man, Yeshua," said Abenadar.

"Is that a problem for us?" asked Iulius Valens.

"No. Yeshua is similar to Yochanan, the man Herod put to death. I gauge that, like Yochanan, Yeshua fancies himself a prophet and not a messiah."

"The gods be praised for that," said the Legatus. "Abenadar, how closely do you think we should watch this man?"

"I have already taken care of that, Legatus. I know when Yeshua is in the city, and when he is here, I keep an eye on him. I receive reports on what he is telling the people in the Temple and the marketplace."

"Excellent. That is precisely what I require," said Iulius Valens. "If you believe we need to take action against this man, you may act as necessary to secure the peace of the city. But can you keep a check on this Yeshua outside the bounds of Jerusalem?"

"I generally know where he is when he is in Judea, but I have not kept a close watch on his movements."

"That is sufficient. If you feel we require a more complete observation, you have my permission to proceed as necessary. Abenadar, you may go now. I will report your vigilance to Pilate. He will be pleased."

Abenadar saluted the Legatus and left the court.

That evening, at home with Ruth, Abenadar said nothing of his conversations with the Primus and Legatus about Yeshua. As he ate, he asked her, "Ruth, did you see Yeshua today?"

In the hearth light, her features became ecstatic. "I saw him, and I heard him speak. He taught in the Temple, and the P'rushim could say nothing to refute his words."

"What did Yeshua teach? Did he answer your question?" asked Abenadar.

"He said he will free us from being slaves to sin."

Abenadar grunted. "I am certain the people of Y'hudah didn't like being called slaves or hearing about their sin."

"They said they were not slaves." In embarrassment, she turned away from Abenadar. "But I was a slave to sin—I...I am a slave to sin." Ruth half-reached toward him. "Abenadar, without your help, I could not escape from the streets. I am free from that life, but I am not pure. I am like a gilt idol full of corruption. Yeshua holds out shalom and the Ruach HaKodesh to all people. He holds out shalom to me—to *me*, though I am a woman and a whore. Perhaps he can take away the guilt of my sin." She spoke on without taking a breath. "He said *anyone* who obeys his teaching will not see death."

"How can that be?"

"You were right before, my lord. Many of his words are riddles to me, but I know he speaks of heavenly things and not about the things of this world. He does offer the Ruach HaKodesh."

"But how can he, a man, know about these things? Unless he is Adonai, how can he give the Ruach HaKodesh?"

"My lord." Ruth bowed her head. "I don't know. I only know I believe him. And he said he is the 'I AM.'"

"He said he is Y'hovah!" Abenadar whispered the word and stroked his chin in thought. "The cohanim certainly tried to stone him?"

"Yes, but he disappeared."

"What do you mean?"

"I watched him. One moment he stood in the court, and the next, no one could find him. The crowd was not large, but he couldn't sneak off with so many eyes on him."

"He disappeared into the crowd. He had to."

"Yes, my lord." Ruth bent her head as if struck.

"What else did you hear about this man, Yeshua, today?"

Encouraged by his softer tone, Ruth came closer to Abenadar. "I heard from Sela, he healed a man born blind."

"That is unbelievable, but from what I saw before, how can I doubt it?"

Ruth said, "The P'rushim interrogated the blind man and his parents. They could find no one to refute what happened."

Abenadar chuckled. "They will certainly be arguing among themselves again. As long as that happens, they can do him little harm."

"Do you think Yeshua, the prophet, is safe?"

"Ruth, no prophet is safe."

The short days of the winter completed their course before Yeshua entered Yerushalayim again.

Ruth met Abenadar before he entered their door. "Yeshua is coming to Yerushalayim for the Pesach. Can we go see him enter the city?" asked Ruth, almost dancing in her excitement.

"When?" asked Abenadar.

"Now, my lord. He is coming into the city now. Yeshua is coming from Beit-Anyah, where they say he brought a man back to life." Ruth took Abenadar's hand and hurriedly led him toward the Temple.

On the way Abenadar asked, "This Yeshua raised a man back from the dead?"

"Yes. The man was El'azar, the brother of Marta and Miryam. Even the P'rushim say El'azar was dead. He lay in the tomb for four days, and Yeshua brought him back to life. Can you imagine life forever?"

Abenadar smiled. "How could anyone live forever? The P'rushim and the Sanhedrin will not like this."

"Yeshua defies them outright, but what can they do against him?" said Ruth.

"I will tell you. Pilate is eager to keep the peace, and the Zealots have been quiet for a while. Pilate thinks this is the influence of the Sanhedrin."

"Isn't it?"

Abenadar chuckled. "My patrols keep the peace. When, all the way to Yericho, Y'hudah is safe for the people and their leaders, there is no need for the Zealots. But with a prophet like Yeshua, the Sanhedrin might conclude he is a greater threat to them than the Zealots. Yeshua's problem is that they may convince Pilate that he is a threat. Then Yeshua will become my problem."

"You would arrest him?"

Abenadar shrugged.

Ruth took a shaky breath and changed the subject. "Do you think Yeshua will clear the merchants out of the Temple again?"

"Why not? He has for the last two years."

"Yeshua's actions enrage the Sanhedrin and the P'rushim, but they are powerless before the people. The people love to see him throw out the merchants."

"What is the price of a certified lamb this year?" said Abenadar.

"I don't know. Yotam has not gone to buy it yet."

"You told Sela that we are buying the lamb this year?"

"Yes, and I have everything we need for the day."

"Good, Ruth."

Ruth and Abenadar heard the roar of the crowds long before they arrived at the Temple. As they came closer, they could make out the words. The people recited the Hallel and cried out, "Hallellu Yah, blessed is He who comes in the name of Adonai. Hallellu Yah!"

Ruth and Abenadar fought their way to the head of the throng.

Many people were waving palms and branches. A gesture like a slow-cresting wave moved through the crowd. The words of the Hallel grew louder. Men took off their cloaks and women their shawls. Suddenly, Yeshua appeared, riding on a donkey. Men and women threw their clothing and palm branches before him. People reached out to him, and they all tried to touch him at once.

Yeshua gazed on the crowd with a gentle demeanor, but every now and then a touch of melancholy crossed his features. He smiled at them, and he stretched his hands out to the people; otherwise, he didn't say a word.

At the sight of Abenadar and his guard of legionnaires, Yeshua's talmidim held back in alarm, but Yeshua, unfazed, moved forward without a change in pace. As Yeshua passed, Ruth reached out to him and touched his shoulder. Yeshua himself reached out to Abenadar, and Abenadar took the hand, wondering why Yeshua singled him out.

After that, Yeshua's talmidim continued close behind Yeshua, but they kept a wary eye on Abenadar and the legionnaires. Behind the prophet, Ruth and Abenadar joined the crowd as it wound through the streets toward the Temple.

Above the noise of the crowd, Abenadar said to Ruth, "What does all this mean?"

"I don't know."

"If Yeshua announces he is the king of Y'hudah, that will be the end of him."

"You will arrest him?" Ruth asked.

"There can be no king but Caesar. The Sanhedrin knows that. They will arrest him themselves."

"In the Temple?" said Ruth. "Last time they couldn't manage it."

"They will try."

Ruth's countenance grew more grave. "The people may resist them."

"The people *will* resist them. The Sanhedrin cannot stop Yeshua, and then it will be up to me," said Abenadar sadly.

"Listen to what he says." There was a touch of desperation in Ruth's voice. "You may have no reason to act."

"Yeshua is no fool," Abenadar said with comforting insight. "He will give me no reason to act and that will infuriate the Sanhedrin. They have desired his blood for a long time."

"He is only one man," said Ruth. "A man without weapons and without ambition."

"All men have ambition, and their weapons are ideas. A wise leader doesn't need a sword."

At the broad steps of the Temple, Yeshua brought the donkey to a stop and slid off its back. As if expecting Yeshua to speak, the crowd immediately quieted.

Yeshua didn't disappoint them. He raised his arms. "The time has come for the Son of Man to be glorified. I tell you, unless a grain of wheat falls into the soil and dies, it is just a grain. Only if it dies will it produce a harvest. If you love your life, you will lose it, but whoever hates his life in this world will keep his life safe for eternal life. If someone is serving me, let him follow me; wherever I am, my servant will be there too. My Father will honor anyone who serves me.

"Now I am in turmoil. What can I say—Father, save me from this hour? No, it was for this very reason that I have come to this hour. This is all I need to say: Father, glorify your name!" Yeshua's words utterly held the attention of the crowd. When he stopped speaking, the court was almost silent.

In the stillness, the wind rose up and a voice thundered out of the heavens. The voice was deep, powerful, and hauntingly sad. "I have glorified my name before, and I will glorify my name again!"

No one said a word, then the people began to whisper to each other.

Yeshua said, "This voice from Adonai did not come for my sake, but for yours. Now is the time for this world to be judged. Now the ruler of this world, Satan, will be expelled. As for me, when I am lifted up from the earth, I will draw everyone to myself."

From the crowd a voice called out, "When you are lifted up? The Tanakh tells us that the Messiah remains with us forever. Do you call yourself the Son of Man? How can it be that you will be lifted up? If that is so, then who is this Son of Man?"

Yeshua said, "The light will be with you only a little while longer. Walk in the light while you have the light or the dark will overtake you. If you walk in the dark, you don't know where you are going. While you have the light, put your trust in the light, so that you may become the people of light.

"Those who put their trust in me are trusting not merely in me, but in the One who sent me. And, those who see me, see the One who sent me. I have come as a light into the world, so that everyone who trusts in me might not remain in the dark. If anyone hears what I am saying and does not heed it, I don't judge him. I did not come to judge the world, but to save the world. Those who reject me and don't accept what I say have a judge—the word, which I have spoken, will judge them on the last day. I have not spoken on my own initiative; the Father who sent me has given me a command. He has told me what to speak and his words are those which bring eternal life. What I say is what the Father has told me to say. I AM who I AM."

The crowd gasped in astonishment. "He said the name of Adonai."

Yeshua ignored them. He turned and entered the Temple. The crowd paused, then rushed forward to follow closely behind him. Ruth and Abenadar pushed their way through the crowd and into the Temple, but, all at once, they couldn't find Yeshua. He was not there.

"Where did he go?" asked Ruth.

"I don't know." Abenadar searched over the heads in the crowd. "I can't see him."

In the crowd they heard similar confusion and the refrain, "Where has he gone?" But no one could find Yeshua.

"Could he have been taken by the P'rushim?" said Ruth.

"I don't know. I don't think so. He disappeared on his own, for his own reasons. Let's go home."

"Only one moment more, my lord. Perhaps he will show himself again."

Abenadar snorted. "Even his talmidim are looking for him." He pointed to where the talmidim searched the crowd.

Ruth peered into Abenadar's eyes. "This is just like the other time I told you about. You didn't believe me then."

"I don't know what to believe now."

"But why would he leave so suddenly?" said Ruth.

Abenadar shook his head, and they pushed their way back through the crowd and returned home.

Ruth and Abenadar ate their evening meal in silence. Their thoughts were obvious to each other—and they were the same. Who was this Yeshua who called himself the Son of Man and compared himself with Adonai?

As usual, before the sun came up, Abenadar left for the legion camp. After the morning muster, Cecilius Bassus found him with his century.

"Centurion Abenadar." The Primus took him aside. "As you know, Pilate is in the city for the Judean festival. He heard about the spectacle at the Temple yesterday, and he wants to know more about the prophet, Yeshua."

Abenadar gave command of the century to Cerus and followed the Primus Pilus.

Abenadar and Cecilius Bassus made their way into the Praetorium and to Pilate's court. As soon as they entered, Pilate ordered everyone but his guards and Iulius Valens out of the court. Pilate motioned for Cecilius Bassus and Abenadar to approach, and they went to one knee before the Procurator.

"So Primus, Centurion Abenadar, what is the word in the city? We heard that the prophet Yeshua returned just as we have for the Judean festival." Pilate struck his palm with his baton. "We heard he entered the city like a king."

The Primus signaled Abenadar to speak.

Abenadar said, "Yes, Procurator, Yeshua returned to the city, but he came on a donkey, followed by an army of a dozen ragged men."

Pilate cocked his head. "So you don't think we should be concerned?"

"My patrols watch him and his men. So far, he never speaks to the people of rebellion."

"You are certain of this?"

"I receive reports on his activities and his words. When he is in the city, I keep an eye on him myself."

Pilate motioned with the baton. "The Sanhedrin warn us that this man is a rebel, an Essene, and they disavow any ties to his ideas or actions."

"The Sanhedrin hate him because he makes them look like fools before the people. I think this man is good for us. He captures the attention of the people but resists their attempts to pronounce him anything more thant a prophet."

"I heard he is a miracle worker," said the Primus.

"He is a miracle worker," stated Abenadar.

Pilate stared at him in astonishment. "Surely you jest."

"Not at all, Procurator. I saw him heal a man."

"He actually cures people?"

"I saw him make a withered limb become whole."

Pilate thought for a moment. "There must have been some kind of trickery."

"He accomplished the healing in the middle of a crowd?"

"If it is as you say," said Pilate, "then we have all the more reason to fear him."

Abenadar said, "Or not to fear him. What can we do against him if he has this kind of power?"

Iulius Valens stared first at Abenadar, then the Procurator. "Indeed, what could anyone do to stop him?"

Abenadar continued, "I suggest you let this play out, Procurator. Right now, Yeshua is no threat. In fact, as I said before, he captures the people's attention—at this moment, the people follow him. In time, they will tire of him. The Judean leaders and priests are beside themselves with rage at him, but they have been able to do nothing against him. They will either capture him themselves or ask you to rid them of him. In either case, you maintain control over the leaders and the populace."

Pilate nodded in agreement. "Your words make sense, and you have not been wrong before, Centurion."

Abenadar bowed.

Pilate continued. He spoke into the air. "You, Abenadar, Primus, will continue the patrols in the city. Bring us news of any change in these circumstances." He eyed Abenadar. "What should we do if the

Sanhedrin ask us to rid them of him?"

"Tell them you are watching Yeshua's every move, and that you will protect the city and people with your legion. Then Yeshua will vex them, with your blessing."

Pilate smiled. "Yes, and they will be divided—leaders and people, prophet and priests. Primus!"

"Yes, Procurator."

"The words of your centurion are wise. Let him proceed as he suggests. Centurion Abenadar!"

"Yes, Procurator."

"In this issue, we are reaching a critical juncture with the Sanhedrin, and I don't want to be misunderstood. Because you speak the tongue of these people, we wish you to accompany us during all future interviews with them."

"Should Abenadar remain here in the fortress?" asked the Primus.

"No, Primus. We will call for him when we need him. The Sanhedrin may wait until the centurion is present. Centurion Abenadar has more important duties to accomplish for us in the city. You may go."

Abenadar and the Primus saluted together and left the Procurator's chambers.

They put me to the test and mocked me;
they gnashed at me with their teeth.
O Adonai, how long wilt thou look on?
Rescue me from the roaring beasts,
and my life from the young lions.

Psalm 35:16-17

Twenty-two

Ruth sat at Abenadar's feet while he ate.

"What did you see in the Temple today, Ruth?"

Her smile brightened, "Yeshua taught from the Torah again."

"Did the Sanhedrin and cohanim try to trick him today?"

"Oh yes, my lord, they asked him so many questions, and he answered every one. His answers astounded everyone. Yeshua asked the P'rushim and Tz'dukim some questions in return, but they wouldn't answer him. Eventually, they went away."

"Their patience will not last."

"What do you think they will do?" Ruth watched him closely.

"The Cohen Hagadol will eventually send the Temple guards to take him and that will be the end of it."

"Surely not, my lord."

Abenadar stared into his cup of wine. He started to speak, stopped, then said, "Do you have everything we need for the Pesach?"

"Yes, yes, my lord."

"Don't go to the Temple tomorrow. The prophet, Yeshua, is tempting the Sanhedrin to act. They will not sit still forever."

"Yeshua said as much."

Abenadar tossed back the last of his wine. "Why does he stay in Yerushalayim? He knows only his death will appease them."

"The people will not allow it."

"Pilate will allow it."

"But you have his ear."

"With all the Sanhedrin and cohanim clamoring for the prophet's blood, Pilate will not listen to me."

Ruth stood up to remove the supper bowl. Abenadar grabbed her arm. "You know the words of the prophets, and, like Yochanan the

Immerser, I know this Yeshua will not live to see another Pesach. Ruth, I don't want you caught up in this."

"You are too late, my lord. I am convinced. Yeshua is surely the Messiah."

"What if he dies? Is he still Messiah?"

"Why...I...I don't know."

"Ruth, this man will die—the Sanhedrin and the cohanim will see to that."

Ruth stared at him. "You know this. You know they will capture him." Ruth knelt at his feet again and covered her face with her hands. "When will they come for him?"

"Tomorrow. Tomorrow night, on the mount where he stays with his talmidim. One of his own will betray him."

"One of his own? On the Mount of Olives?" She stared at the floor. "Are you going too? Are you going to capture him at the Mount of Olives?"

"I will be there."

Ruth cradled her head with both hands. "Why are you telling me this, my lord?"

Abenadar didn't say a word.

Under her breath, Ruth said, "Thank you, my lord."

In the morning, as Abenadar readied himself to go to the camp, Ruth dressed in her robe and veil. She fed and kissed him before he went through the door.

When the sun came up, Ruth left to search out Yeshua before he entered the Temple.

At dusk, Abenadar led two columns of his legionnaires to the Temple. The chief cohen of the current levy of L'vi'im, and not the Cohen

Hagadol, intercepted them before they entered the Court of Goyim. He was a sickle-featured man with heavy lidded eyes. As if a single glance would defile him, he gazed everywhere except directly at the Romans. In simple Greek, the cohen said, "You are Centurion Abenadar?"

"Yes," replied Abenadar.

"The Procurator promised the Cohen Hagadol, if your columns escorted our guards, they could leave the Temple with their weapons."

"You have the Procurator's word."

"Will you help us take the criminal, Yeshua from Natzeret?"

From Natzeret, thought Abenadar, alarmed, but he said, "No. This is your business and not ours. I was present when the Procurator made that clear."

"Yes, certainly." The chief cohen motioned toward the door of the Temple. The large door opened again. For a while no one showed at the shadowed opening, then a tall man stepped out. He was dressed like a tradesman from the Galil. His face was intense and hard. His hands did not look like a workman's hands, but neither was his face soft enough to give the impression that he made a living appeasing other men. This man walked over to the chief cohen and looked up and down the columns of legionnaires.

The chief cohen said, "This is Y'hudah ben-Shimon from K'riot. He will lead you to Yeshua from Natzeret. He is one of Yeshua's talmidim." The chief cohen motioned a second time. A tall gray-haired L'vi walked slowly from the shadows by the door. The man was lean, and his features had a hard and wolfish look, but unlike Abenadar's soldiers, his arms were soft and unscarred. He wore a linen robe covered by leather armor. The protection didn't appear more than ceremonial. Abenadar was certain the armor and the man would not hold up against a determined attack. The old soldier seemed less familiar with military training than Abenadar's greenest legionnaire. "This is Captain Natan, the head of the Temple Guard. Natan, you heard the Centurion's reassurances. You may bring out your men."

Natan called out an order, and a troop of 30 guardsmen crept out of the Court and lined up on the steps before the Temple. In a separate crowd, a group of about 20 cohanim and some of their slaves also exited the Temple. They stood milling in a bunch on the far side of the

Temple guards—the side well away from the legionnaires.

The chief cohen spoke to Y'hudah, Yeshua's talmid, in Aramaic, "You have your silver. Take the Temple guard to Yeshua, and be sure the man is delivered to us."

"I will greet Yeshua with a kiss." Y'hudah ben-Shimon turned toward Natan. "You will know the man by my kiss of shalom. Yeshua will suspect nothing. He knows nothing of weapons and fighting." Y'hudah's words were breathy and disdainful. "Except for a few fish knives, his talmidim will not be armed, and they will do nothing to stop you."

The chief cohen turned to Captain Natan. "After you take Yeshua, bring him to Anan's house."

The Temple guard lit their lanterns, and Abenadar signaled his columns to ignite their torches. Y'hudah ben-Shimon led them out of the Temple area and toward the Mount of Olives. The chief cohen, the Temple guard, and the cohanim with their slaves followed him closely. Abenadar and his columns stayed in the rear. The group exited the city at the Eastern Gate and crossed the Kendron on the great bridge. This time of year, the stream of the Kendron formed little more than a muddy rivulet.

As they started up the mount, on either side, olive trees cast fantastic shadows away from their torches. Their march seemed to light up that entire side of the valley.

Abenadar was certain Yeshua would see them coming and flee. He knew Ruth had delivered her warning. Yeshua certainly wouldn't be waiting to be captured.

The Temple guards and cohanim huffed and puffed as they ascended the steep side of the mount. Abenadar was pleased to see his men silent and their breaths unlabored as they climbed. With Yeshua warned, the Temple guard and cohanim would search the Mount of Olives until daybreak and find no sign of the prophet. Yeshua would be well on his way back to Natzeret. Natzeret, thought Abenadar. He knew a Yeshua from Natzeret. Many years separated the last time Abenadar had seen that man, but could this Yeshua be the same person? The prophet resembled his friend, but Abenadar was not sure. Abenadar's memories threatened to overwhelm him. Just as he had ignored them before, Abenadar ignored them again.

As the men closed on the top of the mount, the ground flattened out and the olive trees became sparse. A clump of men rested in a clearing beside the road. One of them stood. His eyes were closed and he prayed out load. The man was obviously Yeshua.

Abenadar was dismayed that after his warning, Yeshua stayed here in this clearing on the mount. Yeshua had obviously waited for them.

As if on cue, Y'hudah ben-Shimon walked straight up to Yeshua. "Shalom, Rabbi," he said loudly and kissed Yeshua's cheek.

The Temple guard rushed the rest of the way up the steep sides of the mount. Dashing sleep from their eyes, Yeshua's talmidim slowly rose from the ground.

Yeshua stared past Y'hudah and said to the Temple guards and approaching cohanim, "Whom do you want?"

Natan, the Captain of the Temple guard said, "We seek Yeshua of Natzeret."

Yeshua held out his hands. "I AM," he said, using the name of the Lord God Y'hovah. When he said this, the cohanim and Temple guard stepped back in astonishment and fell to their knees.

Abenadar himself was taken aback. Yeshua used the name of Adonai, the name that could only be spoken by the Cohen Hagadol on the highest holy day.

"Get up," cursed the chief cohen. "Get up, you fools, and capture him."

The Temple guard stood up and stared angrily at the chief cohen. Then they stepped again toward Yeshua.

"Whom do you want?" said Yeshua again.

This time the chief cohen said, "Yeshua of Natzeret." He motioned for the slaves around him to set upon Yeshua. With obvious fear, they moved forward with the Temple guards.

"I told you 'I AM,' " said Yeshua. The Temple guards and cohanim stopped in their tracks. "If I am the one you want, then let these others go."

The talmidim beside Yeshua finally stirred themselves to action. A couple drew long knives and one struck at the slave of the Cohen Hagadol as he stepped toward Yeshua. The talmid, in his excitement, aimed his attack poorly, and instead of cutting the slave's throat, the knife glanced off the side of his head. The blade sliced through the slave's ear and left it hanging by a single thread of skin.

The slave cried out and, in agony, holding his head, fell to one knee. Blood poured down the side of his face.

Yeshua reached over to the slave and gently touched the side of his head. In that instant, the ear reattached itself and the blood stopped flowing. Yeshua said to his talmid, "Kefa, put your knife back into your belt. Anyone who lives by the sword will die by the sword. Don't you know that I can ask my Father and He would instantly provide me a dozen legions of angels to help me? But if I did, how would the passages in the Tanakh be fulfilled that say it must happen this way? This is the cup the Father has given me to drink; should I not drink it to the dregs?"

Then Yeshua spoke to the guards and the cohanim. "You have come with swords and clubs to take me like the leader of a rebellion, yet every day I sat teaching in the court of the Temple and you didn't seize me then. You know that all this has happened so that the words the prophets wrote may be fulfilled."

At the sight of the knives, the legionnaires drew their swords, and Abenadar ordered them forward. The Temple guards still did not move. As soon as the Romans stepped forward, the talmidim recognized them. They dropped their weapons and ran off into the darkness. Abenadar knew they would be nearly impossible to capture. Beside Yeshua, one last talmid waited too long to escape. A Temple guard grabbed him by his robe, but the man twisted out of the clothing and ran almost naked into the darkness and down the side of the Mount of Olives.

Natan stepped toward Yeshua with his sword drawn. Before the legionnaires could come any closer, the Temple guards roughly grabbed Yeshua and tied his arms and knees together. Yeshua offered no resistance. He stood silent and motionless while they placed a rope around his neck. Natan grasped the end of it and almost tugged Yeshua to the ground. Surrounded by the cohanim, their slaves, and the Temple guard, Natan led Yeshua roughly back the way they came—down the mount. Abenadar and his men followed closely behind them.

They reentered the city by the Eastern Gate, and Abenadar made certain the Temple guard left their weapons in the Temple. Natan ordered two thirds of the guard back to their posts in the Temple courts. Unarmed, Natan and about eight of his men remained with the cohanim and their slaves. Abenadar and his legionnaires followed them as they led Yeshua to Anan's house in the upper city.

When they arrived at the house, Abenadar didn't enter the court. He made sure the cohanim did not murder Yeshua outright, then he led his columns back to the Praetorium.

Pilate and the Legatus Legionis waited for him in the Procurator's court.

Pilate paced back and forth across the tiled floor. When he saw Abenadar, he immediately asked, "Did you capture the man?"

"Yes, Procurator," Abenadar said. "They took him to Anan's house, and he and Kayafa, the High Priest, are interrogating him."

"Did this Yeshua put up a fight?"

"His followers drew knives, and one struck the ear off the High Priest's slave, but they ran away when they saw my legionnaires."

Pilate and the Legatus chuckled. "Was that all?" said Pilate.

"Yeshua healed the man right before us all."

"He healed the High Priest's slave?"

"I saw it. He put the ear back on his head."

"Amazing." Pilate nodded. "So we were wise to send you?"

"Very prudent, Procurator."

Pilate sat in his chair. "What can we expect next, Centurion?"

"Anan and Kayafa will wait until sunrise and bring the man Yeshua to you."

"What will they want from me?"

"The priests fear you more than they fear Yeshua. They will insist you judge Yeshua guilty of insurrection and demand you put him to death."

Pilate's face took on a sly cast. He poured himself a cup of wine. "How then should we rule, Centurion Abenadar?"

"I would not presume to make this judgment for you, Procurator."

"How would you rule?" Pilate cocked his head.

Abenadar thought a moment. "This man, Yeshua, does not challenge your authority in Judea. He is a challenge only to the

Sanhedrin and the priests. Yeshua's teaching and this conflict with their leaders distract the people, and because of this, we have little trouble in the city or in Judea. He makes our job easy, and the peace brings tribute into your treasury. I say Yeshua is worth more to us alive than dead. And for this reason alone, I would keep him alive."

"That is well spoken, Centurion." Pilate toyed with his baton. "You made a similar recommendation to us before. We must think on this. Both of you keep watch in the court." Pilate stood up. "Send for me when the Judeans come. I believe you are right, Centurion Abenadar. They definitely will come for my judgment."

Abenadar and Iulius Valens bowed as Pilate left for his quarters.

The Legatus turned to Abenadar. "Abenadar, you gave very discerning advice to Pilate." He crossed the court. "Yeshua's followers are armed. Should I instruct the Primus to hunt them down?"

"They are like fools and children. Their swords are fish knives. If they rise up, I will crush them myself."

Iulius Valens sat on a step at the back of the court and pulled his cloak around his shoulders. "You have always read these people correctly before." Abenadar bowed. "Rest yourself, and we will await the coming day and its events."

"I must look to my men first, Legatus."

"Of course, Centurion." Iulius Valens waved him off.

Abenadar set his men on alternate watches in the outer hall. Afterwards, he returned to the Procurator's court. When he entered, Iulius Valens was already snoring on the step. Abenadar pulled his cloak around his shoulders and propped himself in the doorway to the chamber. He quickly fell into an uneasy doze that alternated between watchfulness and sleep.

A light touch awakened Abenadar. He reached instinctively for his gladius, but when he opened his eyes, he stared up into the face of one of his men.

"Centurion," said the legionnaire, "the priests brought the man,

Yeshua, to Pilate. They are standing outside the fortress."

Abenadar stood up and shook himself. The coming daylight barely turned the sky gray, and the court was still dark. Abenadar stepped over to Iulius Valens and woke him. "Legatus, the priests have brought the man Yeshua to us. They wait outside."

"Speak to them. I will get the Procurator."

Abenadar saluted.

Outside, Abenadar's column stood on guard in a loose semicircle before the great gate of the fortress. The cohanim paced back and forth beyond them. When the cohanim spotted Abenadar, they stopped milling around and stood nervously waiting. Yeshua stood in the midst of them still bound by his hands and knees. His bonds didn't look as if they had been loosened since his capture. Bruises covered Yeshua's face and spittle marked his robe.

Abenadar pushed between the legionnaires. Led by the Cohen Hagadol, the cohanim moved toward him. They didn't dare get too close to the Praetorium and stopped about ten feet from Abenadar and his men.

Kayafa held the position of Cohen Hagadol that year. He was an imposing man and stood almost a full head taller than his father-in-law, Anan. Kayafa was not nearly as tall as most of the legionnaires, and his corpulence diminished his stature. Both in girth and height, he was, by far, the largest man among the cohanim. Kayafa stared at Abenadar with his phlegmatic face and, in Greek, said, "We would speak with the Procurator."

Knowing Kayafa wouldn't enter the fortress, Abenadar answered him in the same tongue. "I will take you to him."

The Cohen Hagadol answered without apology. "In respect for our religious law, I cannot enter the fortress to attend the Procurator. He will give honor to all the people of Y'hudah if he will speak with us here."

"I will deliver your message to him." Abenadar turned and reentered the gate.

Pilate awaited Abenadar. The Procurator was regally dressed and perched tensely at the edge of his seat. He supported his chin with his hand and rested his elbow on the arm of the chair. Although his face was fresh and clean, Pilate did not appear rested. He was thoughtful, but with a strange undercurrent to his demeanor. Abenadar read it as fear.

"What do the priests say?" Pilate finally spoke. His words seemed almost an afterthought.

"Procurator, the High Priest requests that you receive him on the portico of the fortress."

"He has a reason for such a request?"

"He did not say, but the Judeans believe they are defiled when they enter the Praetorium. The priests wish to avoid defilement so they can participate in the sacrifice and Passover meal."

"Ah yes, you are right. Since they accommodated us so well in the past, I am willing to accede to their request. How long can we make them wait for the privilege?"

"They will want to wrap up this business soon; the Passover comes when the sun sets."

Pilate wagged his head. "Very well. I also want to see this business finished; we will make them wait only a little." He stood up. "Come with me, Abenadar. We will walk slowly, and you tell me what their Greek words do not."

Abenadar bowed and followed Pilate from the hall.

In the courtyard, Anan stood a little ahead of the group of cohanim surrounding Yeshua. Abenadar guessed that the Cohen Hagadol returned to the Temple for the morning sacrifice. The blast of the Temple trumpets told him he was right. As Pilate passed between the legionnaires on the portico, Anan stepped toward him.

Anan bowed gingerly to Pilate—he was not used to bowing to anyone.

"Well, Anan," said Pilate in Greek, "we granted you the use of your Temple guards to capture a band of rebels and you bring us only one?"

Anan responded in the same tongue, "Procurator, we used your boon to good effect. This is their leader."

Pilate obviously didn't want to extend the interview; in a bored voice he said, "What charge do you bring against this man?"

Anan said, "If he hadn't done something wrong, we wouldn't have brought him to you."

Pilate clenched his teeth. "Then you take him. As our agreement states, you judge him according to your own law."

Anan responded, "We have judged him, but we don't have the legal power to put anyone to death."

"Then, if you ask us to judge, we ask you again, what is the charge against him?"

An older member of the Sanhedrin stepped forward. "He was subverting our nation."

Pilate did not hide his exasperation.

Another cohen said, "He forbade the people to pay taxes to the Emperor."

"He has not the power to forbid anyone anything." Pilate inspected his fingernails. "Or so we would guess."

The ancient Sanhedrin almost screamed out, "He claims to be the Messiah."

Anan held up his hand. "That is a kind of king, Procurator. He claims to be the king of the Judean people. There is no king of our people. We only have an Emperor and a High Priest."

"Very well, we will question the man ourselves. Centurion, bring him into the court." Pilate didn't wait for Abenadar; he turned contemptuously and reentered the gate.

Abenadar walked over to Yeshua, and the Sanhedrin, fearful of defilement, parted quickly before him. Abenadar grasped Yeshua by the arm. Under his hand, Abenadar felt thews like iron. So Yeshua could walk more easily, Abenadar reached down with his gladius and cut the ropes around the man's knees. At first, the cohanim moved forward in protest, then they must have thought better of it and, without a word, stepped back. Abenadar led Yeshua across the portico and into Pilate's court.

When Abenadar brought Yeshua into the court, Pilate was speaking with his wife. Because Pilate guarded her jealously, Abenadar had seen her only a few times. Her name was Claudia Procula, and Pilate valued her advice almost as much as he did that of his Legatus. Iulius Valens told Abenadar that when he needed the Procurator's agreement, he often passed information to Pilate through her first. Claudia Procula was not a beautiful woman. She bore the look of the old patrician families of Rome. Her nose was long, and her face, though made up in the style of the Alexandrians, was ordinary. But an air of wisdom encompassed her presence, and Pilate listened carefully to her every word. She was very agitated and became more so when Yeshua entered the court at Abenadar's side. She spoke quietly into Pilate's ear while he inclined toward her on the arm of his chair. When Abenadar and Yeshua entered the center of the court, Pilate hastily waved her away.

Claudia would not be put off so easily and said loudly to Pilate, "That is the man I told you I dreamed about. Have nothing to do with him." Then, abruptly, she left.

Pilate did not look after her but stared intently at Yeshua. He stared as though he could discern the depths of the man by this simple appraisal. Finally, he said in Greek, "Are you the king of the Judeans?"

Yeshua answered in the same tongue, "Is this your own conclusion or are you repeating what others told you about me?"

Pilate looked startled, then tilted back his head and laughed. "Am I a Judean? Your own nation and High Priest handed you over to us; what have you done?"

Yeshua's expression was bland. "My kingship does not derive its authority from this world's order of things. If it did, the people of Jerusalem would fight to keep me from being arrested by the Sanhedrin. My kingship does not come from here."

"So then—" Pilate tapped his baton—"you are a king, after all."

"You say I am a king." Yeshua's face became more animated. "The reason I was born, the reason I have come into the world, is to bear witness to the truth. Everyone who belongs to the truth listens to me."

Pilate shook his head. "What is truth?" Then he got up and motioned for Abenadar to follow him. As they walked back to the portico, he said to Abenadar in Latin, "What should we do about this man? Surely the charges against him are brought maliciously."

"The response of the people is my greatest concern, Procurator."

"How so, Centurion?"

"You said yourself, the people of the city greeted this man as if he were a king. Many believe he is a prophet, some think he is the Messiah of the Judeans. If we kill him, the people may revolt against us."

Pilate struck his palm with his baton. "While he is alive, the man is an asset. When he is dead, he becomes a threat to us. These people are perverse. What do you suggest we do?"

"If the Sanhedrin could be convinced to proffer a lesser charge against the man, we could scourge him and let him go."

Pilate put his hand to his head. "But what if the Sanhedrin are trying to encourage a revolt?"

"Your legion will decimate them. The Sanhedrin are insolent, but your rule makes them wealthy. The people only think of freedom because their leaders betray them. Again I recommend that we find a way to release this man."

"The Sanhedrin cannot be allowed to kill him themselves," said Pilate. "We embrace your advice, Abenadar, but these people are stubborn and obstinate. If they will accept nothing but this man's death, we must determine how to put the responsibility squarely on their shoulders."

They reached the portico and the legionnaires parted for them. By this time, the morning sacrifice was over, and most of the cohanim from the Temple joined the 71 members of the Sanhedrin. Anan and Kayafa waited at the edge of the steps.

In a loud voice Pilate said to them all, "I don't find any case against this man, Yeshua."

Anan and Kayafa both started to speak, then Anan continued alone. "He is inciting the people with his teaching throughout Judea. He started in the Galil, and now he's here."

"Then he is from the Galil? He is from Herod's jurisdiction." Pilate turned to Abenadar.

"Yes, Procurator."

"Herod is visiting in the city during this festival of the Judeans. Centurion, take this man, Yeshua, to Herod and ask for his judgment."

"Yes, Procurator."

Abenadar sent two of the legionnaires to retrieve Yeshua. They returned with the prisoner between them. Abenadar took a column of his legionnaires, and without another word, they led Yeshua off through the streets toward the ancient palace.

The cohanim and Sanhedrin grumbled aloud, but they fell back before the column. After the last legionnaire passed, they shadowed them at a discrete distance. By this time, the Temple guard joined the cohanim and Sanhedrin. Abenadar and his legionnaires watched the guards closely. As required by Pilate's decree, they appeared unarmed, but Abenadar didn't trust them. They were no better than many of the rebels he faced, but as trained soldiers, they could be more dangerous than any rebel.

When Herod stayed in Yerushalayim, Pilate allowed him to occupy the old palace. Because the Fortress of Antonia was easier to defend, nearer the market, and sat right against the Temple, the Procurator preferred to reside there. The man who ruled the Fortress of Antonia ruled the city. The palace, on the other hand, was rundown and undefendable, and with no king in Yerushalayim, the cohen had no reason to spend a single lepton to rebuild it.

Herod could not complain. The buildings, though aging, were still magnificent. The palace was a low edifice that spread out without much evident plan or consistent design. The outer wall was torn down long ago, so a good 20 feet of open space separated it from the rest of the city. Into this space, the people on the city side built awnings and other extensions. They treated the gap like an open road and slowly took it over. That didn't really matter; without the wall the palace was not defendable, and because of the way the palace was built, it probably couldn't have been defended with the wall in place.

The remains of two watchtowers marked the entrance to the palace. Abenadar conveyed Yeshua there. Herod's guards stood watch by the broken towers. Unlike the Temple guard, Herod's sentries were fully trained and equipped. Pilate, as a courtesy to Herod, allowed them to carry their weapons and wear armor within Y'hudah. The soldiers stood at attention on either side of the rubble that marked the location of the ancient gate. Their officer kept watch behind them. He held a staff of rank in one hand, and a sword hung at his waist. His soldiers were armed with swords and spears, but they would have been no match for Abenadar's legionnaires, and they knew it.

As the party approached the ancient gateway, the guards lowered their spears, but they dared not threaten the legionnaires. Abenadar stepped forward and stretched his vitis toward the officer of the guard.

The officer saluted Abenadar and cried out in Greek, "Hold one moment, Centurion. Herod Antipas, Governor of the Galil and Perea, occupies the palace. Do you have business with him?"

Abenadar answered, "I am the Centurion Abenadar. We come in the name of Pontius Pilate, the Procurator of Judea. Pilate wishes your master well and desires his judgment in a difficult legal case."

"Who are these others?"

"These men are the priests and Sanhedrin of Jerusalem, who come to press their case against my prisoner."

"And who is your prisoner?"

"Yeshua of Natzeret, the miracle worker."

Anticipating the pleasure of his master, the officer smiled broadly. Herod had long wanted to speak to Yeshua of Natzeret. "Wait here, Centurion. I will return shortly with my master's instructions."

The officer left for only a few minutes. He came back at a quick pace. "Centurion Abenadar, bring your prisoner immediately. Herod will gladly assist the Procurator with this difficult judgment."

The officer motioned with his staff, and the guards lifted their spears back to attention. The captain of the guard gestured with his open hand toward Abenadar. Abenadar led his men between the rubble of the towers and into the palace.

The smell of water lay heavy in the low buildings. Herod had opened all the wells in the palace and brought water in from all around the city. Overflowing with fresh cool water, the pools in the palace glistened like clear crystals. The water flowed languidly in them and moved slowly toward some invisible and long-forgotten cistern. Following the captain of the guard, the legionnaires made their way around many decorated pools as they traveled deep into the palace. From the long and low chambers, Herod's court opened up into a wide tall room. Here the water moved with a soft chuckling undertone that blended with the higher pitched sounds of harps and finger cymbals.

Herod lay on his side on a great couch. As the group entered, the captain of the guard announced them in Greek. "Centurion Abenadar with his prisoner, Yeshua of Natzeret. The Sanhedrin and priests of Jerusalem."

Abenadar nodded to Herod; he was a citizen of Rome. The

Sanhedrin and priests, though not under Herod's jurisdiction, were wise enough to kneel.

"Welcome, Centurion Abenadar. So you speak for Pilate now? Not long ago, you spoke for our friend, Iulius Valens?"

Abenadar nodded more deeply at the recognition and accepted Herod's invitation. "Governor Herod, the Procurator of Jerusalem and Judea, sends his greetings. Welcome to the city of Jerusalem during the Judean festival of Passover. The Procurator wishes to hear your judgment of a prisoner. This man called Yeshua of Natzeret." Abenadar signaled, and two legionnaires brought Yeshua forward between them.

Herod examined Yeshua for a moment, then turned to Abenadar. "Who accuses this man? What is he guilty of?"

Abenadar answered, "Governor, his accusers came with him. They can bring their charges themselves."

Anan lost no time. He and Kayafa stepped forward and Anan said, "Greetings, Governor. I am Anan, leader of the Sanhedrin in Judea and Jerusalem, and this is our Cohen Hagadol, Kayafa. This man, Yeshua, has been inciting the people. He calls himself a king—a king of the Judean people and profanes our Laws."

"Isn't this Yeshua of Natzeret the miracle worker who has done so many amazing things across both our lands?" asked Herod.

"Of his purported miracles," said Anan, "I cannot speak. I only know his insurrection firsthand."

"What does he say to these charges?"

No one spoke.

Finally, Herod prodded Yeshua. "Yeshua of Natzeret, we are the Governor of the Galil and your rightful ruler. We will judge you fairly. What do you say to these accusations?"

Yeshua stood without speaking.

Herod motioned for Abenadar to come to him, then whispered to Abenadar, "Does he understand Greek?"

Abenadar bent toward Herod. "Yes, Governor."

"Then why won't he speak?"

"I do not know, Governor."

Herod lay back and said more loudly, "Yeshua, you may speak. Show us a miracle and you shall go free."

Anan started forward to protest Herod's offer of freedom, but Herod pointed toward his guards and, flustered, Anan stepped back.

Yeshua said nothing.

"Centurion," hissed the Governor, "why won't he speak to us?"

"He is an obstinate rebel," cried Anan.

Herod sat up. "You shut up, Priest." He gestured toward his soldiers. "Perhaps he must be placated. Bring a purple robe."

Kayafa started to speak, but Herod cut him off with an angry motion.

"Put the robe on him."

The soldiers placed a purple robe around Yeshua's shoulders.

Herod sat up on his couch. "Come, Yeshua. Now you look like a king. We know you accomplished miracles across the breath of the Galil and Judea. Surely you can show us one. All we ask is a simple one. Make our pool become wine or produce a bit of bread. Demonstrate the foolishness of these priests and show all of us your power."

For breathless minutes they waited, but Yeshua said not a word. He stood with his shoulders drooping. The purple robe flowed gently over his body.

"Strike him," said Herod to the captain of the guard.

The officer unsheathed his sword, and Abenadar stepped forward.

Herod did not miss this silent threat. "Strike him with the flat of your blade."

The captain hit Yeshua across the shoulders, and Yeshua fell to his knees.

"Will you speak to us now, Yeshua?" Herod waited for an answer. "No?" He twisted the end of his manicured beard. "We could have you beaten until you cry for mercy." He motioned to the captain. "Strike him again."

The captain hit Yeshua across his face, and that blow hurled the large man to his side on the tile floor. Yeshua climbed gingerly to his feet. A trickle of blood wound its way from his scalp and down the side of his head.

"That is enough," said Herod. "We find nothing to condemn this man. What do you say to that, priests?"

Anan spoke. "By our law, he is a rebel and a criminal."

"Rebels always have some word to say; it's their curse. Criminals constantly claim their innocence. This man does neither. Perhaps he is your king." Herod turned back to Abenadar. "Centurion."

"Yes, Governor."

"Return this man to Pilate. Except for his mute tongue before us, we find nothing warranting a capital punishment. Tell the Procurator...tell Pilate that he was wise to send us this man to interrogate. We commend this Yeshua to the judgment of the Procurator, but for ourselves, we find him guilty only of silence."

Abenadar stepped to the side of Yeshua and motioned to his legionnaires. He bowed to Herod. "Governor, your judgment is wise, and I will convey it to Procurator Pontius Pilate."

The cohen and Anan shuffled nervously as though they might protest the Governor's words, but knowing Herod's cruelty and unpredictability, they wisely said nothing and followed Abenadar, Yeshua, and the legionnaires back out to the street.

Abenadar returned Yeshua to the Fortress of Antonia and brought him into Pilate's court. The court was empty, so Abenadar sent a legionnaire to inform Pilate that he had returned from the palace with Yeshua.

Then Abenadar took Yeshua to an alcove at the side. There he released Yeshua's bonds and motioned for him to sit. Yeshua let himself wearily down to the stones and rubbed the rope burns on his wrists. He grimaced as the circulation slowly returned to his hands. Then he scrubbed his face with his palms.

Abenadar stuck his head out into the main chamber to check if anyone could overhear them. He saw no one, so he quietly addressed Yeshua in the language of the people of Y'hudah. "You are Yeshua from Natzeret, the son of Yosef and Miryam." His words were a statement.

Yeshua nodded. "You knew me when you stood before me in the Temple three years ago, Abenadar."

"I couldn't believe it was you," said Abenadar over his shoulder.

"But it was me...it is me. Do you believe now?" Abenadar knew Yeshua didn't speak of his origins.

"You should have answered Herod," said Abenadar, turning toward him. "You should have made a miracle for him. That was all he wanted."

"I am not a sideshow, Abenadar. Ask Ruth. She understands what is happening."

"How do you know of Ruth?"

"You sent her to warn me. I know many things that might surprise you, Centurion Abenadar. On the plateau overlooking the caravan road by Natzeret, I once told you, you would find glory in the service of Rome. I told you that you would find a necessary place in the legion."

Abenadar's mouth was dry. "Ruth believes you are the Messiah."

"I am."

Abenadar turned away from him. "If you are, you will likely die if I cannot convince Pilate to set you free."

"I will die."

Abenadar clenched his fists. He stared at the man. "If you die, it will be by my hand."

"Yes. That is your necessary place."

"Yeshua, when I was a child, you were my only friend. I don't want to kill you."

"When the time comes, you must act as Pilate commands you. You are a Roman, after all." Yeshua did not say the word as though it were a curse.

"I would give all of it up to have Ruth's faith."

"There." Yeshua smiled in spite of his bruises. "The faith is yours. All you had to do was ask, but I need Romans. So, a Roman and a centurion you must remain."

Abenadar didn't feel any differently. "And must I kill you myself?"

"You must see to it as your duty to Adonai and to your master Pilate."

"I do not feel the faith you have given me."

"Then you must let it grow. You found me, you must find the fullness of faith in me and in my Father, Adonai."

In the chamber behind him, Abenadar heard the court assembling. He stepped back to the entrance of the alcove. In a voice tinged with desperation, Abenadar said, "We have no more time to speak."

"We have all the time we need. The Father granted that to you. Now I will say one more thing that is on my heart. You rescued Ruth from the streets. In some measure, because of you, she gained her faith. But you have not treated her with the dignity I desire. Make the woman your wife as do the people of Y'hudah, and promise yourself to her. This is my command for you now. You will know my other commands later."

"How?" Abenadar shook his head.

"You will know. Ask Ruth. Just as you guided her from ruin, she can guide you to know the faith I granted you."

Abenadar stared at him sadly. "Yeshua, you must come now. Pilate is entering the court, and I must report with you to him."

They both stood up and moved to the edge of the alcove. Just before they stepped into the court, Yeshua put his hand on Abenadar's arm. "Abenadar, I will require much you will find difficult. Do not shirk your duties as a Roman or as my friend."

Abenadar led Yeshua into the hall.

"Abenadar! There you are," said Pilate as he seated himself on his chair. "What word did Herod give concerning his subject?"

"Procurator, Herod was pleased you sent the man Yeshua to him for judgment. And the Governor bade me convey his greetings to you."

"Very good, Centurion. But what judgment did the Governor give concerning your captive?"

"Procurator, after the priests and Sanhedrin brought their charges, the Governor questioned Yeshua extensively. Herod found him not guilty of any capital charge."

"Did this placate the priests and Sanhedrin?"

"No, Procurator. His pronouncement made them cry louder for his blood."

Pilate said to himself, "Curse their stubbornness. I have no desire to bring a revolt on my head by putting an innocent man to death—especially one who can be of service to me." He gazed at Abenadar and said more loudly, "Where are his accusers?"

"They still wait on the portico, Procurator."

"Very well." He sighed. "It seems we must speak to them again."

"Procurator," said Abenadar, "you might still have a reason to release Yeshua of Natzeret."

"Go ahead, Centurion."

"This is the week of the Passover. In the past, during the festival, you released a prisoner for the Judeans. Right now we possess few popular prisoners for them to choose from. Everyone in our prison is a Zealot—men hated and feared by the people and Sanhedrin for violence at least as much as the Sanhedrin hate this man for his 'truth.'"

Pilate bent his head in thought. "Yes, yes, that is a very good idea. We will ask them to choose, and then perhaps we will be rid of this man. Do you think they will accept this judgment?"

Abenadar shrugged. "Your proposal may surprise them, and their silence may allow you to enact your will."

Pilate smiled. "We will take your advice. Go before us, Abenadar, and summon the high priest and the leaders. We will speak with them again."

"Yes, Procurator."

Abenadar went to the portico and called Anan and Kayafa out of the crowd. After a few moments, Pilate walked out onto the top stair. At the Procurator's appearance, the crowd of Sanhedrin, cohanim, and Temple guards quieted.

Pilate spoke. "You brought the man, Yeshua, before us on the charge of subverting the people. In your presence and in our court, we examined him and did not find him guilty of any crime. Herod sent the man back to us. He also judged Yeshua of Natzeret and did not find him guilty of subversion. Clearly, this Yeshua has done nothing to merit capital punishment."

Both Kayafa and Anan stepped forward to speak, but Pilate waved them back. "You have a custom at your Passover. We have, in the past, released one prisoner to freedom. We will set free for you Yeshua, the 'King of the Judeans.'"

Kayafa and Anan were both taken aback. They conferred for a moment, then Anan said, "We are the Sanhedrin and we speak for the people of Judea. We want you to free the prisoner bar-Abba."

Pilate turned to Abenadar and said in Latin, "Who is this bar-Abba?"

"He is the Blue Shawl I captured at the Pool of Siloam. He is a murderer and a Zealot."

Pilate turned back to the priests and said in Greek, "You are certain this is the man you want returned to you?"

At the prompting of the Cohen Hagadol and Anan, the crowd of Sanhedrin and cohanim shouted, "Give us bar-Abba." As though on cue, they chanted the refrain over and over.

Pilate was filled with rage. He spun on his foot, then recovering his decorum, he stopped beside Abenadar. "Very well, give them bar-Abba. Arm him and tell him the priests have finally agreed to free him."

Abenadar smiled and conveyed the order to one of his legionnaires.

All who see me laugh me to scorn;
they curl their lips and wag their heads, saying,
"He trusted in Adonai; let him deliver him;
let him rescue him, if he delights in him."

Psalm 22:7-8

Twenty-three

Pilate stormed into the court. "Legatus."

"Yes, Procurator," answered Iulius Valens.

"Flog and debase the prisoner, Yeshua. Make him a king of sorrows for these Judeans."

Iulius Valens spoke to one of the legionnaires standing guard in the court. "Get the Centurion Gaius Flaccus. He is the legion's Quaestionaris and executioner. Tell him to bring his tools."

"Yes, Legatus." The legionnaire left at a run.

The Legatus spoke to the other legionnaires. "Prepare the prisoner for the scourge."

The soldiers pulled the purple robe and Yeshua's own garment down to his waist. Then they forced him to kneel in the middle of the court.

Pilate sat in his chair and put his chin on his fist.

With the scourge hanging conspicuously at his belt, Gaius Flaccus entered the court. He knelt to the Procurator.

"Centurion Flaccus," said the Legatus as he pointed at Yeshua, "lash the prisoner."

Gaius unhooked the scourge from his belt and let it play to its full length, "How many strokes, Legatus?"

"Forty…," said Pilate. "Start with forty."

Gaius hefted the scourge, and the pieces of iron at the ends of the leather cords clattered on the tile of the floor. He walked slowly to Yeshua's side and heaved the whip over his head. The heavy cord sang through the air, and the first blow crashed solidly over Yeshua's shoulders. Yeshua grunted with pain and gasped as Gaius drew the metal tipped cords over his back. Blood welled in thick lines where the iron bit into him.

Gaius said, "One," and drew the scourge behind him for the next blow. The cords whistled and came down again. "Two," and again, "Three," and again. Each time, with exact precision, Gaius let the cords hit a little farther up or down from the original blow, until Yeshua's back was a single pool of blood.

When no room remained for the iron to slash new wounds, he varied the angle. "Twenty."

Then, "Thirty." Bright red flecks sprinkled the floor tiles and slowly dried a dirty brown. Drops of blood rolled off Yeshua's back and formed small dark puddles on either side of him.

Finally, Yeshua collapsed to the floor, but the blows continued. Each brought a new grunt and sharp intake of breath. The blood flowed in slow runlets to the tile on either side of him.

"Forty." A sheen of sweat covered Gaius, and great drops fell from his brow and chin.

"Enough," cried Pilate. "Truly, this man has the strength of a king." He motioned toward the Legatus. "Stand him on his feet."

The Legatus pointed to two legionnaires. They lifted Yeshua and held him up. Yeshua stood shaking between them, but when they released him he stood on his own. Pain glazed his eyes, and the blood continued to flow freely down his back and sides.

Pilate addressed the legionnaires. "Find him an appropriate crown." Then he suggested, "Thorns would be the perfect match for a King of the Judeans."

Iulius Valens cocked his head as a command, and in a few moments a legionnaire returned with a plaited circlet of desert thorns.

Pilate snarled, "Place it on him."

The legionnaire jammed the crown of thorns over Yeshua's head. Yeshua winced as the points bit into him. Blood flowed where the barbs pierced his skin. It ran across his face and rolled in large drops off his chin onto the floor.

"Show him the deference due a renegade king," demanded Pilate. "Strike his face!"

Gaius backhanded Yeshua. The legionnaires on either side of Yeshua steadied him, and Gaius struck him again and again. At each blow, Gaius bellowed, "Hail, King of the Judeans." The blood splattered from Yeshua's broken lips.

Finally, Pilate cried out, "Enough." Then he glanced at Iulius Valens. "Does this king look as though he is chastised enough for his crime—whatever crime he may have committed?"

The Legatus Legionis shrugged. "It is enough, Procurator, but whether it is enough for the priests and the Sanhedrin…"

Pilate surveyed the court. "Centurion Abenadar, is it enough?"

"Bar-Abba is now in their hands. If the Sanhedrin are men of honor, we have spilled enough of his blood—" Abenadar lifted his hand toward Yeshua—"to pay for any crime the man might have committed."

Pilate stood up and leaned over Yeshua. He grasped Yeshua's hair and lifted up his head. "Did you hear that, King? I find you guilty of nothing—nothing. Are your countrymen men of honor? What do you say?"

Yeshua's mouth worked for a moment, then with blood and spittle falling from his broken mouth, he whispered, "It will not be enough."

Pilate released his hair. "We shall see. We shall see." Pilate raised his hand. "Come, Abenadar, bring the King of the Judeans, and we shall see if 40 lashes and debasement are enough for these men."

Abenadar signaled the legionnaires on either side of Yeshua, and they followed Pilate out to the portico.

Pilate stepped into the sunlight and angrily motioned the guards out of his way. He walked right to the edge of the steps and shouted at the crowd of cohanim and Sanhedrin, "Here is Yeshua. We are bringing him out to you again to tell you we find no case against him."

Abenadar stood behind Pilate, and the two legionnaires half carried Yeshua between them out onto the portico. The purple robe Herod had placed on Yeshua still clothed his lower body. Blood covered him—some dried, but much still flowing down his face, chest, and back. The thorn crown circled his head.

"Look at the man!" cried Pilate.

"Crucify him. Crucify him," bellowed Anan and Kayafa. Bunched before the steps, the cohanim and leaders took up and repeated their words.

"Crucify him yourselves," snarled Pilate, his voice almost drowned out. "We, representing Rome, find nothing against this man."

Anan raised his hands for silence. The roar of the cohanim and Sanhedrin dwindled to nothing. Almost menacingly, he stepped forward toward Pilate. "We have a law; and by that law, because he claimed to be the Son of Adonai, he ought to die."

Pilate made a savage cutting gesture with his hand. Anan stepped back, startled. In one motion, Pilate signaled Abenadar and spun around on his heel. He strode back into the Praetorium.

Abenadar and his legionnaires, Yeshua between them, followed closely behind.

In the court, Pilate threw himself angrily into his chair. He stared straight ahead and impatiently tapped the tips of his fingers together. The legionnaires brought Yeshua back to the center of the chamber. Pilate erupted out of the simple throne and rushed up to Yeshua. Less than an inch from his face, Pilate screamed, "Where are you from?"

No one made a sound. In the silence, the steady drip of blood against the pavement was deafening.

Still nose to nose with Yeshua, Pilate said, "Now you refuse to speak to me?" He bunched his fists at his sides in frustration. "Don't you understand I have the power to set you free or to have you executed?"

Yeshua answered him more strongly than before. "You would have no power over me if it hadn't been given to you from above—that is why those who handed me over to you are guilty of a greater sin."

Pilate turned away from Yeshua and paced back and forth for a moment, then stared at Abenadar. "Centurion, speak to the Sanhedrin again for us. Speak to them in their own tongue. See if you can convince them against this course." Pilate sat back in his seat.

"Yes, Procurator." Abenadar left the court.

He returned after fifteen minutes.

Pilate sat tensely at the edge of his chair. As soon as Abenadar came in sight, he said, "Speak, Centurion."

"Anan claims if you set this man free you are not a 'Friend of the Emperor.' They say anyone who claims to be a king in Judea opposes the Emperor."

A thin sheen of sweat covered Pilate's face. He sat in silence for a long time, then finally said, "We have decided." He stood up and motioned with his hand. "Take him to the Pavement. We will render our judgment there." Pilate left the court through the passage to his personal quarters.

Abenadar called to his legionnaires and they guided Yeshua out of the court. On the portico, the Sanhedrin and cohanim moved quickly out of the way as Abenadar and his men led Yeshua to the outer court of judgment. All the members of the Temple and the leaders of the people followed closely behind them. Abenadar directed Yeshua to the end of the Pavement and stood him on the dais before the seat of judgment.

When Pilate entered the Pavement, the early morning sunlight already blanketed the open court. Pilate strode from the opening behind the seat of judgment and sat before the crowd. A male slave followed Pilate and knelt at his side. The slave carried a large basin, a pitcher, and a towel.

Pilate examined the crowd. The gathering included the most powerful men in Y'hudah. The men were unusually quiet and alertly watched Pilate. Pilate pointed at Yeshua and, looking at the people, shouted, "Priests, men of the Temple, Sanhedrin, here is your king."

The crowd roared back at him, "Take him away! Take him away! He is no king of ours. Put him to death. He said he was Adonai. Execute him in the Roman manner. Kill him."

Pilate signaled the crowd to let him speak. Slowly the cries decreased, but the men were still frenzied. Finally, Pilate roared over them, "You want me, a Roman, to execute your king on the Roman cross?"

The Cohen Hagadol stepped forward. "Procurator, we have no king but the Emperor."

"Very well. We have tried everything to save a man who is guilty of no crime deserving death." He motioned to the slave beside him. The slave lifted the basin and Pilate placed his hands in it. Pilate nodded to the slave, and he poured water from the pitcher over Pilate's hands. Pilate said, "My hands are clean of this man's blood. His death is your responsibility."

The Cohen Hagadol said quietly, "Then let his blood be on us and our children."

Punctuated by cries of, "Crucify him. Crucify him," the crowd perversely caught up the refrain, "His blood be on us and our children."

Pilate motioned for the Legatus Legionis, Abenadar, and Gaius Flaccus. The three men stood around the seat of judgment. Over the noise of the crowd, they strained to hear Pilate. "I don't want a riot. Abenadar, you are in charge of this. Use all caution against the deception of these people. Take the man to The Skull, and you, Gaius Flaccus, execute him there in the fashion of a king." Then, as almost an afterthought, he said, "Legatus, does this meet with your approval?"

Iulius Valens nodded slowly.

"Very well, go to it. We don't want to be troubled anymore by this man or these religious Zealots." Pilate spat out the last word.

The three men saluted.

Abenadar signaled his legionnaires to form a guard around Yeshua. He motioned for them to draw their swords. As they pushed through the crowd, Gaius Flaccus joined Abenadar on his left.

"This won't be the first time I have executed a man who isn't guilty," said Gaius.

"But have you ever killed a man who is a god?"

"I have never known a man who is a god." Gaius laughed. "But I have two other rebels to submit to the cross, and this is as good a time as any. I need to stop at the Fortress to collect them and pick up the wood."

"Very well," said Abenadar.

Abenadar's column made its way to the lower entrance of the Fortress. There, from the guard, Gaius received two Zealots into his care. They were bound and hobbled, and Abenadar recognized them as the two men he had captured with bar-Abba at the Pool of Shiloach. The guards handed out the execution stakes with crossbars already attached. Gaius placed them on the shoulders of the prisoners. He also took a mallet, wooden pegs, a flask, and some short pieces of rope.

The wooden crosses reeked of carrion, and the legionnaires stood well away from their charges as they began the slow march out of the city. The ropes and wooden pegs were overused too, but Gaius carried them as though he didn't care about their smell, stains, or odor. "This is a dirty business, but it is my responsibility," he said to Abenadar.

Yeshua grunted as Gaius laid the heavy cross on his shoulder.

The prison guard said to Abenadar, "This one will not make it to his own execution."

"Let him take the stake as far as he can. That will make the end easier," returned Gaius.

By the time they started through the upper marketplace, the cohanim and Sanhedrin were already gone. The people of the streets replaced them, and this was a far different crowd than the one that cried for Yeshua's death.

When the execution detail passed the Temple, most of the Temple servers and the Temple guard returned to their duties. From the alleyways and shops, the common people gathered in a growing multitude behind the legionnaires and their prisoners. At the front of the crowd, women, Yeshua's talmidah, walked just behind the legionnaires. They set up a cry of anguish—the wailing preceding a funeral train. The men hung back from the legionnaires, but they filled the streets. They muttered silent curses and loud prayers as disconsolate as the women's cries.

Ruth traveled with the crowd. Abenadar hadn't seen her, but he knew she followed. He knew she cursed him. She understood his orders. She knew he helped capture her Messiah. Abenadar feared he would never see her again. In spite of everything Yeshua said, Abenadar knew Ruth could never forgive him for what he was about to do. Abenadar realized he could never forgive himself.

The crowd pressed against them, and Abenadar's men glanced apprehensively from side to side. They feared the crowd.

Gaius said to Abenadar, "The people are angry and we have only eight men."

"Ten if you count the two of us," said Abenadar. "They will not harm us."

"I hope you are right."

"I will not call for more legionnaires. The people fear Rome more than their god."

"You wish they would act." Gaius stared at him.

"But they will not."

Yeshua fell for the first time at the Market Gate. The legionnaires lifted him to his feet and threw the cross back on his shoulder.

Between his shoulder blades, Abenadar felt Ruth's glare. He stood straighter to ensure the crowd could detect no diminishment in his purpose.

Before they arrived at the Garden Gate Yeshua fell again—he slipped on his own blood. The legionnaires jerked him roughly to his feet, but when they tried to put the cross back on his shoulders, he collapsed again.

One of the men turned to Abenadar. Abenadar nodded for him to speak. "He cannot carry the cross any longer."

"Then carry it yourself or find someone to carry it for him." Abenadar pointed at a tall young man with wide shoulders who walked toward them. "There is a man with a strong back. He will carry the cross for the King of the Judeans."

The legionnaires grabbed the man, and Abenadar said to him in Aramaic, "Don't struggle. We want you to carry the cross for this man."

The man quickly concealed his anger. He shrugged and the soldiers lifted the wooden beams onto them. He took the load easily. The man, now carrying Yeshua's cross, stepped easily into place behind them. The soldiers raised Yeshua and half carried, half dragged him along. After a few steps, Yeshua picked up his feet and staggered on his own. Sweat and blood covered him, and he stumbled repeatedly, but he made his way alone.

At the Garden Gate, the legionnaires escorting Yeshua came to a halt, and Abenadar walked forward to the gate and looked out. Men, women, and children thickly dotted the flat expanse leading up to the small plateau called The Skull. The throng covered the open spaces and the road leading up to the place of execution.

Gaius came up beside Abenadar. "Looks like a pretty tough crowd. Do you think they will stay out of our way?"

"I don't know," said Abenadar, "but just standing here doesn't improve our position."

Wailing women were interspersed throughout the crowd. Their high-pitched voices punctuated the ugly noise of the mob. From the fields and around the legionnaires, the sound swelled like a dirge.

Abenadar turned to Yeshua. "Speak to them!"

Yeshua smiled, and the movement broke open the wounds around his lips. "I will speak to them." He raised his hands and turned to the right and left. The crowd quieted.

"Daughters of Yerushalayim, don't cry for me. Cry for yourselves and your children. The time is coming when people will say, 'The childless women are the lucky ones—those whose wombs never bore a child, whose breasts have never nursed a baby.' Then they will say to the mountains, 'Fall on us!' and to the hills, 'Cover us!' If they do these things when the wood is green, what is going to happen when it is dry? Stand back. Your king is coming into his kingdom just as all the other prophets have come." Then Yeshua turned to Abenadar. "Do not fear them. They will part for you."

Abenadar ordered, "Forward." And the group again started toward The Skull. As soon as they entered the crowd, the people moved out of their way to let them pass. The crowd closed just as quickly behind them.

The march from the Garden Gate to The Skull seemed to take an eternity. Before long, Abenadar felt the ground rising under his feet, and, in moments, the legionnaires and their prisoners stood alone on the top of the flat knoll called The Skull.

The remnants of many executions covered the top of The Skull. At evenly spaced intervals, holes one foot wide and three feet deep covered the area. At one side lay a low mound of human bones, and bones in various states of decay littered the ground.

Gaius chose three holes near the center of the place of execution and motioned for the legionnaires to bring the first rebel forward. He was a gruff-looking Zealot with a bald spot spreading from his forehead. His face was craggy and only partially covered by a ratty and stringy beard. Gaius pointed to the ground and the man dropped his cross there. Panic flickered in his eyes, and he gave a lurch as though he were about to bolt. Even if he wanted to run, the hobbles allowed him only a foot-long stride. The soldiers stripped off his rags, and he stood naked and shivering with fear.

Gaius pointed at the cross on the ground, and three legionnaires grasped the rebel's arms and legs and drew him down on it. Gaius deftly tied the man's upper and lower arms to the crossbar and his ankles to the central beam. At Gaius' signal, the legionnaires heaved up the cross with its human cargo and let it fall into one of the holes on the hilltop. The efficiency was breathtaking—the whole event was over in under a minute. The Zealot made only a single sound; he groaned when the cross thudded home at the bottom of the hole.

For a moment, the Zealot hung unmoving. He wondered why he hadn't tried to escape when he had the chance. Now he couldn't fight back, and he resigned himself to the cross. He felt no immediate pain, and without pain, his anticipation of death became muted. In spite of the evidence all around him, it seemed unbelievable a man could die by being hung on a cross. The cross appeared to provide a mercifully easy death.

But experience would cruelly prove him wrong. Already he breathed with difficulty, and he pressed against the main bar to lift himself up and suck oxygen hungrily into his lungs.

Now Gaius stood ready to hang the second rebel. Except that this man feared enough to resist the inevitable, the execution progressed almost like the first. He tried to fight back when the legionnaires grasped his arms and legs. The legionnaires relished the challenge—his actions were futile. Without a word between them, two grabbed his arms and a third yanked on the hobble. As easily as the first, they lay the man on the cross, and Gaius tied him to it. When this cross thudded home, the only evidence of the rebel's struggle was raw, almost bloody wrists and ankles.

Pleased, Gaius stepped back from his handiwork. Both of the Zealots were still conscious. Gaius used care to keep his prisoners healthy and awake. With unconsciousness, death came too quickly, too mercifully. A man on a cross cannot breathe unless he can raise himself up. Death for the unconscious was rapid. Many of Gaius' prisoners fainted with fear or if the soldiers treated them too harshly. Then he would have to wait to raise them until they were fully awake. The delay in an execution was unsatisfactory, but necessary. Gaius believed there was no need to reduce the pain of an appropriate punishment.

As soon as the second cross rammed home, Gaius turned to Yeshua. Yeshua was not bound or hobbled, but the march and the loss of blood had weakened him. He would not be able to resist execution.

Pilate had told Gaius to execute this man like a king, so Gaius brought wooden pegs to attach him by his wrists and ankles to the cross. The pain and loss of blood would ensure Yeshua died more quickly than the Zealots Gaius had tied to the cross. Each time Yeshua tried to raise himself for a breath, the pegs would grate against muscles, tendons, and bone. Each breath would come at a price in blood, and death would arrive in hours instead of days.

Gaius removed the flask from his belt. He had filled it with wine and myrrh. The mixture would numb Yeshua's brain enough so he wouldn't lose consciousness while Gaius staked him to the cross. Gaius handed the flask to Abenadar. "Tell the man to drink this. It will deaden the pain."

Abenadar pulled the cork and held the flask to Yeshua's lips. Yeshua took a single taste and shook his head.

"It will make things go easier," said Abenadar.

Yeshua smiled grimly and said in Greek, "I have come this far without relief. I will drink the whole cup the Father has given me."

"Make him drink it," said Gaius in Latin. "I don't want to have to wait before we lift him up."

Abenadar shook his head and handed back the flask. "Go ahead, Gaius."

Gaius jabbed his finger at the cross, and without a word, Yeshua lay down on it. First, Gaius tied Yeshua's upper arms and ankles to the beams. Then, he carefully arranged Yeshua's right wrist above the peg-hole on the cross. He motioned two of the legionnaires, and they grasped Yeshua's wrist and held it motionless. Gaius felt for the artery against the bone—he didn't want to pierce it; the man would die in minutes. Gaius prepared for that possibility; if he hit an artery, he would tie off the arm with a rope and stick tourniquet. He put the rope around Yeshua's forearm and picked up the stake and mallet. Gaius placed the sharpened stake against Yeshua's wrist. With a single blow he pierced the muscle and skin and set the peg behind the wrist between the two bones of the forearm.

The crowd gasped; they had never seen this type of crucifixion. Yeshua groaned, and blood bubbled slowly up around the peg. Satisfied he hadn't hit an artery, Gaius gave the stake a second blow to set it.

Yeshua grunted again. Just to be sure he wouldn't need the tourniquet, Gaius watched the peg a moment.

Abenadar surveyed the mob for any threatening movement toward his legionnaires, but when the peg thudded home, the people didn't move toward them; instead, they fell back in greater despair. At that moment, Abenadar caught sight of Ruth. She held her face in her hands, and sobs wracked her slight body. She was not the only one; the execution even affected the men in the crowd.

Gaius moved to the other arm. Reflexively, Yeshua tried to pull his wrist out of Gaius' iron grasp, but he was already weak, and the ropes made movement almost impossible.

In poor Greek, Gaius said, "You are truly a man of strength. The last 'king' I executed cried like a child at the first peg." The second stake brought a single choked cry from Yeshua. Gaius set it as firmly as the first.

Gaius saved the legs for last. They were more difficult to stake than the arms. Just above the ankle, at the point where the two bones of the lower leg came together, Gaius pounded a single peg through both. Then, with a single blow, he set the stake through the peg hole on the beam. When the stake pierced his legs, Yeshua writhed in agony, but his strength was gone and his mouth was so dry he could only let out a long hoarse breath. Gaius lashed Yeshua at his ankles below the stake and removed the rope around his lower legs. Then he stood up, stretched, and said to Abenadar, "He is ready to be lifted up."

Abenadar's own mouth was dry. He watched Ruth's suffering figure through the crowd and ignored the anguish he felt. At first he didn't hear Gaius' remark.

Gaius touched Abenadar's arm. "Abenadar, I said he is ready to be lifted up."

"What?" Abenadar cleared his throat. "Yes, already?" Abenadar kept his eyes from Yeshua and turned to his librarius. "Mark the placard 'This is Yeshua from Natzeret, King of the Judeans.' Write it in Latin, Greek, and Aramaic."

With shaking hands, on the board at Yeshua's bloody head, Abenadar wrote the Aramaic because his librarius did not know the language. When he finished the last letter, Abenadar quickly turned to

Gaius. "It is ready."

Gaius motioned to the soldiers, and they lifted up the cross with Yeshua on it. "Be careful," cautioned Gaius, "let it down gently. I don't want to have to reset the pegs." Straining, the legionnaires lowered the cross gently into a hole between the two other crosses. "Good," said Gaius. "Very good."

At that moment, Yeshua regained his voice. Pain tinged his speech, but the words were clear, and they rolled over the crowd. "Abba, forgive them; they don't understand what they are doing."

The people and the legionnaires peered up expectantly, but that was all he said.

Abenadar spoke to Gaius. "You take half the column with you and return to the barracks. With the remainder, I'll keep the watch over the execution."

"Are you sure? You don't look well, and you haven't slept since the night before last."

"I am certain."

"Then let the men finish dividing the spoils from the prisoners, and I'll go." The legionnaires were already throwing knucklebones for Yeshua's coat. The purple cloak still lay untouched below the cross.

"Gaius, you take the purple cloak," said Abenadar.

"By rights, it is yours."

"I don't want it. I have no stomach for this business. From now on, I will leave all the executions to you."

Gaius laughed. "If these people don't learn to heed their own law, we will certainly see more."

Not long after that, Gaius, with the purple cloak gathered under his arm, took four legionnaires and marched them back into the city.

The horrible repetition of the cross already consumed Yeshua and the two rebels. Each breath required an agonizing pull from their arms and push with their legs. The arms tired quickly.

For Yeshua, intense pain marked each breath. When he pulled

upwards, he knew the agony of wooden stakes grating on the flesh and bones of his arms. When he pushed upwards, he felt the grate of the wooden stake in his legs. With each motion, blood flowed freely from the wounds in his limbs. Yet, to not breathe—in his aching lungs, he savored each breath like a deep mouthful of crisp spring water.

The shadow of the crosses measured an hour before the Cohen Hagadol, Anan, the Sanhedrin, and some cohanim came to ensure that the legionnaires had put Yeshua to death as Pilate promised. They ignored Abenadar and his men and stood at the edge of the hill well away from the crosses. After he read the placard above Yeshua's head, Anan complained to Abenadar, "His crime should not say he was the King of the Judeans, but rather that he *said* he was the King of the Judeans."

"On that account, you will have to speak to Pilate. I followed my orders, and I will not change the words unless the Procurator gives me instructions."

At that, Anan stood back. He and the Sanhedrin conversed in low tones. Finally, the Cohen Hagadol stepped forward and spoke in Aramaic to the crowd gathered around the hill. "He saved others," cried Kayafa. "If he really is the Messiah, the one chosen by Adonai, let him save himself."

Beside him, Anan said, "So he is the Messiah, is he? The King of the people of Y'hudah? Let him come down now from that Roman cross. If we see that, then we'll believe him. As it is, he is defiled, and the day is defiled by his death."

Another cohen cried out, "He trusted Adonai? Let Adonai rescue him—that is, if Adonai wants him."

Some of the people who stood near the knoll jeered along with the Sanhedrin and cohanim, but their voices were few. When they saw that Yeshua would not reply to their taunts, they quickly lost interest. Yeshua stared at them with a look of pity and disapproval. Compassion so ovrwhelmed his features that they felt they and not he were under the threat of judgment. After a while Anan, Kayafa, and the Sanhedrin hunched their shoulders and quietly returned to the city.

The remaining cohanim glanced around expectantly; usually, the crowd continued the mockery begun by their leaders. The people around the knoll just glared sullenly at them. After a while, the cohanim followed the example of the Sanhedrin and dispiritedly returned to the Temple.

After the leaders left, the Zealot on Yeshua's right cursed him between breaths. "Aren't you the Messiah? If you are, then save yourself and us."

But the second rebel shouted back at the first, "Shut up, Machat. Don't you fear Adonai, blessed be He? You're being punished in the same way this man is. With bar-Abba, we robbed and murdered our own people. I know how guilty you and I are. Our punishment is just, but you and I both saw this man. We couldn't help but know who he was and what he did in Y'hudah. This man did nothing to deserve our punishment."

Machat murmured under his breath, but he didn't have enough energy to respond.

The second Zealot stared intently at Yeshua. "Yeshua, please remember me when you come as King."

Yeshua turned his head to look directly at the second man. "Yes, my friend. I promise, today you will sit with me in Paradise."

At that moment, the sun struck its zenith, and a rumbling shook the air. The noise sounded like an earthquake or a thunderstorm, and Abenadar and the legionnaires braced themselves. But the ground didn't shake, and the sky remained clear of clouds. Unexpectedly, the sun went dark. People in the crowd below the Skull screamed and dropped to the ground. The legionnaires drew their swords and fell back into a tight defensive circle.

Above them, in a raspy, pain-filled voice, Yeshua exclaimed, "Do not be afraid. I am the light of the world."

Immediately, the stars became visible in the sky. The people quieted and night sounds imbued the air. Just at the edge of hearing, the almost subaudible sound continued, and Abenadar soon forgot about it.

Almost as quickly as the darkness surprised them, the people accepted the dark as though it were night. Many headed toward their homes. Most wondered how they could sacrifice the Pesach lamb now that it was already night. They all questioned how the Shabbat of the Pesach could come without the Temple horns announcing the sacrifice.

Abenadar's men put away their swords, but they still kept a careful watch. They built a small fire near the crosses, but that glimmered like a tiny candle—overpowered by the darkness raging all around them. Abenadar was lost in thought. He wondered what phenomenon could explain the sound and the darkness. He had seen an eclipse of the sun, but he'd never heard of an eclipse that lasted as long as this. He didn't want to frighten his men, so he said nothing to them. As much as he wanted to deny the evidence of his own experience, he twice had heard the witness of a voice from the heavens. He had seen more than one inexplicable healing, and now this.

In the darkness, a small group of women, including Ruth, he knew, and a couple of men still stood on the plain below The Skull. As the crowd thinned out, the group moved closer and closer to Yeshua. Abenadar recognized the men as two of Yeshua's talmidim. The group carefully watched Yeshua to see what he would do. Abenadar admired their faith. At any moment, he thought, they expected Yeshua to step down from the cross. Abenadar hoped their wait was not in vain.

When the group came close enough for Yeshua to see them unmistakably, he called out in a clear voice, "Mother, there is Yochanan, your son." Then he nodded at one of the men. "Yochanan, this is your mother." The older woman collapsed in tears.

Even in the darkness, Abenadar realized he knew the older woman. She was Miryam, Yeshua's mother. Abenadar was ashamed. Miryam had befriended his mother when no one else in the town of Natzeret would. Now he was the man who executed her son. Abenadar again felt Ruth's glare through the dark. He wished he could speak to her.

Yeshua then turned his head toward Abenadar. "I'm thirsty."

A jar of cheap wine that had long ago turned to vinegar rested against the base of the cross. Abenadar signaled for one of the legionnaires to give Yeshua a drink. The legionnaire put a sponge into the jar and stuck it on a long hyssop branch. At that moment, three trumpet blasts rang out from the Temple to announce the sacrifice of the Pesach lambs. And, as though the trumpets announced the return of the sun, dazzling sunlight covered the earth. Abenadar shaded his eyes from the brightness. The position of the sun declared the time was, indeed, three o'clock in the afternoon, the time of the sacrifice. The water clock in the Temple kept a good record of the time, though the sun refused to do so.

Yeshua lifted his face toward the heavens. The sunlight outlined him like a torch. "My Y'hovah! My Y'hovah! Why have you deserted me?"

Below, someone said, "He's calling for Eliyahu."

The legionnaire lifted the sponge up to Yeshua's lips, and Yeshua tasted the bitter liquid.

At once, the remaining people bunched toward the cross, and they said, "Let's see if Eliyahu comes and rescues him." The talmidim and women on the knoll covered their faces and wept.

The rumbling sound that had been in the background since noon gradually increased in volume, and now the ground began to tremble. The legionnaires again drew their swords and stood with their backs together.

The people in the crowd fell down on their knees and covered their heads.

All at once, Yeshua lifted his face and cried, "Everything is complete."

Abenadar stared directly at Yeshua. The earth shook violently.

Above the clamor, Yeshua pushed his body up and shouted, "Abba! Into your hands I entrust my spirit." He dropped loosely back against the cross and his head fell forward on his chest. At that moment, the earthquake stopped, and the world became completely still. No one moved or spoke.

Finally, his heart engulfed with anguish, Abenadar said, "Surely, this man was the Son of Adonai."

The people got to their feet. The crowd below the cross slowly broke apart. Many tore their clothing and threw dirt on their heads. Many beat their breasts and cried aloud. They all knew Yeshua was dead.

Abenadar threw himself down under the cross and lay back against the upright. The man was dead. For a moment, he thought he saw Ruth at the edge of the crowd moving back to the city, but just as quickly, she disappeared from his view. Abenadar knew he would never see her again. His men were quiet and subdued. A small group of women still stood a ways off. Abenadar recognized some of them. At least one was Ruth's friend, Miryam. She was once a whore and now one of Yeshua's talmidah. None of Yeshua's talmidim was visible.

About an hour before sunset, Gaius Flaccus returned to The Skull. With him, he brought a half-column from his century. Behind them trudged a man of Y'hudah and his servants.

Abenadar stood and saluted Gaius, but said nothing.

Gaius returned his salute. "I told Pilate Yeshua would be dead—long dead."

"Why are you here, Gaius?" said Abenadar.

"The Judeans don't want these corpses to ruin their holy meals. They want them all dead and buried before sunset."

"Then do what you must," said Abenadar.

Gaius pointed to the first Zealot on the cross and motioned to two of his men. "Break his legs."

Machat was exhausted, but he saw the legionnaires coming toward him and pulled his legs tightly against the cross. One soldier stuck the haft of his pila behind the Zealot's legs—between the cross and his knees. The legionnaire pulled back and the legs bent outward from the cross. The second legionnaire struck Machat's legs with the haft of his pila, once, twice, thrice until, with a loud report, the bones cracked. The rebel gave a cry and slumped down. Only supported now by his useless arms, he hung helpless. His legs moved sickeningly. The muscles twitched ineffectually as he tried to push up to breathe. Machat made a burbling sound and foam cascaded out of his mouth and nose and flowed down his chest. In moments, he was dead.

The legionnaires saw so much death during their time in Y'hudah, they didn't even note his passing. They moved on to the second rebel and broke his legs in the same way. He died just as quickly.

Then they came to Yeshua. He hung on the cross limp and unmoving. His color and stillness told them he was already dead. They didn't break his legs, but to make certain, one of the soldiers stabbed him in the side with his pila. The point pierced Yeshua through the chest and lung. When the legionnaire pulled out the barb, blood and clear fluid flowed out in a thin stream. The legionnaire said, "Centurion Gaius, this man is certainly dead."

"Good, I knew he would be. Treat him like a king, said Pilate. He died like a king. In your report to him, Abenadar, tell the Procurator Yeshua died like a king."

"I will, Gaius."

"The Judeans want these off the cross before sunset," said Gaius, "Cut them down!"

They pulled Yeshua's cross from the hole and allowed it to fall to the ground. At that moment, the man of Y'hudah stepped between Abenadar and Gaius. He wore elegant clothing, but he had torn his inner robe in the gesture of mourning of the people of Y'hudah. "I am Yosef of Ramatayim. Centurion Gaius, the Procurator promised me Yeshua's body."

"It is yours," said Abenadar.

The legionnaires cut loose Yeshua's bonds and were about to pry his limbs from the stakes that nailed them to the cross.

"Leave that one alone," Abenadar ordered the legionnaires,

They left Yeshua, and after checking the rebels to ensure they were dead, without lowering their crosses, they cut the bonds with their swords and let the bodies drop to the ground. Gaius led the legionnaires off, and they threw the bodies of the two Zealots into the gorge called Gey-Hinnom.

Meanwhile, Yosef and his servants gently pried the stakes from Yeshua's arms and legs and laid him out on a fine linen sheet. Yosef's servants placed packets of spices in the grave clothes. From where Abenadar stood, over the scent of corruption, he could smell the spices—myrrh and aloes. Yosef himself wrapped the linen around the body.

In Aramaic, Abenadar said to Yosef, "Friend Yosef, because you touched the dead, you are defiled before Pesach. You will not be able to eat the Pesach lamb."

Yosef colored at this remark and replied, "Centurion, you are well known in this city. You follow the ways of our people, but this is a secret few know: read the Tanakh, this man is our Pesach lamb. He is one of the few lambs that will be sacrificed in Y'hudah today. No one should feast tonight—we sacrificed our Messiah." With that, he signaled the others, and they gently lifted Yeshua and carried him toward the garden of tombs on the other side of The Skull.

Under his breath, Abenadar said, "I am also defiled."

At a discrete distance, Abenadar followed Yosef and his servants. The men entered the garden of the tombs and laid their burden at the entrance to a newly cut tomb. Abenadar stood in the garden and watched their work. First, they unwrapped Yeshua's body, and prepared it with the spices they brought. Then, in the style of Y'hudah, they carefully wrapped him and sealed the body and linen with sticky resin. Yosef himself wrapped Yeshua's head with a fine cloth. He placed myrrh and aloe between the swathes and sealed it in the same way. When they were done, they carried Yeshua into the tomb, and all of them together rolled a large stone in front of the entrance. To place the stone required the combined strength of all the men. Without speaking again to Abenadar, they left the garden of tombs and headed back to the city.

Abenadar watched the closed tomb for a while, then he turned and left. At the edge of the garden, but well away from the tomb, in a pathetic group, stood the women who had stayed with Yeshua at the cross. They had also torn their robes, and their faces were streaked with dirt and tears. They stared at Abenadar with fear and loathing, but he ignored them as he trudged wearily past them, and returned to The Skull to gather his legionnaires.

When Abenadar returned, Gaius said to him, "Our job is done."

"Go back to the camp," said Abenadar. "I will take my men and make the final report to Pilate."

The city was quiet. Many of the houses were dark. Abenadar never knew the Pesach to be so quiet or so cheerless. No smell from the

Temple proclaimed the great slaughter of lambs that should have taken place there. At the Praetorium, Pilate had already retired so Abenadar gave his report to Iulius Valens. Abenadar dismissed his men, and walked back to the house he once shared with Ruth.

As Abenadar expected, Ruth was not waiting for him, and the hearth was cold. He took off his clothing and collapsed on their bed. As he lay down his head, the long hours of wakefulness grabbed his weary body and he fell into a fitful slumber.

*I will praise thee, for thou hast answered me
and hast become my deliverer.
The stone that the builders rejected
has become the chief capstone.
This is Adonai's doing;
it is marvelous in our eyes.
This is the day on which Adonai has acted:
let us exult and rejoice in it.*

Psalm 118:21-24

Twenty-four

Abenadar awoke covered with sweat. He faced the back wall of the house. The sun stood high enough to throw itself through the windows and beat down on him. In his sleep-befuddled brain, he heard singing. He thought it was his imagination—the fragment of a dream. Abenadar rolled over. The sun lay beyond the peak of the window. The day was already past noon. His eyes widened, and he rubbed the sleep out of them. The voice wasn't his imagination, and he wasn't dreaming. Ruth sat at the edge of the hearth and sadly sang the words of the Hallel. Her face was turned away from him.

Abenadar breathed a silent prayer of thanks. After the events of yesterday, he couldn't believe she had come home. He winced at his memories, and at the forlorn look he witnessed in her eyes. He had betrayed her.

Had Ruth heard him wake? He didn't want to startle her. In his thoughts she was like a deer—a frightened doe ready to plunge back into the depths of the city and forever away from him. He would do anything to prevent that.

Abenadar moved slowly. He raised himself on one arm, and considered what he should say to her. Could he say anything that would bind her heart back to his and secure it there again?

Ruth hadn't washed since the previous day. Today was Shabbat; she couldn't wash. Mourning-ashes streaked her face, clothing, and hair. Still engrossed in her song, Ruth turned the side of her face slightly toward him. Tears traced twin tracks through the dirt on her cheeks and drew the sad line of her eyes down further. Her face had turned into a mask of grief.

Abenadar couldn't gaze on Ruth without loving her. He wanted to hold her in his arms, but he guessed, at this moment, she would reject any comfort he could give. Her face copied the appearance it wore when he first met her, haughty and inconsolable—untouchable.

Abenadar could not lie there and say nothing. He couldn't let Ruth continue her suffering alone. He couldn't wait any longer, ignorant of whether room remained in her heart for him. Had he become just another of the men she had known? Did she believe he discarded her love like other men discarded her body?

Abenadar knew he had to say something, and when he finally spoke, his voice sounded strange and far away in his own ears. "Ruth." The name hung in the small room. "Did you go to Yotam's feast?"

Ruth's face turned slowly toward him. She stared at him with her sad dark eyes. "There was no feast."

"No feast at Pesach?" Abenadar said, amazed. "Did Yotam keep you out—because of me? I was defiled, not you."

"He didn't keep me out. We couldn't sacrifice our lamb at the Temple."

"But...I heard the horns blow."

"They were too late. Sela told me. The water clock in the Temple kept the time, but without the sun, the Cohen Hagadol feared to make the first sacrifice. At three, the L'vi'im finally sounded the horns, and the sun came back. But the Cohen Hagadol sacrificed the first lamb too late. Before he could cut the animal's throat, the earth shook, and a violent wind tore open the curtain of the Holy Place. Sela said the curtain ripped from top to bottom, and everyone could see right into the Holy Place. After that, before the sun set, the cohanim didn't have enough time to complete all the sacrifices of the first division. They only sacrificed some of the lambs of the Sanhedrin and the L'vi'im. But the Cohen Hagadol took two cuts to slaughter the first lamb and the Holy Place was open to the world, so the cohanim disagreed among themselves about the legitimacy of those sacrifices. And because of this, many who could sacrifice did not celebrate the Pesach."

"There was no Pesach?"

Ruth remained silent for a moment, then said, "Some in the city say Adonai supplied a sacrifice. Some say Adonai provided a Pesach unlike any other." She stared at him.

"What do you mean?"

Ruth tilted her head upward. "I mean that Yeshua, the man from Natzeret, the Messiah, became Adonai's Pesach lamb."

"Yosef of Ramatayim said the same thing." Abenadar hung his head. "And I killed Yeshua." He whispered, "Does that make me a murderer?"

"Or a cohen. Better you than anyone else, Abenadar. You ensured that Yeshua was executed correctly. You made the horrible, honorable."

"You mock me, Ruth, and I deserve your ridicule."

She turned completely toward him and knelt on the edge of the hearth. "I would never mock you, Abenadar, never. Last night I made up my mind not to come back here to you." She turned her head away.

"I...I know. I guessed you would not come back. I murdered your Messiah."

"You're wrong, Abenadar. *We* killed Yeshua. All of us. Even those who loved him best did not love him enough to fight and die for him. But that's all past. You heard what Yeshua said while he was being lifted up on the cross. He said, 'Father forgive them.' He forgave you. He forgave us all. The best we can do now is to live as Yeshua said Adonai, blessed be He, would have us live. Because of that, I forgive you. Because of that, I came back to you. I love you, Abenadar. I will never leave you." Ruth did not look at him. Her voice was full of tears.

Abenadar rolled off the cot and stepped to the hearth. He knelt in front of Ruth and touched her arm. "I'm glad you came back. I love you, Ruth, and I cannot imagine life without you."

Ruth lifted her arms to him. Kneeling, Abenadar folded her in his arms and held her while she wept. He would have cried too, but he had served Rome too long, and no tears remained in him. Praising Adonai in his heart, Abenadar held Ruth and wondered what it could mean to possess a dead Messiah.

Ruth pulled slightly back from his embrace and kissed his face. "You rescued me from the streets of the holy city—you saved me. I will save you by bringing you to the Messiah."

"Yeshua told me something like that." Her face was level with his. "Ruth, I promise myself to you. I am your husband, and you are my wife. Tomorrow I will have a marriage contract written for us."

Ruth stared at him in surprise. "You are already my husband, but you would write a contract for me. For me, though I was a whore?"

"You are no whore. I love you, Ruth, and I will do what I should have done long ago. I only wish I could also give you a canopy."

Ruth threw her arms around his neck. "No, Abenadar, I don't need a contract. Your promise is enough. No rabbi would marry us."

Ruth buried her face in his chest again, and for a long time they said nothing. Finally, she reached up and touched his face. "Will you stay home for the rest of Shabbat?"

"I must check on my century, but I'll be back before the afternoon."

"I have nothing to feed you. I thought the Pesach lamb would be enough."

"I don't need anything. From what you say, many in the city of Yerushalayim fast today."

With Ruth's kisses fresh on his lips, Abenadar drew on his tunic and armor and headed for the legion camp.

After Abenadar arrived at his quarters, he called for Cerus. The optio came immediately.

"Cerus, enter," said Abenadar, looking up from his desk. He paused, unsure how to continue, and put down his writing brush. "How are the men?"

Cerus saluted. "The camp is rampant with rumors, Centurion." Cerus looked at the ground. "Is what I heard about the execution true?"

"Sit down." Abenadar gestured toward his cot. "What did you hear about the execution?"

"The men you took with you told us about the death of a man whom they called a god. Did these savages trick us into executing a god?"

"If he was a god, we can only blame ourselves. I saw many strange things yesterday—things I cannot understand or explain."

Cerus said, "This morning, the Primus, with direct orders from

Pilate, put a guard on the tomb of the King of the Judeans."

"Why?"

"The Judean leaders told Pilate the man said he would rise from the dead. The Primus stationed a half column at the tomb to ensure he doesn't make good on his promise, or at least to keep his followers from stealing the body away."

Abenadar shook his head. "The Sanhedrin still fear Yeshua when he is dead."

"Yeshua?"

"Yes, that was the name of the King of the Judeans."

"Common name for these barbarians."

"Did the Primus set a simple guard, or did he place an officer in charge?"

"He set a simple guard from Gaius' century."

"How long are they to stay at the tomb?"

"The Primus didn't specify a time limit."

"I think I'll inspect the guard. Tell Gaius' optio I am going and send for his tesserarius."

"Yes, Centurion." Cerus saluted and left the room.

Instead of the tesserarius alone, Centurion Gaius reported with his officer of the watch.

"You want to review my troops?" Gaius threw himself onto Abenadar's trunk.

Abenadar glanced up from the duty roster. "Actually, no. I want to view Yeshua's tomb."

"Why not? I have no objections." Gaius turned to his tesserarius. "Demoteless, take Centurion Abenadar when you change out the guard at the tomb. Let him see everything he wants but make sure he comes back in one piece."

Demoteless saluted.

Abenadar said, "Tesserarius Demoteless, when do you plan to leave?"

"Centurion, give me time to organize the next half column guard, and I will be ready to go."

"Good. I'll wait for you here."

Gaius stood up after his tesserarius left. With a laugh, he said,

"Will you also make the dawn rounds for me?"

"I might as well. Or would you rather I didn't?"

"No, go ahead. I don't care."

"Very well, Gaius."

"You have a strange preoccupation with this man, Yeshua. In my mind, he is just another dead Judean. You should forget him and everything about him."

"I can't forget what happened at the execution yesterday. You shouldn't either. When have you ever heard of anything like it?" asked Abenadar.

"In a story told by a priest."

"But this was no story. You and I saw it for ourselves."

"What you say is true, but I, for one, have no time for such things."

"Time or not, you should think carefully about what they mean."

"Because I respect you, Abenadar, I'll consider your words, but I keep alive and sane by not thinking too much. Blissful ignorance is the legacy of a successful Roman soldier. And I advise you to also consider my words." Gaius grimaced and left the room.

Demoteless returned soon after Gaius left. Abenadar followed the principalis of the watch to the camp's gate. The four replacement guards waited there. With Abenadar in the lead, the half-column took off at a normal step for the garden of the tombs.

Their line of march took them through the marketplace and toward The Skull. They traced almost the same path through the city that Abenadar had followed yesterday when he led Yeshua to his execution.

The garden was quiet. As they passed the entrance, the legionnaires' heavy tread became strangely muted. The stone remained unmoved before the tomb, and the legion guards stood in pairs on either side of it. Abenadar could tell the stone had not moved since he saw it rolled into place. It had moved only once; the tracks of this single path were obvious on the rock. On either side of the stone, the Procurator's seal was pressed into a heavy clump of wax; no one could move the stone without breaking the seals.

The fresh guards took the tessera from the men they replaced and hung the wooden placards around their necks. Demoteless marked the time and date on the tessera, and then he was ready to leave. Abenadar took a final look around the garden and led the detail back into the city. At the marketplace, he passed the command to Demoteless and returned home to Ruth.

That night, before Abenadar drifted off to sleep, he asked Ruth, "When did Yeshua say he would come back to life?"

Ruth raised up on one arm. "Where did you hear that?"

"The Sanhedrin knew of the claim, and they insisted Pilate seal and guard the tomb. They're afraid Yeshua's talmidim will steal the body and proclaim he came back to life."

She curled up next to him. "Yeshua's talmidim won't be stealing anyone's body. They're too afraid. They're all in hiding."

Abenadar chuckled. "Tell them they can come out of hiding. No one's searching for them."

"I would, but they won't speak to me anymore."

Abenadar said with surprise, "Why not?"

"When Yeshua was alive, the talmidim tolerated me, but they always believed I was your spy. Since Yeshua's death, they won't even acknowledge my presence."

"I'm sorry, Ruth." Abenadar didn't tell Ruth he did use her as a spy. He guessed she already knew. "But how long after his death did Yeshua predict he would come back to life?"

"He told the talmidim he would come alive in three days, but none of them believed him. They didn't believe him when he said he would die." More softly she said, "I didn't believe him when he said he would die."

"Do you believe he will come back to life?"

"Yeshua was never wrong. He told us exactly when he would die and how." She was silent for a long moment. "I believe he will be back in three days."

"I can't argue against that." Abenadar stroked Ruth's hair in the darkness. "Three days means tomorrow."

"Yes."

In the morning, Abenadar wolfed down the thick wheat gruel Ruth made him. He put on his tunic and started toward the garden of the tombs. Abenadar hoped Gaius had informed Cerus that he was making the morning rounds. He didn't need to have the Primus after him for missing a muster. The sun already crested the horizon, and the heavens blazed clear blue.

As Abenadar made his way through the Garden Gate, a gentle earthquake rolled the ground. At first, he didn't imagine the event was supernatural. But with new awareness, he realized something remarkable must be happening.

Three women walked ahead of him on the path to the garden. They carried sacks and linen similar to the supplies Yosef used to prepare Yeshua's body for burial. He thought he recognized the women as the three who lingered so patiently beside Yeshua's cross. One appeared to be Ruth's friend, Miryam, but Abenadar couldn't be sure. The earthquake startled them too. They paused for a moment, then, gathering their courage, continued down the path. When they passed The Skull, they stared with intensity at the two crosses that remained on the knoll, then forced their eyes away.

The three proceeded unerringly toward the garden of tombs, and Abenadar followed at a discrete distance. When the women arrived at the entrance to the garden, they stopped and acted as though they were afraid to enter. After a moment, they crossed into the garden and out of Abenadar's sight. Abenadar ran the rest of the way to the entrance. When he came to the opening, the reason for the women's apprehension became apparent. Someone had rolled away the stone that sealed Yeshua's tomb. As Abenadar watched, the women entered the tomb.

At first, Abenadar thought the talmidim came to the tomb and opened it, but he saw no sign of any men. Then he thought of the legionnaires. As Abenadar entered the garden, he noticed the four men sprawled on the ground. They seemed uninjured.

Abenadar ran to the first soldier. The man breathed normally and seemed only dazed. Abenadar shook him. "Wake up."

The legionnaire covered his eyes with his hands and cried out, "I am awake. I cannot see."

"What happened?"

"A man in dazzling clothing appeared on the sealed stone. He spoke to us, but I couldn't understand him. When we threatened him with our pila, the ground shook, and he rolled the stone from the tomb. A brilliant light blazed out of the opening and blinded me. I tried to cry out, but I couldn't move or speak. I fell to the ground. I still can't see."

"I am the Centurion Abenadar. Don't move until I come back for you."

"My lord," said the man, "My lord, we didn't desert our guard. We cannot fight against the gods."

"I believe you. Now keep quiet. I'll take care of you."

Abenadar scrutinized the tomb. He could make out the three women's legs as they stood inside. Without warning, a light blazed from the cave, but it wasn't intense enough to blind him. He could now discern the legs of two other people in the grave and he heard a man's muffled voice. The women dropped to the ground and in a low bow almost touched their faces to the floor of the small cavern.

Abenadar rushed to the entrance. In Hebrew he heard, "…Remember how he told you while he was still in the Galil that the Son of Man must be delivered into the hands of sinful men and be executed on a stake as a criminal, and on the third day be raised again?"

With a gentler flash of light, the two other people in the grave disappeared. Immediately, the women stumbled out of the tomb. They saw Abenadar and stood stock-still, unsure what to do. Now Abenadar was confident he recognized Miryam, Ruth's friend.

In Aramaic, he asked, "Who were they? What did they tell you?"

Miryam stepped forward, exuberant. "You must be Ruth's husband, Abenadar the Centurion. Yes. If you are looking for Yeshua, he is not here, and they will not be able to kill him again." Then, as if realizing she was talking to one of Yeshua's executioners, she almost spat out, "I don't care what you do to me. You cannot hurt him any more." Her voice was more tender when she said, "Tell Ruth, Yeshua is risen from death. He is alive."

"Have you seen him?" asked Abenadar.

"Not yet. But we will see him. The angels told us."

"Were those angels?"

"They appeared out of nothing, and they were clothed in light. What else could they be? Now, sir, let us go. We must tell the others." The women backed away from him.

"Wait."

They stopped.

"Yeshua's talmidim don't know?"

"We came to prepare Yeshua's body. The talmidim think he is dead. Please, we must go tell them: he is alive."

"Certainly, go."

Still carrying their unused spices and linens, the women turned and rushed back toward the city.

Abenadar watched them until they were lost to sight, then stooped and entered the tomb. Amazingly, after three days, the smell of death didn't foul the grave. Inside, the cave was about five feet high. A two-foot-deep ledge was carved into the back wall, and that is where the body of Yeshua would have lain. Now the shelf held only the linens used to wrap Yeshua's body. Myrrh, aloes, and resin impregnated the cloth. All together, they created a fragrant, sticky form in roughly the shape of a man. Other than the shape, Abenadar saw no sign they not long ago clothed a dead man. The appearance of the linens gave Abenadar the impression that Yeshua's body melted right through them.

At the far end of the ledge lay the piece of linen that covered Yeshua's head, and as though an invisible head still filled it, the cloth formed a perfectly rounded shape. Abenadar passed his hand through the neck of the covering just to be sure the cloth was empty. Impregnated with pounds of gummy spice, the linen would have stuck like glue to Yeshua's dead body. No man could remove these pieces of cloth. No one could have removed the body and left the burial clothing in this condition.

Abenadar pondered this impossibility, then backed out of the cave.

The legionnaires still lay dazed on the ground. Abenadar gathered them together and led them back toward the city. The legion had no reason to guard the tomb now; Yeshua was gone. Perhaps he had risen from death.

As the legionnaires stumbled back toward the city, they slowly regained their sight. At the legion camp, Abenadar left them in the hands of Demoteless and hastened to the Primus' office.

"Abenadar, welcome," said the Primus as he turned from his desk. "I missed you at the muster this morning. Gaius told me where you'd gone. Do you have something important to report?"

"Yes, Primus, I came to you immediately. The body of the man we executed for the Sanhedrin is gone."

"You mean the one called Yeshua, the King of the Judeans?" Abenadar nodded, and Cecilius Bassus continued, "I set a guard of legionnaires at the tomb to prevent just that occurrence. How could his body be missing?"

"Primus, I can only tell you what I saw." And with that, Abenadar reported, in detail, everything he witnessed at the tomb.

When Abenadar concluded his account, Cecilius Bassus exclaimed, "Can Pilate believe this? Can I believe it?"

"Can you explain these events any other way?" said Abenadar.

"I don't know. I have no idea." The Primus shook his head. He put his head in his hands, then glanced up at Abenadar. "The Procurator will not believe this. We must report to him before he hears about this from anyone else. You must come with me now, Abenadar, and tell Pilate exactly what you told me."

Abenadar and the Primus rushed to the Praetorium. Pilate sat in court, and when he received Cecilius Bassus' message, he called immediately for them. Rumors had already circulated to the Procurator, and when the Primus and Abenadar arrived, Pilate cleared the court except for his legion guards and Legatus Iulius Valens.

The Primus insisted Abenadar repeat everything he saw at the tomb. When Abenadar finished his report, Pilate gripped his heart and said under his breath, "My wife was right. I should have had nothing to do with this man." Then, more loudly: "But now what can we do?"

"I think we can do nothing, Procurator," said Abenadar. "Anything we do may make the situation worse for us."

"You advise us to take no action?"

"The Sanhedrin don't desire this information to become common knowledge. They fear the people will believe their Messiah has come alive, and if the people believe this, they may reject the Sanhedrin's authority."

"Such a scenario would be catastrophic for us." Pilate tapped his lips with a finger.

"But the people may not believe it. And if they do, how can our situation be any worse than before Yeshua's death? If he has really been raised from the dead, and he advances on us from heaven at the head of a legion of angels, how can we fight against him? We cannot defeat a god. If he does not oppose us with the host of heaven, your legion is enough to keep the people of Judea under control."

Pilate stared at the floor for a moment. He raised his gaze, first to Abenadar, then to the Primus. He sat back in his chair with a sigh. "Your words make sense, Centurion Abenadar. For the moment let us accept them without argument. But another matter concerns us: what should we do about the guards? If they have not told the truth about this missing Messiah, they deserve death."

Abenadar continued. "I agree, Procurator. If they have not spoken truthfully, they deserve death. But they are all veterans, and their story has already circulated around the camp. Many of our men are going to the tomb to see for themselves. If we put the guards to death, we give credence to the idea that a band of weak rebels stole the body right from under our nose. In the eyes of the Judeans and their leaders, we lose credibility. If we kill the guards, we also lose four veteran legionnaires, and that we cannot afford. For our sake, it would be better if everyone believed Yeshua truly came out of the tomb alive. The prestige of your legion is at stake. We can defeat men, but no one expects us to defeat a god."

Pilate searched the face of every man in the room. His stare finally settled on Iulius Valens. "Legatus? Do you agree with this reasoning?"

"I, for one, cannot fault Abenadar's counsel."

"Very well, they may live. Primus, we are still uncomfortable with the idea we can do nothing to subvert this cult. Instruct the legionnaires, all of them, to keep this matter quiet. We do not want to hear of this incident again. For now, we will accept Centurion Abenadar's advice and handle any future problems related to this event as they occur. Legatus, do you have anything further to add?"

"Yes, Procurator," said Iulius Valens. "Centurion Abenadar's advice and leadership have guided us well through this very difficult situation. I commend his actions to you."

"Have we not said before, it's a pity he's not a full-blooded Roman?" Pilate held up his hand. "We acknowledge the truth of your assertion, Legatus. His performance and advice have been exemplary. You needn't fear on that account; our records will so read.

"Now, Centurion Abenadar," the Procurator went on, "we charge you anew to keep us informed of the events that transpire in all the quarters of this city. The Passover is over, and you must take your patrols into the streets again. You must watch for rebellion more carefully than before. Now, you may go."

Abenadar and the Primus both saluted and exited the court.

Before they parted in the camp, the Primus took hold of Abenadar's arm. "Abenadar, what do you really believe about this whole thing?"

"After all I have seen, how can I not believe the body of the man we executed was supernaturally removed from a sealed tomb? Yeshua was surely a god, but I don't know what that means."

The Primus grunted in thought and walked away slowly. He seemed as though he would turn back to speak to Abenadar, but he made up his mind and continued on.

The next day Abenadar organized two columns of his century and led them on an uneventful patrol through the Ophel. The rest of his men were busy with other duties. He heard from Gaius that the Sanhedrin paid the guards from Yeshua's tomb to keep the matter quiet. The Sanhedrin were too late; the news had already circulated through the whole city and out into the countryside.

Yerushalayim was quiet. It was as if, this time, on this Pesach, the Angel of Death had not passed over. Or that, this time, too many of the people, like the Egyptians, were unprepared, unready. On that night, too many of the doorposts were not marked with the blood of a lamb.

In the evening, Abenadar made his way home. Ruth greeted him with a warm lamb stew and a warmer kiss. "The lamb was our Pesach," she said. "Yotam butchered it, and this is our share."

"The city was quiet today."

"The people are afraid." Ruth sat beside him on the cushions.

"Afraid of what?"

"Rumors fill the marketplace," said Ruth.

"What do the people say?"

"Many think Yeshua is alive again, and that makes them fear. Many believe he was the Messiah."

"What do you know about it?"

"One of Yeshua's talmidah spoke to me today, and she told me what is going on among the talmidim."

"What do Yeshua's talmidim say?"

Ruth was breathless. "She says, they saw him alive."

"They saw him?"

"Yes, and more than just one or two of them. Many who knew Yeshua and who believed say they saw him."

"Have you seen him?"

"No...not yet."

He glanced up from the stew. "But you expect to see him."

She turned her head away. "Tomorrow...maybe. I told you, since Yeshua was executed, his talmidim don't welcome me."

"I want to see him, myself."

"They may not want you to see Yeshua."

"The talmidim?"

"Yes. Because you executed him."

"What more can I do to him?" said Abenadar. "No one can stop Adonai." Abenadar hunched over his bowl. "Why is Yeshua hiding?"

"He is not hiding."

"Then I expect he will show himself to whomever he wants."

"You are surely right, my lord." Ruth bowed her head, but he could hear the smile on her lips.

"Tomorrow I want you to take me to his talmidim."

"They would shun me for it." Ruth's features became set.

"Then tell me where they are."

"They would know who told you." She was defiant.

A voice came from behind them. "You don't need to go to my talmidim."

Abenadar jumped up, and Ruth covered her face.

"Yes, Ruth. Yes, Abenadar. It is I. I am Yeshua." At once, Yeshua stood in the center of the room. He was dressed in a white robe, and a brilliant light shown all around him.

"My lord." Abenadar fell to his knees and touched his face to the ground.

Ruth didn't seem surprised. She stood and walked over to Yeshua. "You were dead."

"But I am alive." Yeshua smiled. He held out his hand, "Come, Abenadar, take my hand."

Abenadar leapt up and grasped the hand in his. A jagged pink scar creased Yeshua's forearm. Abenadar stared at it.

"Yes, the stake pierced me there." Yeshua showed Abenadar his other arm. "And here."

"I'm sorry," said Abenadar. He didn't know what else to say.

"My death was necessary. You obeyed me, Abenadar. You acted just as I commanded you."

Abenadar said, "What do you want us to do now, Lord?"

"That's simple. I want you to tell everyone what you saw, and teach others everything I taught you."

"Is that all?" said Ruth.

Yeshua smiled broadly. "It is enough. I give you a Pesach that is permanent and complete. Perfect salvation comes not from the blood of lambs and goats but by the blood of the Son of Man. Now I must go. I have many others to visit." Yeshua held them both in his arms, then released them. He unlatched the door and let himself out. When Abenadar closed the door, Yeshua was gone.

Abenadar looked at Ruth and she stared back at him.

"He is the Messiah. The Messiah did come."

Their music goes out through all the earth,
their words reach to the end of the world.
In them a tent is fixed for the sun,
who comes out like a bridegroom
from his wedding canopy,
rejoicing like a strong man to run his race.

PSALM 19:4-5

Twenty-five

In the fall, Ruth conceived, and Abenadar received orders to report to Rome. During the senatorial review of Abenadar's commission as a Primes Ordines Centurion, the record of the Roman from Natzeret came to the Emperor's attention. Pilate's reports gave an exemplary record of Abenadar's leadership that were backed by correspondence from both the Primus Pilus and Legatus Legionis. In a letter, Herod through the Governor Tiberius also provided Abenadar a strong recommendation. Abenadar's new commission came a month later. The Emperor ordered him to report to the Praetorian Guard and take over a century in the Primus Cohort.

"I don't want to go to Rome," said Ruth in no uncertain terms, "but I will go with you, Abenadar." She bowed her head. "It is right that we go, and right that we bring the message of Yeshua to Rome."

Abenadar was less certain than she. He knew the prejudice of the Romans for anyone they considered inferior. He foretold only hardship for Ruth and him. The challenge was one he never thought he would have to endure, but he could not turn down the commission—not a commission from the Emperor. If he rejected the orders of the Emperor, the next message might demand his head.

Ruth packed their goods. They were meager, but she filled two large chests: Abenadar's and a new one she bought in the marketplace.

In the chest Ruth bought for travel, between clothing, blankets, and linens, she carefully placed their chethubah, the marriage contract, and her dowry. Abenadar paid all the marriage costs, and though the two of them had not stood beneath a canopy, by the law of the people of Y'hudah, they were legally bound to one another.

When the time came for them to leave for Rome, their friends and most of the legionnaires from the camp came to see them on the road to

Caesarea. The Legatus Legionis assigned a turmae of cavalry to escort them. He mounted both Ruth and Abenadar on the legion's horses. Because Ruth had never ridden a horse before, Abenadar led hers.

Ruth peered over her veil with quiet pride as the Legatus and Primus saluted her husband. She passed tearful farewells to Yotam, Sela, Ya'akov, Shoshanah, and more than half of the families from the Marketplace.

Before they rode, Iulius Valens came to stand beside Abenadar. "Abenadar, you and I have made a fine course through the wilds of this place. Have we not?"

Abenadar said, "I sought to serve you and Rome as well as I was able, Legatus."

"I am proud of you, Abenadar. As proud of you as I would be of the son I never had. The legion does not know yet that I will soon be sent back to Rome. I suspect that I will be given a place of authority in the Empire's Officium of the legions." He handed a sealed scroll to Abenadar. "When you get to Rome, go to my father's house. Ask for the family Valens by name. With this letter, my father will receive you into my house with honor. You and your family—" he smiled at Ruth— "will be my guests. I don't want you to stay anywhere else while you're there."

"Thank you, Legatus. I don't know what to say."

"Say nothing, friend Abenadar. You will honor me by accepting this hospitality." Iulius Valens took hold of Abenadar's arm. "Godspeed to you. A safe trip and much honor to you."

The Legatus released Abenadar and stepped back. The decurion called out the order to march, and Abenadar, leading Ruth, followed them out of Efrayim's Gate. Over six years ago, Abenadar and Iulius Valens together had entered Yerushalayim through this gate. The time had passed so quickly, yet to Abenadar it seemed a lifetime.

When the escort started to ride, the legionnaires and the people from the marketplace cheered and waved. As Abenadar and Ruth passed through Efrayim's gate, the sounds diminished and soon disappeared.

Ruth turned her head toward Abenadar and smiled at him. "Yeshua is sending us to Rome. Adonai willed this."

"Who else could make a half Roman a centurion in the Emperor's own legion?" Abenadar stared out over the mountain road. "It will not be easy, Ruth, but in the name of Adonai, I will serve Yeshua, the Messiah."

Ruth reached out to him. "Then we will serve Him together."

"Together, we will serve Him," said Abenadar, firmly grasping her hand.

Lexicon

AWARDS

Ranks lower than Centurion
torques—necklace
armillae—armband
phalerae—discs
corona civica—laurel leaf crown

Centurion
vitis—vine-staff—baton of office
corona aurea—golden crown
corona vallaris—first over ramparts
corona muralis—first over wall
corona civicae aurea—oak leaves, saving a fellow citizen
corona obsidionalis (or graminea)—wreath of grass, deliverer of a besieged army

Ranks above Centurion (Primus Pilus+)
hasta pura—silver spearshaft
vexillum—small standard mounted on silver

COMMON ROMAN TERMS AND ITEMS

ambulatura—military training and practice of marching out 10 miles while practicing basic training and formations
aquila—staffs bearing the legion's eagle
armatura—military training and practice with real weapons
buccellatum—hard tack rations

caligae—sandals
cibaria—regular wheat rations
cornicen—horn blower
forum—store and marketplace
frumentum—corn ration
gladius—Roman short sword
imagines (imago)—staffs bearing portraits of the deified and reigning emperors
lorica hamata—banded armor
muli marinani—fielding training with heavy loads
pila (pilum)—roman spear
pila praepilata—spear for practice with leather buttons on the tips and reinforced
quaestorium—equipment issue, storage, and smithy
scutum—large rectangular shield
signum—spear-like staff with phalerae
stipendia—legionnaires' pay
tessera—watchword, plaque marked by the tesserarius for the guards

Money

Roman
as (asses)—copper
obol (obols)—copper, 2 obols = 5 asses
denarius (denarii)—silver, 4 obols = 1 denarius, 16 asses = 1 denarius
quadrigatus (quadrigatii)—silver, 15 asses = 1 quadrigatus
aurie—gold, 25 denarii = 1 aurie

Judean
kodrantes—copper, 4 kodrantes=1 as
lepton—copper mite, 2 lepton=1 kodrantes

Legion

10 Cohorts
Each cohort 6 centuries
Each century 80-100 men (80 more commonly)

Legatus Legionis—head of the legion
Primus Pilus—centurion head of first century of first cohort
Primus Cohort—1st Cohort
Primes Ordines—centurions of the Primus Cohort

1st Cohort (5 double centuries, 160-200 men); names of the centuries:
Primus Pilus 1st
Princeps 2nd
Hastatus 3rd
Princeps Posterior 4th
Hastatus Posterior 5th

Other Cohorts 2-10 (6 standard centuries); names of the centuries:
Pilus Prior 1st
Pilus Posterior 2nd
Princeps Prior 3rd
Princeps Posterior 4th
Hastatus Prior 5th
Hastatus Posterior 6th

Cohorts: 10 Decimus (added to the name of the century to delineate it)
Praefectus Legionis—head of training and judge of training
centurion—officer, head of century
principalis (principales)—noncommissioned officer
optio—principalis, second in charge of century
signifer—principalis, carried the signum, third in charge of century
tesserarius—principalis, officer of the guards, fourth in charge of century
librarius—clerk for century, only one step above common legionnaire
officium—legion headquarters and headquarters staff

Praetorium—building housing the headquarters
Praefectus Castrorum—trainer of the recruits and legionnaires
Cornicularius—senior principalis in charge of the librarii
Quaestionaris (Quaestionarii)—torturers
cornicen—hornblower
Aquilifer—Eagle (aquila) bearer—usually veterans near end of service
Imaginiferi—imagines (imago) bearers

Transliterated Aramaic Names and Their Common Anglicized Translations

Abba—father
Adonai—Lord God
Avraham—Abraham
Beit-Anyah—Bethany
chethubah—marriage contract
Chizkiyahu—Hezekiah
cohen (cohanim)—priest
Cohen Hagadol—high priest
David—David
Efrayim—Ephraim
Elisheva—Elizabeth
Gavri'el—Gabriel
Gey-Hinnom—hell (valley around the west and south of Yerushalayim)
Goyim—Gentiles
Hordos—Herod
Kanah—Cana
L'vi (L'vi'im)—Levite
Miryam—Mary
Natzeret—Nazareth
Parush (P'rushim)—Pharisee
Pesach—Passover
Ruach HaKodesh—Holy Spirit
Shabbat (Shabbatot)—Sabbath

Shiloach—Siloam
Shomron—Samaria
Sukkot—the Feast of Tabernacles, Feast of Booths
talmid (talmidim (p), talmidah (f))—disciple
Tanakh—Books of the prophets and history, books of the Bible not including the Torah and the Psalms
The Galil—Galilee
Torah—Books of Moses, the first five books of the Bible
Tzadok (Tz'dukim)—Sadducee
Tzippori—Sepphoris
Y'hoshafat—Jehoshaphat
Y'hudah—Judea
Ya'akov—Jacob
Yafo—Joppa
Yarden—Jordan
Yericho—Yericho
Yerushalayim—Yerushalayim
Yeshua—Jesus
Yochanan the Immerser—John the Baptist
Yosef—Joseph
Yotam—Jotham
Z'kharyah—Zechariah

Coming Soon...

Aegypt

L. D. Alford

*An unspeakable evil
and an unbelievable power
is about to be released into the world...*

Lieutenant Paul Bolang, stationed at Fort Saint in Tunisia in the 1920s, discovers a hieroglyph. Suspecting that the fort might have been built beside an ancient Egyptian foundation, he summons an archaeological party. When a tomb is discovered and opened, death strikes immediately...and reveals a grisly secret.

Lt. Bolang soon uncovers two other tombs: the tombs of the Goddess of Light and the Goddess of Darkness. As the first tomb is opened, a being escapes into the desert...and is pursued by Bolang. What will the next tomb hold? Will opening it unleash a great evil and suffering on mankind, as many believe? Or is all that simply a myth?

A fascinating tale of technology, cultures, and ancient magic

For more information about L.D. Alford and *Aegypt*:
www.LDAlford.com
www.AegyptNovel.com

Coming Soon by L.D. Alford...

The Chronicles of the Dragon and the Fox

*Fantasy ladies and knights come alive
in this sci-fi/adventure portrait of futuristic societies, vengeance
and betrayal, warfare and honor.*

The End of Honor
Book One

An intragalactic war threatens to tear apart
the Human Galactic Empire and the lives of
Prince John-Mark and his bride-to-be, Lyral Neuterra.

The Fox's Honor
Book Two

It was a time of treachery and vengeance...
of nobility and redemption...all because of love.
But the ultimate price could be Devon Rathenberg's life.

A Season of Honor
Book Three

Baron Shawn du Locke must choose between
honor and desire...with the fragile peace of the
Human Galactic Empire hanging in the balance.

The End of Honor

An intragalactic war
threatens to tear apart
the Human Galactic Empire…

The death-knell of the Human Galactic Empire has sounded—it is the crash of an axe against the virgin white marble of the Hall of Accords. It is the bitten-off cry of the Lady Lyral Neuterra, whose head lies sundered from her smooth shoulders. It is the death of the Emperor at the hand of his own son. It is the whirlwind of a thousand ships sent to enforce the new Emperor's will. And only Prince John-Mark, the Emperor's youngest son, can bring the Empire back from the edge—back to peace and honor.

Prince John-Mark had intended to wed the Lady Lyral—now he can only mourn her. Revenge is his great desire, but he cannot be revenged without tearing apart the civilization and people he loves….

For more information about L.D. Alford and *The End of Honor:*
www.LDAlford.com
www.TheEndofHonor.com

The Fox's Honor

It was a time of treachery and vengeance…
of nobility and redemption…
all because of love.

Prince Devon Rathenberg, the Emperor's Fox and chief of intelligence, has fallen in love with the Lady Tamar Falkeep—the third daughter of the least Duke in the Human Galactic Empire. But custom dictates they can never marry.

Then the unthinkable happens. In the insurrection that threatens to tear apart the Human Galactic Empire, Devon designs a plan to reveal the Empire's internal enemies. It's a plan of desperation that, by design, will result in the ultimate sacrifice: his own death. But before he dies, Devon is determined to win the heart of Lady Tamar and declare his love….

For more information about L.D. Alford and *The Fox's Honor:*
www.LDAlford.com
www.TheFoxsHonor.com

A Season of Honor

Baron Shawn du Locke must choose between honor and desire…with the fragile peace of the Human Galactic Empire hanging in the balance.

Shorn of his lands, regency, title, father, lady, and name, the only thing left to the Baron Shawn du Locke is his honor. Nothing in the past has shaken it and nothing would cause him to compromise it—until he meets the Lady Elina Acier.

Elina Acier is the last hope of the Noble Houses of the Human Galactic Empire. To protect the planet Acier from the Emperor, she must marry a Duke's son.

Before Shawn meets Elina, he vows to convey her to the Imperial Capital to marry Duke Nior's son. But Elina is a startling lookalike for her cousin, Shawn's long-dead love, the Lady Lyral Neuterra. Shawn once loved Lyral enough to grant her his House and fight a war in her name. Now he is honor-bound to deliver Elina, Lyral's "twin," to marry another man.

Shawn must safely deliver Elina to the Imperial capital before the Emperor discovers and kills Elina, and before her presence drives him insane…or he falls in love.

For more information about L.D. Alford and *A Season of Honor:*
www.LDAlford.com
www.ASeasonofHonor.com

About the Author

"The finest escape in literature is an escape into a real and inviting culture," asserts novelist **L.D. ALFORD**. He enjoys exploring with originality and intimacy those cultures and society we think we already know in order to build compelling tales that make ancient people and times real to his readers. His stories uniquely explore the connections between events close and familiar and the events of the past—all woven together with threads of reality and fascinating technology that bring the past alive.

L.D. Alford is familiar with both technology and cultures. He is an experimental test pilot with over 6000 hours in more than 60 different kinds of aircraft. He also served in worldwide military operations as a member of three different operational combat squadrons. L.D. earned a B.S. in Chemistry from Pacific Lutheran University, an M.S. in Mechanical Engineering from Boston University, and is a Ph.D. candidate in Aerospace Engineering at the University of Dayton. He is a graduate of Air War College, Air Command and Staff College, and the US Air Force Test Pilot School. He is widely traveled and has spent long periods in Europe and Central America. He is a featured writer for www.WingsoverKansas.com, and his writing includes over 40 technical articles and a previous novel of historical fiction, *The Second Mission*.

For more information about L.D. Alford and *Centurion*:
www.LDAlford.com
www.CenturionNovel.com
www.capstonefiction.com

CAPSTONE FICTION

The place for inspirational fiction . . .
a place to call home.

We're all about respecting an author's hard work
and creating a new market for inspirational fiction.

For more information
Visit **www.capstonefiction.com**

or write:

CAPSTONE PUBLISHING GROUP LLC

P.O. Box 8, Waterford, VA 20197

Printed in the United States
200987BV00003B/160-207/P